About the Author

Andrea Laurence is an award-winning contemporary author who has been a lover of books and writing stories since she learned to read. A dedicated West Coast girl transplanted into the Deep South, she's constantly trying to develop a taste for sweet tea and grits while caring for her husband and two spoiled golden retrievers. You can contact Andrea at her website: andrealaurence.com

Writing romance for Mills & Boon is truly a dream come true for **Soraya Lane**. An avid book reader and writer since her childhood, Soraya describes becoming a published author as 'the best job in the world'. Soraya lives with her own real-life hero and son on a small farm in New Zealand, surrounded by animals and with an office overlooking a field where their horses graze. Visit Soraya at sorayalane.com

Kate Hardy has been a bookworm since she was a toddler. When she isn't writing Kate enjoys reading, theatre, live music, ballet and the gym. She lives with her husband, student children and their spaniel in Norwich, England. You can contact her via her website: katehardy.com

Friends to Lovers

Friends to Lovers:
A Little Surprise

ANDREA LAURENCE

SORAYA LANE

KATE HARDY

MILLS & BOON

First Published in Great Britain 2024
by Mills & Boon, an imprint of HarperCollins*Publishers* Ltd,
1 London Bridge Street, London, SE1 9GF

www.harpercollins.co.uk

HarperCollins*Publishers*
Macken House, 39/40 Mayor Street Upper,
Dublin 1, D01 C9W8, Ireland

ISBN: 978-0-263-34495-0

THIRTY DAYS TO WIN HIS WIFE

ANDREA LAURENCE

To the Dedicated Soldiers of My Street Team
Andrea's Army of Awesomeness—

I can't list all of you individually, but know that this dedication is for you! Thank you for all the hard work you put in to help make each of my books a success. It may not seem like a lot, but every review you write, every bookmark you hand out, every post you share with friends…makes a difference. I am happy to reward all of you with books and goodies because it's worth every penny to have you on my team. Thank you for your support and friendship. You're awesome. *(Obviously!)*

Prologue

"Do you want to get out of here?"

Amelia Kennedy turned and looked up into the cool blue eyes of her best friend, Tyler Dixon. Of course he would be the one to save her. "Yes, *please.*" She got up from the banquet table and accepted his hand, happily following him out of the ballroom, through the casino and out to the glittering lights of the Las Vegas Strip.

Just breathing in the cool desert air made her feel better. Why had she thought her high school reunion would be fun? It was just a room filled with people she never liked, gloating about how great their lives were. Even though she couldn't care less about what Tammy Richardson—cheerleader and all-around stuck-up brat— had done with her life, hearing Tammy brag had some-how made Amelia feel less enthusiastic about her own achievements.

It was ridiculous, really. She co-owned her own company and was very successful, but the lack of a ring on her hand and toddler photos on her phone made her the odd girl out tonight. This entire trip was a waste of her precious vacation time.

Well, not the whole thing. It was worth it to see Tyler. They had been best friends since the ninth grade, but recently they had both gotten so busy they were lucky to see each other once a year. The reunion was a good excuse.

They stumbled down the sidewalk hand in hand with no destination in mind. It didn't matter where they ended up. Every step they put between them and the reunion improved Amelia's mood. That, or—if her softening knees were any indication—the tequila was finally kicking in. A low rumble caught their attention, and they stopped outside the Mirage to watch the periodic eruption of the volcano out front.

They leaned against the railing, Amelia resting her head on Tyler's shoulder and sighing with contentment. She really missed spending time with him. There was just something about being with Tyler that made the world seem better. There was a comfort and ease in his arms that she'd never found in another man. Although they'd never dated, Tyler had set the bar high for her future relationships. Maybe too high, considering she was still single.

"Feel better?" he asked.

"Yes, thank you. I just couldn't look at any more pictures of weddings and babies."

Tyler wrapped his arm around her, chasing away the January desert chill. "That's what happens at reunions, you know."

"Yeah, but I didn't expect it to make me feel like such a…"

"Successful, talented businesswoman in control of her own destiny?"

Amelia sighed. "I was thinking more along the lines of a relationship failure on the fast track to a house with too many cats."

"Quit it," he said in a stern voice. He turned toward her and tipped her chin up so she had to look him in the eye. "You are amazing. You're beautiful, talented, successful... Any man would be lucky to have you in his life. You just haven't found one worthy of you yet."

That was a nice thought, but it didn't change the fact that she'd been on a fruitless quest for Mr. Right since she'd come of age. "Thanks, Ty," she said anyway, as she wrapped her arms around his waist and buried her face in the lapel of his suit.

He held her tight, resting his chin on the top of her head. It was a simple hug. One they'd shared a hundred times before. But tonight, somehow, it was different. She was suddenly very aware of the movement of his hard muscles beneath his shirt. His cologne tickled her nose, so familiar and yet so enticing in the moment. It made her want to bury her face in his neck and inhale the warm scent of his skin. Run her palms across the rough stubble of his jaw...

A wave of heat licked at Amelia's cheeks, and she realized it had nothing to do with the flames shooting across the water beside them. There was a warmth curling in her belly, a need building inside her. It was a familiar arousal, but one she'd never associated with Tyler. He was her best friend. Nothing more.

But in that moment, she wanted more. She wanted him to show her how beautiful and talented he thought she was with his hands and his mouth instead of his words. It was a dangerous thought, but she couldn't shake it.

"Do you remember graduation night?"

"Of course," she said, pulling away to put an end to the physical contact stirring the blood in her veins. She couldn't forget that night. They had suffered through family parties, and then they'd snuck off together to camp in the desert. Amelia had driven them out to the edge of town, where they could finally see the stars. "We drank wine coolers and stayed up all night watching for shooting stars."

"Do you remember the pact we made?"

Amelia thought back to that night, the details blurred by a combination of time and fuzzy navels. She remembered them pinky swearing something. "What was it about? I don't remember."

"We agreed that if we weren't married by our ten-year reunion, we would marry each other."

"Oh, yeah," she said, the moment flooding back into her mind. In their eighteen-year-old brains, twenty-eight was nearly ancient. If they weren't married by then, all hope was obviously lost. They'd sworn they would save each other from a lonely middle-aged existence. "Twenty-eight sure doesn't feel the way I expected it to. I still feel young, and yet sometimes I feel like the oldest, most boring person I know. All I do is work. I never have adventures like we used to have together."

Tyler studied her face, his light brown eyebrows drawing together in thought. "Do you feel up for an adventure tonight? I guarantee it will cheer you up."

That was exactly what she needed—the kind of night that would make for a great story. "I am definitely up for an adventure. What did you have in mind?"

Tyler smiled and took her hand in his. The touch sent

a surge down her spine, and she knew she'd agree to anything when he smiled at her that way. Then he dropped to one knee, and she realized she was in for more than she'd bargained for.

"Amelia, will you marry me?"

One

"Amelia," Gretchen pressed, "tell me you didn't elope in a Las Vegas wedding chapel."

Amelia took a deep breath and slowly nodded. Her stomach was turning somersaults, but she managed to get the words out anyway. "I did," she admitted. "The details are a little blurry, but I woke up married to my best friend."

"Wait." Bree held up her hands in disbelief. "Did you just say you're married? *Married?*"

Amelia looked at her two friends and coworkers, not entirely certain she could repeat the words. It had been hard enough to say them the first time. She actually hadn't admitted it aloud until that very moment. The past few weeks it had all seemed like a fuzzy dream, but with Gretchen and Bree staring at her as though she'd grown a second head, it was suddenly very, very real.

"My high school reunion didn't go the way I planned,"

she explained. "I thought going back to Las Vegas would be fun, but it wasn't. Everyone was passing around pictures of their wedding days and their kids..." Her voice trailed off.

The sad state of Amelia's love life had hit her hard that night. She'd been in the dating scene for ten years with nothing to show for it but a string of almost-but-not-quite relationships. It wasn't for lack of trying—she put herself out there time after time, but with no luck. She refused to settle for anything less than a timeless love, and it seemed just out of her reach.

Her hectic career hadn't helped matters. She'd spent the past few years since college focusing on building the business she and her partners had founded, From This Moment. Running a wedding facility was a stressful job, and her area of expertise—catering—was no small task. Between menu tastings, prep work and wedding cakes, the wedding day itself was the least of her troubles. She loved her job, but it left little time to seriously dedicate herself to finding the love and family she'd always fantasized about.

She was only twenty-eight. Hardly old-maid material. But then she'd gone to the reunion and found that her schoolmates had left her in their familial dust. Even dorky Dave Simmons had come with his wife, and she'd been certain he'd never find a woman. Not even having Tyler there—equally single—helped. He was single by choice, too happy to play the globe-trotting CEO to have the burden of a serious relationship.

"I was feeling sorry for myself. My best friend, Tyler, kept bringing me drinks, and eventually we decided to blow off the party and go down to the Strip."

"Skip to the part where you eloped," Gretchen pressed,

with an odd mix of wonder and glee on her cherubic face. She enjoyed living vicariously through others.

Amelia shook her head. "It's kind of a blur, but Tyler reminded me about this stupid pact we made on graduation night. We swore that if we weren't married by our ten-year reunion, we would marry each other."

"You didn't!" Bree said, her large blue eyes growing wider by the minute.

"We did." She couldn't believe it either, but they'd gone through with it. When Amelia woke up the next morning, the giant diamond ring on her hand and the naked man beside her in bed had confirmed her worst fears. The night before had not been just a vivid dream. It had really happened. She was married to her best friend.

"We did it for a laugh, you know? In high school, the two of us were always coming up with crazy ideas. I think Tyler was trying to cheer me up, offering to marry me so I wouldn't feel like the single one at the reunion anymore. It seemed like a brilliant solution at the time."

"It always does," Gretchen noted, as though she'd had her share of impetuous experiences.

"What the hell kind of liquor were you drinking?" Bree asked at last, sliding away the bridal magazine she'd been reading to plan her own upcoming nuptials.

"Anyway," Amelia continued, pointedly ignoring Bree, "the plan was to annul it as soon as we can. He lives in New York. I live here. It's obviously not going to work long-term."

Work? What was she even talking about? Of course it wasn't going to work. She'd just married her best friend from high school! *Tyler.* She knew everything there was to know about him and she was certain Tyler was not husband material. He worked too much, he traveled constantly and he had a bad habit of falling off the face of the earth for weeks at a time. She loved him, but she couldn't count on him. And yet, here she was. Married to him.

"So far the annulment plan isn't panning out the way I'd like. Turns out you can't annul a marriage in Tennessee just because it was done on a whim. New York may have better laws, but if not, that means a full-on divorce. Either way, Tyler has been traveling too much to start the process. I've only gotten a few texts from him in between stops in Belgium, Los Angeles, India... I haven't even spoken to him on the phone since I left Las Vegas."

"So do you think he's really busy, or is he avoiding you?" Gretchen asked. "I would think that might be an awkward situation to deal with. I can't even imagine sleeping with one of my guy friends from high school. If the sex was bad it would be hard to face him later. If the sex was good...that might be even worse."

"The sex was amazing," Amelia confessed, quickly clamping a hand over her mouth. Had she really said that out loud? She shook her head. The words had spilled out because they were true. Tyler had been the most talented and attentive lover she'd ever had. Their wedding night had easily left her top five encounters in its dust. She wasn't entirely sure what to think about that.

"Well, then," Bree noted with a smile twisting her lips. "Do tell."

"Oh, no," she said. "I've already said too much."

"Maybe he's dragging his feet in the hopes of getting some more of that sugar," Gretchen suggested.

"There's no more sugar to be had. That was a one-night thing and we both know it," Amelia argued, even as she felt the untruth of her words. She wanted more, she just knew she shouldn't. "He's just busy. He's always busy."

Tyler obviously wasn't that concerned with fixing this.

In the few texts she'd received, he'd told her to relax. If annulment was off the table, there was no rush, so unless she was madly in love and needed to marry someone else right that minute, it wasn't a big deal. He, of all people, knew about her relationship struggles and knew that the odds of that were extremely low.

But it was a big deal to her. Especially considering the extenuating circumstances. She couldn't even wrap her brain around that, so she continued to ignore it. It wasn't a pressing issue...yet.

"So you're really just going to walk away from the man that gave you the greatest orgasms of your life?" Gretchen frowned. "I don't think I could do that, even if I couldn't stand the guy. You and Tyler love each other, though. It's not much of a hop from friends to lovers, is it?"

"It is a huge hop over a massive chasm, I assure you." Amelia knew for certain they shouldn't go there again. Tyler had been her best friend since ninth grade, but she had never really allowed herself to consider anything between the two of them. For one thing, there was no way she wanted to risk their friendship in an attempt to take it to the next level. If it failed—and the odds were that it would—she'd lose the most important person in her life.

For another reason, there was a big difference between being friends and being lovers. Being friends was easy. She tolerated Tyler's jet-setting, bossiness and extended radio silences just the same as he tolerated her romantic drama and pickiness. It wasn't a big deal because as friends, it didn't impact them directly. Dating someone magnified those personality quirks, and suddenly they were deal breakers.

Her raw emotional state at the reunion had apparently forced all those concerns out of her mind. The next thing she knew, she was on the verge of consummating her marriage. In that moment, nothing mattered more than peeling away Tyler's clothes and getting a taste of the forbidden. His hard body and sure touch had been an unexpected surprise, and she hadn't been able to get enough of him. Even now, the mere thought of touching him again sent a thrill through her body, awakening parts of her that should never, ever throb with need where Tyler was concerned.

Since she'd gotten home from the reunion, their night together had haunted her. The marriage could be undone. But the memories... Those couldn't be erased. The way he'd touched her. The way he'd coaxed pleasure from her body as though he'd studied his whole life for that moment... She could never go back to the blissful ignorance they'd once had. They had eaten the forbidden fruit.

A chime like a kitchen timer went off on her phone, rousing her from the mental spiral she'd just dived into. It was a new text. She frowned down at her phone when she saw the name. Speak of the devil, she had finally gotten another text from Tyler. Unfortunately, it didn't address her million questions or make up for the weeks of waiting he'd put her though since they'd married. All it said was, Are you at work?

He must be ready to talk about all this at last. Perhaps his jet-setting had abated for a few days and he was finally able to move forward.

Yes, she replied to his text. She would be able to call him back after the staff meeting was over. At that point, she could go into her office, shut the door and have the much-needed discussion to put this behind them. Natalie, the wedding planner and office manager, would arrive any moment with coffee, as she did every Monday morning. Not even Amelia's latest life catastrophe would throw off Nat's schedule.

On cue, Natalie pushed open the door of the conference room and stopped in the doorway. She had the cup holder clutched in her hands, four paper cups held tightly in place, as usual. But there was a strange look on her face. Her normally calm expression was pinched, her mouth tight. Something was wrong.

"What's the matter, Natalie?" Bree asked.

Natalie turned from Bree to look at Amelia, her long dark ponytail sweeping over one shoulder. "There's an incredibly hot guy here to see you, Amelia. He says that he's your, uh…*husband*."

Someone gasped. Amelia wasn't sure which of them it was. Probably her. She launched up out of her chair, her expression no doubt panic-stricken. He couldn't possibly be here. He'd just texted her and hadn't made any mention of being in Nashville. Natalie was surely mistaken. "What does he look like?"

Natalie's brow shot up. "Five minutes ago, I didn't think you had *a* husband, period, much less so many that you wouldn't know who he was immediately when I mentioned him."

"Tall, dark blond hair, bushy eyebrows, icy blue eyes?"

Natalie nodded slowly. "That would be him. He's waiting in the lobby with a shiny wedding ring on his hand. Have I missed something?"

"Oh, yeah." Gretchen snorted.

Moving into the room, Natalie set the drinks on the table and then crossed her arms over her chest. "You're married? To the guy in the lobby?"

"Yes," she admitted.

"Amelia—the one who's had her wedding planned since she was five? Amelia—the one who just a few weeks ago was complaining that there was no one special in her life? I mean, you *are* the same person, right? You're not a pod person that just looks like Amelia?"

She wished she could blame her rash behavior on alien influences, but it was all her doing. Natalie was right to be surprised. Amelia quite literally had had a wedding planned for twenty-three years. Her files of cartoon drawings and magazine cutout collages had evolved into Pinterest boards and spreadsheets, but the content was basically the same. And considering she had never been engaged, it was an excessive level of detail. She occasionally updated the color palette, but the rest was the same. She'd always fantasized about a big wedding with hundreds of guests, tons of good food, dancing and all the elegant touches she adored. All she needed was the love of her life to slip into that Armani tuxedo and make her dreams a reality.

To throw all that away so she could get walked down the aisle by Elvis and marry her best friend was... unthinkable. But Vegas seemed to have that power over people. "It's a long story. They can fill you in." Amelia started toward the door.

"Do you at least want your coffee?" Natalie asked, holding up the paper cup with her white chocolate–caramel macchiato.

Amelia started to reach for it, and then she caught a whiff of the strong aroma. Her stomach immediately started to turn, making her wince and step back. "Ugh—no, thanks. Maybe later. I just can't face it right now."

Turning quickly, she disappeared down the hallway. Natalie's voice easily carried the distance. "Will someone *please* tell me what the hell is going on?"

Tyler Dixon waited longer in the lobby than he expected to. When the dark-haired woman disappeared down the hallway to deliver his message, he was certain Amelia would come rushing out to him immediately. She would run and jump into his arms, greeting him with a big hug and a kiss on the cheek the way she always did.

Glancing down at his Rolex, he started to wonder if he'd miscalculated. He'd known she was here, even before she'd texted him back—he'd recognized her car in the parking lot. That meant she was either angry and making him wait for ignoring her, or she was avoiding him because she was embarrassed by the whole sex thing.

He didn't know what she had to be embarrassed about. With a body like hers, walking around naked could be considered a public service. Sure, they'd crossed a line, but they could work through that. They'd weathered rough patches in their friendship before.

It probably had more to do with him not calling her back. His schedule had been pretty hectic since the reunion, but it had to be. He'd bought some raw diamonds and taken them to India to be cut. He'd hit an auction in Belgium and picked up an antique sapphire brooch formerly owned by French royalty before the revolution. He'd closed a huge deal with a Beverly Hills jewelry designer to provide diamonds for their pieces. Whenever he'd thought to call her, the time zones were off. She wouldn't have appreciated getting those calls at 2:00 a.m.

This was why he didn't get in serious relationships anymore. He'd gotten burned with Christine and learned his lesson. He knew that most women didn't appreciate his schedule, even if they appreciated the money that resulted from it. At first, his diamond airline status and exotic travels seemed exciting, but it didn't take most women long to realize that meant he was always on the go. No, he wouldn't be able to go to that work thing with you. No, he couldn't talk about your crappy day when he was ten times zones behind and busy working.

Amelia had never minded his schedule before. Had that changed along with their marital status?

What was the rush anyway? She hadn't found Prince Charming in the ten years leading up to now. Certainly she hadn't found him in the past month while he'd been gone. He loved Amelia, but she wasn't known for her successful relationships. He'd only met one woman in his whole life who was as high maintenance as she was, and that was his ex. He'd known that about Amelia going into this, but she was his best friend and he would do anything to make her happy. Apparently.

They'd take care of the divorce. That was why he was here at his first opportunity. Despite what Amelia might think, Tyler wasn't deliberately dragging his feet. Although, if he was honest with himself, there was a part of him that was sad that he'd never get to touch those soft curves again. He'd always been happy to be Amelia's friend, but he wouldn't mind spending a little more time exploring her body before they went back to being just friends. He'd only had one brief taste, and that wasn't nearly enough for a woman like her.

But in the end, he knew their friendship would outweigh his erection. Amelia was the most important person in his life and he wouldn't risk that, even to make love to her again. She wasn't just his best friend; she was a driving force in his life. As a kid, he'd been a nobody lost in the chaos of his large family. At school, he'd been just as invisible. Amelia had seen him when no one else did. She'd seen his potential and lit a fire in him to make something of himself. Over the past ten years he had built up his own company, dealing in precious gems and antiquities. He lived a lifestyle he never could've imagined as a poor kid growing up in Vegas. Amelia had made him believe he could do all those things.

No, he wouldn't risk his friendship with her for the greatest sex ever had in the whole universe.

Tyler looked up to see Amelia watching him from the doorway. She didn't run and leap into his arms, but at this point, he was no longer expecting an enthusiastic greeting. He was just happy she hadn't left him standing out here indefinitely.

She took a few hesitant steps into the room, not speaking at all. She looked amazing today. There was a glow about her that lured his gaze to travel over her body, admiring the fit of her sweater dress. The dark purple tunic was gathered beneath her ample breasts and flowed to her knee. She was wearing black leggings and boots with it that enhanced her shapely legs.

The deep V of the dress's neckline displayed an amethyst pendant he'd sent her for her birthday. The fat teardrop gemstone fell just at her cleavage, drawing his eyes to her breasts. Amelia was petite in many ways, but the Lord had blessed her with enough assets for three women.

He knew he shouldn't look, but the memories of their wedding night rushed into his brain, and he couldn't turn away. In an instant, he could see her naked body sprawled across the hotel bed. His palms tingled with the memory of running his hands over every inch of her flawless porcelain skin. Tasting those breasts. Hearing her cries echo through the room.

The lobby was suddenly very warm. It was a cruel trick of the fates to give him a woman so desirable for a wife, then not let him keep her. And he couldn't keep her. He had to remind himself of that. They'd only disappoint one another and ruin their friendship.

"Hey, Ames," he said, finally meeting her gaze.

She swallowed hard, watching him warily. With her big dark brown eyes, she almost looked like a doe, easily spooked by any sudden movements. He hated that. She'd never looked at him with anything other than adoration and love before. He supposed getting married had ruined that. This was just his first taste of what it would be like to be in a real relationship with his demanding, high-maintenance best friend. The honeymoon was barely over and he was already in trouble. He definitely shouldn't have waited this long to talk to her.

"What are you doing here, Tyler?"

Apparently they were skipping the pleasantries. "I came to talk to you."

Her arms crossed over her chest, her breasts nearly spilling from the dress with the movement. "*Now* you want to talk? What about the past few weeks when I've tried to get hold of you and you just blew me off? When I wanted to talk to you, all this didn't seem to matter. Am I just supposed to drop everything to talk to you now because you've decided you're ready to deal with this mess?"

Tyler's lips twisted in thought, his hand rubbing over the rough stubble on his chin. Now did not seem like the time to try to convince her it wasn't a big deal. She had always been a very emotional person, her temper as easily lit as the flames of her red hair. He'd seen her unleash that fury on past boyfriends and he didn't ever want to be the recipient. "I'm sorry I didn't get back with you. I needed to take care of a few things."

"And I needed you to talk to me!" She took several steps toward him, a strand of auburn hair falling from its clip to frame her face. A red flush rushed to her cheeks and décolletage, marring her pale, creamy skin. "We're *married*, Tyler. Married! You can't just keep ignoring this. As much as I'd like to pretend this never happened, we've got to deal with it. Talk about it. Of all the times to ignore me for business, this is the wrong time."

"I know." He held out his hands in an appeasing gesture. It hurt him to hear how distraught she was over their situation, but there was nothing to be done. Business was a priority over a fake marriage, even with his best friend. "I should've called, I know. I'm sorry. I hopped a flight out here as soon as I could so we could deal with this in person."

That seemed to calm her down. Her hands fell to her sides, the tension in her shoulders relaxing. Even then, there was a concern lining her eyes. Something was wrong. More than just her irritation with him. He knew Amelia better than anyone else on the planet. A thousand miles apart, he could detect that she was upset over the phone. In person, it was hard to ignore that something wasn't right.

She crossed her arms over her chest, and he noticed she wasn't wearing her wedding ring. He could feel his own wedding band encircling his finger. He didn't know why, but he'd worn it faithfully since the ceremony. Somehow it felt tighter and more irritating when he knew he was the only one wearing it. "Where's your ring?" he asked.

"It's at home in my jewelry box. Until five minutes ago, no one knew I was married, Tyler. I can't strut around here with that giant rock on my hand and not get a million questions."

She was right about that. Subtlety was thrown out the window after you moved past a couple carats. Her ring was a flawless eight-carat D-color cushion-cut diamond. He'd purchased it a few weeks before the reunion and had been taking it, and a selection of other jewels, with him to

LA for a potential buyer. The reunion had only been possible because he could fit it in on his way. When they'd scrambled for last-minute wedding rings, he'd pulled it from the hotel vault. They'd agreed that when the prank was done, she'd return it.

"I've wanted to keep this whole situation pretty quiet," she continued. "The fewer people that know, the better. What's an adventure to us is a ridiculous mistake to others."

That was probably true. He slipped his own ring off and dropped it into his lapel pocket, noting how his finger suddenly felt naked. It was amazing how easily he'd adjusted to wearing that ring. He'd only gotten close to putting one on the one time, years ago, and since then he hadn't given much thought to it. "Is there any way we can go somewhere to talk?" He glanced down at his watch. "It's still early. I'll take you out for pancakes, my treat."

Her face fell into another frown, this time with her delicate brow furrowing. "I can't right now, Tyler. I'm supposed to be in a staff meeting. You may be able to work whenever and wherever you want, but I'm not a jewel dealer that zips around the country whenever I please. I run a business with partners that count on me. And on Mondays, we have a standing meeting."

"I'm sure they'd understand. Come on, Ames. It will be like senior ditch day all over again. We can have eggs and sausage and pancakes. Maple syrup. I caught a dawn flight from LaGuardia and came straight here without eating anything. I'm starving."

Amelia's eyes narrowed for a moment, then widened with a touch of concern. Her free hand flew to her mouth. "Shut up about the food," she said.

"What?" What did he say that was so offensive? Breakfast was hardly an unpleasant concept.

"I said, shut up, *please*." Her eyes were squeezed tightly shut, her muscles tense as she fought for control. It concerned him. He wanted to run to her, do something, but he didn't think the gesture would be welcome.

After a moment, she took a deep breath and seemed to recover. "I can't talk to you right now, Tyler. You just show up out of the blue with no thought to my schedule. I'm not fifteen anymore. I *will* meet with you, but you've got to respect the plans I have. I can meet you for lunch if you want."

He nodded, knowing she was right. His schedule was flexible, but to assume the same of hers was inconsiderate. "Whatever you need to do, Ames. I'll take you for barbecue, if you want. I haven't had some good ribs in a long time."

She started to nod, then froze as a look of panic spread across her face. "I—" she began, then turned on her heel and dashed around the corner.

Tyler started to follow her but stopped when he heard the unpleasant sound of retching. Apparently barbecue was not terribly appealing to her.

She returned a moment later, her face flushed and her eyes watery. "I'm sorry about that."

Why was she apologizing? "Are you okay? Did you eat something bad?"

She shook her head, a somber expression in her eyes. "No," she said. "I'm fine. I'm just…pregnant."

Two

This was a bad dream.

This was not how her life was supposed to go. Not how this moment was supposed to be. Her first child was supposed to be a blessed occasion. She was supposed to be joyous, not nauseous. Telling her husband the news should be a gloriously happy moment.

Gloriously happy were not the words she would use to describe the look on Tyler's face. His square jaw was slack, his pale blue eyes wide with panic. Not even his expensive suit could keep her superconfident, successful best friend from instantly transforming back into the startled, unsure teen on his first day at a new school.

She still remembered the day her father, the principal at El Dorado High School, had walked into her freshman English class with a new student in tow. She'd pointed out an empty seat beside her and befriended the new boy. It was the best decision she'd ever made. Tyler was the best friend a girl could have.

Today, looking at that same lost expression on his face, she didn't know what to do. Hugging him seemed awkward considering the state of their physical relationship and the legal ramifications of their marriage. She didn't have any words of comfort or wisdom to offer. If she did, she'd say them to herself. She was still reeling from the morning's dose of unexpected news.

She was pregnant with Tyler's baby. She just couldn't figure out how something like that could be possible. From the moment she'd seen the two pink lines on the pregnancy test this morning until she'd announced it to him, it had felt surreal. She loved Tyler more than anyone else. She'd known him since she was fourteen. But having his baby had never been a part of her plan. And Amelia had big plans.

Apparently, it wasn't part of his plans, either. Before she made her announcement, his gaze had drifted over her body, bringing a flush to her cheeks. It didn't take much to realize that he was mentally reliving their night together. She understood. Seeing him standing there in his tailored suit with that charming smile had made it hard for her to remember she was supposed to be irritated with him.

Now all he could do was stare at her midsection, looking desperately for some kind of evidence that she was wrong. She wished she were wrong, but she hadn't needed that test to know the truth. It had only confirmed what the past few days' misery had made abundantly clear.

"Say something," she pressed at last.

Tyler cleared his throat and nodded, her words snapping him back into the moment. "I'm sorry," he said. "I wasn't expecting…" His voice trailed off.

"I don't think either of us was expecting *any* of this. Especially me being pregnant." Or her throwing up into the lobby trash can. "But what's done is done. As much as I'd like to go back in time and change things, we can't. Now we have to figure out what we're going to do."

She needed his input desperately because she didn't know what to do. In any other scenario, Tyler would've been the one Amelia ran to for support and advice. If she'd found herself pregnant by another man, he'd be the first person she called in a panic. He would be the one to talk her down and tell her everything was okay. But it was his baby, and somehow that made everything more difficult.

"So do you still need to go to your meeting?" he asked.

Now that the baby was out of the bag, so to speak, the meeting didn't seem as critical. Her stubbornness had really been more from irritation about his disregard for her plans than anything else. She loved Tyler, but sometimes he forgot he wasn't the CEO of everything and everyone. He'd steamroll people if they let him. Amelia was one person who never let him.

The meeting wasn't her number one priority at the moment. She could catch up on the high points later. It was more important to talk to Tyler about what they were going to do. She needed a story, a plan, before she faced her friends again and had to tell them what was going on in any depth whatsoever. They'd be like a firing squad, lobbing questions at her that she didn't have any answers for. Yet.

"No, let's just…" She eyed her office, and her gaze strayed to the open doors of the wedding chapel just beyond it.

The white-and-gray chapel was so elegant. Beautifully detailed, yet understated enough not to upstage the bride or her chosen decor. Since the day construction was completed, Amelia had envisioned herself getting married in that same chapel wearing a strapless ivory Pnina Tornai gown. She could easily picture sprays of white and pink roses filling the room with their delicate fragrance. The rows of friends and family crying happy tears.

That was the way her big day was supposed to be. Not at 1:00 a.m. in the Li'l Chapel of Love with the pink bismuth—colored upholstery and dusty silk flower arrangements. She'd been wearing a black cocktail dress, for chrissake. Married in black! No old, no new, no borrowed, no blue. It was blasphemous. And obviously very bad luck. The whole thing made her want to curl into a ball and cry the tears of a five-year-old who'd had her dreams destroyed.

Her office was a convenient place to talk, but the sudden urge to get as far away from the chapel as possible nearly overwhelmed her. "Just get me out of here," she said.

"You got it."

She moved quickly, slipping into the coat she'd hung nearby. She should tell the others she was leaving, but she didn't dare stick her head back in the conference room. She'd text Gretchen once they were on the road and let them know she'd be back later.

They walked out of From This Moment together, Tyler holding the door for her like he always did. He led her through the parking lot to a black BMW parked out front.

"Nice rental," she said. Whenever she flew somewhere, she usually ended up with some tiny compact car, not a luxury car. That was the difference between her and Tyler, with his jet-set lifestyle and wealthy business associates.

"It's okay," he said, opening the door to the passenger side. "I wanted an Audi, but they didn't have any available."

"Aw, you poor thing," she muttered as she climbed inside. Such a hardship. The leather interior was soft, and the car smelled brand-new. Fresh from the factory. She hadn't experienced that in a long time. She was still driving the little crossover she'd saved up for after graduation. It was ideal for hauling catering supplies, but it was more practical than posh.

It must be nice to have money. She'd never really had a lot. Her father was a math teacher turned high school principal and the sole breadwinner in the family. He did okay, but she'd never considered her family to be more than middle class. As an adult, every penny of her own had gone into making From This Moment a success. Tyler had had even less when they were kids. He was one of six kids in a family that could barely feed two despite his parents' best efforts.

Driving a brand-new BMW around had been a pipe dream when they were kids. Tyler had done well for himself over the years. No one was prouder than she was of everything he'd accomplished. If he could get his eyes off his smartphone and stay in the country for more than a day at a time, he would make some woman a great husband one day. She just couldn't fathom that person being her.

"Where are we headed?" he asked.

"There's a coffee shop a few blocks up, if that's okay."

"Sure." Tyler started the car, pulled out of the parking lot and headed in the direction she'd pointed. A nearby commercial district had restaurants and coffee shops where they could sit down and talk. Considering the state of her stomach, she would pass on the food, but she could get some hot tea. And maybe, if that went okay, a scone.

They didn't speak in the car on the way there, which was odd for them. They always had a million things to catch up on. They could talk for hours about anything and everything. Now, as she feared, there was tension between them. Sex changed things, as she'd known it would. She'd never wanted their relationship to cross that line for that very reason.

She sighed and looked out the window instead. There would be plenty of things to say, but she could tell neither of them was ready to say them. He'd just found out he was going to be a father. That needed time to sink in. Tyler had never mentioned having an interest in a family—at least, not since he'd broken up with Christine. After that, he'd focused 100 percent on business. This had to be an unexpected blow for him. Amelia had always known she wanted children, but it had still been a shock for her.

Eventually, they arrived at the small independent coffee shop. He opened her door, helped her out and then followed her inside. Tyler bought them both drinks and got himself a giant cinnamon roll while Amelia found a plush couch in the corner away from the others in the shop.

Tyler came over a few minutes later with their things on a tray. He put the drinks on the coffee table and sat beside her. His knee barely grazed hers as he did, but even that simple touch was enough to awaken her nervous system. It was the first time they'd touched since that night. Being in such close proximity to him again was confusing. Her body remembered his touch, aching to lean closer to him and feel his hands on her again. Her brain knew it was a bad idea, but she didn't want to act childish. It was a simple touch, an innocent one. Just because her libido lit up like the skies on the Fourth of July didn't mean it meant anything.

Amelia busied herself preparing her tea and distracting herself from Tyler's nearness. She added a pack of raw sugar and stirred it, waiting for him to say something. She'd already said enough. Now it was his turn.

"So," he began, after a few bites of cinnamon roll and a sip of his coffee, "do you want to tell your parents first, or mine?"

She tried not to choke on her tea. That was not where she'd expected him to go with this. "Tell them what, exactly?"

"That we've gotten married and we're expecting a baby."

She shook her head furiously. He must still be in shock. "Neither."

Tyler frowned at her. "We have to tell them eventually. We can't just show up at their house with an infant and say, 'Here's your grandchild.'"

"I know that," she argued. "We will have to tell them about the baby eventually. I meant about the wedding. I don't see why anyone needs to know about it if we're just going to file for divorce anyway. I'd rather my father not know what we did, to be honest. You know how he is. The only reason he let me go to college in Tennessee was because my grandparents live here. He's just waiting for me to get into some kind of trouble so he can point out he was right."

Tyler nodded thoughtfully. "I understand your concerns. I wasn't planning on telling my family about the wedding, either. I mean, I came to Nashville so we could get the ball rolling on the divorce. But...everything is different now."

She flinched. "How? How is everything different now?"

"We're going to have a baby together," he said, as though it were the most obvious thing in the world. "I know we've got to work out the logistics, but starting a family is a complicated thing."

"A f-family?" she stuttered, a feeling of dread pooling in her stomach.

"Well, yeah. I mean, obviously, since you're pregnant with my child, the divorce is off the table."

Amelia's face flushed as red as her hair, and Tyler knew immediately that he'd said the wrong thing. Or at least, he'd said it in the wrong way. He knew he was right about what they needed to do. Convincing her would take more finessing than just blurting it out the way he had. Amelia didn't take well to being told what to do. *Good job, Dixon.*

"Divorce is off the table," she mimicked with a bitter tone. "You act as though you're the only one with any say in the matter. I know you're Mr. Big Shot and you're used to your word being law, but you aren't the boss of me, Tyler. You can't bully me into staying married to you."

"Of course I'm not the only one with a say," he soothed. "And I'm not bullying you. As if I even could. You're the most stubborn woman I know. But we have a child to consider now. What about the baby?"

The baby. Tyler could barely believe he was saying those words out loud. After his engagement with Christine had ended, he'd told himself that he wasn't going through all that again. The joy and high of love weren't worth the inevitable crash and destruction at the end. He'd shelved the idea of anything more complicated than sex and focused on his work. Business came a lot easier to him than romance.

That meant that any idea of marriage or family had been put to bed, as well. He'd been okay with that. How were a wife and a family even possible when he was jet-ting from one place to another and working long hours? He had five siblings to carry on the family name and give his parents the grandchildren they craved. No one would miss his genetic contribution to the world.

And yet, faced with the eventuality of a family, he found the idea didn't bother him as much as he thought it would. The image of a rambunctious toddler with wild red curls running through the coffee shop formed in his mind. It was so real, he could almost reach out and snatch the giggling child up into his arms. He suddenly wanted that, down to the depths of his soul. When Amelia had told him, he'd been startled, of course, but now he knew what had to be done.

Tyler had been given the chance to have the family he hadn't realized he wanted, and perhaps he could keep his heart from being destroyed a second time. He was having a child with his best friend. That child needed a stable, loving home, and he and Amelia could provide that. Why would they divorce now?

Amelia's gaze fixed on his. "What *about* the baby?" she asked. "You know I'm not the kind of woman that would insist on getting married to someone I didn't love just because I got pregnant. Why would I insist on *staying* married to someone I didn't love just because I got pregnant?"

Tyler tried not to be offended. This wasn't about him, and he knew that. And he knew that she loved him. She just wasn't *in* love with him. He wasn't in love with her, either. But they could make this work. They had affection, mutual respect and history. Some shotgun marriages started with less. "I know that our marriage and our child are not what you have down in your big notebook of life plans. But don't you think it's at least worth giving our relationship a try, for our baby's sake?"

"Why can't we just be friends with a baby? We can raise it together. If you're in Nashville, it makes things easier, but we can do it. We don't have to be married to have this baby. We don't have to pretend that our wedding night meant more than it did just because I got pregnant."

She made it sound as though they'd just had a random hookup. It might not have been love, but it certainly ranked higher in importance than picking up some girl at the bar and taking her home. It had been an amazing night, one that had haunted him the past few weeks as he'd traveled the globe.

As much as they might want to forget it, they'd made love. And it had meant something. He wasn't sure exactly what, but he knew he didn't want to just be friends with a baby. He wanted the benefits, too.

"Okay, fine. Let's set the issue of the baby aside for a moment. I just want us to sit down and seriously talk all this through. It's too important to make a rash decision."

"You mean like eloping in Vegas in the middle of the night?" she snapped.

"*Another* rash decision," he corrected. "Let's not compound the issue. We have time to figure this out, so let's do it right. What's so horrible about the idea of us staying together?"

"I know that the concept of failure is something you're not comfortable with, but I don't think you understand what you're asking of me. Of us. This is about a hell of a lot more than just creating a happy home for our baby. You're asking me to choose you as the man I want to be with for the rest of my life and potentially compromise my ability to find my real soul mate. I love you, Tyler, but we're not *in love*. There's a difference."

Tyler couldn't help flinching with the sting of her sharp words this time. He was asking her to settle for him. He hadn't thought of it that way, but when she said it like that, it was painfully obvious that he didn't meet her sky-high standards. That was okay, though. He was used to being the underdog in any fight; he actually preferred it. That was just a detail. His parents had struggled his whole life, but they'd always put their kids' needs first. Not loving Amelia wasn't a good enough reason for him not to make the sacrifice and provide a stable home for their child. "People have married for reasons other than love for hundreds of years and it's worked out fine."

"Well, I don't want to be one of those people. I want love and romance. I want a husband who comes home every night and holds me in his arms, not one that texts me every other day from his latest hotel room."

Tyler sighed and took a sip of his coffee. This was bringing back uncomfortable memories of his last fight with Christine. Nothing he did was ever good enough for her. She'd wanted him to be successful and make lots of money, but she'd also placed all these demands on his time. He couldn't win, at least not playing by her rules. Maybe with Amelia it could be different. If they both made the effort, he was certain they could find something that worked for them. If that meant she had to fall in love with him, he would work to make that happen.

Staring into the polished wood of the coffee table, he asked, "Do you think loving me is a total impossibility?"

She scoffed. "That's a ridiculous question, Tyler."

His head snapped back to look at her. "No, it's not. Tell me—do you find me physically repulsive?"

"Of course not. You're very handsome, obviously, or we wouldn't have made this baby to begin with."

"Okay. Am I obnoxious? Pretentious? A jerk?"

Amelia sighed and leaned back against the cushions. "No. You're none of those things. You're wonderful."

Sometimes Tyler didn't understand women. And Amelia in particular. But he'd decided they were staying together for this baby. If he knew nothing else, he knew how to sell something. He was going to market himself like one of his finest gemstones until she couldn't resist saying yes.

"So I'm good-looking. I own my own business and make good money. I'm fun to be around. You've trusted me with all your secrets. You enjoy spending time with me. The sex was pretty awesome, if I may say so myself… I must be missing something, Amelia. Is there a crimson *F* stitched to the front of my shirt, because you refuse to see me as anything but a friend? If there was another person on the planet exactly like me, you'd date him."

Amelia frowned. "You're talking nonsense."

"No, I'm not. Tell me your top five must-haves for a man you could love. Seriously." He knew the list was probably closer to a hundred must-haves. After each of her relationships ended, she'd add a new thing or two to the list.

She thought about it for a moment, holding up one hand to count off on her fingers. "Smart, a good sense of humor, compassionate, ambitious and honest."

He twisted his lips in irritation. If he'd asked her to name the five things she liked best about him, she might have recited the same list. "And what on that list do I not have? I'm all of those things and more."

"Maybe, but you're not around. I'm not going to sit at home alone with this baby while you hopscotch around the planet."

"What if I said I could be better about that? Maybe having a wife and a family will give me something to come home to."

"We're still not in love," she argued.

"Love is overrated. Look what it got Christine and me—a bunch of heartbreak. I'm not saying it will work. We might end up being totally incompatible, and if we are, we end it and you can go back to your quest for the White Buffalo. But why can't we at least try? Pandora's box is open. There's no going back to where we were."

She sighed and shook her head. "I don't know, Tyler. I can't…lose you. You've been the person in my life I can always count on. You're my rock."

"You're not going to lose me, no matter what." A wicked smile curled his lips as a thought came to mind. "We've slept together and the world hasn't ended. I'm still here. And since I've seen you naked, I've got even more incentive to stick around. I've touched and tasted every inch of your body, and if there's the potential I'll get to do it again, I'm not going anywhere."

Amelia's eyes widened, her cheeks flushing. "Tyler…" she chastised, but he wasn't hearing it.

"I know you're attracted to me. You just have to admit it to yourself."

"Wh-what?" she sputtered. "What makes you say that?"

"Oh, come on, Amelia. You can't blame that whole night on tequila. You were wildly passionate. You couldn't get enough of me, as though you'd finally let the floodgates open and allowed yourself to have something forbidden. It was the sexiest thing I've ever witnessed," he added, and it was true. He hadn't lusted over his best friend in the past, but since that night, he couldn't get her out of his head.

He placed a hand on her knee and leaned in close. "If that night was any indication, we might have a chance. So why not see what could happen if you opened your mind to the possibility of us? Forget about Tyler the friend and think of me as the hot new guy you're dating."

That, finally, made Amelia smile, and relief washed over him all at once.

Her eyes narrowed at him, her lips twisting in deep thought. "Okay, fine," she said at last. "We'll give this relationship a trial run. I will *date* you, Tyler, but there are some ground rules I want to lay down first. Number one, no one is to know we're married, or that I'm pregnant. Especially not your family. Did you tell anyone?"

"No," he said quickly. He'd never thought their marriage would last as long as it had. His family loved Amelia, but he wouldn't get their hopes up for nothing.

"Okay. My three coworkers found out this morning, but they're the only ones and that's how I want it to stay. Number two, I'm putting a time limit on this so it doesn't drag on too long. You've got thirty days to win me over. And I mean it. I want to be wooed, Tyler. I want romance and passion and excitement. You're not going to get off easy because we're friends. I'm going to be harder on you because you should know what I want and need."

A wide grin broke out across his face. Tyler never backed down from a challenge, and this wouldn't be any different. He could win her over in thirty days, no problem. He knew her better than he knew himself. She just had to let him try. "That's fair."

Amelia turned to look across the coffee shop and survey her surroundings. She sighed heavily and shook her head. She seemed disappointed by everything that had happened. Worn down. He didn't like seeing her that way. If there was one thing he loved the most about her, it was her optimism when it came to love. She believed—really, truly believed—in the power of love. But she didn't believe in them. He would change that. To make it happen, he would lift her up, make her smile, make her believe this was the right choice for them both, even if he wasn't entirely sure of it himself.

"All I've ever wanted," she said softly, "was a marriage like my grandparents have. They've been happily married for fifty-seven years, and they're just as in love today as they were the day they got married. That's what I want, and I'm not going to compromise that for anything or anyone."

Tyler took a deep breath, wondering if she was on the verge of changing her mind. He knew all that about her. She'd always talked about her grandparents and how she wanted a love like theirs. That was a high bar to set, but he was up to the challenge. If she didn't fall in love with him, it wouldn't be for lack of effort on his part.

No, he wouldn't even allow the negative thought. Amelia would fall in love with him. There could be no doubt of his success.

"At the end of thirty days," she continued, "we'll decide how we feel about each other. If we're in love, you'll propose again—properly—and we'll announce our engagement to the world. I want to get remarried with the big ceremony and all our family and friends there. And if one of us doesn't want to continue, we quietly agree to end it."

"And then what? Are we just supposed to go back to how things were and pretend it never happened? That will be pretty hard with a child."

"If we divorce, we make the best of things. I hope there won't be any animosity between us. We stay friends, okay?"

"Okay." Tyler knew failure wasn't an option, but he was comforted by the idea that he would have her friendship no matter what. She was notoriously picky when it came to men. He refused to become just another guy thrown onto the reject pile with the rest. "Anything else?"

"I think that's it," she said with a smile that betrayed she already knew it was too much.

"Okay, then, I have one demand of my own." If she was only going to give him thirty days, he needed to make them count and get every advantage he could. That meant proximity. There was no way this was going to work if they went to dinner a couple times a week and went to their separate corners when it was done. He couldn't disappear to Antwerp or work eighteen-hour days. If they wanted to figure out whether they could cut it being married, they needed to go all the way. "I want us to live together the whole time."

He watched Amelia frown into her lap with dismay. "My apartment isn't really big enough for two people. It's just a one bedroom, and my closet is already over-flowing."

Tyler had zero intention of living in her tiny little apartment with her. There was a difference between prox-imity and being locked in a cage together for thirty days. He was certain only one of them would make it out alive. "I'll get us a new place," he said simply.

"I have a lease."

"I'll pay the fee to break it."

She sighed, obviously irritated with his ability to shoot down her every concern. "And what if at the end of thirty days, we're not in love? I'll be pregnant and homeless."

He sighed. "You will be nothing of the sort. If we don't work out, I'll help you find a new place that's big enough for you and the baby. I'll buy you whatever you want."

"You don't have to buy me a house, Tyler. I'll just keep my apartment for the month, stay with you, and we'll figure out what to do about it when we've made a decision about us."

He chuckled, knowing there wasn't much sense in continuing to argue about this when that wasn't how it was going to end. "Fine, but you've got to get used to the idea of someone else helping out. You're having my child and I'm taking care of you. That point is nonnegotiable. Have we got a deal or not?"

"It's a deal. Congratulations, Tyler," she said, holding out her delicate manicured hand to shake on their agreement. "You may now date your wife."

Game on.

He took her hand, shaking it for only a moment before pulling her knuckles to his mouth to kiss them. She was soft and warm against his lips, reminding him of how he'd spent an entire night kissing every sensitive curve. His skin prickled where it touched her, the sudden rush of need to have her again rocketing through his veins like a shot of adrenaline.

Amelia's reaction was just as potent. Her lips parted softly and she sucked a soft gasp into her lungs. Her eyes fluttered closed for a moment as his lips pressed to her skin and she leaned in to him.

He was going to enjoy this challenge. Pulling her hand to his chest, he leaned close. The air was warm and charged between them, her eyes widening and her pupils enlarging as he neared her. Her breaths were short and rapid, and her tongue moistened her lips on reflex. She wanted him to kiss her. Winning her over might be easier than he thought if she reacted to him so easily.

He pressed his lips to the outer shell of her ear and whispered in a low, seductive tone, "What do you say we seal the deal with a real kiss?"

When he pulled back, he noticed that a smile had lit

Amelia's eyes and curled her lips. She moved ever so slightly closer to him, placing a hand on his cheek.

"Sorry," she said with a shake of her head. "I don't kiss on the first date."

Three

Amelia watched a flicker of emotion cross Tyler's face before he leaned back and sighed. He seemed tired. The familiar blue eyes she'd looked into a million times were lined with fatigue, and the muscles in his neck and shoulders were tense. She didn't know if it was the early flight, the stress of their marriage or the pressing worry of impending fatherhood that had him tied in knots.

She wanted to reach out and rub his shoulders to loosen him up, but she realized that probably wouldn't help. She might be the reason he was exhausted, as she was refusing to play by his rules and making everything harder than he probably thought it needed to be.

"If you won't let me kiss you," he said at last, "will you at least let me buy you another cup of tea?"

"No," she said, shaking her head. She didn't want anything else in her stomach. Right now, she felt okay, but she didn't know how quickly the balance could tip. "I could actually use some air. This coffee shop is a little stuffy." The combination of the heater and the smell of roast coffee were verging on overwhelming. Amelia loved the scent of coffee, but her tolerance was limited today.

She could also use a little breathing room from Tyler. She should've known he would shoot out from the starting gate at the proverbial sound of the gun, but she hadn't prepared herself for the sudden assault. Nor had she been prepared for her body's response to him.

"How about a walk?" Tyler suggested. "I know it's a little chilly today, but the sun is out."

That worked for her. Amelia always thought better when she moved anyway. Of course, that meant she might take three steps and realize she was a fool. If she was honest with herself, she already knew that. As she watched Tyler devour the last of his cinnamon roll and toss their empty cups into the trash, she felt the worry pooling in her already tumultuous stomach.

She had very nearly kissed her best friend just a moment ago. She'd covered her weakness with a joke, but for a second, it had been a very real impulse. The skin of her knuckles burned where he'd seared her with his mouth. Her heart was still thumping at double the speed. The goose bumps continued to stand tall across her arms. Fortunately, she was able to hide all that beneath her blouse and the jacket he was currently helping her into.

Kissing Tyler shouldn't be a big deal considering she'd let him do a hell of a lot more only a few short weeks ago. But this time she was stone-cold sober, and she still wanted him. She supposed she should be happy about that fact. That was the path they were on now. She'd agreed to date him. Move in with him. They were having a baby—

the best thing she could do was fall in love with Tyler. That would make everything easier.

But if she knew anything about relationships, it was that none of it was easy. Amelia wasn't the kind to slip and fall in love. She was too analytical, too driven to find just the right guy. With over seven billion people in the world, the odds of running across the one who was meant for her were astronomical. Yet every day, happy couples came into From This Moment, ready to get married. Were they settling, or had fate really brought them together?

Fate had certainly thrust her and Tyler together. Did that mean he was the one she was meant to be with? She didn't know. But whether dating him was a good idea or a bad one, she'd given her word to try. And almost immediately, she'd found her body was on board with the plan, even if her mind was resistant.

It was official—her life had spun out of control. Could she blame her reaction to him on pregnancy hormones?

Tyler opened the door of the coffee shop and they stepped out onto the sidewalk. It was a beautiful day. The sky was a brilliant robin's-egg blue with no clouds to be seen. There was a cool breeze, but the warmth of the sun on her face made it worth the chill. Winter had been rough this year, pounding them with uncharacteristic snow and ice storms. Her coworker Bree had even been trapped in a Gatlinburg mountain cabin by a wicked winter storm just a few weeks before Amelia went to Las Vegas.

The weather in Nashville was usually pretty mild, but she was certain today was the first time she'd seen the sun since November. Having a taste of it made her look forward to the summer. She couldn't wait for flowers, ice cream trucks, sandals, cute pedicures and spending a little time cooling off in her bikini at the pool of her apartment complex.

Wait, she thought. Summer might be very different this year. For one thing, she'd be four or five months pregnant, so the bikini was probably out. And based on their discussions, she wouldn't be living at her apartment much longer. She was moving into a place with Tyler. At least for thirty days. After that, who knew?

Tyler tugged his leather jacket over his navy blazer. They were barely half a block down the road when she felt his fingers reach for hers.

They held hands a lot—in a goofy, best friend sort of manner. She and Tyler had always been physically affectionate in a nonthreatening way. At least, nonthreatening to her. The guys she'd dated had never cared too much for the male best friend she talked about all the time. They'd never believed her when she insisted they were only friends. Perhaps they'd seen something in the two of them that even she couldn't see.

Amelia laced her fingers though his until they were palm to palm. As much as she didn't want to admit it, holding his hand felt different somehow. Maybe it was the soft shudder that ran through her when his warm skin pressed against hers. Perhaps it was the occasional whiffs of his cologne that drifted past her nose. Or her sudden awareness of his body so close to hers. It was most likely that all three were combining to remind her of that night together—the one when she'd realized what he was hiding under those expensive suits, and that she couldn't wait to explore every hard, muscular angle of it.

"This area has built up a lot since I was here last," Tyler said, oblivious to where her thoughts had strayed.

"Yes. None of this was here when we first bought the land to start building From This Moment. Fortunately, it filled in with a nice residential area and some higher-end shopping centers. I wish I could afford to live closer to work, but we found a good spot between two really expensive residential areas, so it's not happening. There's not even an apartment complex anywhere around."

"It's nice. I like it. Close to the interstate, but not too close. Nearby shopping and restaurants. Not too congested. What do you think about looking for a place around here?"

Amelia turned to look up at him with a frown. "Did you miss the part where I said it's really expensive?"

"Did you miss the part where I auctioned off a thirty-one-carat canary diamond at Christie's auction house last month?"

He had mentioned it, but she hadn't thought much of it. He was constantly buying and selling stones. "But it's not like you made pure profit. You've got what you paid for it originally, company overhead, insurance, fees to Christie's... If you got it recut, there's that expense, too." There had been a time in Amelia's life when she'd known nothing about the world of jewels and gemstones. There had also been a time where she hadn't owned any jewelry worth more than fifty dollars. Tyler had changed all that.

Every year on her birthday, or for Christmas, he sent her something. The large teardrop amethyst around her neck had arrived on her twenty-sixth birthday. She also had sapphire earrings, a ruby-and-diamond tennis bracelet, an emerald ring and a strand of pearls. She never dared to ask how much he spent. She didn't want to know. She just bought a small fireproof safe to store it and increased her jewelry insurance policy every year.

"Of course I have expenses," he argued. "My point is that we don't have to rent a tiny place in a cheaper neighborhood on the other side of Nashville. If you'd like to live around here and be closer to work, I'll have a real estate agent start looking."

The average home in the area ran about half a million. A good number of them were twice as much. She couldn't imagine what the rent would be on a place like that. "You can look," she said with a tone of disbelief, "but I doubt you'll find something that works in this area. We don't need a four-thousand-square-foot mansion with a five-car garage and an indoor pool."

He shrugged, leading her down the sidewalk as though discussions of multimillion-dollar real estate transactions were nothing to him. "You don't know that. I live in Manhattan. Real estate is at such a premium that some people live in apartments the size of a dorm room. The idea of a ridiculously large house—with private parking—sounds awesome to me. Why not? You might like having an indoor pool."

"Get real, Tyler," she said with a wry chuckle. "We may only live in this place for a month. Even if we stay longer, we need at most a three-bedroom house with a decent yard. Maybe a good-size kitchen so I can cook. And that's only if we like the place enough to put in an offer to buy it. Right?"

"Right," he said, looking thoughtfully off into the distance.

Amelia knew him well enough to know he wasn't paying any mind to what she said. He'd pick whatever caught his fancy, regardless of price or practicality. All she knew was that if he picked a massive house, he'd better hire a housekeeper to go with it. It would be a full-time job keeping it clean, and she already had one of those.

They paused at an intersection, waiting for the light to change. "I'll see what I can find. But like you, I'm not going to compromise, either. This isn't just about finding a place to stay for a few weeks or months—it's about finding a home where we can start our life together. It's the house to which we'll bring our child home from the hospital. It's where he or she will take their first steps."

Tyler had only known about this baby for an hour, but it didn't matter. It was still an almost abstract idea in her mind, and yet he'd already revised his entire strategy to accommodate and care for his surprise family. He couldn't just settle for a house to spend the next few weeks. He wanted a home for his family. He wanted to take care of her and their child. She didn't understand how he could roll with the punches like that.

"You know, you don't have to be so confident and positive about everything. You're allowed to be upset and scared by the prospect of what's happening. I threw a grenade at you and you're just standing there holding it with a smile. I know that you don't want to be tied down, and a family wasn't on your radar. I'm freaking out. Tell me you're freaking out, too, so I'll feel better."

Tyler turned to look at her with a frown. "What good would it do to get upset? Worrying just wastes valuable time. When I'm feeling uncertain, having a plan to go forward and executing it is the only thing that makes me feel better. No, a child wasn't what I was expecting or wanting. Yes, a part of me wants to get in my car and disappear. But I won't do that to our child. I have an obligation to step up and take responsibility for my actions, and I'll do whatever it takes to make it work."

It wasn't a romantic declaration, but she'd asked for his honesty and gotten it. Having Tyler's child wasn't her plan, but she knew she would be hard-pressed to find a better father for her baby.

"You're only thinking short-term, Ames, but I have no intention of us getting divorced in thirty days. Successful people plan for success, so I'm going to find the perfect house for us. We'll rent until we're sure we love it, and then we'll see if we can convince the owner to sell it. It will be the place where you and I will raise our family."

His words should've been reassuring, and yet she felt a cold chill run through her as the concept started to sink in. He wasn't resigned to his obligation or even optimistic about their future together. He was treating this like a challenge to be overcome.

Until that moment, she hadn't fully realized that she'd waved red in front of a bull. Laying down a thirty-day challenge to Mr. Overachiever wasn't very smart if she didn't want to be with him in the end. Whether or not his heart was in this, he would likely get his way, be it with the house, their child or their relationship.

She felt a sudden pressure against her chest; the air clamped down in her lungs. Suddenly, a thirty-day trial period had just changed to the rest of their lives.

What had she really agreed to?

"I'm serious about us making this work, Ames. Our baby deserves it," Tyler said. Before he could elaborate, he noticed a bit of the color draining from her face. She was fair complexioned, but she was approaching the shade of a sheet of paper. "Are you okay?"

She grimaced a little but didn't answer, making him wonder if she was battling morning sickness again. "Are you going to be sick?"

"No," she said with a shake of her head. "Suddenly, I'm just a little tired. I didn't sleep well this weekend and it was a big wedding with three entrée choices. I think it's just catching up with me."

He had witnessed two of his older sisters' pregnancies, and their biggest complaint was always exhaustion.

It started earlier than you'd expect. Taking her elbow, he led her to a bench around the corner.

Tyler sat her down on the wooden seat and crouched at her knee. He looked up at her, realizing for a moment that he was in the same position he'd been in when he'd proposed to her on a sidewalk along the Las Vegas Strip. The memory made him smile despite his concerns for her. He wasn't sure what had made him remember their teenage pact that night, but it had seemed like the perfect remedy for her frown. In that moment, he would've done anything to cheer her up. He'd never dreamed that their adventure would ever go this far. He'd never even expected them to consummate the marriage, much less have a baby together. Would he have gone through with it if he'd known? That was a question with an irrelevant answer, unless someone had invented a time machine he didn't know about. He returned his focus to her.

"Can I get you anything? A bottle of water? Or do you need something to eat? There's a convenience store across the street. I can bring you anything you want."

"Stop fussing," Amelia said, although her eyes were pinched tightly shut as she spoke. "I'm fine. I just need a minute."

"Are you sure I—"

"I'm pregnant, not helpless, Tyler. I just needed a little break from walking around."

Tyler ignored her, jogging across the street to the store and returning with an ice-cold bottle of water. He pressed it into her hand.

Amelia sighed but twisted off the cap to take a sip anyway. "Are you going to be like this for the next eight months? 'Cause I don't think I can take you hovering over me all the time. It reminds me too much of my dad."

"Hey, now," Tyler argued in an offended tone. "There's

a big difference between trying to take care of you because I want to and doing it because I think you're incapable of taking care of yourself. I'm not your father. And you're not your mother."

Visiting Amelia's home when they were kids had been an eye-opening experience. In Tyler's home, everyone pitched in. Both his parents worked. The older kids helped take care of the younger ones. The boys and the girls all did their share, equally. That was the only way they could get by, day to day.

Then he went to Amelia's house and watched with surprise the way Principal Kennedy fawned over and protectively guarded his wife and daughters. He treated them as though they were delicate and helpless, a perception Amelia's mother worked hard to create. She was fragile and often ill with headaches or other ailments, although Amelia insisted there was nothing actually wrong with her. It didn't matter. Amelia's father took care of everything. He made all the decisions, earned all the money. He hired a cleaning woman to come a few days a week and relieve her mother of that burden. The two Kennedy girls were expected to do nothing but be pretty and shop, just like their mother.

It had made Amelia crazy growing up. She was far from helpless and fragile—she had a spine of steel. She was smart and independent, but her father never gave her enough credit for anything she did. He expected her to marry well and carry on the way her mother had.

And he supposed she had done that, even if she hadn't meant to. Tyler was successful. His business in gemstones and antiquities was amazingly lucrative. The markup on diamonds was insane. A quick trip to his suppliers in India or Belgium would set him up easily with a stash of high-quality stones at an amazing price. On any given day, he could have a quarter of a million dollars in precious gems tucked into his lapel pocket. If Amelia wanted to quit her job, he could take care of her and their child for the rest of their lives.

But he knew she would never allow that. He wouldn't even suggest such a thing for fear of bodily harm. She wasn't her mother. Not even close. "You might not like it," he continued, "but I've got a vested interest in your welfare. For one thing, I haven't had a chance to get a life-insurance policy on my wife yet." He grinned wide and was pleased to see her reluctantly smile and roll her eyes at his joke.

"And for another," he said, getting to his feet and sitting beside her on the bench, "that's our kid you're hauling around in there. It's my job to make sure both of you have everything you need to stay happy, healthy and safe. You can complain all you want and it won't make any difference."

Amelia searched his face for a moment, looking for something he didn't understand. Then she nodded and placed her hand over his, squeezing gently. "Thank you for that. I'm sorry for being difficult today. I feel as though my whole life has been hijacked and shifted off course. I've gotten used to being on my own and taking care of myself. It may take a while for me to adjust to anything else. But I do appreciate it. You. No matter what happens between us, I know you'll be a good father."

Tyler watched a bright red lock of hair slip from its clip and curl around the curve of her heart-shaped face. The peachy tones of her skin had returned, beckoning him to reach out and caress her velvet-soft cheek, pushing the hair behind her ear. Today, he would do it because he could.

He reached out to her, letting his knuckles softly graze

across her cheekbone as they swept the errant curl away from her face. The pale peach of her skin was replaced with a rosy pink as her cheeks flushed. Her dark eyes watched him, but she didn't pull away from his touch.

"I've always wanted to do that," he said.

"Really?" she said, her voice betraying the disbelief that reflected in her eyes.

"Absolutely. You've got the most beautiful hair I've ever seen. It's like liquid fire."

"Tyler," she began, hesitating, "I know I can be difficult in a relationship, and you know that better than anyone. Part of me has begun to wonder if I'll ever…" Her gaze dropped into her lap. "Do you really think you can fall in love with me in thirty days?"

Tyler didn't want to lie to Amelia, but he knew he had to. If he told her that he had no intention of ever falling in love with her—or anyone, for that matter—it would all be over. If he wanted to succeed for their child's sake, he had to play along and keep those dark secrets inside. He couldn't let his own doubts spill over and taint Amelia with his negativity.

As it was, he was stunned by her fears. How could a woman so smart, so beautiful, so talented have any doubt that a man could love her? At least, a man capable of opening himself up to loving someone?

"Are you kidding me? You are incredible in a hundred different ways. Your cooking is the best thing I've ever tasted. You tell better dirty jokes than any guy I've met. You're strong of will and spirit. You care so deeply for others that I don't know how you don't get your heart crushed every day. You amaze me in a new way every time I'm with you."

Amelia listened to him speak with silent tears welling in her eyes. He couldn't bear to see her cry, ever. He opened his arms to her and pulled her tight against his chest. She rested her head against his shoulder, allowing him to press a kiss into the silky strands of her hair.

"I didn't want to make you cry, but you need to know how important you are. I measure every woman I date against the bar you've set, and each of them has fallen miserably short. You're the best thing that ever happened to me. You need to think like a winner and erase all those doubts. Then you need to ask yourself, how could I *not* fall in love with you?"

When he finished speaking, she sat back and looked up at him. She studied his face with a curious expression that wrinkled her delicate nose.

He didn't know what she was thinking, but he was hyperaware of how close she was. The scent of her body lotion perfumed the air with tropical flowers. He breathed it into his lungs and held it there, remembering that scent from their night together. The muscles in his neck tensed as the memories rushed into his mind and flooded his veins. It would be so easy to touch her. Kiss her. And he wanted to, first date be damned.

As though she'd read his mind, Amelia reached up and rested her palm against his cheek. Then she leaned into him. She closed the gap slowly, her eyes focused on his until their lips touched and their eyes closed. Her mouth was soft and hesitant against his own. He tried not to push too hard or too fast, applying just enough pressure, but letting her take the lead this first time.

It was hard. The sweet, gentle kiss was enough to start a hum of electricity traveling through his body. Tyler wanted to tug her against him and drink her in. He wanted to caress her silken tongue with his own and press his fingertips into her ample flesh. But he knew she was testing the waters. If he pushed too hard, he would lose valuable time trying to coax her back to this place.

She finally pulled away and he reluctantly let her go. Tyler opened his eyes to find her looking up at him with a dreamy smile curling her lips. She took a deep breath and sat back, tugging down at her tunic. "I've, uh…" She stumbled over her words. "I've really got to get back to work."

"Okay."

Tyler swallowed hard, trying to suppress the heated need she'd built up inside him. His every muscle was tense, his fingertips tingling with the need to touch her. It would have to wait. But not for too much longer. She'd kissed him. That was an important first step on the road to success.

He stood and stepped back, helping her get up from the bench. They walked to his rental car and made their way back to the wedding facility she owned with her friends. Once there, he parked the car and came around to open the door for her. Amelia got out but didn't get far. Before she could escape, he leaned in, pressing a palm against the car and blocking her exit.

"So I'll let you know when the real estate agent finds us a place and I can arrange the movers to pack your apartment. In the meantime, can I take you out to dinner tomorrow night?"

She looked up at him with surprise in her dark eyes. "So soon?"

Tyler had to laugh at her. She really had no idea what she'd done. His beautiful wife was a smart woman, but the terms of their agreement weren't the most intelligent choice she could've made. He had been willing to take their romance slow, but she'd cranked up the dial on the intensity when she'd set her time limit.

He leaned in to her, pinning her with his intense gaze. "You've given us thirty days to fall in love, Amelia. Do you really think I'm going to let a single day go by without seeing you? Touching you? Hearing the melodic sound of your voice?"

Her gaze dropped to the pavement to avoid his eyes, her teeth nervously chewing at her bottom lip. "I understand that," she argued, "but I have a job to do. So do you. You know I pretty much spend Thursday, Friday and Saturday in a kitchen. I can't run off on a date with you every night."

He understood that. They both had responsibilities. He just wasn't going to let her use them as an excuse. She'd agreed to a test run of their relationship, but he knew this would be a battle to the finish. She wouldn't give in easily, and neither would he. "That's fine. That's why we'll spend our nights together at our new place. And during the day, I may very well be by your side, too."

"What?" Her nose wrinkled in confusion. "In the kitchen with me? At work?"

Tyler nodded. "Whenever I can, I'm going to be where you are, Amelia. If you're baking a cake, I'm going to be washing the pans. If you're dicing vegetables, I'll be peeling carrots and taking out the trash. You insisted I be present, not zipping around the world, so for the next thirty days, I'm your shadow. You only get a reprieve today while I make all the necessary arrangements."

Her mouth dropped open and her auburn eyebrows knit together, but she didn't say anything. She hadn't thought this through, and the consequences would come back to haunt her. She'd be begging him to take a business trip before too long.

"Don't you have a job to do? Aren't there precious gems to be sold? Diamonds to be cut?"

He shrugged nonchalantly. "I have plenty of work, I assure you. But I have a flexible schedule and employees that can handle some things. I can conduct business where and when I want to. That's the beauty of what I do. Right now, I'm more interested in focusing all my attention on you. So again," he pressed, "dinner tomorrow night?"

Amelia drew her mouth closed and nodded. "Okay. About seven?"

Seven was perfect. That was his lucky number—an omen of his success on the horizon. He pressed a soft kiss to her lips and stepped back to give her some room. "It's a date."

Four

"She's ba-a-a-ck!"

Amelia winced the moment she crossed the threshold into the lobby and heard Gretchen announce her arrival. She'd been hoping they would have clients in this morning. If someone was booking a wedding with Natalie or taking a tour, her friends couldn't fuss over her. No such luck.

Bree and Gretchen spilled into the hallway. Natalie popped her head out of her office, her headset on. She held up a finger to wait and then continued her phone conversation.

Amelia went on into her office so she could hang up her coat and stow her purse away. She grabbed her tablet in the hopes they would talk about what she'd missed at the staff meeting, but she knew the conversation would be about anything but work.

She carried her half-empty bottle of water with her to the conference room. By the time she got there, her three partners at From This Moment were assembled there, waiting, although not patiently. Bree looked as if she was about to burst with excitement. Gretchen had wicked glee lighting her eyes. Natalie seemed concerned, as she was prone to be. She was suspicious about love in general, and marriage was a bridge too far in her opinion. At the moment, Natalie was probably the smarter of the two of them.

Amelia sat down in one of the chairs. "So what did I miss this morning?"

"Please." Bree groaned. "You are going to tell us everything that's going on with you and that guy, right now!"

"Yes, and start from the beginning," Natalie said, "since I missed the discussion this morning."

With a heavy sigh, Amelia repeated the tale about the high school reunion gone awry. She went into as much detail as she could, hoping she wouldn't have to repeat the story again. She left out the part about it being the most incredible sex of her life and tried to focus on how she ended up married to her best friend while on vacation.

"So," Natalie began with a furrowed brow, "did he just come to town so you can start the divorce proceedings?"

"Pretty much, although I'm not sure we're going to do that just yet."

Bree's eyebrows shot up. "What does *that* mean?"

"It means," Amelia began, "that we're going to date for a month and see where it goes. It's a lot easier to get married than it is to get divorced, so we're going to put more thought into the latter than we did into the former."

"You're going to date your husband? This is all just so wrong," Natalie said with a slow shake of her head.

"Is he moving here? Doesn't he live in New York or something?"

"Yes, his company is based out of Manhattan. He has more flexibility with his work than I do, so he's going to rent a place here for a month." Amelia hoped they didn't ask what they would do after that, because she honestly didn't know. Could Tyler stay in Nashville long-term? She couldn't leave. Amelia was From This Moment's caterer. A wedding without food was…a tacky Vegas elopement. She sighed.

As it was, they would have to figure out what they would do while she was on maternity leave. They would cross that bridge when they got there, she supposed. She hadn't even dropped that bomb on her friends yet.

"You and Tyler never dated before, did you?"

Amelia took a sip of her water and shook her head. "No. We've only ever been friends. You know how I am with men. If we'd dated, we would've broken up by now. It was always more important to have him in my life than to act on some physical impulse."

"Natalie said he was hot. Like, *Chris Pine* hot. How could you go all those years without so much as kissing him?" Gretchen asked.

The simplest answer was that she just hadn't allowed her mind to go there. Yes, he was handsome. All the things they'd talked about in the coffee shop earlier were correct. He had a lot of the attributes she valued in a prospective partner. But in the end, he was just Tyler. That canceled out a lot. "We did kiss once, in tenth grade. This stupid girl dared us at a party in front of everyone."

"And?"

"And—" she shrugged "—it was awkward. I only have a sister, but I thought that might be what it was like to kiss your own brother. Zero chemistry. A very uncomfortable experience. After that, it was easier to keep things platonic."

"Tell me it was better the second time around," Gretchen groaned.

"It was. A million times better." Amelia should've taken into consideration that their first kiss had been with an audience of their peers. On a dare. They'd been fifteen and she had braces. Neither of them had had much experience to go on. It had been a recipe for disaster, but what a difference a dozen or so years could make! "I honestly couldn't believe I was kissing the same person. Even knowing it was Tyler and I shouldn't be doing that, I couldn't stop myself."

"What happens in Vegas…" Gretchen said, as though that explained everything.

And in a way, it did. The lights and the alcohol and the heightened emotions inspired you to move out of your comfort zone and do something exciting for a change. Unfortunately, not everything that happened there stayed there. The consequences had followed her home.

"What did Tyler say to change your mind about getting divorced all of a sudden?" Bree asked as she thoughtfully twirled her long blond hair around her finger. "You've already had a month to think about it, and I was pretty sure you were set on that when you left."

And now they came to the part she was avoiding. "I was. We were. But um…things changed. I, uh…"

"You're pregnant," Natalie stated. There wasn't an accusatory tone to her voice, just quiet resignation. She gave Natalie a lot of grief for being uptight, but she was very observant. She saw everything, even the things people tried to hide.

Amelia couldn't respond so she just nodded, thankful that Natalie had saved her from saying the words aloud a second time today.

"Wait, what?" Bree nearly shrieked. "You're pregnant

and you haven't mentioned it yet? How could you leave that massive detail out of the story?"

"One bombshell at a time, okay?" Amelia frowned. "I just found out and I'm still a little shell-shocked by the whole thing. I mean, it's as though my whole life has gone irrevocably off course. You think it's bad to marry your best friend on a whim? Find out you're having his baby, too. There's no pretending it didn't happen anymore. There's no annulling it and sweeping the memory of it under the rug."

"That's why you're trying to stay together," Gretchen noted, the pieces finally clicking together for her. "What will you do if it doesn't work out? Get divorced and work out a custody arrangement?"

"Yes. It will be okay, though. We've agreed that no matter what, we'll stay friends."

"Um, Amelia," Natalie said, "you don't really think that's going to happen, do you?"

"Of course it will," she insisted. They'd been friends for fourteen years. They could do it. Of course, that had been without sex and emotions and custody agreements in the way.

"I'm not trying to upset you," Natalie clarified, "but you need to be prepared for this. At the end of the month, you two might break up. And it may go okay for a while, but eventually things are going to fall apart. You'll try for the good of your child, but it will get hard. I've seen it happen. He'll show up late to bring the kid back from his weekend and you'll get irritated. You'll want the baby for a holiday that's supposed to be his and you'll argue about it. Make the most of these thirty days, Amelia. If you don't have a husband when the time is up, don't plan on having a best friend for much longer after that."

She hadn't thought about that at all. She was certain

they would be okay, but she had seen it happen to other people. If she thought sex might ruin their friendship, shared custody and a strained relationship would certainly do it.

Natalie reached out and placed a hand over Amelia's. The supportive gesture made tears threaten in her eyes. She never cried. Hated to, actually. She always saw it as a weak feminine gesture her mother used to manipulate her father. But in the moment, all the emotions and worries of the past few weeks came to a head and before she could stop them, teardrops started spilling over her cheeks.

"Damn hormones," Amelia lamented.

"Aw, honey, it will be okay." Bree got up and snatched a tissue from the other side of the room to give to her. "Everything is going to work out, I know it."

"It absolutely will," Gretchen chimed in. "No matter what happens with Tyler after the thirty days are up, you're going to be a great mom. We're going to throw the greatest baby shower in the history of baby showers. And I'll paint a mural in the nursery. We can even turn the extra office into a playroom with toys and a crib so you can bring the baby to work. Bree's getting married soon—we could have babies all over the place before too long."

Bree's eyes widened a touch and she choked on the last sip of her latte. "Um, yeah," she said with a rough cough to clear her lungs. "Babies all over the place."

Amelia had to smile through her tears. She really did have amazing friends. Gretchen was right. No matter what happened with Tyler, things would work out. Neither the marriage nor the baby had been planned, but she would make it through this. "Thank you, guys. I feel a lot better, now."

"That's what girlfriends are for," Natalie said with a

soft smile. "You know we're always here to celebrate, commiserate or eviscerate. Whatever you might need."

"Okay. For right now, all I need is to keep this quiet. Please don't mention it to anyone. Really. No Facebook posts, no offhand comments when clients are here, no telling my mom I'm at the obstetrician if she calls and I'm not around. We're keeping all of this a secret until we decide what we're going to do. You guys are the only ones that know."

"Sure thing," Bree said. "I won't tell a soul."

"Me, neither," Gretchen agreed. She looked up at the clock on the wall and sighed. "We'd better get back to it. I've got the future Mr. and Mrs. Edwards coming by to pick their invitations on their lunch break."

All four of the women stood and started back to their various tasks. Mondays were Amelia's Fridays. She was off the next two days, so she needed to get things in order for the upcoming weekend. That meant submitting her grocery order to the food suppliers. She also needed to email the finalized reception menu to a couple doing a '50s rockabilly-themed wedding. There wasn't time to sit around and mope about her situation for long.

Life went on. And so must she.

Tyler was pretty certain today might qualify as one of the longest days of his life. Probably because he hadn't slept since he arrived in Nashville and the two days had blurred together into one. By the time Tyler rang the doorbell of Amelia's apartment to pick her up for their dinner date Tuesday night, he had been awake for forty hours straight.

He'd learned early on that sleep was for the guy who came in second. He'd accomplished a lot since he dropped Amelia back at the chapel. He'd made arrangements to manage his business dealings from Nashville. He got some of his employees to take on more business travel to free up his calendar. There was still a trip to London on his schedule in a few weeks, but he would play that by ear. He really needed to be there for the Sotheby's auction. Perhaps he could talk Amelia into joining him for that trip.

Work handled, he met with a real estate agent and toured half a dozen potential homes. He was pretty certain he'd found the one, but he wouldn't decide until Amelia had seen it. He'd also turned in his rental car and picked up something more suitable for the next few weeks.

With the logistics in place, he directed his attention toward more romantic pursuits. He made dinner reservations and set out in search of a nearby florist that carried her favorite flower. She'd said she wanted romance and that she expected him to know exactly what she would like. Well, mission accomplished.

Amelia opened the door of her apartment. Before she could even say hello, her gaze dropped to the bouquet of roses in his hands. Not just any roses—green beauties. They were a pale-green-and-ivory rose with darker green edges. The flowers reminded him of tiny cabbages, really, but she'd always loved them. Her favorite color was green after all.

"Wow," she said. She looked up at him with a wide smile brightening her face.

"I was about to say that same thing." Amelia looked amazing. She was wearing a plum-colored dress that popped against the ivory of her skin. It almost looked like strips of fabric wrapped around her body. It had cap sleeves with straps crisscrossing over her collarbones. It molded to her shape, making her incredibly voluptuous figure even more outrageous. She had the kind of dangerous curves that required two hands or a man could lose control. "You look beautiful tonight."

"Thank you. This is a Herve Leger bandage dress I saved up to buy, and I've never had the opportunity to wear it. It's on the snug side to begin with, so I figured I should wear it tonight while I can. If I could get away with it, I'd wear it every day until I hit my second trimester, but it's just not that practical."

Fashion before comfort with Amelia, always. "I would vote for that. I wouldn't get anything done staring at you the whole time, though."

"You're sweet," she said, a rosy color rising to her cheeks. "I can't believe you remembered my favorite flower."

"Of course I did," Tyler said as he held the bouquet out to her. "For you."

"Come in," Amelia said as she took a few steps back into her apartment.

He followed her into the cozy one-bedroom corner unit she called home. Golden overhead lighting shined down from an antique-looking fixture. It illuminated every detail she'd worked hard to put in place. It was a cute little apartment, spacious by New York standards, and very much Amelia. The furniture was shabby chic in style, mixing older, worn antiques with a few newer, brighter pieces. There was a mishmash of throw rugs, embroidered pillows and candles scattered around the space.

She had always had a keen aesthetic eye, be it for fashion, furniture or food. Even back in high school, when Tyler's daily uniform had included jeans and a T-shirt, she had always gone above and beyond when it came to her style. To her, decorating an apartment was like getting her place dressed up to go out. He couldn't be bothered. He wanted things to be functional and not too fussy. Like his clothes.

He watched Amelia disappear into the tiny kitchen and put the green roses in a tall crystal vase filled with water. She had been right when she said there wasn't room for him to live here with her. It was comfortable, welcoming, but not really big enough for more than one person. And she certainly would have difficulty raising a child here, too. There was no room for a nursery. No yard to play in. A couple toys on the floor could create a treacherous obstacle course.

"What?" she asked, coming toward him with the vase in her hands. "You look disgusted about something."

"Not disgusted. I was just thinking of how small your place is. Reminds me of the first apartment I rented when I moved to New York to apprentice at Levi's jewelry store."

"It suits me just fine." She placed the flowers in the middle of her square white dining room table. "It's quiet, I have reserved parking and the price is good. I'm really not home that much anyway."

"Well—" he frowned "—no matter what happens with us, we'll need to find you a new place. Either you'll move in with me or we'll get you something bigger for you and the baby." He raised his hand to halt her protest. "Don't start. You and I both know you'll need more space when the baby comes."

Amelia shrugged and scooped up her purse. "I had been thinking about getting a townhouse before all this started. But there's no sense in worrying about it now. We've got time to figure out things like that."

"Absolutely. Right now, we need to focus on not missing our reservation."

"Where are we going?"

"The Watermark, downtown."

Amelia smiled as she picked up her jacket and followed him outside. "Nice choice."

He escorted her to the parking lot, but Amelia stopped abruptly at the curb. "What's the matter?"

"Where's your BMW?"

"I'd only rented that for a couple days. I turned it back in when I realized I was going to be staying awhile." Reaching into his pocket, he pulled out his keys and hit the button to unlock the doors of the white Audi SUV parked beside hers.

"I see you finally found a place that would rent you an Audi. I bet you're happy now."

Tyler held open the passenger door and helped her inside. "Actually, I bought it," he said before slamming the door shut.

By the time he got in on his side, Amelia was shaking her head. "You're from another planet, you know that?"

"Why?"

"Because," she argued, as they pulled out of her apartment complex, "you buy luxury cars on a whim—with cash, I'm certain. You think a mansion in Belle Meade is a reasonable suggestion. You gave me an eight-carat engagement ring for a spur-of-the-moment wedding in Vegas. That's not normal, you know?"

Tyler smiled and focused on the freeway stretched out ahead of them. "I worked hard to be abnormal. Would you prefer I have a dead-end office job and scrape pennies together for the monthly payment on my practical sedan like everyone else?"

"No..." she said thoughtfully. "I suppose it wouldn't make a difference. Even when you were broke, you were abnormal. Just abnormal with less money."

He chuckled. "I'm not sure if I should be offended or not."

"Don't be. I've kept you in my life this long with you the way you are. If you're abnormal, then I guess I am in my own way, too."

Tyler had to heartily agree with that assessment. For whatever reason, he had lasted in Amelia's life far longer than any other man. Probably because they weren't dating, so she didn't try him on like a pair of shoes and cast him aside when he didn't fit just right. When they'd crossed the line in Vegas, he'd known he was putting their friendship at risk. Despite their long-standing relationship, adding sex to the mix could potentially land him in the discard pile. Even with their agreement to remain friends no matter what, that was still a very real danger.

That was why he'd come to Nashville fully anticipating they would file for divorce and pretend that night in Vegas never happened. He'd never dreamed they might continue their romance, much less stay married.

The wild card in this scenario was their baby. It was Amelia's anchor; it might be the only thing that would keep her from bolting from this relationship like every other one before it.

Might be.

Tyler had agreed to Amelia's thirty-day arrangement for their child's sake. He would put everything he had into convincing Amelia to love him. Everything but his heart. His wasn't any good to anyone anymore. It had been irrevocably broken, and he didn't dare expose it to more damage.

If she fell in love with him, everything might work out, but even then, Tyler wasn't holding his breath. He was fighting an uphill battle with Amelia. Even if he did everything right, she could find fault in him. No one was perfect, not even her grandparents. It made him wonder how much of their idealistic marriage was truth and how much was fantasy built up in Amelia's mind.

Tyler slowed the Audi and pulled to the curb outside the restaurant. He handed over the keys to the valet and rounded the car to escort Amelia inside.

The interior of the Watermark was dim, with pot lights illuminating the tables from the exposed beams overhead. The hostess escorted them to a white linen-draped table for two near the window. Amelia chose to sit on the side with the long white leather banquette, and Tyler sat opposite her. A server quickly took their drink orders and disappeared, leaving them to look over the menu and admire the view.

Tyler knew he should be looking at the impressive cityscape or deciding on his appetizer course, but he found himself distracted by the view directly in front of him. A square glass-and-chrome candleholder in the center of the table cast a mesmerizing glow across Amelia's face. It highlighted the subtle cleft in her chin and soft apples of her cheeks. Her skin looked peaches-and-cream flawless, nearly glowing with radiance.

It took everything he had not to reach across the table and brush his thumb over her full, coral-painted lips. They looked soft and shiny with some sort of gloss that made them shimmer in an utterly kissable way. He wanted to kiss her again tonight, and keep doing it until every drop of that gloss was gone and her lips were bee-stung from it.

That was how she had woken up in his hotel room the morning after their wedding. Her red hair had been everywhere, her mascara had been smudged and her lips had been pink and swollen. She'd looked like a woman who had been well and truly loved the night before. Tyler's whole body stiffened as he thought of being able to make love to her again. It was a masochistic thought, one that wasn't likely to get him through dinner without discomfort, but he couldn't shake it. Once they'd crossed the line in Vegas, he couldn't force himself back.

"Have you ever eaten here before?" he asked to distract himself with conversation.

She shook her head, oblivious to his thoughts. "No, but I've been dying to get into their kitchen. The executive chef here is well-known for his amazing creations. I'm certain nothing we eat will be bad."

"So I chose well?"

Amelia smiled. "You chose very well."

"All this rich food won't be too much on your stomach, will it?"

She shook her head, making the sleek auburn waves dance over her shoulders. "I hope not. But really, I've only had trouble early in the day. By midafternoon I'm starving. I'm anxious to try the duck. It is so hard to find well-prepared duck. What about you?"

"I'm thinking the cobia. Or the lamb."

"Ooh…" Amelia's dark brown eyes lit up with excitement. "Get the lamb and let me try some. You can try my duck, too, if you want."

"Sounds good," he said with a smile. Very few things got Amelia as excited as food. The old saying about the way to a man's heart being through his stomach was just as true with her. Whenever they were together, he went out of his way to find someplace they could eat that would be new and exciting for her.

She was a fashionista at heart, but her first love was cooking. He hadn't been at all surprised to see her go into a culinary program. She had been bringing him food all through high school, using him as a guinea pig when she wanted to try out a new recipe. It was almost always good. And beautiful to look at. Rarely was food both, and that was where her talent really came into play.

Tonight was where his talents came into play. He was a successful jeweler because he knew exactly what the client was looking for, even if they weren't entirely sure. He had the ideal night planned for Amelia. After two hours of talking and dining, including a decadent chocolate soufflé to share, they strolled through the trendy downtown area known as the Gulch. They wandered together, hand in hand, looking in shop windows and listening to the live music streaming out of some of the bars. The conversation flowed easily, the way it always had with them, not stifled by the fact that this was a real date.

By the time they returned to her apartment, Tyler was confident they'd had a successful date. Amelia was smiling and laughing, relaxed for the first time since he'd arrived in Nashville. It was a good night. But it could be better.

He walked her to her door, hesitating as she unlocked it. He wanted to go in pretty badly, but he wouldn't. Thirty days didn't seem like long, but it was long enough not to rush.

"Dinner was great," she said as she turned back to face him. "I had a nice time."

"Me, too." Moving closer, Tyler rested his hand on her waist.

Amelia didn't pull away or stiffen at his touch. Instead she looked up at him with a soft, inviting smile. He accepted the invitation, leaning down to cup her face in his hands and capture her coral-painted lips with his own.

She melted into him, pressing her ample curves against the hard wall of his chest. As his tongue glided across her lips, she opened her mouth to him. Her own silky tongue met his, a soft moan muffled in the back of her throat.

The sound conjured memories of their wedding night. His body instantly stiffened, his palms tingling to touch her. He moved his hands back to her waist, letting them roam over the stretched fabric that clung to her every curve. Tyler boldly cupped the swell of her rear and pressed her hips against the hard ridge of his desire.

The growl deep in his throat made Amelia chuckle softly against his lips and pull away. Her hand caught his, moving it back to her waist. Her eyes were closed, her breath fast and shallow. He understood. That was enough for tonight. He withdrew his hand, placing one last soft goodbye kiss on her lips.

"I want to take you somewhere in the morning."

"I suppose you aren't going to tell me where."

He smiled wide. "What's the fun in that?"

She sighed and shook her head. Although she acted exasperated by him, he could see the glint of excitement in her eyes. When that was there—the way it had been on that sidewalk in Las Vegas—he knew he had her intrigued. That was key to getting her to go along with whatever harebrained idea he'd come up with.

"I'll pick you up at nine."

Five

"So seriously, where are we going?"

Tyler shook his head. "Ames, I haven't told you the past three times you've asked. What makes you think I'm suddenly going to change my mind?"

She sighed and crossed her arms over her chest. "I'm your wife. It's now my job to nag at you until I wear you down and you do what I want."

He chuckled and slowed the SUV to turn off the main commercial thoroughfare and into a large, sprawling subdivision. "I thought we were trying to date. You're not supposed to pull those tricks out of the bag until later."

"Tricks?" she replied in mock outrage. "What about those tricks you pulled on me last night? Those flowers, that restaurant…"

"That kiss," he added.

Amelia didn't reply to that. Instead she turned and looked out her window to watch the houses they rolled past. She wouldn't give him the satisfaction of knowing he'd made an excellent impression on their first official date. She'd had a better time with him than she had on half the dates she'd been on in the past year. Perhaps the fates knew better than she did. Or maybe they were just having fun messing with her head.

The houses they passed were large. On meticulously groomed lots. And not far from work. That was when everything clicked into place. They were going to look at a house. But here? Despite her attempts to dissuade him, he'd apparently sought out a place in Belle Meade. They were obviously not on the same page when it came to the real estate market.

Finally, Tyler turned into a driveway that was barricaded by a large iron gate. He punched in a code and the gate opened, revealing the incredible estate hidden beyond it. They drove down a narrow lane lined with trees and hedges, then circled around a courtyard fountain, stopping in front of the double-doored entrance of stacked stone stairs.

Thoughts of denial swirled in her mind as she looked up at the house. Correction—*mansion*. This was no three-bedroom starter home. To buy it would cost several million dollars, easily. The rent was probably high enough to give her heart palpitations. Was this what he'd envisioned when he'd talked about a home where they could raise a family together? She couldn't even fathom it.

"Tyler…" she said in a warning tone as she looked out the window.

"Just wait until you see the inside," he said, holding his hands up defensively. "It's amazing."

She bet it was. The Biltmore House was nice, too, but she wasn't moving in there anytime soon, either. "Did you already rent this place? Without asking me? That's really not the best way to start out. A woman likes to have a say in where she lives."

"Of course I know that. I did not rent it yet, but I was confident enough that the real estate agent gave me the key to bring you here today. When we're done, I'll either return the key or sign the lease."

Amelia didn't wait for his assistance to get out of the car. She opened the door and stepped onto the cobblestone driveway. The cream-and-gray-mottled brick of the mansion's facade seemed to sprawl on forever, broken up by large arched windows and tall square ivory columns. The house was beautiful, but ridiculously large for a family of two and a half.

"Whose house is this? And why on earth would they rent it out to strangers?"

"Apparently some musician had the place built, then ended up going on a world tour and never moved in. The real estate agent seemed pretty confident that if we liked the place, the owner would entertain an offer."

She sighed and shook her head. It was a rock star's house. She'd never fathomed she'd step across the threshold, much less ever live in the home of a rock star. "Let's go inside and see it before you sign your life away, hmm?"

Tyler offered his hand to help her up the stairs, then escorted her through the entrance to the large marble foyer. Amelia was stunned by the size and luxury of the space. There was very little furniture and nothing on the walls, but the details of the house itself were amazing. There was intricate crown molding, carved stonework and sky-high ceilings with shimmering chandeliers dripping crystals from their golden branches. A split staircase of dark, polished wood encircled the room and met at a second-floor landing.

"I don't think the two of us combined will ever have

enough stuff to fill a house this big." The expansive rooms were so empty, their steps echoed through the space.

"I'm only going to have the movers bring down my personal things from my apartment. It's a lot more modern, and I don't think much of the furniture would work here anyway. We'll need to go shopping for some of the basics to get us through the next month—a bed, a couch, that sort of thing. Then, if we decide to keep the place, we'll start looking for the rest. I want you to decorate however you want to."

Amelia fought the frown threatening to pull the corners of her mouth down. They'd agreed to date only two days ago, yet he was moving forward with the intention of them living here forever. Her head was still spinning, but Tyler was a master of rolling with the punches.

As it was, they'd put the cart before the horse and were scrambling to build a relationship to go with their marriage and their baby. Thirty days was really not enough time to fall in love, but she'd known she had to pick a deadline to put an end to this madness. This would either work or it wouldn't, and now they would know in a month. She couldn't take the uncertainty any longer than that. Tyler didn't seem to acknowledge that failure was even an option. It rarely was in his eyes. It didn't matter if it was a jewel auction or a game of cards with friends—he had to win. This time, she'd made her future the prize he was out to claim.

"I don't know, Tyler… This place is intimidating. As much as I enjoy decorating, I wouldn't even know where to start."

"I know," he admitted. "I had an interior designer do my place in New York. You're welcome to pick stuff for the house, but we can hire a decorator if you need help."

He reached down and took her hand in his. "Come on," he said with a gentle tug. "I'll show you the upstairs first."

They went up the stairs to the second floor, where he led her through a labyrinth of bedrooms and bathrooms. There was another family room and a large open bonus room that was bigger than her whole apartment.

"I was thinking we could turn this into a game room. Maybe get a pool table and a couple of pinball machines. What do you think?"

She thought this house was way too much space for them. It was too big for five or six, even, but she kept that to herself. "That would be fun."

"And through here," he continued, "is the movie theater."

Amelia stopped. "You're kidding, right? Why on earth would we need our own movie theater?"

Tyler grinned wide. "Nope, I'm not kidding. I think the real estate agent officially called it a media room, but it's all the same to me. This is one of the reasons I really love this house."

Amelia walked ahead of him into the windowless room with dark burgundy–painted walls. There was a large screen on the far wall with a projector mounted in the ceiling overhead. The floor was a staggered incline with two rows of leather media chairs that could seat eight people. One row was a step down from the first so everyone had a prime view. It was the craziest thing she'd ever seen.

"When I started looking for a place to rent, I wanted more than just luxury. I wanted functionality. With this, it made me think about how much we both love movies. You and I have wasted hours of our youth watching films together. I think we were at every Saturday matinee for four years. Having a place to screen our own movies in comfort seemed like a good investment for the future."

"It's amazing," she said, nodding blankly. "If you can afford it, why not? I'm sure we'll get a lot of enjoyment out of it."

Tyler continued on with the tour, heading downstairs to show her the luxurious master suite with a bathtub she could swim in. Amelia followed, only half listening to what he had to say about the house. Her mind was being pulled in ten directions, her chest tight with anxiety over this whole situation.

Things seemed to get more complicated minute by minute. Eloping with Tyler had been a mistake, but a correctable one. Getting pregnant was a curveball, but women had children every day with less suitable fathers. She could handle it. Tyler would be a great father, even if they didn't have a romantic relationship. Moving in together, temporarily or otherwise, was a big leap for her. But this place… It was like moving to an alien planet.

She'd known her best friend was a strategist. He always looked at every angle before making a decision, routinely kicking her rear in chess and rarely making a wrong move on the game board or in life. He didn't just win, he won intelligently. Still, it was hard to believe Tyler had pulled all this together in a day's time. He'd bought a car, found an amazing house he knew she'd love… She had no doubt he had movers on standby both here and in New York, just waiting for the call that he'd signed the lease on the house.

What did she expect? She'd laid down a challenge— thirty days to fall in love. Tyler was taking it seriously and would tackle it with the same drive and commitment that had gotten him from an old, overcrowded apartment to a multimillion-dollar mansion in ten years' time.

She would be hard-pressed to fight him off, especially when his opening volley included a mansion with a movie room. He was playing to win. What would he do next?

"I saved this room for last because I think it's going to be your favorite." He led her through what would probably be the living room to the kitchen. That was where her heart stopped and her worries vanished in an instant.

It was a chef's dream. Gorgeous cherry-stained cabinets, gold-flecked granite countertops, ornate tile work on the backsplash, professional stainless-steel appliances... It was gorgeous. She couldn't help rushing past him into the space to look more closely. The kitchen in her apartment was average. Nice, but nothing special. The one at the chapel was large, sterile and industrial, for cooking for hundreds of people at once. Neither of those places had anything on this.

She opened the deep drawers for pots and pans, sliding out built-in spice racks. The massive gas stove had two ovens, six burners and a grill in the center. There were two farm sinks on opposite sides of the kitchen, one beside a full-size dishwasher and the other with a small drawer dishwasher for quick washes of glasses. The French doors of the refrigerator opened wide, revealing enough space for countless platters and large serving dishes. There was even a warming drawer built in beside the stove.

It wasn't just a beautiful kitchen, it was a well laid-out one with all the latest amenities. She knew better than anyone how important it was to have the space designed properly to get work done with the fewest steps possible.

Amelia could cook up a storm here. She could throw some of the most amazing dinner parties ever thrown. Maybe an engagement party for Bree and Ian. They'd gotten engaged right before her reunion and had yet to have a party. Thoughts of gatherings with champagne and canapés started spinning through her head, but a glance at Tyler's smug grin brought everything to a stop.

She'd fallen for it, she realized with a silent curse. What was better than a movie room? The kitchen of her dreams. He knew exactly what he was doing, bringing her to this house and seducing her with stainless-steel appliances. He knew better than anyone that the route to her heart went through the kitchen. She'd underestimated how easily she could be had by someone who knew her every weakness.

Amelia wasn't ready to lose herself to the fantasy quite yet, though. Even if they did rent this place and move in, she couldn't get attached to any of it. In four weeks, everything could be different.

Tyler was confident they could build a successful relationship, but they had a steep hill to climb. She'd take a great love in a camper over a so-so romance with a mansion.

"Well, what do you think of the place?" he asked.

"You've done well, Tyler," she said with a polite smile. She ran her hand over the cool granite countertop. "I can't believe you turned up a place like this in a day. This kitchen is amazing. It's a shame you're the worst cook I've ever met."

He smiled and ran his hand through the messy strands of his dark blond hair. "Well, honestly, I have no intention of ever doing anything more complicated than making a bowl of cereal in here. But when I saw it, I knew how much you'd love it. This is all for you, really."

His pale blue eyes were focused on her with unmatched intensity as he spoke. She could feel the truth of his words and the depth of what they really meant. He could've rented a lesser house with average amenities, but he'd wanted to find the one that would make her eyes light up and her heart flutter with excitement. The kitchen had done that, easily. And he knew it.

Looking around her, it was obvious that her life had taken a very surreal turn. Tyler would rent this house, she was certain of it, and they would be living here by the weekend.

The flowers, the dinners, the granite countertops... She'd demanded Tyler woo her, and he was doing a damn fine job. She could already feel her resolve weakening, and it was day two. What would happen over the next twenty-eight days?

The mere thought scared the hell out of her.

"I didn't say anything because it's a temporary arrangement." Tyler rolled his eyes as his brother Jeremy needled him. He shouldn't have answered the phone when he saw his brother wasn't accepting his text at face value.

"Moving to Nashville doesn't seem temporary."

"I never said I was moving, just that I would be here for a while. I kept my apartment in New York," Tyler argued. "And I'm not moving my business. I'm only telling you so someone knows where I am." He'd chosen to text his younger brother Jeremy so someone in the family knew where he was if something happened. He had his cell phone, of course, but at least one person needed to be able to find him in an emergency. He regretted the decision now. Jeremy wouldn't accept the fact without the justification.

"What's going on that would make you drop everything and run to Nashville? Wait..." Jeremy hesitated. "Amelia lives in Nashville, doesn't she?"

"Yes," Tyler confirmed, feeling anxiety pool in his

stomach. The conversation was unraveling faster than he'd like.

"Is she okay?"

"She's fine. She just…needs me for a little while."

A long silence followed. "Needs you? Cut the crap, man. What's going on? I'll tell everyone you've moved to Nashville if you don't tell me why. Your life will be hell."

Tyler sighed. Better Jeremy know than the whole family. "Okay, but you can't breathe a word to anyone. I mean it."

"Of course. I'm not the blabbermouth in the family. I never even told anyone about that trip to Tijuana where you got arrested."

Tyler frowned at the phone. "I've never been to Mexico, Jeremy."

"Oh, that must've been Dylan," Jeremy said. "Crap, I just told a secret. It's normally not a problem, though. I've kept that secret for five years."

That didn't make him feel better, but he didn't have a choice. "Okay…I'm going to stay in Nashville for a few weeks because Amelia and I got together at the reunion and we're trying to make it work."

"You hooked up with Amelia?" Jeremy asked with an edge of incredulity in his voice. "Finally! I thought you guys would never—"

"We're married," he interrupted. "And she's pregnant."

"Holy crap!"

"I'm telling you, Jeremy, no one can know." That was Amelia's first and most important rule. It couldn't get out.

"Okay," Jeremy said. "It's safe with me, but when Mom finds out, she's going to kill you."

Tyler hung up the phone and shook his head. That hadn't been how he'd wanted that conversation to go, but it actually felt good to get that news off his chest. At least he had one semireliable person to talk to about all this. If all went well, when the rest of his family found out, it would be good news and no blood would be shed.

His phone rang again, and this time it was the moving company. There was no time to dwell on this. The clock was ticking.

The next few days were a blur of activity that made Amelia dizzy just thinking about it. Tyler signed a short-term lease on the house, and his moving companies went to work packing up both their apartments. The real estate agent referred them to an agency that provided domestic contract work, and they hired a part-time housekeeper named Janet, much to Amelia's relief.

After they left the agency, Tyler took Amelia to brunch, and they went furniture shopping to pick out the few things they needed in the interim, including a king-size bed and a desk where Tyler could work.

It was a good thing Tyler had the money to make all this happen, because Amelia certainly didn't have time to do it all. She'd spent all day Thursday baking, filling and crumb-coating a five-tiered wedding cake. Although chefs tended to specialize in culinary arts or in pastry arts, Amelia had studied both. That came in handy when she and her partners had decided to open From This Moment and did pretty much everything themselves.

By Friday afternoon, the cakes were iced, covered in her famous marshmallow fondant and stacked high on the cart she would use to move the cake into the reception hall. Today's cake was a simple design, despite being large in size. All she needed to do was load a pastry bag with buttercream and pipe alternating tiers of Swiss dots and cornelli lace. The florist was bringing fresh flowers for the cake Saturday afternoon.

Leaning back against the stainless-steel countertop to eye her accomplishment of the day, she came to the sad realization that soon she would have to let the cakes go. Cakes took hours. There were some days when Amelia was in the kitchen working on a cake until two in the morning. On more than one occasion, she'd just stayed over and slept on the chaise in the bridal suite.

Those days were coming to an end. They'd need to bring in help anyway to assist her late in the pregnancy when she couldn't power through a sixteen-hour day on her feet in the kitchen, and to bridge the gap of her maternity leave. That would be much easier if they started contracting out the wedding cakes.

Reaching for her tablet, she brushed away a dusting of powdered sugar from the screen and made a note to talk to Natalie about that. When that was done, she loaded her piping bag and started working on the final cake decorations.

"That's a big cake."

Amelia looked up from her work to see Tyler standing in the doorway of the kitchen. She was surprised to see he'd shed his suit today and was wearing a snug-fitting green T-shirt and a pair of worn jeans. It was a good look for him, reminding her of the boy she knew in school. "That's an understatement. It weighs over a hundred pounds."

He whistled, strolling into the kitchen to stand beside her and admire her handiwork. "Pretty impressive. Does it taste good?"

She frowned at him. "Of course it does. It's my special lemon–sour cream cake with a fresh raspberry-and-white-chocolate buttercream filling."

"No real chocolate?"

"This is the South," she said. "Chocolate is for the

groom's cake, which, fortunately, I do not have to make. The groom's aunt is making him one that looks like Neyland Stadium at the University of Tennessee."

Tyler nodded thoughtfully and eyeballed the bowl with leftover raspberry filling. "What are you going to do with that?" he asked.

Amelia sighed and went to the other side of the kitchen to retrieve a plastic spoon. "Knock yourself out," she said, holding it out to him. She waited until he'd inhaled a few spoonfuls of icing. "What brings you by today, Tyler? I really need to get this finished. I've got several hours of prep work ahead of me for tomorrow when I'm done with this."

He swallowed and set the bowl aside. "By all means, continue working. Primarily, I came by because I haven't seen you yet today."

Amelia smiled and climbed up onto her stepladder to pipe the top tier. "Once we're living in the same place, that won't be a problem any longer."

"Speaking of which, I also needed to let you know that you have a new address." He reached into his pocket and dangled a set of keys. "These are yours. I also have a gate opener for your car."

"Wow, your people move quickly. Is everything really out of my apartment?"

"Yep. I even had Janet go by and clean once everything was gone."

Amelia nodded thoughtfully and went back to piping the cake. She was keeping her apartment for another month, but the odds were that she wouldn't move back. As they'd discussed, she would either stay with Tyler, or she would get a new place big enough for her and the baby. He'd been right—her apartment was too small. It was easier to just get everything out now instead of having to go back and get the rest later.

"Janet also went to the store with the list you put together and stocked the pantry and refrigerator with food. And she got all the necessary cleaning supplies to keep the house shipshape."

Amelia was going to like this Janet. While she loved to cook, cleaning was at the bottom of her list. The industrial washing machine in the kitchen made it easier to clean up here, but keeping up with cleaning her apartment had always been a burden. She'd developed a process of immediately cleaning up anything she did as she did it to avoid having to deal with it later. She'd never lived with anyone else, but she assumed that would make it exponentially harder to manage.

"Sounds great. Hopefully I'll get to see what the house looks like before I collapse facedown in the mattress tonight." She had a long list of things that had to be done before she went home today.

"Don't you have anyone to help you in the kitchen?"

At that, Amelia chuckled. She added the last flourish to the top tier and climbed down the steps. "Not really. We bring in a crew of servers the day of the wedding, but I'm pretty much on my own until then."

"What about the other girls? They don't help you?"

Amelia pushed the cart with the cake over to the walk-in refrigerator. Tyler rushed ahead of her to pull the door open and she slid it inside. "It's Friday afternoon," she said, stepping out and shutting the door behind her. "Natalie is in headset-and-clipboard mode, counting down to the wedding. She's probably meeting with the officiant and the musicians right now to go over the schedule. She will be coordinating the rehearsal, then the rehearsal dinner. Bree will be with her, taking pictures. Gretchen is currently in the reception hall setting up tables, laying out linens and doing all the decorating she can do in advance. When the rehearsal is over, she'll start decorating the chapel and lobby. They would help me if they could, but we all have things to do."

"What a circus," Tyler observed with a shake of his head. "I don't recall our wedding being this complicated."

"Yeah, I know," she replied, her tone flat. "Unfortunately, the circus is necessary for a beautiful, smoothly run wedding day. We've got it down to a science."

Amelia picked up her tablet and pulled up her task list for the afternoon. At the top of the list was prepping a hundred servings each of filet mignon, chicken breast and salmon to marinate overnight. She pulled out a large plastic tote and started mixing up the steak marinade.

She kept expecting Tyler to make noises about leaving, but he continued to hover a few feet away. Whereas she normally didn't mind company, he was a distraction. A glance at his smile, a whiff of his cologne, and she'd likely slice off her thumb. Dumping in the last ingredient in the marinade, she turned to him. "Tyler, honey, you don't need to stand around and look at me. I'm sure you have something more important to do today."

Tyler leaned against the counter beside her and shook his head. "No, I don't. I'm here to help you. I'm no chef, but I'm another set of hands. Tell me what you need done."

That was the sexiest thing she'd ever heard. She resisted the urge to throw her arms around his neck and let him take her against the industrial refrigerator. Fridays were a day for work, not play. Instead she took a deep breath and decided where they should start first.

"If you insist." She pointed to a sink on the opposite side of the kitchen. "Scrub up in the sink and grab an apron off the shelf. When you're ready, glove up and grab the beef tenderloins from the refrigerator so we can get them broken down into portions."

If he was going to be a sexy distraction, he could at least be a useful one.

Six

"If I never see another potato, it will be too soon." Tyler opened the front door of their new home and held it for Amelia to step through ahead of him.

"You were a trouper. Thank you for all your help today." She looked down at her watch. "Home by eight. I think that might be a Friday-night record."

He followed her into the kitchen, where she dropped her purse on the breakfast bar and slipped out of her coat. She hopped on one foot, then the other, pulling off her shoes with a happy sigh.

"All your things are in the master suite," he said. Tyler had had to make a command decision when the movers arrived, so he'd given her the nicest room on the main floor and hoped that at some point they would share it.

Amelia followed him, shoes in hand, down the hallway to the master suite. The new bed dominated the formerly empty space, with a green-and-gold embroidered comforter in place. They continued into the master bathroom, where a door led to the walk-in closet.

"All your clothes are in here," he said. "Everything that was in your dressers is in the built-in armoire here. All your shoes are in the cubbies there."

Amelia slipped her sneakers into an empty slot in the shoe display and nodded. "Thank you for taking care of all of this. Since it's all handled, I think I might take a bath in the big whirlpool tub. It might help me relax after a long day. Just not too hot, right?"

He remembered his sister saying something about that because she'd found out she was pregnant with his niece right before her fifth-anniversary cruise. *No drinks, no hot tubs! What a vacation,* she'd lamented. "I think so. I know hot tubs are bad, but they keep the temperature up. The bathwater, especially with the jets running, will cool over time."

"I'm more interested in the jets than the heat anyway. I'll go online on my phone and check first. I've got quite a list of things to talk about with my doctor when I go to my first appointment."

Tyler paused. "When is your first appointment?"

"Tuesday afternoon."

"May I come?" he asked, hesitantly. He was teetering on the edge of wanting to be involved in the process and not wanting too many of the less-appetizing details.

Amelia nodded. "I don't think the first one will be very interesting, but you're welcome to join me and ask questions. We're both new at this."

"Great. Thanks. I'll, uh…" he took a few steps toward the hallway "…let you take your bath now."

Tyler slipped from the room and went back out into the kitchen. He had set up his temporary office in the keeping room off the kitchen. Turning on his laptop, he settled into the new office chair. He was exhausted. He really couldn't understand how Amelia worked that hard week after week. As a steady stream of emails downloaded into his inbox, he realized he wasn't in the mood to deal with any of it. Instead he closed his email program and started playing a game.

Even that was hard to focus on. He could hear the water running in the master bath. It seemed to take an eternity to fill the tub, but eventually the water stopped and the soft hum of the jets started. He lost multiple rounds of solitaire, his mind more interested in imagining Amelia stripping out of her clothes. Dropping them to the floor. Clipping her hair up so it didn't get wet. Lowering her body into the warm, churning water, inch by inch. Rubbing her body with a slick bar of fragrant soap until bubbles formed across her skin.

A prickling sensation traveled down his spine, every muscle tightening with anticipation for something it wouldn't have. He suddenly felt constricted by the clinging cotton T-shirt and jeans he'd worn today. Especially the jeans. Tyler swallowed hard and squeezed his eyes shut, but it wasn't enough to block out his imagination. Nothing could drive the image of her wet skin and steam-flushed cheeks from his thoughts.

Their date had brought his need for her to the forefront of his mind. Their wedding night had been weeks ago, and although he would never forget that experience, his hands could no longer feel her skin, and his tongue could no longer taste her. The kiss on her porch had refreshed everything, making it hard for him to focus on anything else. Not even long hours working in the kitchen had helped with her so nearby.

About fifteen minutes into her bath, Tyler leaped up from his chair and marched toward the staircase. Maybe a little distance would help. He might take a shower of his own. Or bury his head under a pillow and smother the fantasy.

He was halfway up when he heard Amelia's voice. "Tyler?" she shouted. "Tyler, help!"

His heart jumped into his throat. He spun on his heel and sprinted back downstairs, not stopping at the closed door of the suite. Instead he charged in, fearful he would find she'd slipped and hurt herself, or worse. She was still in the bathroom. He headed that way, his loafers skidding across the tile to a stop.

Looking around the bathroom, he couldn't spot an immediate problem. No blood, nothing broken. The air was heavy with steam and a tropical scent she must've added to the water. Amelia was in the tub with the jets turned off. She was watching him with large, surprised eyes, her hands protectively attempting to cover her nakedness in the clear water of the bath.

"Yes?" he asked, breathless. "Are you okay? What's wrong?"

Amelia bit her bottom lip. "I'm sorry, I didn't mean to send you into a panic. Nothing is wrong, at least nothing serious. I'm fine."

Tyler took a deep breath of relief, feeling his fight-or-flight response dwindle away. It was replaced with a different kind of tension as his eyes shifted over the uncovered patches of her ivory skin in the water. Nothing scandalous was visible, but it didn't need to be. He had an excellent memory and could easily fill in the blanks without fail. Damp strands of red hair were plastered to her neck, a rosy flush painted across her cheeks. "What do you need?"

"There's no towels," she admitted with a pained wince. "I'm an idiot and I didn't grab one before I got in. I didn't want to drip water all over while I hunted for one. Do you know where they are?"

Towels. Yes. That he could do. "Sure thing." He turned and opened a narrow door that hid a linen closet. He pulled out a fluffy yellow towel that had come from her apartment and carried it back over to the tub. "Here you go."

"Thank you," she said with a sheepish smile. "I'm sorry to scare you."

"No problem. Let me know if you need anything else." He turned and started walking out of the bathroom.

"Tyler?"

He stopped and turned. "Yes?"

Amelia had stood in the tub and quickly wrapped the towel around her. "Would you like to watch some television with me tonight? I was thinking we could pile up in the new bed and watch something together. I know the list I left for Janet had popcorn and chips, if you'd like some."

Tyler was a little surprised by the invitation, but he was more surprised by the seemingly shy expression on her face while she asked. It was almost as if she was a teenager again, asking if he'd like to sit with her at lunch or something. She was his best friend. Of course he'd like to watch television with her. He hadn't suggested something like that because…things were different now. They had shared a bed on several occasions throughout the years, but lying beside one another in bed now felt more complicated than it used to. Feelings had been unleashed between them.

The last thing he wanted was to lose the parts of their friendship he cherished the most as their physical relationship changed. Perhaps once they made the decision to cross that bridge again it wouldn't seem like such a big deal any longer, but for now, they were in limbo.

Married. Having a baby. Yet dating as though none of it had happened.

"That's a great idea. Are you getting out of the tub already?"

"Yes. I'm not very good with sitting idle, even when it feels nice."

"Okay, well, while you're getting dressed, I'll see what I can find in the kitchen for snacks."

A smile lit up Amelia's face, distracting him from the sight of the tiny towel wrapped around her curves. It was a contagious grin, and one spread across his own face just as easily.

Tyler left the room so she could put on some clothes and started to hunt through the kitchen. Fortunately, Janet had put everything in very sensible places. He found a box of microwave popcorn on a shelf in the pantry. Score.

About ten minutes later, he strolled cautiously back into the bedroom with two cans of soda, a roll of paper towels and a large bowl piled high with movie-theater butter-flavored popcorn.

He found Amelia dressed—thankfully—and sitting on the bed cross-legged. Her hair was still clipped up on top of her head, but she'd removed her makeup, leaving her skin clean and fresh. She was wearing her pajamas— a pair of pale blue cotton lounging pants with a matching tank top. The top had thin spaghetti straps and a lacy edge that gave the impression of modesty where there was none. There was no disguising Amelia's assets in anything short of a turtleneck.

Tyler went around to the other side of the bed and unloaded the contents of his arms into the space between them. Currently, the only television in the house was from Amelia's apartment. He'd opted to put it in the bedroom, since they really didn't have much in the way of living room furniture for now.

Amelia flipped on the television, then piled the pillows up behind her. She accepted the can of soda from Tyler, resting it between her thighs since they also didn't have nightstands yet. "Ooh," she said, looking over at the bowl of popcorn. "That looks like the really buttery, nasty kind. I love it."

Tyler chuckled. "I would've thought that such cheap, pedestrian fare might offend your refined palate."

At that, she snorted. "People like that make me crazy. Whenever I watch those cooking competitions and the chefs are whining because they have to use canned ingredients or something, I just roll my eyes. The average working mom does not have the time to deal with freshly preparing a meal from scratch every night. Real people eat canned foods sometimes. And microwave popcorn," she added, shoveling a handful into her mouth.

They flipped through the channels, finally agreeing on a mermaid mockumentary on the Discovery Channel. They heckled and joked, laughing throughout the show and polishing off all their snacks. It was just like old times, Tyler thought with an overwhelming sense of relief.

Tyler didn't have much time for dating, but when he did, this was always what he was missing from his other relationships. He liked to keep things light and fun, but for some reason, the women were always so serious, as if he was the Lombardi Trophy in the Super Bowl of marrying well. Those women wouldn't dare to be seen without makeup or to be silly with him, but he supposed in the end it didn't matter what was lacking. He wasn't going to fall in love with them. If he wanted friendship and compatibility, he would go to Amelia.

Looking over, he realized Amelia had drifted to sleep beside him. Her red-gold lashes rested against her cheeks, her pink lips softly parted. She must have been exhausted. He felt an ache in his chest as he looked at her lying there. All those other poor women had been doomed before they'd even started. He hadn't really needed them for anything but a sexual release when he had Amelia in his life. His ex-fiancée, Christine, had known that. Even though he'd loved her, even though he'd proposed to her and wanted to start a life together, she'd felt like a third wheel. Maybe she had been.

Through a strange turn of events, it seemed Amelia was going to be the woman in his life. Fortunately, she was the one woman with whom he knew it was possible to have it all. They had the friendship. The sexual compatibility was there. He hadn't stopped wanting her since he'd allowed himself to think of her that way.

As for love, she just had to be open to loving him. He had twenty-six days left. If she loved him by then, that would be as good as it could possibly get. They would stay married, raise their child together... Tyler could be happy with that. He didn't need or want love for himself. In the end, it just made things harder.

Tyler slowly lowered the volume on the television and turned it off. He picked up the empty bowl of popcorn and eased toward the end of the mattress, trying to slip out of bed without waking her. He failed.

"Stay," she muttered into her pillow without opening her eyes. "This house is too big and I don't want to be alone down here. Please."

With a sigh, he put the bowl on the floor and switched off the lights before he climbed back into bed.

"Yay." Amelia yawned, snuggling up next to him and immediately falling back asleep.

Tyler wished he was so lucky. The scent of her perfumed skin so close to him and the soft heat of her body pressed against his made sleep impossible. He shut his eyes and tugged her close. If he couldn't sleep, he could at least lie contented with her in his arms.

It was going to be a very, very long night.

Amelia was burning up. She woke up in the middle of the night with an unfamiliar warmth pressed against her back and an arm draped over her. It took a full five to ten seconds for her to remember where she was and who was touching her.

Tyler. She'd asked him to stay with her tonight.

That she didn't mind, but at the moment, his internal furnace was making her back perspire. It was like sleeping with a hot water bottle. Turning her head to look over her shoulder, she found him on his side, snoring softly near her ear.

She eased ever so gently away from him. The movement was enough for him to mumble and roll onto his back, liberating her. She sat up in bed, looking down on him as he slept. The poor guy was still wearing his clothes from today. Those jeans couldn't be comfortable, but she knew he would rather be uncomfortable than get into bed without them and make her ill at ease.

Reclining onto her elbow, she looked down at him. His face was perfectly relaxed in sleep, something he never seemed to be anymore. There was no tension in his square jaw, no crinkles of thought around his eyes. Just peace. She wanted to reach out and touch his cheek to feel the rough stubble of his perpetual five-o'clock shadow. She wanted to feel his soft lips against hers again. But she wouldn't. He'd worked hard today, and she wouldn't wake him up for something so trivial.

As if he'd heard her, his eyes opened and he looked at her. There was no confusion or dreaminess in his gaze. Only a powerful need that hit her as surely as if she'd been punched in the stomach. Without hesitation, his palm went to her cheek. His touch was a match to a forest in drought. It started a pleasurable heat spreading like wildfire through her whole body.

"Amelia?" he asked, his voice gruff with sleep.

"Yes," she replied to his unasked question.

He buried his fingers into the hair at the nape of her neck and tugged until her mouth met his. Neither his hands nor his mouth were gentle, and she didn't mind. She liked the rough feel of his stubble against her cheeks and the sharp press of his fingertips into her flesh.

His tongue thrust into her mouth and slid along her own, making her core pulsate with the anticipation of more. She wanted to be closer to him, to touch him again. He had been right before—once they'd crossed that line there was no sense holding back any longer.

She threw one leg over his hips and straddled him. The move put her sensitive center in direct contact with the throbbing heat of his desire. The thin cotton of her pajama pants did little to dull the sensations that shot through her when they touched.

Amelia was desperate to liberate him from his jeans. Her palm slid along the hard muscles of his stomach, seeking out the button of his fly and stroking him through the denim.

Her fingers had barely brushed the button when in one swift move, Tyler rolled them across the bed. Amelia found herself with her back to the mattress and him between her thighs. His palms sought out her wrists, pinning them over her head. All through this, he never stopped kissing her.

When he finally let her mouth free, it was to taste her throat. Still holding her wrists with one hand, he used the other to gently tug her tank top up and over her head, leaving it tangled around her wrists with her breasts exposed. He didn't hesitate to capture one hardened pink nipple in his mouth, drawing on it until Amelia cried out and bucked her hips against him. His teeth and tongue worked her flesh, sending pleasurable shock waves through her whole body.

"Let go of my hands," she whispered.

"No," he answered between flicks of his tongue across her sensitive skin.

What did he mean, *no*? "Please," she begged. "I want to touch you."

"I know," he said, looking at her with a wicked smile curling his lips. "But if you do, it will be all over. I can't take it." His mouth returned to her breast, effectively ending the conversation.

All she could do was writhe beneath him, drawing her knees up and thrusting her hips forward to rub agonizingly against the hard ridge of his jeans.

He growled low against her sternum. "Two can play at that game." He glided his palm over her hip and under the drawstring waistband of her pants. His insistent fingers easily found her moist center, stroking hard.

Amelia cried out, the sound echoing through the mostly empty bedroom. "Tyler!" she gasped as he rubbed her again and again. She felt herself start to come undone, but the more desperate she became, the more he eased back, leaving her teetering on the edge.

At last, he let go of her arms, but it was only to sit back on his knees. He whipped his T-shirt over his head and threw it to the ground. With the use of her hands back, she did the same. His hands gripped both sides of her pajama pants, tugging them and her panties down over her hips and to the floor.

Standing at the end of the bed, he stopped to look down at her. Only the moonlight from the nearby window lit the room, which made Amelia feel a little less self-conscious about being sprawled out in front of him like this. That, and the look on his face. It was as though he was in a museum admiring a piece of art. A piece of art he wanted to devour.

Without looking away from her, he unzipped his jeans and slipped out of the last of his clothes. Crawling back up the bed, he covered her body with his own. Without hesitation, he found her entrance and moved into her.

Amelia gasped, her body tightening around the sudden invasion. He filled her completely, leaving her biting her lip and pressing her fingers desperately into his shoulders.

"Amelia," he groaned at her ear, slowly withdrawing and filling her again. "I never imagined..." he began, his voice drifting away. Shaking off a shudder that made his whole body tremble between her thighs, he started moving in earnest.

Rational thought slipped away as only the physical drive inside of her remained. Amelia wrapped her legs around his waist and tried to absorb every wave as it washed over her. "Yes" was all she could say. It was an encouraging plea, a desperate demand and an enthusiastic consent all rolled together at once.

And then it happened. The dam broke inside of her. A sudden rush of pleasure swept her up and carried her away. She cried out, bucked her hips against him, clung to him, all the while aware of his soft, encouraging words in her ear.

Her own release had barely subsided when she felt

Tyler tense in her arms. He surged forward like never before, pounding hard into her body before roaring loud into the night.

Amelia held him until it was over. She expected him to distance himself, to roll away the minute it was done, but he didn't. He stayed there, inside her, examining the curves of her face.

"What is it?" she asked after a few minutes under his intense scrutiny. She brought her hands up to smooth the unruly strands of her hair. "I probably look a fright."

His gaze met hers and he smiled softly. "No, of course not. You look perfect. The sexiest thing I've ever woken up to. I just...never imagined being with you would be like this. If I'd known..." His voice drifted away.

Tyler never finished the sentence, but he didn't need to. Amelia knew exactly what he meant.

Seven

Thank goodness it was Saturday.

For some, Saturdays were days for barbecues, college football games and relaxation. For Amelia, Saturday meant all-day wedding chaos, but today she was grateful for it. Her mind had to stay focused on work, so there was zero time to sit and analyze what they'd done last night. Well, aside from fifteen minutes in the shower when she washed the scent of him from her skin and tried to ignore the memories of making love to Tyler only a few hours earlier.

Amelia had not intended on that happening so soon. They were dating, but it was still early on, despite moving in together. None of that had seemed important at the time. She'd gotten caught up in the moment. The fuzzy edge of sleep had blurred her thoughts. When he'd touched her, all she could think about, all she'd wanted, was to fall into his arms again. So she'd gone with it.

In the end, sleeping with the man who was technically her husband was hardly newsworthy. The reality seemed more complicated than that when your husband was your best friend and you were starting an impromptu family together. Of course, this whole process would be easier if she stopped fighting it. The thirty-day challenge wasn't supposed to be a battle; it was supposed to be a trial run. And Tyler was doing his part. He'd done everything she'd asked of him so far, and then some. His every action seemed to be motivated by his thoughtful nature. He was kind. He cared about her and what was best for her and the baby. They didn't always agree on what those things were, but marriage was about compromise.

For once in her life, maybe she just needed to relax and let things happen. Something wonderful could come from it if she allowed the universe to unfold as it should. That was a tall order for Amelia, but she'd think on it. The alternative, as Natalie had pointed out, was unacceptable. She couldn't lose her friendship with Tyler over this.

Once she stepped from the shower and dried off, she had to let that line of thought go and get ready for work. It took a little longer than usual, but she was still adjusting to the new house and trying to figure out where everything was. Since she now lived so much closer to From This Moment, she would still get there well before eight, even when it took five minutes to find her blow-dryer.

Tyler had still been asleep when she got up. When she finished in the bathroom, she moved quickly through the bedroom to the kitchen so she wouldn't disturb him. She wanted to get out the door before he noticed. Yes, she was being a chicken, avoiding an awkward conversation, but she had a good reason to leave.

As she rounded the corner into the kitchen, she realized it was a pointless exercise. Tyler was sitting at the counter hunched over his tablet, reading, with a mug of coffee in his hand. He still had on the rumpled clothes he'd slept in, his dark blond hair wildly standing up in several different directions. Instead of looking messy, the look was charming. An intimate portrait of the man behind the suit. It made her want to come up behind him and wrap her arms around his neck, plant a kiss on his rough cheek and tousle his hair.

Even though they'd had sex, that somehow seemed too intimate. Instead she turned her attention to a tall glass beside him with something greenish brown in it. She was certain it would look unappetizing even if she wasn't having her daily battle with morning sickness.

Amelia knew there was no avoiding a discussion before she left. Maybe he would want to ignore last night's encounter, as well. That seemed like a topic for after noon, at least. With a deep breath, she continued on into the kitchen.

"Morning," she said as cheerfully as she could without sounding suspicious. She opened the door to the pantry and started nosing around for something quick and easy she could take with her for breakfast. Eating was not high on her priority list at the moment, but when the nausea faded, she'd be starving and up to her elbows in twice-baked potatoes for the reception. She picked up a high-protein granola bar with chocolate chips. A bundle of bananas was sitting on the counter. One of those would slip easily into her purse for later.

"Good morning," Tyler replied, his voice low and gruff from sleep. He looked up from his screen. "I already made your breakfast. I hope you don't mind. I know you're the chef, but I thought you might be in a hurry this morning."

Amelia turned around and noticed he'd slid the tall

glass of green sludge closer to her. "Thanks," she said, although she didn't feel very grateful. Her stomach rolled unpleasantly as she neared it. "What is it?"

"It's a pregnancy smoothie. I found the recipe online. It's got cocoa and peanut butter, which you like, plus bananas to soothe a queasy stomach, milk for calcium and spinach for the iron and folic acid needed for healthy fetal development."

She eyed the glass with suspicion. It sounded like a good idea. Maybe it tasted better than it looked. Even if it didn't, Tyler was looking at her with such a pleased and hopeful expression, she'd have to drink it anyway. Lifting the glass to her nose, she sniffed it. It smelled like peanut butter and bananas, mostly. Nothing to make her recoil. Bringing the straw to her lips, she found it tasted the same. The spinach seemed to disappear, adding nutrition while letting the other flavors shine.

"Mmm," she said, swallowing a large sip. "This is pretty good. You can feel free to make me one of these every day."

"Absolutely," he said with a smile. "Taking good care of our child means taking good care of you. I'm glad to do it."

Amelia fought a small twinge in the back of her mind as he spoke. She recognized the feeling as the pang of jealousy, but that didn't make any sense. Who was she jealous of? Their baby? That seemed silly. She should be happy that Tyler wanted them to have a happy, healthy child. And he most likely wanted her to be happy and healthy, too. Amelia was just being oversensitive. She would blame the hormones.

"And after what I experienced yesterday," Tyler continued, "you're going to need all the good nutrition you can get. Are all of your days like that?"

She swallowed another sip and set down the glass on the shiny granite countertop. "Just Thursdays, Fridays and Saturdays. Saturdays are the worst. I have no idea when I'll get home tonight. I probably won't get back until one or two a.m., so don't wait up. What are you doing today?"

Tyler set down his tablet. "I'm going to the estate auction of a country-music singer. She died last year, but her lawyers have finally gotten her estate settled. Her heirs just want to liquidate for cash."

"Who is it?" Amelia asked. There were a lot of country-music stars in Nashville to choose from.

"Patty Travis. That woman was the country-music equivalent of Liberace. She spent almost every dime she earned on jewelry, and her famous roster of lovers over the years bought her even more. It's almost as good as the Elizabeth Taylor auction a few years back. I'm hoping to snap up a few nice pieces."

Amelia frowned at Tyler. "That's why you really came to Nashville!" she accused at last.

He opened his mouth to argue but must have decided against it. "I came to Nashville," he said, seeming to choose his words very carefully, "to see you and work out the details of the divorce we're not getting. It was my first opportunity to come, and I was able to make the time because, yes, I was planning on coming to this auction and I could do it all in one trip. You'll notice I arrived a full five days ahead of the auction so I could devote the time to you. I didn't intend to spend those days renting a house and moving here."

"That's true," she said, carrying her mostly empty smoothie glass over to the sink. She took one last sip and rinsed it out. "Do we need to schedule an auction here in

Nashville the week of the baby's birth so I'll be certain you're in town?"

"Very funny," Tyler said without laughing.

"I'm not entirely kidding." Amelia walked back to the counter and planted her palms on the cool stone. "It took over a month to nail you down about our elopement. If Patty Travis's estate wasn't having an auction this week, it might have taken even longer. I know you've reorganized what you can to make the thirty-day arrangement work out, and I appreciate it. But what are we going to do after that? Even if we stay together, I'm going to spend most of my time in this huge house, alone, while you trot around the world chasing flawless gemstones."

"You could come with me, you know."

Amelia snorted. As alluring as the idea might sound, it would never work. "I have a job, too, you know."

"Do you not get vacation time?"

"It's not a question of benefits, Ty. I am part owner of the company. If I'm not there to do my share, everyone else has to scramble to fill my space. We were lucky when I went to the reunion that the wedding that day was light appetizers and we were able to bring in a contractor. My maternity leave is going to be a huge impact to the business. Traveling with you is impossible."

Tyler frowned. She could tell he wasn't used to someone shooting down his great ideas. He needed to understand that From This Moment wasn't just some job she was keen to cast aside once she had a rich man to take care of her. It was her career. Her passion. A rich husband only seemed to be complicating the issue.

"What if I could arrange the trip to depart on a Sunday night and come back on Thursday or Friday?"

"That would still be pushing it. It would have to be really important. And somewhere I'd like to go. I'm not getting a bunch of shots with weird side effects so you can haul me to India when I'm four months pregnant."

"What about London?" he asked with an optimistic tone.

Damn it if he didn't pick the perfect location right out the gate. Amelia had always wanted to go to London. "Yes, I would like to see London, but timing is key. And," she added, "that wasn't really my point, Ty. In a few more months, I'm not going to be able to travel anywhere. After that, I'll have an infant. More than stamps in my passport, I need you to *be here*."

She looked down at the clock on her phone. "Just think about it. We can talk later. I've got to get to the chapel. Good luck at your auction."

Tyler nodded thoughtfully and waved a hand at her. "Okay. Hope the wedding goes well. I'll see you tonight."

Amelia picked up her purse and went out the door. Tyler could be aggravating at times, but when it came down to it, he knew her better than anyone else. He could use that against her to get his way. Dangling a trip to London was just cruel because he knew how badly she wanted to go. But if she agreed to one trip, he'd find a reason she had to take another. And another. Then after the baby was born, they might as well just bring in a full-time caterer to replace her.

She might be softening on compromising for their relationship, but her job was her dream and she wouldn't lose that. Even so, the whole drive to work she was taunted by thoughts of a proper English tea with fresh scones and the potential to lick clotted cream and strawberry jam from Tyler's bare chest.

"I told you not to wait up for me."

Amelia stumbled in the door around two-thirty in

the morning, her eyes glazed with fatigue and her purse weighing so heavily on her shoulder it could've been filled with concrete.

Tyler frowned and got up from his laptop, where he'd been working. He hadn't intended to stay up, but work had beckoned and the later it got, the more he worried about her. He knew her job was important to her, but she worked too hard. He had seen that same expression on his mother's face when she'd come home from a double shift at the manufacturing plant—bone tired. Too tired to sleep, sometimes. He would make her a cup of tea and sit up talking with his mother until she finally relaxed enough to go to bed.

"You should've called me to pick you up," he chastised gently. "You look exhausted enough to wrap your car around a light pole. Who will cater for them then?"

She shrugged and dropped her purse on a stool in the kitchen. "It's not a long drive home now. I'm fine."

Tyler came up behind her to help her slip out of her jacket. "I thought you had help on Saturday nights."

"I do. There's the waitstaff and a couple people that help cook, like Stella. She was a godsend tonight. Normally it's not a problem. I thrive on the adrenaline rush of the kitchen chaos." She climbed onto the next stool and slumped against the counter. "But lately, I just don't have it in me. A couple hours in and I have to sit down and take a break."

"You're pregnant, Ames."

"So? The baby is the size of a blueberry at best. It shouldn't be giving me this much grief so soon."

"That's not how it works. My sisters complained about the exhaustion far more than anything else. It starts earlier than you'd think."

"I need to get a baby book—*The Moron's Guide to*

Procreation or one of those *What to Expect When Your Body Is Taken Over by a Tiny Alien* books."

"I think we can manage that," he said with a smile. Amelia was really tired if she was getting this crotchety. "Would you like some chamomile tea?"

Amelia sighed, shaking her head and then stopping. She looked up at him with hope beaming in her big doe eyes. "Do we have any hot chocolate?"

"I don't know, but I'll look." Tyler went into the pantry, scanning for the tiny packets of instant mix, but came up empty-handed. He spied a bar of milk chocolate on the shelf and decided to improvise. It had been a long time since he'd made hot chocolate for his little brothers after school. Once his older sisters had gotten part-time jobs, Tyler had been the one at the apartment when the school bus dropped off the little ones. He'd been the one who had made sure they'd done their homework and given them snacks. Hot chocolate had been one of their favorites. Back then he'd made it with bottled syrup, but this would work.

"From scratch?" she asked as she watched him put a small pot of milk on to boil.

"Only the best for you," he said with a grin. He broke up small pieces of the chocolate and dropped them into the heating mixture of milk, vanilla and cinnamon. A few minutes later, it had come together into a frothy brew that he poured into a mug for her. "Here you go. Be careful, it's hot."

"Looks yummy. Thank you."

Tyler rested his hands on the granite countertop and watched her sip the cocoa with a blissful expression on her face. In that moment, he realized just how much he enjoyed making her happy. Over the years, he'd always liked sending her pretty gifts for her birthday or Christmas. That was fun because he knew she would never buy anything like that for herself, and jewels were his business. Seeing her wearing something sparkly and decadent seemed like the perfect treat.

But lately, even before the reunion, their relationship had started to feel different. With their hectic schedules, they rarely saw each other in person, but as life had started encroaching on their technological interchanges, he'd found the idea of it was bothering him more than it used to. He missed talking to Amelia on the phone. Finding emails and texts from her. When he'd arrived in Vegas for the reunion, he couldn't believe how much he'd missed the sight of her. He hadn't even wanted to go to the party. Tyler would've been just as happy ordering room service and spending hours talking in his hotel room.

Now that they were spending almost all their time together, he certainly couldn't miss her. But he still found himself feeling the same little thrill every time she walked into the room. Doing little things like making her breakfast and helping her cut up beef tenderloin gave him a warm feeling in the center of his chest that was more satisfying than giving her some expensive bauble.

She looked at it as being fawned over or taken care of, but that wasn't how he thought about it. He wanted to do things for her because he...cared about her. She was his Amelia. Of course he wanted to do what he could to make her life better. If cocoa made her happy, he'd make it. If this kitchen and a private movie theater that seated eight made her smile, he'd rent this house at twice the price. If marrying her would make her feel better about being single at the reunion...apparently he'd do that, too.

She was the most important person in his life. He'd never expected that she would also be his wife. But now that she was, and the clock was ticking, he was having a hard time envisioning his life without her. He didn't want to go back to just seeing Amelia every now and then. The baby would bring them together more often, but somehow even that wasn't enough. He wanted her here. With him. Every day. This was one challenge he couldn't fail at.

"This was very good," Amelia said, draining the last of her cup. "You're better in the kitchen than you give yourself credit for."

Tyler shrugged and rinsed her mug in the sink. "I am just painting by numbers when in the presence of Michelangelo."

At that, Amelia snorted and burst into exhausted giggles. "I'm more like Bob Ross painting happy little trees, but thank you."

"You should give yourself more credit, too."

"Maybe later," she said with a yawn. "I'm about to fall out with all that warm, chocolaty milk in my tummy."

Tyler wrapped his arm around her shoulder and walked her toward the bedroom. "All right. Come on, let's get you into bed before you collapse on the kitchen floor."

They walked down the hallway to the master suite. There, he sat Amelia down on the bed and knelt in front of her to take off her shoes. He unlaced her little sneakers and slipped them off with her socks, revealing dainty, pink-painted toenails.

"Thank you," she said, pulling her shirt up over her head and throwing it to the floor beside him. "I'm so tired, my feet seem as if they're a million miles away. In a few months, they might as well be. I'll have to get some slip-on shoes."

"You don't need them," Tyler argued. "I'll be here to help you."

"Tyler?"

He sat back on his heels and looked up, catching a glimpse of her large ivory breasts held in the tight confines of her white satin bra. He swallowed hard at the sight of them and focused on her eyes, trying not to look at the temptation on display in front of him. Amelia wasn't trying to tempt him—she was exhausted. "Yes?" he said, clearing his throat.

Her brow furrowed in thought, her eyes glazing over slightly. Even this discussion was tiring her out. "What if thirty days come and go and we don't fall in love?"

That was a good question, and one he hadn't really allowed himself to consider. Having a winning attitude in life had gotten him far. He'd accepted her challenge, never doubting he would be successful. But this was the first time he wasn't fully in control of the variables. No matter what he did, it was possible that Amelia wouldn't fall in love with him. Then what?

That was too deep a conversation for three in the morning. "You mean you're not mad for me already? After last night?"

She shrugged coyly. "I'm getting there. Maybe we should try again tonight to see if it makes a difference."

Tyler chuckled. As much as he'd like to, he didn't relish the idea of Amelia falling asleep in the middle of it. He stood up, planting a warm kiss on her forehead. "Tomorrow night," he promised. "Tonight, all you need to do is slip out of these pants and get to bed."

She nodded slowly, fumbling at the waistband of her black slacks. "Are you staying in here with me?" she asked. "I'll keep my hands to myself."

Last night he hadn't given her request a second thought. Now her question was plaguing his mind with unproductive fantasies about what might happen at the end of their time together. He'd always avoided a relationship with Amelia because he was certain it would end badly, like all the others before him. Now, because of the baby, he hadn't allowed himself to consider any other alternative than them being successful. There was no way he would be sleeping anytime soon. Tossing and turning was more like it. Amelia needed her rest, and that meant he needed to sleep in his own room tonight.

"No," he said, stepping away as she slipped off the last of her clothes.

Amelia slipped under the covers and Tyler pulled the comforter up as if he was tucking a small child into bed. She pouted a little, but the soft pillows quickly lured her into the twilight before sleep, wiping worries from her mind. "Good night, Tyler," she said as her eyes fluttered closed.

"Good night," he replied, looking down as she drifted off to sleep. Tyler couldn't make himself walk away, like he should. He just stood there, watching the soft rise and fall of her chest and the faint smile that curled her pink lips in her sleep. She was the most precious thing he'd ever had in his life. And soon, they would have a child—maybe with the same rosy cheeks and flash of red hair.

Failure was simply not an option. That had been the motto of his life since he was eighteen years old and decided to get into the jewelry business. He hadn't had a family legacy or a lick of experience, but that hadn't stopped him. He had drive. Ambition. A fire that pushed him to succeed in everything in life. It was a passion Amelia lit in him.

That same passion would carry over into their relationship, as well. At the end of thirty days, Tyler would be successful in making Amelia fall in love with him. He might not be in love with her, but it didn't matter. He wasn't the one hell-bent on a perfect love. He just wanted a happy family, and he didn't intend to let this woman and their child slip through his fingers.

Eight

"I can drive, Tyler." Amelia frowned at him as she stared down his new Audi with disdain. "You don't even know where my doctor's office is."

"You can tell me," he said as he opened the passenger door for her to get in. Why would she rather ride in her old SUV than his brand-new luxury vehicle? He had heated leather seats. Individualized climate controls. It was like floating on a cloud to their destination.

She crossed her arms over her chest. "How can I convince you that pregnancy is not a disability? I'm perfectly capable of driving my own car to the doctor's office."

Ah, it wasn't the car. It was him driving it. Too bad. His willingness to do whatever made her happy went only so far. He was going to take care of her whether she liked it or not. "If I had truly thought that about you, the acrobatics in bed last night would've persuaded me to believe otherwise."

Amelia's eyes grew wide, then a smile chased away her irritation. "Quit it," she scolded.

"I will, but how can I convince *you* that letting other people help you isn't a crime?" He stood looking at her expectantly until she finally gave in and climbed into his car. "See?" he said. "That wasn't so bad, was it?"

She didn't respond. Once he got in the car and they started out toward the doctor's office, she turned to look at him again. "You make me crazy sometimes."

He gave her a sly smile in return. "Ditto, sweetheart. You know, you gave me this big, looming deadline to steal your heart, but you fight me at every turn."

Tyler's thoughts drifted to her concerned question from Saturday night. She hadn't broached the subject again since then, but he hadn't been able to put it aside in his own mind. If she didn't love him at the end of thirty days, it wouldn't be for his lack of trying. But would their friendship survive it? He'd insisted everything would be fine and dismissed any concerns because he didn't intend to lose, but could they be friends with a baby? Could they go back to where they came from, knowing what they knew about each other? "How am I supposed to woo you when you won't let me do anything for you?"

"We must have different definitions of wooing. I don't consider it very romantic to drive a woman around everywhere against her will and treat her like a fragile flower."

"That's your problem," Tyler noted. "I don't think you know what love is really about."

"What?" She looked at him with wide eyes as she scoffed at his suggestion. "Love is my business."

"Food is your business. Love is your obsessive ideal, but you don't really understand it. You think love and romance is just about those big gestures—expensive gifts, fancy dinners and moonlit declarations of undying devotion."

"What is wrong with all those things?"

Tyler sighed. "Nothing is wrong with them. It's just that none of that lasts. Flowers die, food gets eaten, words are forgotten. Fifty years from now, when we're sitting in our favorite chairs watching our grandkids play, that's not what you'll remember about our life together. You'll remember the little things, the things you don't give me credit for doing now because they don't fit your ideal."

"You get credit for everything you do," she argued. "I just feel helpless when you drive me around and carry things."

"That is your hang-up, not mine. I'm just being nice. But I could go bigger if you want me to. Would you like me to buy you a new car? That would be a big romantic gesture."

"You are not buying me a car. No way. I don't care how much money you have just lying around, it's a ridiculous suggestion."

"See?" he said, with a shake of his head. "I can't win."

At that, Amelia chuckled. "You're married, Tyler. You'd better get used to that."

That was certainly right. He wished Amelia didn't question the motives of every little thing he did. Somehow being nice seemed to get him in trouble, although he didn't really mind it. He didn't do it on purpose, but he got a little thrill when Amelia got irritated with him. A becoming flush would rush to her cheeks and a flash of emotion would light up her dark eyes. She was a beautiful, passionate woman. He'd had the good fortune to share her bed the past two nights and had taken full advantage of that fire in her. That didn't mean that he didn't enjoy winding her up and watching her spin in the daytime.

He hadn't wanted to push their physical relationship too hard. They'd come together suddenly that first night in the house, and he could tell she was apprehensive about it. Their night together in Vegas had been fueled by raw emotions and alcohol. The second by the delirium of sleep and fierce desires. Since then, he'd thought she'd want some space, but it had been the opposite. She seemed to have abandoned all her reservations about their physical connection. Which he didn't mind at all. But somehow it didn't feel as though they were making relationship progress. It just felt like sex.

What universe was he living in where just having sex with a beautiful woman was somehow less than fulfilling? He was turning into a teenage girl.

Speaking of girls, the doctor's waiting room was crawling with women when they arrived. They checked in, then found a pair of seats among the sea of other ladies waiting. Tyler wasn't certain he'd seen that many women together at once. Young ones, old ones, pregnant ones, ones with babies in carriers... At the moment, he was the only man and feeling very out of place.

"Maybe I should—" he began, but stopped when another man came in with a pregnant woman.

"Are you trying to punk out on me?" Amelia asked with a teasing smile.

"Well, I just wasn't sure. I didn't know what the protocol was for this kind of thing."

Amelia patted his arm, reassuringly. "Daddies can come. Relax. You may just have to look the other way when there are lady parts involved."

"Lady parts?" he asked with a frown.

"I know you're familiar with them, but this is a whole new ball game. Just remember, if you're uncomfortable seeing them, just think how uncomfortable I am putting them on display and subjecting them to various…things."

Things? Tyler swallowed hard. There was a lot to this baby-having business he hadn't considered before.

"Amelia Kennedy?" the nurse called from the doorway.

Amelia got up and slung her purse over her shoulder. Despite his trepidations, Tyler followed her to the doorway, pausing only when the nurse smiled at him and held up her hand to stop him.

"Sir, we're going to take her back to change, get her health history and do a quick pelvic exam. If you'd prefer, I can come back for you when that's done and the doctor is ready to do the ultrasound and chat with you both."

"Absolutely," he said, looking visibly relieved.

Amelia smiled and patted his shoulder. "Saved by the nurse. It shouldn't be long. Read some parenting magazines."

Tyler nodded blankly and returned to his seat. About a half hour later, the same nurse returned and waved him over. He followed her through a maze of corridors, finally stopping at an exam room with a closed door. She knocked softly and entered.

He paused just as he crossed over the threshold into the domain of the female. Amelia was lying back on the table with her feet up. She had a paper sheet draped over her, but his eyes still widened as he took it all in. "The nurse said we were going to do an ultrasound. I thought that meant rubbing gel on your stomach."

"That's for later trimesters," the doctor explained, gesturing toward a stool where he could sit by Amelia's side. "A transvaginal ultrasound gives us a better picture of what's going on early in the pregnancy."

Amelia took his hand and tugged until he sat down.

"We're watching the television screen. Stay north of the sheet and you'll be fine."

Tyler nodded and watched the screen intently as the blurry gray images swirled around. A black circle came into focus and inside it, a tiny gray blob that looked a little like a pinto or kidney bean.

"There's your baby," the doctor announced.

Tyler watched the screen with a touch of disbelief. It didn't look anything like a baby. And yet, his focus narrowed in on the image as if everything else in the room ceased to exist. Up until this moment, the baby had still been a vague concept to him, a challenge he had to face head-on. He'd accepted its existence and had planned how he would care for it when it arrived, but it was still an idea. Suddenly seeing it on the screen made it a person—a tiny little person that he and Amelia had made.

"Wow," Tyler said.

Amelia turned to him and smiled. "Look what we did." Her cheeks were flushed pink and she had glassy tears in her eyes.

Truthfully, he was fighting the same reaction himself. Tyler gripped her hand tightly as the doctor took size measurements and put information into the system.

"What is that little flicker of movement there?" Tyler pointed at the screen. For the most part, the baby was still, but a small section seemed to be pulsing.

"That is the heart beating," the doctor said. "It looks good, too. Nice and strong, considering how early it is."

"Can we hear it?" Amelia asked.

"It's too early to pick up with the Doppler, but it should certainly be audible when you come back in four weeks for your next checkup. That will give you two something to look forward to. Laura is going to print out a couple shots of the ultrasound images for you to take home and show the grandparents," the doctor said. "It's your baby's first picture."

A soft sigh slipped through Amelia's lips as she watched the blurry image. The expression of awe on her face had faded to a faint sadness. Maybe Tyler only noticed it because he knew her so well. It was no surprise that the doctor's words would distress her. A lot of these early milestones in the baby's development would go uncelebrated by friends and family. The excitement, the hugs, the discussion of baby showers and nursery furniture… There would be none of that, at least for now. At some point they would make the happy announcement of her pregnancy to their parents, but would it be tempered by the news that they weren't marrying or even in love?

Little Bean's grandparents would have to wait awhile before they got to learn about his or her existence, much less see the ultrasound photos. Everything would stay under wraps for at least another twenty-two days while he and Amelia figured out what they were doing.

"Okay, we're done here," the doctor said. He helped Amelia sit up and scoot back on the table. "You can go ahead and get dressed, then Laura will bring you back to my office, where we can go over the new-pregnancy packet and you can ask any questions you might have."

They thanked the doctor and Tyler waited outside while Amelia redressed. The meeting with the doctor was pretty short. All their questions seemed to vanish when they were put on the spot, but the doctor laughed and said that was common. That was why they sent parents away with all the paperwork that would answer the questions they remembered once they got home.

When they got back into the car to leave, Tyler noticed Amelia flipping through the massive package with a wide-eyed expression of panic. "There's a lot of stuff in here to read."

"We'll go over it tonight. What do you say we go by the bookstore and pick up some of those baby books you wanted? Then we can get some Chinese takeout, and we can spread all of it across the bed and go through it together. How does that sound?"

"Better," she said with a soft smile. Amelia might be worried about what they faced, but the idea of tackling this together seemed to soothe her concerns for the moment. "Thank you. There's just a lot to think about."

"Sure. But we can handle it. Humans have done it for thousands of years, and most of them without books or handouts to help them. It will be just fine." Tyler tried to think of a distraction, and the weight of the box in his coat pocket reminded him he had a gift for her. He'd had it for a couple days but hadn't found the right time to give it to her yet. "I've got a surprise for you."

She set the paperwork aside and looked at him suspiciously. Amelia wasn't big on surprises, good or bad. "Will I like this surprise?"

"I think so. I bought you something at the Travis auction the other day."

Amelia's nose wrinkled. "I have enough jewelry, Tyler. I know that's your business, but I don't know what to do with all the pieces you've already given me."

"It's not jewelry." He pulled the long, narrow box from his lapel pocket.

"It looks like jewelry," she argued as she took it from him.

Tyler watched her open the box, revealing the delicate silver spoon inside. It had a long, thin handle with a grip designed to look like a crescent-shaped man in the moon. A small diamond was embedded in the eye of the moon. "What do you think?"

Amelia's brow knit together as she examined the box, but no words came. She lifted it, turning the spoon in her fingers and examining the excruciatingly detailed handle.

"It was a gift to Patty from Elvis Presley when she had her first son, Martin. I thought you might like it. You said I wasn't allowed to get any furniture or things like that until after we make it out of the first trimester, but this is a little thing. I hope you don't mind."

"No, I don't mind. It's beautiful." She ran her fingertip over it and placed it back in the box. "Thank you."

He noticed a hesitation in her. He'd noticed it a lot lately. She seemed to second-guess everything he did outside of the bedroom. "But?" he pressed.

"Well," she said with a smile, "I just never dreamed I'd have a baby born with a silver spoon in its mouth."

"These are super yum. I vote for Tasty Temptations."

Amelia turned to look across the conference room table at Gretchen. Between them was an assortment of platters and dishes, food courtesy of the five catering companies they'd interviewed today. Each company had been asked to bring menus, customer references and a sample each of an appetizer and a main course. They were also each asked to replicate one of Amelia's trademark dishes in case a customer requested something specific while she was gone.

"I don't know," Bree said. "We've used Bites of Nashville a couple times, like when Amelia went to Vegas. I feel like they should get priority."

"The only thing I'm loyal to is this little cheeseburger." Gretchen was enamored with a tiny Kobe beef slider by

Tasty Temptations. It had tomato aioli and a tiny, fresh-baked yeast bun.

That was all nice, but Amelia didn't feel charitable. None of the catering companies had really blown her away. "They were okay," she said.

"Okay? Come on, Amelia." Natalie groaned, putting her tablet down on the table beside a platter of Bellinis with assorted toppings. "I'm as big a stickler for perfection as anyone, but you're unreasonably nitpicking. Every company we saw today was great. They were professional and the food was tasty and creative. Chef on Wheels replicated your gorgonzola-and-cracked-black-pepper tenderloin flawlessly. I couldn't tell you hadn't made it."

Amelia frowned at her coworkers. Maybe the hormones were making her oversensitive, but she couldn't help it. Flawlessly? Why should she be happy that someone had been able to copy one of her featured dishes so easily? "I'm sorry, but I'm not that enthusiastic about being supplanted. It's hard to think about someone coming into this place and doing my job. Taking over my role. We'll see how you guys like it when we interview your replacements."

"You know we could never replace you," Bree soothed. "You make the most amazing cream puffs on the planet. But remember, you're the one that got pregnant. We wouldn't be going through this if you weren't going to be out for weeks at a time. And before that, you're going to need help when you're in your third trimester and can't stay on your feet for sixteen hours straight."

"That's not going to be for months," Amelia argued.

"We've got to start the process now, even though you're still perfectly capable of doing the job." Natalie put a hand on her shoulder. "Think about this with your businesswoman cap on, okay? If one of us was going to be away for weeks, we'd need to get a backup set up as soon as we could. Right?"

Amelia sighed. "Yes, I know. You're right. It's just hard."

"Frankly," Natalie continued, "we need to have a backup on standby for all our roles. With your pregnancy we have advance warning, but the blizzard snapped up Bree with no notice at all. Fortunately, we had Willie to fill in, but there's nothing like that for the rest of us."

"Maybe this will help with the vacation issue," Bree said. "We're all pretty burned out, but we're booked solid until the end of next year. We need to be able to take time off. I'm going to want to go on a honeymoon after Ian and I get married. Gretchen has been dying to go to Italy for years. I'm sure there's something you'd rather do than sit behind that desk and work every day, Natalie. Even if one of us just wants to lie on the couch for a week and binge on television, we can't as things stand now."

"How about this?" Amelia offered. "Instead of bringing in a catering company, why don't we hire someone else to help in the kitchen? I didn't realize how much help I could use until Tyler pitched in last weekend. We bring someone in, and then I can spend the next few months getting them trained and comfortable. Maybe we keep Bites of Nashville or one of the others on standby for big events, but there's always someone from our team here."

Natalie thought over her suggestion and nodded. "That's not a bad idea. That way we always have one of our people with eyes on the product. Any ideas on a candidate?"

"I was thinking about Stella."

"From the serving team?" Natalie asked.

Amelia nodded. On wedding days, a restaurant agency provided them with a team of servers to work the front and back of the house with her. Stella was one of the employees who was consistently sent over. She preferred working in the kitchen and had told Amelia she was about to graduate from culinary school in the spring. "She's finishing school in May. That will give us all summer to get her up to speed. By the time my due date comes, she'll do fine with smaller projects and managing the outside caterer if we need one."

"Okay, I'll get her information from the agency and we'll bring her in for a chat." Natalie started tapping on her tablet, capturing the important information. "Now, in the meantime, we still need to pick a backup caterer. I want to have someone on standby."

"Yeah," Gretchen said with a sly grin on her face. "One of us might up and go to London on short notice or something."

Amelia's head snapped up in Gretchen's direction. London? Why would she say London? She and Tyler had discussed that very possibility two weeks ago, but she hadn't said anything to them. Not even in casual discussion. "Is someone going to London?"

Bree snorted into her hand. "You are, dummy."

Amelia's eyes widened in surprise. "I am? Since when?"

"Since Tyler came by last Friday," Natalie informed her. "Before he went into the kitchen to help you, he stopped by my office and asked about the possibility of taking you on a business trip with him. I thought it was nice of him to check before he broached the subject."

Amelia felt the heat of irritation rise to her cheeks. Tyler had the ability to coax an emotional response from her faster than anyone else, for good and bad reasons. She should've known he was up to something. Things had been going too well. It had been over a week since the doctor's appointment, and it had been smooth sailing. They'd enjoyed their evenings together, read baby books together, argued about names and laughed together. "Well, it would've been nice if he'd said something to *me* about it! Anyone care to tell me when I'm going to London?"

"Sunday," Natalie replied.

It was Thursday afternoon. "*This* Sunday? You're kidding, right?"

"No, he told me the date." Natalie looked down at her tablet. "Yep, March 8. That's Sunday."

Amelia gritted her teeth together. This was *so* like Tyler—doing whatever it took to get his way without considering what she wanted or how she felt about it. "I'm gonna kill him. We'll need a backup caterer because I'm going to be in jail for fifteen to life."

"Are you mad?" Gretchen asked. "Seriously? Your husband wants to take you on a spur-of-the-moment trip to London and you're upset about it? I can't get a guy to take me on a spur-of-the-moment trip to Burger King."

"I'm not mad because he wants to take me to London. I'm mad because he went behind my back and set it all up without asking me first."

"That's because you would've said no," Bree pointed out.

Amelia sat back in her chair and crossed her arms over her chest. "So what? It's irresponsible of me to leave on short notice. I just took off time for my reunion, and as we've discussed, I'll be out again in the fall. I shouldn't take off more time just for the hell of it."

"Tyler said he'd have you back Thursday night," Natalie reasoned. "Technically, you wouldn't miss anything. We're not doing the cake next week. They're ordering a cupcake display from a local vendor. But I think you should take the rest of the weekend off anyway."

"Why?"

"You'll be jet-lagged, for one thing," Natalie said. "You're not going to feel like working when you get back."

"You also need to spend some quality time with Tyler," Bree added. "The clock is ticking down on this relationship trial run of yours. You guys have been so busy worrying about renting a house and dealing with baby stuff. Going someplace romantic might be nice. Go and try to enjoy yourself. Roam the streets of London and let yourself fall in love."

In love? Things had been going well, but somehow the thought of that still seemed ridiculous. Amelia did love Tyler, but she was pretty certain being in love was not going to be an option. There were only two weeks left. They were comfortable together, yes. And the sex had been…noteworthy. But love? Amelia had never been in love, but she figured it would take a lot more than a stroll along the Thames to get them there.

Nine

"I think I might be sick."

Tyler snapped to attention, moving to Amelia's side as they stood on the curb in front of Sotheby's auction house. Her color looked okay, her cheeks pink from the chill of the early-March London air. "What? Are you nauseated again? There's a trash can over there."

Amelia smiled and took his hand. "Sorry, I didn't mean I was really sick. The idea of all those diamonds and millions of dollars changing hands was just enough to make me ill."

"Oh," he said with a chuckle as relief washed over him. Amelia had seemed to be doing better with her morning sickness, especially since they'd arrived in London, so he'd been surprised by her sudden declaration. An auction of this caliber could be intimidating to a first timer. Some of the world's greatest jewels and antiques passed through the doors of this auction house, along with the ridiculous amounts of money that went with them.

"I thought maybe the chocolate tea at the Landmark Hotel had turned on you. We ate so much I was miserable through half the auction."

"Oh, no," Amelia argued. "That food was amazing. The one at Fortnum and Mason yesterday was good, too. French macarons are my new favorite thing and I plan to master them the moment we get back home. I think they'd make a lovely item for a dessert display, especially in the wedding colors."

They'd arrived in London early the previous day. The jet lag had been rough on them both, so he'd taken her on a quick drive around the city and they'd had a classic tea before checking into their hotel. Today they'd tried the tea at their hotel before coming to the auction. They were eating their way through London.

"I just love the idea of having afternoon tea," she continued. "That's usually when I get peckish, so it's perfect. A scone and tea is preferable to the soda and candy bar I typically end up eating. I don't know why Americans don't have teatime. It makes us seem so uncivilized, somehow."

"I just spent two hundred and twenty thousand dollars on a diamond-and-pearl tiara from the nineteenth century. That seems pretty civilized to me."

Amelia shook her head and tugged him down the street. "Maybe if you wore the tiara while having tea."

Tyler laughed, following her. Looking the way she did today, he'd follow her anywhere. She was wearing a stunning cobalt-blue wool jacket that came down past her knees to keep her warm. The bright color popped against her fair skin and fiery red hair. Combined with the pregnancy, she was damn near glowing. Beneath her coat, she was wearing a more muted dress with a gray-and-blue geometric design. She'd paired the outfit with sapphire earrings he'd sent her for Christmas the year before. Seeing how radiant the color was on her, Tyler regretted passing up a brilliant sapphire choker that had been auctioned off earlier that afternoon.

"Where are we headed?" he asked when they'd traveled several blocks away from Sotheby's and in the opposite direction of their hotel.

"You're going to take me for a ride on the London Eye."

"I am?" The giant Ferris wheel overlooking the Thames hadn't been in Tyler's plans at all, but he didn't mind going. He'd never ridden it. His past trips to London had been focused on jewels and finding a good chip shop. "I thought we were going to dinner after the auction."

"We will, but I'm not hungry yet after that big tea. We'll eat after you take me on the Eye."

"Okay," Tyler relented, raising his hand to hail a cab. It was probably a good night to ride the Eye anyway. London had remarkably clear skies for this time of year, so they'd have a nice view. By the time they got there, it would just be sunset, when the sky would glow orange and the lights of the city would start to illuminate. It would actually be a great romantic opportunity if not for the herd of other tourists in the capsule with them.

Of course, he could fix that. She wanted the big romantic gestures, right?

After climbing into a cab, Tyler pulled out his phone and found the number of the agency that handled special events on the Eye. By the time they reached the busy plaza and long, winding queue, he'd arranged for a private go-around.

The London Eye was massive, dominating the landscape along the river. It seemed ridiculous to call the large white structure with its space-age pods a Ferris wheel, but he supposed that was what it was.

As they approached the VIP entrance he'd been directed to, a small woman with short brown hair and an immaculate black suit greeted them. "Mr. Dixon? I'm Mary, your personal London Eye hostess. We have your private capsule waiting for you."

Amelia looked at him with surprise lighting her eyes. She'd obviously gotten too used to tuning out his phone conversations, assuming they were all about work. She hadn't paid a bit of attention to the intentionally vague yet still decipherable discussion he'd had with the Eye offices. He hadn't been trying to make it a surprise, but he was pleased to see she hadn't anticipated it.

"A private capsule?" she asked with a wide grin. "Really?"

Tyler smiled and gestured for her to go ahead of him and follow behind Mary. They bypassed the hundreds of people lined up and were escorted onto the next available capsule.

"Your three-hundred-and-sixty-degree maps are on the bench. Enjoy the ride," Mary said before the capsule was closed and locked.

"Off we go," Tyler said as the glass bubble moved up and away from the platform. He followed Amelia to the far side of the car overlooking the Thames. The sun was just setting, and the blazing orange-and-red sky illuminated the boats traveling up and down the river and the cars crossing the bridges beside them. The Parliament building, Big Ben and Westminster Abbey beyond it glowed brightly in the evening light. Turning to look the opposite direction, he recognized other famous buildings, like the Gherkin and the Shard, against the skyline.

It was an amazing view at any time of day, but Tyler was certain he'd hit the jackpot tonight. Not only was it the perfect time, but he had a beautiful woman there with him. She had been resistant to coming on this trip at first, especially since he'd planned it as a surprise and gone around her, as she'd put it, but she'd really warmed up to the idea. He'd been to London enough that he didn't get the surge of excitement when he saw one of the famous landmarks. With Amelia here, he was experiencing the city anew. It made him want to take her with him everywhere he went, and if he couldn't do that, he'd rather stay at home and send one of his employees instead.

Amelia's back was to him as she gazed out at the panorama before them. Her red hair was pulled up today, revealing the long line of her neck. He wanted to lean in to her and place a kiss against her sensitive skin. He wanted to hear her gasp with surprise and moan softly as the sensations he coaxed from her rushed through her body.

Stepping up behind Amelia, he leaned in and grasped the railings on each side of her. He rested his chin on her shoulder, breathing in the scent of her.

"It's beautiful," she whispered.

"You're beautiful," Tyler countered, and wrapped his arms around her waist. She leaned back against him, sighing with contentment as their tiny bubble rose higher and higher around the wheel. The view was spectacular, but the longer they spent pressed against each other, the less interested Tyler was in the landscape.

He swept a stray strand of red hair out of the way and pressed his lips to her skin. Amelia gasped and tilted her head to the side to give him better access. He moved across her throat, teasing her with his lips, teeth and tongue. She held still, only her rapid draws of breath giving away her building arousal. His desire for her was harder to disguise. The minute he touched her, the blood rushed to his extremities and he was overwhelmed by the throbbing need to possess his wife.

His wife. Funny how he'd come to think of her that way in only a few short weeks. He'd gotten used to spending the evenings with her, watching her cook and testing her new recipes. He liked falling asleep with her in his arms and waking up to her grumpy morning face. Tyler needed Amelia to fall in love with him. He couldn't bear to lose all this in a week's time.

Just as they crested the top of the Eye, he slipped a hand beneath her coat and cupped one large breast. He could feel the nipple form into a hard peak beneath his touch, straining through the fabric to reach him. Amelia arched her back as he stroked her flesh, pressing her round backside into the firm heat of his desire.

Tyler groaned aloud, the sound echoing in the capsule. He was overcome by the driving need to touch her, bury himself in her and lose all rational thought in loving her. But damned if they weren't four hundred feet in the air, enclosed in a clear bubble with tourists on both sides of them and a closed-circuit camera recording their every movement. It was the most seemingly private yet agonizingly public scenario he could've possibly put them in.

Amelia turned in his arms to face him as they started descending back toward the ground. She slipped her arms around his neck, lacing her fingers together at the nape. She did look beautiful today. And this was an amazingly romantic moment. And yet he couldn't stop from voicing the concerns that had been plaguing him for over a week. They had to get past this.

"Amelia?" he said, his voice near shaking with adrenaline and need.

"Yes?"

"Will you love me?" he asked.

A seductive smile curled her lips. "Absolutely."

Tyler softly shook his head. She'd answered too quickly, so he was certain she misunderstood. "That's not what I meant," he corrected. Amelia had given him her body, but it wasn't enough. He wanted more. He wanted to break through her walls and topple all her misconceptions about love. He knew her well enough to know he couldn't force his way into her heart. She had to let him in. "Will you give me your heart?"

Her eyes widened, her mouth falling open without words.

"I want this to work between us, Amelia. I want you to fall in love with me, so we can have a family and all the wonderful things you've always dreamed of. But you have to stop fighting it. Are you ever going to let yourself fall in love with me?"

There was a long silence, a painful one, but when she finally did speak, it made him yearn for the quiet again.

"You're asking me to give you something with nothing in return."

It was Tyler's turn to look at her with wide-eyed surprise. "What do you mean?"

"Through this whole thing, you've been on a mission to make *me* fall in love with *you*—and you're succeeding, even if you don't feel that way. But you're right, I am holding back, and it's because I get the feeling that *you're* not letting yourself fall in love with *me*. You had it rough with Christine. I know that. Breaking off the engagement a week before the wedding was just cruel, especially if she knew she'd had doubts about the two of you. She hurt you. You wouldn't ever talk about it, but I can tell by the way you changed after that. All work, all the time."

He didn't like talking about what happened with Christine, even with Amelia. Talking about it meant that he would have to face his first big failure in life. To talk about how he couldn't measure up, no matter what. He'd rather just pretend it hadn't happened. "I have a business to run," he argued.

"So do I. That's no excuse. You're just hiding away. You might have lost her, but in the process, I almost lost you, too. You buried yourself in your work, flying so much the flight attendants know you by name. But you need to clip those wings of yours if we're going to make this work. I think both of us are trying so desperately to protect our hearts, so afraid this isn't going to succeed and we're going to lose everything we have.

"I will let myself fall in love with you, Tyler," she continued, "but you have to let yourself do the same."

Tyler swallowed hard, hearing the truth in her words but not knowing quite how to address it. He had held a part of himself back, and he still wasn't certain he could give all of himself the way he had before. It was a scary prospect, even as desperately as he wanted the life they could have together. But they'd never have the chance if he didn't give in. Or at least, let her think that he had.

"You're right," he said, forcing himself to smile at her reassuringly. "From now on, no holding back. I will let myself love you and you will let yourself love me."

A brilliant smile lit her face. Before he could react, her lips met his. He was happy to close his eyes and lose himself in the physical contact that had been his comfort these past few weeks. This was the kiss that was supposed to mark the change in their relationship for the better. They were giving in, and he needed to make her believe his words.

He pressed into her, pushing her back to mold her

against the concave wall of the capsule. Her mouth was soft and welcoming in juxtaposition to his hard advance. His tongue forced its way into her mouth, demanding she give him more, and she gladly complied. She pressed her breasts against his chest and met his every advance.

How had he been so blind to this for so long? Amelia was perfect for him in so many ways. She knew just how to touch him, just how to handle his every mood. She wasn't afraid to call him on his crap. And when it came down to it, he'd never been as attracted to a woman in his life as he was to her. From the first day he laid eyes on her freshman year, he'd known he was hers, be they friends or lovers. When they'd decided on friends, he'd shelved the attraction and kept his distance. Why, even now, he was resistant to let go. The minute he gave in to how badly he wanted her everything would fall apart.

At that unnerving thought, he pulled away. The moment their lips parted, the lights of the Eye illuminated and they were suddenly surrounded by its haunting blue glow. Amelia looked up at him, the lights and shadows highlighting the contours of her delicate features. Her smile was devoid of the pink lipstick she'd had on when they entered the Eye.

"Let's go back to the hotel," Amelia said, her voice breathy.

"You don't want to go to dinner?" he asked.

"No," she replied adamantly. "Take me back to the hotel right now or risk me doing something scandalous to you in this plastic bubble where everyone can see us."

As appealing as that sounded, Tyler could see the loading platform approaching below. They wouldn't have enough time to start anything interesting—or at least not to finish it—before the cops arrested them both.

"To the hotel it is."

* * *

The moment they touched back down on solid earth, they rushed to get a cab to the hotel. Amelia's heart was racing in her chest the entire way there, and when they pulled up outside the Landmark Hotel, she felt a tightness, like a vise closing down on her rib cage.

It wasn't making love to Tyler that made her anxious. She had a thirst for him that never seemed to be satiated. It was their conversation on the Eye that worried her. She'd told him that she sensed he was afraid to give himself fully to the relationship, but there was more to it than just fear. Yes, he might be worried about losing their friendship or afraid of getting hurt again, but there was something else. He'd never seriously pursued her before now. Not once in all these years. But the moment a baby had come into the picture, Tyler had been ready to swoop in and claim her as his own.

Which raised the painful question she didn't really want to face—was Tyler only here for the baby?

Did he really want them to fall in love, or did he just want Amelia to love him enough to stay in the relationship for the sake of their child? She had a miserable track record—she knew that. If not for the baby, she probably wouldn't have let their relationship go on this long, in truth. She would've found some reason why it wouldn't work. But now she was having feelings for Tyler. Real feelings that went far beyond friendship. Far beyond loving him, but not being *in love* with him.

But she didn't get the same vibes from Tyler. It felt more like…an obligation, despite him telling her he was going to stop holding back.

Amelia shuddered at the thought. She never wanted anyone to be with her just because he thought he had to be. Tyler was attracted to her—there was no doubt of that—but could they have more?

The thoughts weighed heavy in her mind, even as they made their way through the stunning eight-story atrium of the hotel. She barely saw it, or any of the other remarkable features about their historic, hundred-year-old hotel. It wasn't until they reached their suite that Amelia pushed the doubts out of her mind, just as she pushed Tyler's suit coat over his shoulders. As they had nearly every night since they'd shared a home, she wanted to lose her worries in Tyler's arms.

His jacket fell to the floor along with her own blue coat. Tyler pulled her into his arms and kissed her until she was nearly breathless. "I've never wanted a woman as badly as I want you tonight," he said, his voice low and rough.

Amelia's anxiety faded at the sound of his voice. It wasn't all about the baby. His desire for her was real enough. She gave him a wicked, knowing grin and tugged at his tie. They shed clothing as they made it through the seating area to the large ivory-draped bed. Tyler whipped back the duvet and the flat sheet, then slipped out of his pants and eased onto the bed. Their make-out session on the Eye had certainly fired up his engine, and he was clearly ready for a long, exhilarating drive.

Kicking out of her heels, Amelia didn't waste any time joining him in the bedroom. She'd been feeling a little feisty when she'd packed for this trip. Beneath her modest dress today, she'd opted for a lacy black demibra with matching panties and garter belt. The sheer black silk stockings were topped with lace that contrasted sharply with her pale skin.

Tyler's mouth dropped open when her dress fell to the ground and she exposed the sexy lingerie she'd kept hid-

den all day. She did a little twirl, showcasing the revealing thong cut of the panties before slipping her thumbs
beneath the sides and sliding them down her legs. She'd
worn them outside the garter belt just for this reason. "Do
you mind if I keep the rest on?" she asked innocently.

A frantic shake of his head was all she received in
reply. Approaching the bed, she crawled slowly across
it, putting the brakes on his rapid-fire seduction. When
she reached the hard-carved muscles of Tyler's bare abdomen, she threw one leg over his torso and straddled
him. The movement immediately brought their most sensitive parts into contact, and the sensation brought a gasp
of pleasure to her lips and a wicked smile to her face.

"All day?" He groaned. "You've been wearing that
all day?"

"Mmm-hmm," she hummed, reaching for the pins
holding up her hair. When she removed the third and
final one, her red curls spilled down over her shoulders,
and she shook them out to great effect.

Tyler's palms slid up her silky thighs, running his fingertips over the silver snaps of the garters and lacy tops
of the stockings. "I…" he began, but Amelia brought a
finger to his lips to quiet him.

They had done enough talking for today. There had
been too many emotions and too much angst. Right now
she just wanted to lose herself in making love to him. He
wanted her to let go, and tonight, she would.

Rising up onto her knees, Amelia planted her hands
on the pillows on both sides of Tyler's head. Her breasts
nearly tumbled from their confines as she moved, but
he was quick to offer his hands to support them. As he
kneaded her flesh, she slowly moved back, finding his
firm heat and easing the length of him inside her hot,
aching body.

Sitting up, Amelia rocked her hips forward, the pleasure of the moment forcing her eyes shut. It was better that way, so she kept them closed. With her eyes shut, she could focus on the feeling of Tyler's hands cupping her breasts and teasing her nipples through the lace. She could absorb every powerful sensation as she moved her hips and forced the length of him deeper inside her body. She could hear Tyler's murmurs of encouragement, her own soft gasps, the faint squeak of the bed as she moved…

But most of all, she could focus on the feeling deep in her chest. It was there, as she gave herself to Tyler, that she really opened up. He'd asked her tonight to let him in, to allow herself to love him, so she would. As though she'd turned the key in a rusty, old lock, she opened herself up to the emotions she'd held at bay for so long.

It was a stunning moment when the feelings hit her. The warmth of love heated her from the inside out, with tears forming in the corners of her eyes. But along with the feeling was a revelation she'd never expected—she not only loved Tyler, but she always had. No other man would ever meet her stringent qualifications because no other man could be Tyler. He was her better half, the part she'd always searched for and failed to find because she'd refused to look in the most obvious of places.

And now she was giving herself to him, heart and soul.

"Amelia…" Tyler groaned, bringing his hands to her hips. His palms cupped the lace-covered curve of her rear, guiding her movements, and she knew neither of them would be able to last much longer.

She placed her hands on his chest, one covering the rapid tattoo of his heart. Moving more forcefully, she quickly drove herself to the edge. When her climax came, her whole body shook with the strength of it. Every nerve lit up; every muscle tensed. She cried out to the dim room, gasping for breath.

Tyler rode out her orgasm, then pressed his fingers hard into her soft flesh and drove into her from beneath until he shouted his own pleasure.

Unable to hold herself up any longer, Amelia collapsed against him. She buried her face in his neck, their bodies both trembling with the power of their release. She kept her hand over his heart as they lay there, feeling the beat slow along with their breaths.

She had given Tyler her heart. It was too late for her to consider fighting the feelings anymore. She just didn't have the strength. The thirty days would be up soon after they returned to Nashville, and she knew what her answer would be. She wanted to stay with him and start their family together.

The only problem was that Amelia wasn't entirely sure if she would ever have Tyler's love. He would stay for their child. She knew him well enough to know that. But that big fantasy of love she'd always dreamed of? That still seemed out of reach.

She couldn't have it when only one of the people had fallen in love.

Ten

"London was amazing," Amelia said to her coworkers seated around the conference room table of From This Moment. It seemed like forever since she'd been in the office, although it had just been a week. As Natalie had insisted, she didn't come in over the weekend. She'd been right about the jet lag. Friday, she'd nodded off whenever she had a quiet or still moment. "I take back every ugly thing I said about Tyler."

"I told you," Gretchen said. "What was the best part of the trip?"

"That's a hard one. The food was great. Seeing all the historic landmarks was nice, too. I think I ate my weight in scones."

"Has your morning sickness gone away?" Bree asked.

"Actually, yeah." She hadn't felt anything even close to queasiness since they'd gone to London. She'd had more energy, too, which had been nice to have on the trip. "I was so happy to be able to eat. Our hotel was beautiful. Everything there is so different, yet familiar. Well, aside from driving on the other side of the road. I very nearly got hit by cabs two or three times because I looked the wrong way before crossing the street. They even have big painted letters on the street that say 'look right' for idiots like me."

"You're probably not the only one to nearly get hit," Natalie noted.

"What about the lovin'?" Bree asked with a sneaky smile. Amelia could tell she wasn't the least bit interested in discussions of scones or old churches. "You've got a look about you today—a rosy, well-loved look."

"Bree!" Amelia complained, but she couldn't help smiling. Things had changed between her and Tyler in London. Once they'd both agreed to let down their barriers, their physical and emotional connection had become stronger than it had ever been. She still had a mountain to climb where Tyler and his emotions were concerned, but they'd made significant progress. "I do think we've had a bit of a breakthrough in the relationship."

"Are you in love?" Gretchen asked, perking up in her chair. "He has until Wednesday to make it happen, and judging by the fact that you can't stop smiling, I think Tyler was successful."

"I think he was, too," Amelia admitted.

"Have you said it to him?"

Amelia wrinkled her nose. "No. I want to wait until we reach the end of the thirty days and make it official. Besides, I've never said that to a man before. I'm a little nervous."

"Make him say it first," Natalie noted, her eyes never leaving her tablet.

That probably wasn't a bad idea. She still had her worries and reservations about how Tyler felt. Outwardly, he hadn't given her any reason to doubt he had feelings for her, but she couldn't shake it.

"Oh, I have gifts!" Amelia announced. "Hold on." She scuttled back to her office and returned with three goodie bags. Each held a Union Jack tin of buttery shortbread cookies, a canister of English breakfast tea and a sleeve of French macarons she'd bought at the Ladurée bakery inside Harrods department store.

Everyone was cooing over their gifts when Amelia's phone started to ring. She looked down to see her sister's number. That was odd. She and her sister weren't particularly close. Whitney took more after their mother, and they didn't see eye to eye on very much. They rarely talked on the phone unless it was a special occasion like a birthday or a holiday, and even then, it was a stilted conversation. The women around the table were closer to sisters than her biological one.

Amelia hit the button to dismiss the call. She would call Whitney back when the staff meeting was done. She'd already avoided too much of her work duties around here lately.

"I thought you guys might like them," she said, feeling her phone buzz with a voice mail message. Before she could say anything else, a text from her sister popped up.

Call me right now!

Amelia sighed. "Do you guys mind if I step out for a minute and call my sister back? She seems to be freaking out. I'm sure my parents have just done something to set her off."

"Sure, go ahead," Natalie said. "I'll just start going

over the weekend wedding with them. We can talk about how the catering went when you get back."

Amelia slipped out of the room and went to her office. A discussion with her sister meant sitting—and eventually taking some pain medication for the headache it would inevitably set off. She pulled a bottle of Tylenol out of her drawer and swallowed a couple with her bottle of water. Her lower back was already bothering her today, so she might as well take some pain relievers and kill two birds.

The phone rang only twice before her sister picked up. "You're married?" Whitney nearly squealed in her ear. "And I find out on Facebook. And pregnant, too! Are you kidding me? I know we aren't super close, but you could at least have done me and our parents the courtesy of telling us this directly before it hit the internet."

Amelia was so stunned by her sister's sharp accusations, she didn't know how to respond at first. It actually took her a moment to even process what she was going on about. Facebook? How the hell had any of that information gotten on Facebook? Of course she would've told her family, when she was ready to. Someone had just beaten her to the punch. She swallowed hard and tried to collect the wild emotions that had just been jump-started in her veins. "What are you talking about, Whitney?"

"A woman named Emily posted, and I quote, 'So excited to hear that my little brother Tyler has settled down and started a family with his best friend, Amelia. We've been waiting years for those two to get together. And a baby! So exciting!'"

There were no words. Her sister's fury was nothing compared to the hot blades of anger running through her own veins. He'd told his family. And his sister had put it on Facebook, tagging her so her own family and friends could see it.

They'd had an agreement. No one was supposed to know until they decided what they were going to do. Things had been going so well. The trip to London was amazing. She had finally let go of the last of her reservations and let herself fall in love with her best friend. There was absolutely no reason to go behind her back and tell his family.

Why would he do such a thing? Was he afraid that when the thirty days were up, she was going to walk away? Tyler was the kind of man who won at all costs. Was this his backup plan? A way of strong-arming her into doing what he wanted in the end? Did he think she would be coerced into staying with him if all their friends and family knew they were married and having a baby?

"Amelia!" her sister shouted through the phone when she didn't get a response. "What the hell is going on? Is it even true?"

There was no point in lying about it. That would just cause more confusion and lead to more phone calls. "Yes, it's true. I'm sorry I didn't call, but I didn't expect the news to get out before I could talk to everyone about it. Listen, I can't talk right now, Whitney."

Amelia hung up the phone and turned off the ringer. She was certain her sister would immediately call back and demand answers, but she wasn't ready to give anyone anything—aside from giving Tyler a piece of her mind.

Grabbing her purse from the bottom drawer of her desk, she got up and headed for the door. The short drive back to the house only served to make her angrier, especially when she rounded the fountain out front of their ridiculously big home.

Standing in the driveway, looking up at the massive

house, she realized this place was a metaphor for their entire relationship. Everything had been his way since the moment he arrived in Nashville. They didn't divorce because he didn't want to. They were dating because he insisted on it. They drove around in his car, moved into the house he chose, took the trips he needed to take, even when she had to work.

He knew just how to dangle the carrot to get her to go along with the way he wanted things to be. But this time he'd gone too far. She stomped up the stairs and through the living room to the keeping room, where Tyler had his desk and computer. He was happily typing away on his laptop, his mind probably focused on rubies and diamonds, giving no thought at all to what he'd done.

"You know," she started to speak, her voice trembling with anger she could barely contain, "I thought we had an agreement."

Tyler looked up, his pale eyes wide with sudden concern. "What? What's wrong, Ames?"

She held up her hand to silence him. "We went into this with just a few ground rules, but they were important ones. One rule was that we would give it thirty days, and if necessary, we'd part friends. Another was that we'd live together in this house the whole time. But the most important of all was our agreement that no one would know we were married and pregnant until we were ready to tell them. No one, Tyler! How could you do this?"

Tyler's expression hardened for a moment, his eyes unfocused as he seemed to be trying to piece things together. "What do you mean, how could I—"

"Facebook!" she shouted. "Of all the places."

"Facebook?" His eyebrows drew together in a confused frown. "I don't even have a Facebook account."

"Well, you know who does? My sister. And my

mother. And apparently, your bigmouthed sister Emily, who just announced to God and country that we eloped and we're having a baby."

The color instantly drained from Tyler's face as he processed her words. "Emily posted that on Facebook?"

"Yep," she said. A quick check of her account had confirmed that, plus a few more details that made it all the worse. She hadn't logged in since she'd gotten back from London, but there the post was, big as day, with lots of likes and congratulatory messages for the happy couple. It was when she saw the responses from her own friends, people who didn't even know Tyler, that she realized she'd been tagged in the post. "And Emily tagged me so it showed up in the news feed of everyone I'm friends with, too. The cat is out of the bag in a big way, so thanks a lot."

"Oh, no." Tyler groaned and covered his face with his hands. Now *he* was the nauseated one. He knew it. He knew he shouldn't have said a word to Jeremy. Now it had come back around to bite him. "Amelia, I had no idea that was going to happen."

She crossed her arms over her chest and narrowed her gaze at him in disbelief. "You told your gossipy sister the biggest possible secret and actually expected her to keep it? Are you insane? You should know better than that."

"No," Tyler insisted. "I never would've told Emily, and for that very reason. I told my brother. *Only* my brother. And it was almost a month ago, right after we got the house. He was needling me about why I was moving down here and wouldn't let it go. I told him in confidence. He was the only person I told. If my sister found out, it's Jeremy's fault."

"No, Tyler," Amelia corrected with a sharp tone. "It's

your fault. You're the one that told our secret when you knew you shouldn't. I don't understand why you would do that."

"I told you why!" He stood up from his seat and his fists pounded into the top of his oak desk to emphasize his answer. "I wanted someone in my family to know where I was, because unlike your neurotic crowd, I actually like my family. I chose Jeremy because I thought he would be the least likely to pry, but I was wrong and I ended up having to tell him. I assure you that he and I are going to have a long talk about keeping confidences."

Amelia shook her head and planted her hands on her hips. She winced slightly and squeezed her eyes shut, not responding immediately.

"It was an accident," Tyler continued. "I'm sorry that it got out, but we're only a few days away from telling everyone anyway. Of course, I didn't want my family to find out on the internet, but there's not much we can do about it now. The sooner we stop fighting, the sooner we can start calling everyone and doing damage control."

"And tell them what, Tyler?"

Tyler opened his mouth but paused. "What do you mean, tell them what?"

"What are we telling them? The thirty days aren't up. We haven't declared our undying love for one another. You haven't proposed. None of this is wrapped up in a neat bow yet. Tell the truth, Tyler. You leaked this to your family because you were afraid you weren't going to get your way."

"You think I did this deliberately? To what? Blackmail you into staying with me?"

"You always get your way, no matter what. The clock will be up come Wednesday. Falling in love so quickly is nearly impossible. Were you nervous that you might not succeed this time? There's nothing like taking out a little insurance policy to make sure you still got what you wanted."

Somehow this whole scenario seemed to be his doing. Why? Because he didn't want to raise his child bouncing between two homes like a Ping-Pong ball? Because he was willing to sacrifice his own personal needs to do what was best for everyone? That made him the bad guy? The big manipulator, pulling all the strings, tricking her into moving into a beautiful house and going on expensive trips. He was such a bastard.

Tyler chuckled bitterly and shook his head. He was tired of handling her with kid gloves. "And what makes you think that *any* of this is what *I* wanted?"

Amelia opened up her mouth to argue, but the sharp tone of his words silenced her. He watched as her cheeks flushed red and glassy tears rushed into her eyes. The words had been harsh, and he knew it, but he couldn't keep them from flying from his mouth.

"You think I'm just like your father, trying to manipulate and browbeat you into getting my way. Well, guess what? This isn't what I would've chosen, either. I came to Nashville to get a divorce, and instead I got a whole damn family and a life a thousand miles away from my business and my home. I've tried to make the best of a bad situation, but you make it really hard, Amelia. You want to talk about telling the truth? Here's a dose of honesty for you—you're a coward!"

"A coward?" she gasped, taking a stumbling step back as though he'd slapped her.

"Yes. You tell people you believe in love and that you want it so desperately, but you'll use any excuse to avoid any relationship with potential. You use the guise of looking for this mythical, perfect love to reject anyone that tries to love you."

"You don't know anything about me and my relationships," Amelia said through her tears.

"I know everything about you. Remember, I'm your best friend, not the latest guy you've tried on like a pair of shoes and cast aside when you decided they don't fit. I know you better than you know yourself. I thought we had something good going between us. I thought that in a few days we would be telling our parents some good news. But you're such a chicken, you're grasping at the tiniest excuse to destroy this relationship and throw all the blame on me."

"I am not! You broke our agreement."

Tyler shook his head. "You're so deep in denial, you can't even see it. The only reason you've even given our relationship half a shot is because of the baby."

"Then that makes two of us, Tyler. That's the only reason you're here, so don't be so self-righteous. I—" Amelia paused, her eyes widening with fear, but they weren't focused on him. She gasped and doubled over, clutching her lower belly. "Oh, no," she cried.

Tyler rounded his desk and ran to her side, clasping her shoulders to offer support. "Are you okay? What is it?"

"Something's not right. I think I'm—" she started, and then groaned. "Help me to the bathroom, will you?"

He helped Amelia to the master bathroom, waiting patiently outside the door. It wasn't until he heard her agonized sobs that his stomach sank and he realized what was happening. She was having a miscarriage.

"Come on, we'll get you to the hospital right now," he shouted through the door.

"I just need to call my doctor."

"No. We're going to the hospital first. Let them tell us to go home."

When she came out a moment later, her skin was as white as paper and covered in a thin sheen of sweat. He could see her hands shaking as she gripped the door frame to come out. She was in no condition to be walking around. He grabbed a blanket from the bed and wrapped her in it, then swept her up off her feet. He carried her out to his car and loaded her into the passenger seat. He didn't stop to lock the door or worry about anything other than getting Amelia to the hospital as quickly as he could. St. Thomas West wasn't far; hopefully they could make it in time to save the baby. If they could.

Tyler's heart was racing in his chest as he flew through the streets. This couldn't really be happening. It just couldn't. She'd said this baby was what was keeping them together and she was right, but only to a point. The baby wasn't the glue that held them together, but it was the steel beam that reinforced them so that even strong winds couldn't knock them down. It was what gave him hope that they could make it. It was what made her stay even when she had reservations.

And now, he was certain, they were losing that. What would happen to them? Would this relationship spiral out of control without the child to anchor them? Would the loss bring them closer together or rip them apart? Tyler didn't know.

He occasionally stole a glance at Amelia as they drove. She was bent over in the seat, curled up against the door with her eyes closed. She was biting her lip, holding back tears of pain and fear. Even with the blanket, she was trembling. It broke his heart to see her that way.

Especially knowing that it was all his fault.

He had ruined everything. He'd opened his big mouth

and betrayed her trust. He'd used her own harsh, hurtful words as an excuse to lash back at her and say the most horrible things he could think of. And now she was losing their baby.

Tyler whipped around the corner to enter the emergency area. Coming to a stop, he threw the car into Park and leaped out. Scooping Amelia into his arms, he rushed through the front door. "Please!" he shouted to the women at the front desk. "Please help, I think my wife is losing our baby."

A nurse rushed into the lobby with a wheelchair. Tyler stood helplessly as Amelia was transferred to the chair and taken away. "Please wait here, sir," another nurse told him. "We'll take you back as soon as we can."

Tyler's knees gave out and he slipped down into one of the waiting room chairs. He wished to God he *could* go back—back in time so he could keep this from happening.

Eleven

"There was nothing you could have done, nothing you did to cause this. About ten to fifteen percent of pregnancies fail in the first trimester."

"The baby was fine at our first appointment. The doctor even said he had a strong heartbeat," Tyler argued with the doctor even though he knew it wouldn't change the outcome.

Amelia was lying silently in her hospital bed, recovering from the procedure she'd undergone shortly after arriving at the hospital. Tyler didn't know all the details, but the end result was the same. No more baby.

"At this stage, a lot changes in two or three weeks. And from the sound of things," the doctor said, "the baby stopped growing at around seven weeks, and it just took this long for your body to deal with it."

Tyler frowned. "How can you know that?"

"Ms. Kennedy said her morning sickness had suddenly ceased and she had more energy. This early in the pregnancy, that's a big sign that the baby is no longer developing."

"So it wasn't anything that happened today...?" Tyler's voice trailed off. He didn't want to outright ask if the emotional upheaval he'd put his wife through had caused her to lose the baby, but that had been the question tormenting him all afternoon.

"No, no. This was just nature dealing with a problem. But the plus side is that there's no reason why you two can't try again. Take some time to recover from this, give your body a few months and then you can give it another try. Just because you miscarried this time doesn't mean it will happen again. You don't have any of the risk factors, Ms. Kennedy, so I wouldn't worry."

"Thank you, Doctor," she said at last. It was the first time Amelia had spoken since she'd greeted the doctor and told him how she was feeling.

"Well, everything else seems to be okay, so the nurse will be around shortly with your discharge paperwork and a few prescriptions to help with the discomfort. Take it easy for a few days. Feel free to have a glass or two of wine to help you unwind, just don't overdo it until your symptoms fully clear up. If there are no other questions, I'll get out of your hair." When they didn't speak up, the doctor shook Tyler's hand and then slipped out of the room.

Tyler slumped down into the chair beside her bed, not certain what to do now. He felt completely helpless, and he hated that. She'd accused him of always being in control, of always getting his way, and she was right. He didn't like it when he couldn't fix things, and this was one thing he simply could not fix.

How quickly things had changed. A few weeks ago,

neither of them had even considered having a child, much less together. And now that the child was gone…he felt as though a part of him had been ripped away. He knew that it was a piece of him that he could never get back.

At this point, he didn't even know what to say to Amelia. She was his best friend, and he'd never felt the awkward lack of words when he was with her. But now, he wasn't sure where they stood. He was fairly certain that she wouldn't want to try getting pregnant again. Where did that leave them? Their last real words to one another before the miscarriage had been cutting and painful. He wasn't even entirely sure he would walk out of the room with a best friend, much less a wife.

"Tyler?" Amelia said at last.

"Yes?" Tyler leaped up from his chair to stand at the rail of her hospital bed. She seemed so small with the oversize hospital gown and all the wires and tubes hooked up to her. Her color was better now, but that wasn't saying much. The faint gray circles under her eyes spoke volumes. She might be healthy, but she was not fine. "Can I get you something?"

"No." She shook her head and winced slightly. "I'm okay."

"How are you feeling?"

"Better than I was," she said, attempting a small smile, but it didn't make it to her eyes. "Tyler…I want you to go home."

"I'm not going home without you. The doctor said you'll be released shortly."

"You don't understand. I want you to go home to New York."

Even though a part of him had been anticipating this eventuality, he didn't expect the painful blow to his midsection that accompanied it. It was excruciating, worse than anything he'd experienced, even his breakup with Christine a week before their wedding. "Amelia—" he began, but she held up her hand.

"Tyler, please. You were and are my best friend. But we never should've been anything more than that. We made a mistake and compounded it by trying to force ourselves into a different mold for the sake of our baby. I'm sorry that all this happened and that I put you through this, but now it's done. Things have worked out the way they were meant to. Without a baby, there's no reason for us to continue on."

Tyler tried to swallow the lump that had formed in his throat, but it remained stubbornly lodged there as he struggled to breathe.

"If you don't mind," she continued in his silence, "I'll stay in the house a few more days until we can arrange the movers to put my things back in my apartment."

"We don't have to make any quick decisions. Give yourself a few days."

Amelia sighed and reached out to pat his hand. "Tyler, you and I both know we don't need a few days. We were ending it this morning before everything else went wrong. Now we just don't have to face the endless custody complications and awkward eventuality of seeing each other with other people. You can travel the world without worrying about me and the baby at home. I can go back to my little apartment and continue my quest for love. This is the way it needs to be."

Tyler felt his grief morph in his veins to a low, simmering anger. She'd been angry with him this morning, yes, but if they had finished that fight, he would've seen to it that it was just a fight. Couples fought from time to time; it didn't have to put an end to the whole relationship. She was using the Facebook leak as an excuse to push him away, just as she was using the miscarriage to push him away. Whenever she got close to anyone, she panicked.

"This wasn't just about the baby, Amelia. Look me in the eye and tell me you don't have feelings for me. Tell me you're not in love with me and I'll walk right out the door."

Her dark gaze flicked over his face for a moment, and she looked intently into his eyes. "I'm not in love with you, Tyler."

She was lying. He could tell she was lying. Her fingers were rubbing anxiously at the blanket, the same way she used to fidget with a pencil or pen in class. But why would she lie about something like that? About something so important?

Tyler took a deep breath and sighed, the fight draining out of him. Even if she did love him, for whatever reason, she didn't want him. Nothing had changed over the years. She hadn't wanted him when they were sixteen and she didn't really want him now. The last thing Tyler wanted to do was force himself on a woman who didn't want to be with him. This wasn't the first time he'd fallen short where a woman was concerned. If she wanted him gone, he'd go. He had work in New York. A life there. An apartment. If there wasn't a reason to be in Nashville, he didn't want to stay another minute.

"Okay," he said with a sigh of resignation. "If that's what you want. I'll let the real estate agent know we'll be out in a week or so and arrange the movers."

"I've called Natalie to come pick me up."

Tyler looked up at her. She didn't even want him to drive her home? "Okay. Well, then, if there's nothing else I can do for you, I won't subject you to my presence any longer."

"Tyler…" Amelia began with a coddling tone he wasn't in the mood to hear.

"No, it's fine. You want me gone. I'm gone." He reached down and squeezed her hand, his eyes not able to meet hers. He didn't want to see conflict there. That might give him hope, and if he knew Amelia well enough, he knew there was no hope. "Have your lawyer draw up the divorce paperwork and send it on when you're ready. Feel better."

With those last words hanging in the air between them, he slipped into the hallway and let the door shut behind him. There, he slumped against the wall and dropped his head back, hard. His chest was so tight he could barely breathe, his hands aching to reach out for her and pull her into his arms. But he wouldn't. He would forfeit for the first time in his life, because that was what she wanted.

And in that moment, he realized it was because he loved her enough to give her what she wanted, even if it killed him to do it.

Amelia had thought their house was large with the two of them in it. Tyler had taken his personal things, some clothes and his laptop before she came home from the hospital. The rest, she assumed, the movers would pack up. The house had hardly been full before, but Tyler's absence made it just that much emptier. When she was alone, it was like being locked in the Metropolitan Museum of Art at night. Room after room surrounded by eerie silence and unfamiliar shadows.

The first night there alone hadn't bothered her as much, but she hadn't really been alone. Natalie had picked her up from the hospital and all the girls had met her at the house with reinforcements. They'd piled up in the bed and had pizza, wine and copious amounts of chocolate while watching a couple of sappy chick movies. It was an excellent distraction, and crying during the movies had been a much-needed outlet for all the emotions she hadn't allowed herself to process yet.

Tonight was her first night by herself. Gretchen had offered to come by, but Amelia had shooed her away. She could use some time by herself, and really, she was used to being alone. She'd always lived on her own. She wasn't sure how living with Tyler for only a few weeks could make it feel as though somehow he'd always been there.

He was back in New York now. He had texted her that much. Other than that, he had thankfully left her in peace. When she'd told him to leave, she hadn't been sure he was going to. She'd seen the resistance in his pale blue eyes, the curl of his hands into fists at his sides. He'd wanted to fight, and for a moment, deep inside, she'd hoped he would. She'd lied when she said she didn't love him, but she wasn't about to admit to something like that when he wouldn't do the same. If Tyler truly cared about her, and hadn't just been sticking it out for the baby's sake, he would've told her no. He would've proclaimed that he loved her and he wasn't going anywhere no matter what.

But he'd just walked away, confirming her worst fear. And breaking her heart.

She'd lain in her hospital bed and sobbed after he'd left, only pulling herself together when she'd heard the nurse coming. Amelia had managed to hold the fragile pieces of herself together since then, but it was hard. In one day, she'd lost the man she loved, her best friend, her husband and their child. Despite the promises they'd made, Natalie was right. She really didn't think their friendship would survive this, and that was what hurt the most. She had never felt so alone in her whole life.

Amelia was standing in the kitchen, attempting to replicate Tyler's hot cocoa, when she heard the buzzer on the gate. She made her way over to the panel by the door, where the screen showed a fuzzy image of her grandmother waiting impatiently to be let in.

She had made the obligatory call to her parents and her sister the day before to tell them what was going on. One of them must have passed along the information to her grandmother and had dispatched her from Knoxville as soon as she could finish curling her hair.

Amelia swallowed hard and pressed the button that would open the gates. She unlocked the front door and left it ajar as she ran back to the kitchen and pulled the milk off the stove before it boiled over. By the time she got back to the foyer, her paternal grandmother, Elizabeth Kennedy, was standing in the doorway.

The woman had recently celebrated her eightieth birthday, but you wouldn't know it to look at her. Amelia was a clone of her grandmother. Elizabeth's flame-red hair was as bright as Amelia's, but maintained now by a fine salon in Knoxville. Her dark eyes saw everything, with the thin curl of her lips giving away her wry sense of humor. She was sharp as a tack, as nimble as ever and drove her old Buick around like an Indy driver.

The moment her grandmother saw her, she opened her arms up and waited. In an instant, whatever threads that were holding Amelia together snapped. She rushed into her grandmother's arms and fell into hysterical tears.

"I know, I know," Elizabeth soothed, stroking Amelia's hair and letting her tears soak through her sweater. When Amelia finally calmed down, her grandmother patted her back and said, "Let's go to the kitchen, shall we? I think a time like this calls for a warm drink and something sweet. I, uh…" She looked through the various doorways. "Where is the kitchen? This place is enormous."

Amelia chuckled for the first time in a long while and took her grandmother's hand, leading her through the maze of halls and rooms to the kitchen. Elizabeth's eyes lit up when she saw the kitchen, reminding Amelia of her first day in the house. "It's beautiful, isn't it?"

Her grandmother nodded. "It's amazing." She went around opening drawers and investigating. "If this is any indication of the rest of the house, I'm moving in."

"It's available for rent," Amelia said with a sad tone in her voice. "The current occupants will be out by the end of the week."

Elizabeth spied the pot of cocoa on the stove. "You sit down. I'm going to finish this cocoa and you're going to tell me what's going on."

Amelia did as she was told, climbing gingerly onto a stool and watching her grandmother cook the way she had as a child. Her grandmother had passed along her love of cooking to Amelia. Most of her childhood they lived apart, but she had looked forward to summers spent with her grandparents and visits at Christmas. It was her favorite time of year.

Elizabeth restarted the cocoa, stirring it with a spoon before going into the pantry. She came out a moment later with peanut butter, cornflakes and Karo Syrup, making Amelia's eyes light up with delight.

"Cornflake cookies?"

Her grandmother smiled. "Of course, baby. Now, what is this I hear from your father about you getting married to that little boy you used to run around with?"

Amelia took a deep breath and started at the beginning. She told about the elopement in Vegas, the pregnancy and the whirlwind romance that followed. She ended the tale with its new, sad conclusion. "And now he's gone, and once I'm out of this house, it will be like none of it ever happened."

Her grandmother placed a steaming mug of cocoa and a plate of still warm and gooey cornflake cookies on the counter in front of her. "I doubt that," she said. "From the sound of things, nothing is ever going to be the way it was before." She pushed up her sleeves and started scrubbing the pans in the sink.

"Just leave those, Grandma. We have a lady for that."

Elizabeth scoffed at the suggestion. "I think better when I'm working in the kitchen. So what are you going to do now? Move back to your apartment?"

"Yes," Amelia answered. "Until my lease is up. Then I think I might buy a townhouse, something with a little more space, although not as much as we have here."

"And what about you and Tyler?"

Amelia shrugged and shoved a cornflake cookie in her mouth to avoid the question awhile longer. "I'm hoping we can still be friends. Obviously we're not meant to be together romantically. I knew from the beginning he wasn't my big love. I was just hoping I was wrong."

"Big love?" her grandmother said with a frown drawing her wrinkled brow together. "What kind of nonsense is that?"

"The big, grand love. The kind of romance that you and Grandpa have. The kind that moves mountains and lifts spirits and makes you certain that you can weather anything with that person at your side. The love that makes you happy to wake up to that person every day. I should've known I couldn't achieve that in thirty days. I mean...how long did you and Grandpa date before you got married?"

Elizabeth considered the question for longer than

Amelia expected her to. Her lips twisted together in thought before she finally planted her palms on the counter. "A week."

Amelia sat bolt upright in her chair. "What?"

"Now, don't you go running around telling people that. No one knows. Your granddaddy and I met when I was working at the university bookstore. He was there studying to be a lawyer. I thought he was so handsome, but I was too shy to speak to him. One day, he asked if I would join him for the football game on Saturday. We went for ice cream. We went out for breakfast," she said with a naughty smile, "and the following Friday, we ditched classes to elope at the courthouse."

This was not the story Amelia had been told all her life. "What about the big church wedding? I've seen the pictures!"

"That happened a year later. We kept our marriage a secret and told our families and friends we were dating. Months down the road, we announced that he had proposed, and we set the wedding day for our first anniversary. No one but your grandpa and I ever knew the truth until now."

Amelia didn't even know what to say. How was it even possible? "But you and Grandpa have the perfect love! The great romance I've always strived for. How could you have possibly known he was the right man for you, your soul mate, in just a week?"

Elizabeth sighed and made her way around the counter to sit at a bar stool beside her. "There is no such thing as a perfect love, Amelia, just like there is no such thing as a perfect person. Your grandpa and I had to work very hard on our relationship. Maybe even harder than other people, because we wed so quickly. There were times I wanted to hit him with a frying pan because he kept leaving his slippers where I could trip over them. There were times I'm certain your grandpa wished he'd taken me on a couple more dates before he proposed. But we made our decisions and we made the best of it."

The cornflake cookies felt like lead in her stomach. It was as if she'd just been told the truth about the Tooth Fairy, the Easter Bunny and Santa all over again.

"In the end, yes, marrying your grandfather was one of the best decisions I ever made. I acted on instinct, on passion, and I was right. If I had overthought it, we probably never would've married. We had ups and downs like any couple, but I don't regret a minute of the time we've spent together."

Tyler's words popped into her mind. *We might end up being totally incompatible, and if we are, we end it and you can go back to your quest for the White Buffalo.* The White Buffalo. Magical. Rare. A fantasy. She'd spent the past ten years of her life chasing a myth and she was the last to realize it.

"I think part of this is my fault," Elizabeth admitted. "When you were little, I filled your head with romantic stories, treating our marriage like one of your fairy-tale books. When you were older, I never thought to go back and tell you differently. I guess I imagined you'd grow up and shelve those fantasies with Cinderella and her glass slipper."

"No," Amelia spoke at last. "No, it isn't your fault. You were right, you were telling a little girl stories. When I grew up, I should've realized that there's no such thing as perfection. When I think about all the men I've driven out of my life because they weren't just so… I feel awful."

"Honey, it's possible that none of those men would've been right for you anyway. But I wonder about this last one. It sounds to me as if he loves you very much."

Amelia perked up in her seat. "What makes you say that?"

"The way you described him. The way he did so much for you, even when you didn't want him to. I know that sort of thing can make a girl like you crazy, but you have to understand why he does it. Moving here on a dime, getting this house, doing everything in his power to make you happy, comfortable and safe... Those aren't the actions of a man who feels obligated because of the child. Those are the actions of a man so desperately in love with a woman that he will do anything and everything to see her smile."

Amelia shook her head. She wished her grandmother was right, but it just couldn't be true. "He's not in love with me, Grandma. He left. He wouldn't have walked out if he'd loved me."

"I thought you loved all the fairy tales with the big romantic gestures? *The Little Mermaid*, *The Gift of the Magi*, *Beauty and the Beast*... In each of those stories, the character sacrifices the most valued thing in their life for the one they love. If you think Tyler left because he didn't care, you're a fool. He left, and gave you up, because he thought that was what you wanted."

Amelia felt the dull ache of regret start to pool in her stomach. Was it possible she had driven away the man who loved her, the man she loved, because she was too blind to see the truth?

And more important...would he ever forgive her?

Twelve

Tyler hesitated only a moment before turning the knob and opening the front door of the home he used to share with Amelia. He could see the lights on in the kitchen, but the rest of the house was dark and empty. "Amelia?" he called, hoping not to startle her. "Hello?"

No one answered, so he traveled down the corridor to the kitchen. Amelia was standing at the counter, her wary eyes watching him as he came in. Apparently she'd heard him but hadn't had anything to say. Or didn't know what to say. Either way, she wasn't about to leap into his arms and kiss him. That was disappointing. At the same time, she hadn't immediately thrown him out either, so he'd count his blessings.

"Hi," he said.

"Hi."

She looked better than she had at the hospital. Her color was vastly improved and she didn't look nearly as tired. Her hair was pulled up into a ponytail, a casual look that went well with her little T-shirt and jeans. The rest of her was anything but casual. Her whole body was stiff. She had a bottle of wine clutched with white-knuckled intensity in one hand, the opener in the other.

"Would you like some wine?" she offered. "I was just about to open it."

"Sure, thanks. Let me—" he started, and then stopped. His instinct was to offer to open it, but that was the wrong tactic with Amelia. She hadn't wanted to be helped with everything when she was pregnant; she certainly wouldn't want to be coddled when she wasn't. "I'll get some glasses," he said instead.

He went to the cabinet and fetched two glasses. By the time he returned, Amelia had the bottle open. He held them by the stems as she poured them each a healthy serving.

"Would you like to go sit outside?" she asked. "It's been a pretty warm day. It would be a shame to move out of here without at least taking advantage of the back-yard once."

"Okay." Tyler followed her through the door to the backyard he hadn't set foot in since he toured the home with the real estate agent. There was a kidney-shaped pool and hot tub with a waterfall to one side. A fire pit was surrounded by stone benches just off the patio. To the right was a large stretch of lawn that would've been perfect for a swing set someday.

The thought brought a painful pang to the back of his mind. Since he'd left the hospital, he'd done the same thing Amelia accused him of doing after his breakup with Christine—he'd thrown himself into his work so he didn't have to think about everything he'd lost. He'd grabbed his computer and a suitcase full of clothes and toiletries and hopped the first plane back to New York. He'd bypassed his empty apartment and gone straight to the offices, where he'd worked until he was blurry eyed and hallucinating at his computer screen. The next morning, he got up and did it again.

Today, he'd woken up missing the warmth of her body only inches away on the mattress beside him. He'd wanted to make her a smoothie and kiss her as she headed out the door. Then he'd realized he was a bigger coward than he'd accused her of being. He got back on a plane to Nashville and came straight to the house to tell Amelia how he felt. Which he would do. Any second now. If he could just figure out *how* to tell Amelia how he felt.

She'd already rejected him once. He wasn't too excited to stick his neck back out again and get his head chopped off, but he knew he had to. He'd regret this for the rest of his life if he didn't.

Amelia strolled out to the stone fire pit and sat down on one of the benches. Tyler resisted the urge to give her personal space and sat right beside her. He leaned forward and turned on the switch the agent had shown him, and there was suddenly a raging fire in the gas fireplace. It was just enough to take the mid-March chill out of the air.

"Nice," Amelia said, leaning in to warm her face. "As much as I complained, I am going to miss this place. It's going to be hard to go back to my tiny, plain apartment after this. We never even got to use the movie theater."

Tyler nodded, but the words fighting to get out of him made it hard for him to focus on conversation. "How are you feeling?" he asked.

"Okay. I'm still sore and achy, but I'll live," she joked with a small smile. "How are you?"

Tyler sighed. That was a loaded question, or at the

very least, a loaded answer. "I am…a little numb. A little overwhelmed. Sad. But mostly, I'm feeling guilty."

"You shouldn't feel guilty, Tyler. It wasn't anybody's fault."

"I know. But there are plenty of other things that I am responsible for. I told my brother about us when I shouldn't have. I said things to you that were hurtful. And I walked away from you when every fiber of my being was screaming at me to stay."

He could sense Amelia stiffening beside him. She hastily took a sip of her wine before she responded, "I told you to go," she said, her voice flat and emotionless.

"You did. But since when have I ever done what you've told me to do?"

Amelia snorted softly, covering her mouth with her hand to smother it. "Practically never."

"Exactly. I picked the wrong damn time to start doing things your way."

"Hey, now—" Amelia started in a sharp tone, but Tyler cut her off.

"I didn't come back to argue, Amelia."

She looked at him with large dark eyes, taking in every detail of his face as though she were trying to catalog it, memorize it somehow. "Then why did you come back, Tyler?"

Tyler took a deep breath. "I came back to tell you that I'm going to be breaking our agreement."

Her auburn eyebrows drew together in confusion. "What do you mean, breaking our agreement?"

"Well," he began, "when all this started, we agreed that when the thirty days were up, if both of us were in love, we would get married. But if one of us still wanted a divorce…we would part as friends."

Amelia swallowed hard and focused her gaze on the

glass in her lap. "So you've come to tell me we're not going to be friends any longer?"

"No. I've come here to tell you that divorce is off the table."

Amelia nervously chuckled, a tone of disbelief in her lyrical laughter. "I think I've heard this out of you before. A couple weeks ago, in fact. And look where it got us."

"That was completely different. The last time, it was because we were having a baby and I thought it was the right thing to do. This time, we're not getting a divorce because I am in love with you. And *you* are in love with *me*, even if you don't want to admit to it."

Amelia's mouth dropped open, a soft gasp escaping her lips. "You *what*?"

"I love you," he repeated. "And I'm not going to let you run away from this. I can't just stand idle while you try to ruin everything we have together. I tried to just sit back and let you lie to yourself and to me, but I can't do it anymore."

Tyler set his wine on the ground and turned on the bench until he was facing her. He scooped up her hand and cupped it between his own. "I love you, Amelia. And I loved you long before there was a baby, even before our wild night in Las Vegas. I've realized that I've loved you since study hall and shared lunches on the lawn by the football stadium. I've loved you since the day you called me over to the empty seat beside you in freshman English and introduced yourself. You were the most beautiful, sweet, loving creature I had, or have, ever met in my whole life."

"How could you have been in love with me all these years?" she argued. "You never said anything. You never acted like you had feelings for me."

"I didn't fully realize it. All these years, I knew that

I loved you as a friend. I didn't allow for the possibility of anything more than that. But the feelings were there, simmering under the surface. Every time I dated a woman and something just didn't click. Every time I saw your number come up on my phone and my heart leaped a little in my chest. Christine knew it, but somehow it took the possibility of losing you forever to make me see the difference."

Tyler slipped onto the patio on one knee and looked up at her. "You're everything to me, Amelia. And I want you to marry me."

"We're already married, Tyler."

"I know," he said with a wicked smile that curled his lips. "But my wife once told me that if I loved her and wanted to stay married, I'd have to propose again—properly—so we could have the big romantic church wedding with our family and friends."

Tyler reached into his coat pocket and pulled out the same black velvet jewelry box he'd offered to her the night they eloped. He opened the box to display the eight-carat diamond they'd used at their first wedding ceremony. Once they'd moved into the house, she'd given it back to him. At the time, she either didn't think they would make it, or if they did, he wouldn't want her to have such a large, expensive piece. She was wrong on both counts.

"I gave that back to you," Amelia frowned. "That was never intended to be my ring. You were supposed to sell that to a dealer in LA so it could become one of the Kardashians' engagement rings."

"Whether or not that's what I intended when I bought it, a fact is a fact. This is my wife's ring, so it belongs to you. Even if I went shopping for a new one, I wouldn't be able to beat it. I've come across larger stones, flashier stones, well-known stones, but this one is the most perfect specimens of diamond I've ever had in my possession. It's flawless and colorless. The cut is perfect, allowing the diamond to truly shine. It's a classic beauty, just like you, and it belongs on your finger. No one else's."

Tyler felt an unexpected nervousness in his stomach. He'd already proposed to Amelia once. They were already married, as she'd pointed out. But this was different. The last time was a joke that went too far, an adventure they'd never expected. This time was for real. He loved her. He wanted to spend the rest of his life with her. He swallowed the anxiety rising in his throat and looked up into her eyes. "Amelia, will you marry me?"

Amelia didn't know what to say. She was stunned. Well and truly stunned. This was not at all how she'd expected this day, or even this conversation, to go. When she'd heard Tyler's voice in the hallway, there had been a moment of elation, followed by panic, with caution bringing up the rear. Her conversation with her grandmother had given her a lot to think about. She had been on the verge of pouring a glass of wine to gather her courage to call Tyler. To tell him that she'd lied and she did love him.

Then, suddenly, he was standing in their kitchen and she didn't know what to think. He probably hadn't come all this way to fight. Or to get his things. The movers could do that. She figured he wanted to talk in person, without the emotions of the hospital and the miscarriage fueling the discussion. At best, she'd been hopeful they could stay friends. She'd never dared or dreamed for more.

But a marriage proposal?

"I don't know what to say," she said with a stunned shake of her head.

Tyler frowned. "I'll give you a hint. The key word is *yes*, quickly followed by *I love you, Tyler.* We'll try this again. Amelia, will you marry me? Okay, now it's your turn."

Amelia smiled. He was right. She felt it. She wanted this. All she had to do was say it. "Yes, Tyler, I will marry you."

"And?" he pressed with a hopeful grin.

"And...I love you. Very much."

Tyler slipped the ring onto her finger and kissed her knuckles before standing up and pulling her into a gentle embrace. Amelia melted into the safety and comfort of his arms, a place she'd thought she might never be able to return to. She tipped her head up to kiss him, pressing her mouth against his soft lips. The moment they made contact, she felt a rush of excitement run through her body. The thrill of new love, the delight of finally experiencing the moment she'd always dreamed of. His proposal was all she'd ever hoped for and more, because it was Tyler. The man who knew her better than anyone. The man who could make her laugh, make her smile and even make her cocoa.

She had always fantasized about perfection. It didn't get any more perfect than this.

Breaking away, Amelia clung to his neck, burying her face in the lapel of his suit coat and breathing in the warm scent of his skin. She sighed in relief as he held her, grateful she hadn't lost him with her foolish fears.

"You know what?" he asked. "It's Wednesday. Day thirty."

Amelia smiled up at him. He was right. Everything had ended just the way it was supposed to. "It looks as though we've made it. It's kind of hard to believe it, but a lot has happened in the past month."

"It certainly has. And one of the things I've learned over the past few days is that I don't want to keep this a secret. We need to call our families. Tonight. We can't make that same mistake twice."

"You're right. But let's wait a little while longer so I can bliss out in this moment."

"Okay. And I'm sure after that, we start planning the big wedding you've always dreamed of. Do you still have that giant notebook?"

Amelia shrugged. "I do, but you know, I've done a lot of thinking since you left. The idea of that isn't as appealing anymore. My big wedding plans were focused on everything but starting off a new life with the man I love. I'd rated cake and flowers over the groom. I guess it's because I was planning a wedding when I wasn't in love yet. Now that I am, I don't think I need all that anymore. We're already married. We love each other. I think that's all I need."

One of Tyler's eyebrows raised curiously at her. "You say that now, and it's sweet, but I know you'll regret it later. One day, ten years down the road, we'll have an argument and you'll throw out there that we eloped in Vegas and you were wearing black and you never got to have your dream wedding. Somehow it will be all my fault. You'll be a total Momzilla when our daughter gets married as you try to live the dream you lost. No way. We're having a wedding. I insist."

Amelia twisted her lips in thought. "Okay, then. Maybe we can come up with something in between. Not quite as grand an affair as I have in my notebook, but one with a white dress, a pastor that doesn't look like Elvis and our friends and family there to share the moment with us."

Tyler smiled and pulled her into his arms. "That

sounds like the perfect wedding to me. Plan whatever you like. All I ask is that you don't make me take dance lessons."

Amelia laughed aloud. Tyler was a confident, powerful businessman, but he had zero rhythm. "I've seen you dance before, Tyler. No amount of lessons is going to help."

"Hey!" He laughed. "Okay, you're right. Just tell me when to show up and what to wear."

"It's so easy for men."

Tyler laughed. "That's because we're far more interested in the honeymoon."

Amelia laughed, then felt the light moment fade. When she looked up into his pale blue eyes, she felt the urge to tell him everything. Why she'd done what she'd done. Why she'd lied. "Tyler..." she began, running her fingers through his messy blond hair. "I'm so sorry for how I've acted. I was terrified of being in love with you and not knowing if you felt the same way. I just couldn't believe that you were here because you loved *me*, so I convinced myself it was just because of the baby."

"That's my fault," Tyler admitted. "I was afraid, too, so I tried to focus on the baby because no matter how you and I felt about each other, the child was going to be a part of my life. I felt things for you that I'd never felt for another woman, but I was waiting for the other shoe to drop. I thought that if I kept my feelings locked inside, when you pushed me away, it wouldn't hurt as badly."

Amelia winced. "And I did push you away. I fulfilled your biggest fear."

"And it didn't hurt any less by keeping my secret. It probably made it worse. I should've just said it right there in the hospital room and not cared what you might say. If I'd told you I loved you and I wasn't going to let you push me away, would you have still told me to go back to New York?"

She wasn't sure. Would she have believed him? She didn't know if her heart had been strong enough in that dark moment to take the risk. "It doesn't matter," she replied. "We can't change the past, and I think this happened the way it needed to. Being apart helped us both realize how much we love each other and want to be together. Sometimes that's what it takes."

"I know it made me realize I hate my apartment in New York. I can run my business from here just as easily as I do there. I really don't want to give up this house. I know it's too big, but..."

"We'll work on filling it up," Amelia said with a smile. She didn't want to get rid of the house, either. It would take some time, but eventually it would be filled with children and laughter and life, and it wouldn't feel so large and empty. Losing the baby had made her realize how badly she really did want children. Searching for the perfect mate had put that dream on hold. The doctor said they should wait a few more months, but when it was time, she wanted to try again.

"You know, I grew up with five brothers and sisters crammed into a three-bedroom, two-bath apartment. We've got thousands of square feet to work with here. If you want to fill this place up, we can fill it up."

"Sounds like a challenge," Amelia laughed.

"I don't know," Tyler warned. "For a girl so focused on perfection, you may find a house full of kids to be a very messy prospect."

"I've decided that perfection isn't so perfect after all. While you were in New York, I had a much-needed and enlightening conversation with my grandmother."

Tyler looked at her with surprise. "The one with the perfect, long-lasting marriage I'll never live up to?"

"The one I *thought* had a perfect marriage. To make a long story short, I had apparently been given the romantic fairy-tale version for little girls. But in reality, I think I got what I wanted anyway. I've always dreamed of having a marriage like hers and, ironically, we've gotten pretty close to achieving that. At least the start. We've just got fifty-some odd years of togetherness to go."

Tyler smiled and kissed her again. "I can't wait."

Epilogue

It was happening. The day Amelia had been waiting for since she was five years old had arrived, and sooner than she'd expected.

When a late-summer wedding was postponed, she and Tyler had jumped on the chance to book their moment in the chapel. From there, it was months of excitement and planning. While she had toned down the event, once she started putting together their wedding, there were some details she found she just couldn't skimp on.

Her gown was the most beautiful dress she'd ever worn, a dazzling ivory-and-crystal creation. Her veil was long, draping down her back and spreading across the gray carpet. The pastor was reading a passage about love and the bonds of marriage as Amelia stood on the raised platform and looked into the eyes of the man she loved.

Turning briefly toward the crowd that filled the chapel of From This Moment, she could easily pick out the faces of the family and friends who had joined them here today. It was just the way she envisioned it—the important people in her life witnessing this important moment.

For years, Amelia had planned a wedding with no groom in mind. But looking into Tyler's eyes, she knew that he was the most important part of this day. More important than a beautiful dress or a fancy cake.

They had arranged this wedding because he'd wanted her to have the moment, but it wasn't necessary. The key ingredients—him and her—had been there at their first wedding. The only difference was going through the ritual and repeating the words with love and tears making their voices tremble as they spoke. The words meant so much more this time.

"And now, I pronounce you man and wife. You may kiss the bride."

Tyler pulled her into his arms, a smile spreading across his remarkably clean-shaven face. Amelia felt her heart skip a beat in her chest when he looked at her that way. She hoped and prayed he would look at her like that for the rest of their lives.

"I love you," Tyler whispered.

"I love you, too. And," she added with a smile, "I'm pregnant."

His eyes widened for a moment before an excited grin changed his whole face. "Really?"

"Yes, really."

His lips pressed to hers in an instant, and she melted into him. The hundreds of people around them faded away. The roar of applause was just a faint buzz in the background, the flash of Bree's camera no match for the fireworks going off beneath her eyelids. She felt a thrill run down her spine and a warmth spread through her body. It wasn't until the pastor cleared his throat that they pulled apart. "Later," the pastor assured them. A rumble of laughter traveled through the audience.

Amelia blushed as her sister, Whitney, handed back her bouquet. She slipped her arm through Tyler's, and they turned to face the crowd and their new, exciting future together.

"Ladies and gentleman, I'd like to present Mr. and Mrs. Tyler Dixon."

Arm in arm, they marched down the aisle of scattered rose petals to start their life together. As they stepped through the doorway as man and wife, she realized this was the moment she'd dreamed of. Not the wedding, but the beginning of their life together. At last, they had a happily-ever-after for them both.

* * * * *

HIS UNEXPECTED BABY BOMBSHELL

SORAYA LANE

For Carly and Kathryn. I truly feel like I hit the editor jackpot with the two of you!

Thank you for all your wonderful ideas, and for making my books so much stronger.

CHAPTER ONE

REBECCA STEWART GULPED as the door to the restaurant opened. *Ben McFarlane*. It had been almost four years, but she'd have known him anywhere. Dark blond hair cropped short, broad shoulders stretching the material of his T-shirt and a stare that still managed to make her heart beat too fast. He was exactly as she remembered him and then some.

"Long time no see."

His gaze softened as he came closer, the corners of his mouth turning upward into a smile, but she could tell he was angry. Those eyes had caused her heart to break and heal all over again so many years ago, the last night they'd had together still burned into her memory as if it was yesterday. *She knew every expression he had.*

Rebecca swallowed, smiled back, her stomach flip-flopping. *He didn't know. Couldn't* know. That angry gaze, determined stride…she'd thought he was coming in with a purpose when she'd first recognized him. That he knew about his daughter.

She pushed those thoughts away and tried to remind herself of how they'd been before that night, back when they'd been best friends and nothing more.

"Hey, stranger," she said. "I had no idea you were back."

Rebecca moved out from around the counter, hands smoothing the soft cotton of her apron. She didn't know what to do—whether to embrace him, touch him. What did you do to a man, formerly your best friend, once your lover, who you hadn't seen or heard from in years?

"Hey." His voice was surprisingly gruff.

Rebecca stepped into his arms when he opened them, gingerly at first, until he pulled her in, giving her an awkward kind of bear hug. She tried to relax, focusing on breathing in and out. *They were just friends.* But after all this time he still had that effect on her. The smell of his cologne, the strength of his body, everything about him took her back to that night, when a decade of friendship had turned into something more. The night before he'd left and she'd encouraged him to leave her behind even though it had shattered her heart into a million pieces.

"How are you, Bec? Haven't heard from you in a while."

Ouch. The hug must have been a formality.

She took a step back, his hands falling from her waist. It was warm but she shivered, wrapping one arm about her body, the other hanging awkwardly at her side.

"I've been good, Ben. Really good," she said, forcing a big smile, avoiding the question. It wasn't as if he'd emailed her lately, either.

"Your folks?"

Rebecca smiled. Her parents would love to know that Ben was back in town.

"They're great." This time she didn't have to force the grin. "Very busy, enjoying their retirement, so I'm running this place on my own most of the time."

She looked over her shoulder, catching a glimpse of commotion in the kitchen. When she turned back to Ben she noticed he was watching, taking everything in. He'd known her parents' Italian restaurant just as well as she had when they were teenagers. They'd both worked waiting tables over their last summer break, before he'd had the opportunity of a lifetime and left for Argentina.

"Anyway, how about you? What brings you back?"

Ben jammed both hands into his jeans pockets, eyes down before he looked up and met her stare. She knew something was wrong. Why was he even back here?

"Has something happened to your grandfather?" Rebecca heard the falter in her own voice.

"He's not doing great, even though he'd hate me telling you that." He squared his shoulders and pushed his feet out wider. "It was time to come home anyway. I've done my time overseas, for now."

"Really? It's not like you were getting too old to play." She ran her eyes over his superfit frame. He was all muscle, *all athlete*. It wasn't like polo players had a use-by date, so long as they were still performing, and she'd never expected him to give up his career voluntarily. Not for anything.

That made him laugh. "I'm not too old, and I'm fit as hell, so don't go feeling sorry for me." His voice was dry. "I just decided I'd been away for long enough, and Gus needs the help. Argentina was fun, but I missed the old fella."

Oh. She tried to digest his words. It sent a cold streak down her spine. "So you're back for good?"

"Yeah, for the time being, anyway," he said. "If you'd been better at emailing me back, I might have given you a heads-up."

Ouch again. "Ben, I just got busy and there was so much happening. I'm sorry." She knew it sounded like a cop-out, and it was. But he hadn't emailed for a long time, so it wasn't all her fault.

He looked up, gave her a long, hard stare before training his eyes past her head.

"So tell me, how long have you been back? What are your plans?" she asked.

"I'm just playing it by ear. I'll see how it goes, how much I can do around the farm."

Rebecca tried not to react, digested the information as if it meant nothing to her. Polo had always been his life, his dream to play as a career, and now he'd just given it up like that? As if it wasn't the single most important thing to him after years of being desperate to make it happen?

"So that's it. You're just not going to play anymore?" she asked.

A shrug of his shoulders told her he was uncertain. Ben always pushed them up, then hunched them when he was uncomfortable.

"Things change, Bec. You know how it is."

Yeah, she did. Only she was pretty certain that he hadn't just had a change of heart—something else had to be going on. If he was doing it for Gus, she completely understood, but she smelled a rat.

"Anyway, I've only just arrived back in. I'm still going to be training horses, I'm just taking time out from playing." He smiled. "I'm heading for Geelong in the morning."

Rebecca turned and walked back toward the counter, trying to ignore the rising heat in her cheeks. Her pulse had started hammering hard at her temple. *Geelong.* The place where his grandfather's horse training establishment was. The place she'd spent every school vacation and weekend, hanging out with Ben and dreaming about their future. Only she hadn't realized how much of a man's sport polo was—she'd ended up bravely waving Ben off while she stayed behind. It had been tough for him to make it, and even tougher for her to try to make a career out of it. But they'd only been friends, it wasn't as if he'd left his girlfriend behind.

"My granddad turned eighty last week, and I know the cancer's probably worse than he's letting on. I'm heading there to learn everything I can and slowly take the reins from him. Excuse the pun."

"He must be so happy to have you back," Rebecca said, refusing to think about what-ifs just because Ben was back in town and standing before her. It wouldn't have mattered if he'd stayed or not, they'd both wanted different things, and their one night together had been the result of too much to drink. He hadn't owed her anything. She took a deep breath. "You're going to love being home."

He smiled, but his eyes told a different story. He was annoyed with her, and she didn't know what to say to him except sorry for not staying in touch. But she hadn't been able to keep emailing him and not mention what was going on in her life, which meant that losing contact with him had been the only option. She'd always sworn that if he came back she'd tell him, but the guys he played polo with had become his family, he'd always said he loved what he did and wouldn't give it up for anything.

"It was what we always talked about, huh? The two of us playing polo overseas then coming back to run a horse stud together."

"Yeah," she said softly, not wanting to go back in time because thinking about the past only hurt. "Yeah, it was."

"But, anyway, tell me about you? I heard a terrible rumor yesterday that you have a daughter." He chuckled. "Is it true?"

Rebecca placed one hand on the stainless steel counter, trying to stop the quiver as it ran up and down her body. *Her daughter.* How much did he know? *She'd wanted to be the one to tell him.*

"Yeah, I'm a mom now," she said, struggling to keep her voice steady and her breathing even. "To Lexie."

"Lexie," he repeated the name, the word on his lips sending another wave of worry down her back. "And who's the lucky man?"

"Man?" she asked.

"Your husband?"

Gulp. Husband. *Hmm.* "I, ah, well, there is no lucky someone. It's just me and Lexie."

"You mean some bastard left you, after you'd had his child? That why you didn't stay in touch with me? Because you knew I'd hunt him down?"

She did *not* like where this was going. Mmm, what did she say. *Yes, Ben, and that bastard was you? That's exactly why I stopped returning your emails.* But she didn't think of him like that, because she'd made the decision to keep Lexie a secret, to protect both of them, but mainly to make sure she wasn't the one responsible for clipping his wings.

"Let's just say I was better off bringing her up on my own, at least for the time being," Rebecca said, being careful with her words. "My folks have been great and she's a happy little girl, so it's all worked out okay."

The look on Ben's face told her he was unconvinced.

"And your dad didn't try to do something about it? Or your brother, for that matter?"

Rebecca needed to change the subject. Fast. She needed time to think about how she was going to tell Ben, how she was going to break it to him. "They weren't thrilled about the whole thing, but sometimes life throws a curve ball and you just have to deal with it."

He opened his mouth, looked grumpy as hell and about to say something else about her solo parenting situation so she quickly interrupted him.

"Do you want something to eat?" she asked. "We can still rustle up your favorite seafood linguine if you like?"

The frown on Ben's face almost instantly spun upward into a smile. "You still do it?"

"We still *can* do it," she said with a laugh. "It's an oldie but a goodie, that one. Not officially on the lunch menu, but a version of it's still a dinner favorite so we have the ingredients."

This time when he looked at her he didn't break the stare, not for a second. His eyes were locked on hers, his dark brown irises flecked with gold in the bright light.

"I have to go, but how about I take you up on that offer another day? Maybe when you're not so busy and you can join me?"

She forced herself to keep breathing, which felt like the most unnatural thing in the world all of a sudden with Ben standing in front of her. The last thing she needed was to sit down and have lunch with him.

"Sounds good. It would be nice to catch up."

Someone in the kitchen called out her name, giving her an excuse to break away, to finally glance away from the eyes that had been holding her captive.

"I'll see you around, Bec." Ben held his hand up in

the air and took a few steps backward before turning and heading for the door.

Rebecca watched him, didn't move a muscle until he'd disappeared from sight, ignoring the chaos behind her. Her heart was thumping with what she knew was excitement, but the rest of her was a quivering mess of nerves, ready to slip into a puddle on the floor. Because there was no part of Ben being back that was okay, none at all.

Ben stuffed his hands deep into his pockets and walked down the street, through the crowded lunchtime buzz of inner city Melbourne. He loved Australia, loved being back on home turf and knowing he was where he belonged. Living overseas had been a blast, but the idea of dividing his time between the city and his granddad's farm was what he wanted now, and he knew he'd made the right decision coming home. As hard as it was leaving his polo family behind, he couldn't stay away from Gus any longer.

And seeing Bec? *Wow.* He'd only been home one day and it had been a fight not to turn up at the restaurant that first night, just to lay eyes on her again. The girl who'd waved him goodbye, his best friend, and then slowly disappeared from his life. But who could blame her? He hadn't exactly been the best at staying in touch, but then she'd been downright terrible.

And then she'd met some other guy and had a kid? Little Bec all grown up and a *mom*? Now, that he hadn't been expecting. In his mind he'd imagined her life on hold, expected he could come home and somehow he'd be able to convince her that their night together had been a good thing, that they were supposed to be more than just friends. He'd been a fool, naive at best, and after seeing her today he knew he'd waited too long, that she'd moved on and he'd missed his chance.

Because even though he'd had the time of his life away, ridden some of the best polo ponies in the world and traveled to the most incredible countries, he'd never stopped thinking about Rebecca. Not for a moment. At the time, he'd been so desperate to belong, loved being part of a big extended polo family, when in reality he'd had a little family here with Gus and Rebecca all along, only it had taken being away so long for him to realize it. It wasn't until his granddad had finally admitted how sick he was that it had really hit home.

Rebecca's soft, smiling face, pillowy lips and shining eyes had been the memory he'd clung on to, and almost four years on, he was darn pleased she didn't have a husband. He could never stay angry with her and seeing her today had proved it. He'd gone in all tough guy, wanting to demand why she'd lost touch. *But he hadn't.* And they might have been drunk that night together, but he hadn't forgotten a moment of what had happened between them.

He'd kill the guy who'd left her, on her own and with a child, and he'd bet her parents would be happy to help him find him. Rebecca had been his best friend, and for one night she'd been his lover. Ben grimaced as he jumped behind the wheel of his car. *And that one night had ruined everything between them.*

Rebecca strolled in to the preschool center and locked eyes on her daughter. Lexie was running around the room at high speed, arms spread out as if she was flying, her little lips bouncing off one another to make a noise like a plane. Her heart fluttered and she turned away, not wanting Lexie to see her yet. Her little girl was clingy enough as it was, and she loved seeing her play with the other kids.

"Hey there."

Bec turned to find Julia, one of the teachers, behind her. She was holding out a colorful, smudged sheet of paper.

"Lexie painted this today and insisted I put it somewhere safe for Mommy."

The grin that followed made her smile, and she reached out to take it. "She has quite a talent, don't you think?"

Both women laughed then as Bec held out the painting and squinted, trying to decipher exactly what it was. "A house covered in green slime?" she guessed.

"Day at the beach?"

A little voice interrupted them. "Mommy!"

Bec turned and scooped up her girl, planting a kiss on her shiny blond head. "Hey, sunshine."

"Do you like my painting?"

"Of course!"

"It's me on a horse. A horse, Mommy!"

"Mmm." She tried not to grin as she looked back at her. The teacher had to walk away to keep from laughing. "We were just saying what a lovely horse it is."

"It's a polo horse." She fought to stand on the ground. "Me on a polo pony."

Rebecca's smile fell from her face, until she realized Lexie was still watching her. She forced her panic away. A polo pony? How did she even know about polo ponies?

"Let's go, sweetheart. Grab your bag and say goodbye to Julia."

She watched as her daughter darted away, reached a hand to push back her hair as she stared at the picture.

Lexie had never even been around horses, let alone rid-den one, but she'd been obsessed about them since she could say the word. *Just like someone else she knew.* As much as she didn't want to admit it, Lexie was more like her dad than she'd let herself believe.

"Mommy?"

She dropped to her knees, taking the bag from her daughter and zipping it up. "Yes, sweetheart."

"Granddad says you used to ride horses. That you used to ride *polo ponies.*"

"Did he now?" She would kill him for even talking to Lexie about her riding. That was a part of her life she'd left behind. She'd never even been near a horse since Ben had left, and she'd long since given up any dreams of making a career out of the sport she'd loved since she was fourteen. The last horse she'd had…she didn't even want to think about the accident.

"He said you were real good, too, until you fell off one day. Did it hurt?"

"And when was Granddad telling you all this?" she asked.

"Yesterday."

Lexie skipped off toward the door, waiting for her, her hand outstretched.

"Can *we* go horse riding?" she asked.

"Maybe."

"Why maybe?"

"I don't know anyone who owns a horse." It was a lie, but what else was she going to say?

"Could *we* get a horse, then?" Lexie asked.

"Get in the car."

She closed the door after her and stood on the side-walk for a few seconds, eyes closed, taking a deep breath to calm her nerves. Once upon a time she would have done anything to spend her life around horses, but that was in the past, and that was exactly how she wanted to keep it. She had to tell Ben, she knew that, but she still didn't want to go back.

CHAPTER TWO

BEN SMILED AT his granddad and walked over to the young colt. The animal's nostrils were flared, body rigid as he approached him.

"Keep your hands down. Don't touch him until he touches you first."

Ben listened to him, and followed his instructions. More and more he was realizing that his grandfather's instincts were always right. He'd argued with the trainers he worked with overseas until he was blue in the face, and he'd been tired of their old-fashioned attitudes. Some trainers liked to force horses into submission, but that wasn't something they did at McFarlane Stables. Just because half the polo trainers out there thought they were crazy for practicing natural horsemanship didn't mean he was going to change their approach. And it was one of the reasons he'd finally had enough of being overseas, one of the reasons he'd finally broken ties with the guys he'd loved working alongside for so long to come home.

"Good. Once he turns his head in, pat him and then move the rope over his neck."

Ben did as he was told. The horse responded to him, moving quietly, but all hell broke loose once the rope was over.

"Keep hold, even if he goes right out to the end."

A damp line of sweat graced his forehead, but he kept hold. This was the only rough part of the exercise and he hated it, but if he got it right this time, it wouldn't need to be done again. Because *animals* and *force* were not two words he liked used in the same sentence.

The horse stopped bucking and rearing and came to a halt, eyeing him cautiously from a small distance.

"Good boy." He said the words softly before approaching him again. "What a good fella."

"Give him a pat and then put the halter on him," his granddad called out.

Ben moved forward, smiling at the horse as he stood calmly. He gave him a scratch behind the ear and then lifted the halter, rubbing his sweet spots as he did so.

Nice and gentle, Ben reminded himself, reaching up and folding the leather strap over the horse's nose and behind his pricked ears. The horse stood still, ears flickering as he listened to him, accepting what was happening.

Ben stood back and grinned. Working with his grandfather for just one morning was worth having come home for.

"Good job, son. Well done."

He gave the horse one final pat and then opened up the gate out of the yard, letting him canter off over to the other young stock. Ben moved toward his granddad, pleased to see the smile on his weathered face.

"It's in your blood, always has been, always will be."

His granddad's voice was strong and deep, but the slap he gave Ben on his shoulder wasn't as powerful as it used to be; his gnarled, weathered hands failing him after years of hard work. Gus McFarlane was a strong man, the kind of man who was used to commanding attention when he wanted it, but he was deteriorating fast. There was something the old man wasn't telling him, he just knew it.

"So have you been coping okay? On your own I mean?"

Gus used a cane, walking slowly over the grass. Mind as sharp as a tack, but the body just not keeping up. Guilt washed over Ben—he'd been so desperate to leave Australia and follow his own dreams, but now that he was back he was seriously regretting leaving his granddad for so long.

"You ever hear from the Stewart girl?"

Ben's body went rigid. "Rebecca? Yeah, well, sort of. I mean, I went to see her when I got back." He tried to sound nonchalant. "Yesterday, actually."

"Great girl that one. You should have married her, you know that, right?"

Yeah, he knew. But Bec was...well, *Bec*. It was never that he hadn't been attracted to her, or that he hadn't wanted her, but he'd always known he could never give her enough and he still couldn't. Settling down with a nice girl just hadn't been part of his plan, what he'd imagined for himself, because he'd always been focused on what he wanted. And now that he didn't have polo, he was at more of a loss about what he wanted from life than he'd ever been.

"She gave up returning my emails a long time ago, Granddad." He wasn't going to let Rebecca off the hook, not when he was getting *the look* from the old man. The fact their friendship had fallen by the wayside was as much her fault as it was his. "And we were only friends, you know that. Nothing more." His granddad didn't need to know they'd spent a night together, and that's all it had been—one night, not a relationship.

"Great little rider, that one. Hard worker and a good seat in the saddle. Not to mention darn nice to look at."

"Yup," Ben agreed.

"Bring her out here sometime. I've a filly that needs to be ridden by a woman, and there ain't none of them out here anymore."

Ben thought about Bec, about having her out here again. Would she even come if he asked her to? Four years hadn't quelled his desire for her, but things had changed, heck, *she'd* changed.

"She won't have ridden in a long time." He doubted she'd make the trip. "And I'm not sure we're on the best terms." It had been awkward between them the other day, even if he had enjoyed seeing her again.

Gus stopped then, resting heavily on his cane.

"Don't matter how long it's been, because a woman like her? She's a natural, just like you." He chuckled. "And unless she's already married, don't be a quitter, son. You don't give up on her if she's what you want."

Ben cleared his throat. His grandfather was unbelievable—he'd only been home a few days and already he was giving him advice on his love life.

"I haven't got long now, doc said maybe only six months. I'm not gonna beat the cancer this time, son." He shrugged. "Tell Rebecca I want to see her. What kind of girl would say no to a dying old man, huh?"

It was his turn to give Gus a slap on the shoulder. Thinking about his granddad dying was not something Ben wanted to give in to, and if the old man wanted Rebecca, then who was he to say no?

"We'll be right, Granddad. Cancer won't beat you."

But it would and they both knew it.

* * *

"Table six! No menus yet."

Rebecca hurried to the kitchen as the bell dinged. She hated keeping her customers waiting, especially the regulars she saw seated at her tables every week.

"Phone for you, Bec."

"Take a message," she hollered back.

"Sure?"

She gave the young waiter a hard stare and he shrugged. Who the hell would be calling her during a lunch shift?

She placed the empty plates down and hurried out back.

"It wasn't about Lexie was it?" She regretted her sharp tone and gave the young guy a smile.

"Nah, someone called Ben. Said you'd know how to get in touch."

The name hit her like a thump to her lungs. *Ben.* Why was he calling here? She glanced around, saw that everything was under control and stepped back from the counter. "I'm taking ten," she called out, heading out the back door, suddenly desperately in need of fresh air and sunlight.

She ignored the noise of the city, the streets filled with all kinds of people rushing back and forward, and took a deep breath, pulling her mobile from her pocket. She should have ignored his call, stopped thinking about what she'd had with Ben before he left, but it was an impossible task and she knew it.

Seeing Ben had reminded her, what they were both missing out on, of how nice it would be to have a man around. *Not just any man, but a Ben kind of man.* But she'd made the decision to let him go without saying anything about how she felt, and no amount of regrets was going to change that.

And now she had to decide whether to return his call or not. *And at the same time figure out what the hell I'm going to do about telling him he has a daughter.*

She bit down hard on her lower lip and dialed the number, quickly as if the speed was going to make a difference. The number was still ingrained in her memory, digits that she had never, ever forgotten. Hell, it had once been her favorite number, and not just for Ben being at the other end of it. Because Gus had been as much her lifeline back then as Ben had. When he'd offer her a ride it had been like a junkie getting a fix.

She kept repeating the number in her mind, silently, lips barely moving as it rung.

"McFarlane Stables."

Phew. It wasn't Ben.

"Gus!" At least she didn't have to hide her excitement with him. "I've missed you so much."

"I don't have many young ladies call me, so I'm guessing that's you, Rebecca."

His voice was strong, but it crackled more than it used to. Those soft, kind tones that had soothed her and taught her when she was a girl—he'd been the grandfather she'd always wished was her own.

"How did you guess?"

His laughter rumbled down the line. "Something to do with me telling that grandson of mine to get you out here before I kick the bucket."

"Gus! Don't talk like that."

"Ah, but it's true, love."

"*Gus*," she said, not knowing what else to say to the man she still cared so much about.

"Let's not talk morbid. Just promise me you're coming to see us."

The silence was all her doing this time. She hadn't expected an invitation to McFarlane's, in fact, she hadn't even considered the possibility of going back there. But it was tempting, just the thought of taking a step back in the past even if it was just for a few hours.

"So, are you coming or not?" He never had been one to waste words.

"I, ah…" She'd kept her secret for so long, the last thing she needed was for it to all unravel now before she had time to figure everything out and deal with it properly, and she'd have to ask her folks to look after Lexie.

"Rebecca?"

A tightness in her throat made it hard for her to say *anything*. "Well…" She paused. "Yes."

"Yes?"

"How about I come down this Saturday?" she asked.

"Bring your bag, love. I want you to enjoy the weekend here. Got a horse that needs your help."

She choked. The thought of going back in time, of horses, of Gus…*it was hard*. Exciting, thrilling, terrifying …but still hard.

"I'll tell the boy you're coming."

Uh-oh. The silver-tongued old fox had talked her into a weekend away, all without a hint of protest from her, and she'd forgotten about the reality of Ben. About the fact that it wasn't just going to be her and Gus reminiscing, that it wasn't about being old friends and catching up. *Just like old times*. That's what he'd said, but there was no way anything between her and Ben was like it used to be.

At least she had nothing to feel guilty about where Lexie was concerned—she spent every Saturday night with her grandparents anyway, but still…she usually didn't feel bad about having Saturday night off from parenting each week because she worked, but having an evening to herself seemed wrong somehow. Even though she'd never done it once in her daughter's three years before.

But she deserved one weekend to herself, and she just couldn't risk taking her with her.

A butterfly-soft shiver ran the length of her spine. But this was Ben, this was a step back into the past for one night, and the idea of seeing him again… She shook her head as if it would somehow push her worries away.

She was going to do it. And then she'd figure out how to break the news to him, because now he was home, and if he was home for good, then all the reasons she had for keeping Lexie from him were gone.

CHAPTER THREE

THIS WAS HARDER than she'd thought. Just the idea of seeing Ben had her stomach turning, twisting into a cavalcade of knots. She focused on the road and gripped the wheel tighter, pulling over just near the turnoff and trying to slow her breathing, trying to stop her hands from trembling, too. If she could only still them enough to smudge some gloss over her dry lips, run her fingers through her hair and press a smidge of perfume to her neck, she'd be fine.

The driveway loomed ahead; as immaculate as she'd remembered it. Gus was an old man now, but his standards hadn't slipped, and she found herself hoping the stables and house were unchanged, too. Her memories were so vivid, colorful in her mind as if she'd been here merely months ago, instead of years.

She pushed the lever down into Drive again, satisfied that she looked passable in the mirror, and pulled slowly into the driveway. Gravel crunched under the tires and trees softly waved against the metal of the vehicle as if welcoming her. Bec took a deep breath and found emotions getting the better of her. Up until a week ago, she'd never expected to see this place again, but it was so good to be back.

Up ahead she could just see the house, a triple brick, beautiful residence that was as immaculate as the drive. Roses were neatly clipped, windows thrown wide, one of the most gorgeous houses she'd ever seen. Her own family home was nice, better than modest, but this place was something else. And then her eyes settled on her once favorite part of the property—the row of stables, in an L-shape, to the left of the house.

She slowed the car to a crawl as she surveyed the place, looking for any sign of life and seeing none. There were no horses in sight, but then at this time of day it wasn't to be expected. Apart from a ginger cat stretched out in the sun, it was as good as deserted. In a way she was glad, it gave her time to walk around and reminisce before figuring out what to say to Ben.

She pushed open the car door and let it shut behind her as she stretched her legs. The sun was warm on her bare arms and she moved toward the stables, eyes wandering everywhere. What she loved about this place was the privacy, with only the side of the stables visible. Bec had heard there were fewer horses here than ever now that Gus had slowed down, but as soon as she rounded the building it became obvious that reduced numbers for him were still impressive.

The property had been purpose built with horse rearing and polo playing in mind. The old stables had been meticulously cared for and maintained over the years, and Rebecca stopped to look. The stables stretched in a long line, flanked by larger, box stalls tying up bays. The wooden structures were faded yet clean, the white and navy colors still vivid in her mind from years ago. Wisteria curled down over the edges, pots of bright flowers infusing color into the well-kept area. The door to the tack room was wide-open, and Rebecca could smell the aroma of saddle soap and sweaty horse blankets. It was a blast from the past that made her smile.

She continued on, stopping to rub a nose poking out from one of the boxes. The smell of hay, the sight of horseflesh, it sent a shiver of both excitement and worry through her body. The same kind of feeling she got thinking about Ben.

Rebecca looked ahead to the land before her. The most sheltered field was still kept for young stock, and from the looks of them, recently weaned fillies and colts. Frisky-looking babies who were having a ball of a time, playing and scolding one another in the safe, well-fenced environment. Working with the young stock had been something she and Ben had both enjoyed. Teaching them their manners, how to respect humans, all without needing to use a firm hand. Back then, she and Ben had always had their heads buried in a Monty Roberts book, the legendary horse whisperer who flaunted industry-standard horse breaking rules.

Rebecca walked on and let her eyes wander, taking in the sights, but it was the noise out to her right that had the blood pumping that little bit faster in her veins, that had a smile turning her mouth upward.

She could just make out someone, who she presumed was Gus, excitedly waving what looked to be a cane as some young guys trained. At least six horses rushed past in a blur, hooves pounding hard on the ground as they thundered fast alongside each other. Her feet picked up speed and she rushed toward them, desperately wanting to watch the game as the horses and riders galloped around the polo field.

She didn't want to disturb Gus, so she approached

quietly once she was close, watching the riders compete for the ball, heading toward the goal. From her vantage point, she snuck a quick glance at the old man before her and felt sad, it was like he'd shrunk a little and aged so quickly, but it was unmistakably the same kind person who had been so good to her for so many years.

"Go, go, go!" She jumped as Gus screamed, waving his stick again.

As one of the players made a goal he threw his stick, one hand pumping up in a fist. She couldn't help but laugh.

"Gus." Her voice was soft but he turned immediately on the spot, his eyes meeting hers.

Gus looked her over for a moment before a big smile spread out wide over his face.

"Rebecca! Well, look at you."

He held out his arms and she reached him in no time, embracing him fondly.

"It's so good to be back here, to see you," she mumbled, holding him tight.

He smiled at her as she stepped back, his eyes shining.

"Just look at you. Look at you, huh? All grown-up."

She beamed, embarrassed yet flattered. Before she could answer a voice interrupted them, sending her almost a foot in the air with fright.

"Becca."

Ben. She would recognize that voice anywhere. Deep, rich and delicious. He sat astride a blowing, sweaty polo pony that was now dancing very close to her.

"Good goal, son. I'll walk him back for you."

Ben jumped to the ground and passed Gus the reins.

"You sure you're okay taking him?"

The older man just looked skyward, eyes rolling. Bec

knew it would take more than a highly strung horse to keep him from where the action was, walking cane or not.

Bec stole a glance at Ben while his attention was still directed at the horse before looking away. If only he wasn't so handsome, so charming, so...*not available*. Or possibly available, she had no idea if he had a girl-friend or not, but not available to her. She was all about no complications, being a mother, nothing else. *Nothing else*, she repeated inside her head just in case her body was thinking of disagreeing. She'd been happy being friends with him for so long, but ever since that night...

"Hey."

He was talking to her. *Damn it!* And there she was away in fairyland.

"You looked good out there." It was all she could think to say, but the truth was she hadn't even realized he was the one in the saddle.

"Yeah, well, I'm happy to be home, but I'm still crav-ing some saddle time." He grinned at her and pulled his helmet off, turning toward the field where some of the guys were still training, and ran a hand through his short hair. "You ever think about getting back up again?"

It had been a long time for her, a dream she'd long since given up, and now she was a mom she was way more cautious than she'd once been. The allure of the polo field now was more about watching than actually doing. And besides, that fall had almost broken her. It had taken everything away from her; her dreams, her future. And Ben.

"Maybe," she lied. Or maybe it wasn't a lie. Being back here was giving her all sorts of mixed emotions, making her question everything. "It's not something I've really thought about, to be honest."

Ben turned to her then and reached out a hand, touching her arm so lightly she almost wondered if she was imagining it.

"It's great to have you here, Bec."

She struggled for words, her skin tingling where he'd touched her. They'd been best friends for years, before one night had changed everything, and now she could hardly look at him without thinking about the fact she'd seen him naked. *And how darn good he'd looked.*

"It feels good being back here." She hardly trusted her voice.

He started to walk and she followed his lead, his long legs eating up the ground.

"There's something about this place, Bec. It's good for the soul."

He stopped then, turning to face her, pulling her hands into his and holding them tight. He studied her with such intensity she didn't know where to look or what to say.

"I'm sorry, Bec, for expecting you to stay in touch after what happened, for leaving you in the first place," he said, his voice low. "I never stopped thinking about you, but it all just got so complicated. So much for best friends, huh?"

Until we ruined it. They were the unspoken words hanging between them.

Bec gulped, her eyes burning with tears. Their friendship? Was that all he wanted from her? Lexie's beautiful little face flashed before her and she almost told him, so wanted to tell him that he was the father of her beautiful daughter, but she didn't. Couldn't yet, even though she knew she had to. Because she also knew that he never wanted children—he'd told her since they were in high school that he wasn't ever going to be a dad after what he'd been through—and she knew nothing would ever change his mind. But she couldn't deny him the chance, couldn't keep this from him any longer.

"I've missed you, Ben. But things change, and I guess we just grew apart, right?"

"Maybe we should have both stuck to our plan. Gone to the UK together and both played."

"It would have been good, huh?" Only the reality was that Ben had been picked up by a team in Argentina, and she hadn't, and instead of telling him the truth, she'd made out like she couldn't leave her family. That it wasn't what she wanted. Maybe if he'd asked her to go as more than friends, maybe if her confidence hadn't been shattered after the fall and she'd not been such a mess over everything. Maybe then things could or would have been different.

His eyes were as sad as hers as he watched her. "Come on, let's show you around. There's something I want you to see."

Her eyebrows dragged together as he turned and started to walk again, tugging her along with him.

"Well, more like Gus wants you to see it. Just come and take a look."

Her curiosity was piqued, and she hurried to keep up with him. Make her hair longer, she thought, take away the soft crinkles around his eyes and they could have gone back five or so years. To a time when everything had seemed possible, when they were both in charge of their own destinies, before fate and life had intervened. Before she'd fallen pregnant to a man she'd loved with all her heart, and instead of asking him to stay behind because she loved him, she'd let him go. She couldn't help but wonder if he would have left and not come home, had she told him how she really felt. If she'd called him and told him that she was pregnant. But then deep down she knew the answer to that.

Ben would *never* have left her, not if he knew how she felt, if he knew that she was carrying his baby. And that was precisely why she'd lied, told him they'd made a mistake that night, that they were better as friends. Because she didn't believe in clipping the wings of a bird to keep it at home, and Ben had been like an eagle ready to soar through the sky. And she never wanted to be responsible for ruining Ben's life, and seeing him repeat the same mistakes his mother had.

CHAPTER FOUR

"SHE'S BEAUTIFUL."

Rebecca ran her eyes over every inch of the horse. It wasn't hard to act interested—the filly was one of the most beautiful animals she had ever seen. Endless black legs, four white socks and a silky long tail. Her face was framed by a wide white blaze, stretching all the way to her nostrils; dark brown eyes like pools of trust, following every movement she and Ben made.

He didn't say anything, just watched the horse, arms slung over the corral fence, one foot resting on the lowest tread of timber.

"So, what's the deal with her?"

Ben shrugged, broad shoulders moving under his shirt. She was glad to have the distraction of the horse, because she was finding it almost impossible not to stare at him.

"She's had all the guys on, doesn't seem to like them."

"How about you?" Rebecca asked. "Does she like you?"

He laughed. "Nope, not particularly."

They looked at one another. They were both thinking the same thing, Rebecca could tell by the look in his eyes. There had always been the odd horse that had worked better for one of them or the other, it was about personalities, the rider clicking with beast. But there had been one very special mare who'd only ever worked for Rebecca, to the point where Gus had decided the horse was useless for anyone else, and had given her over to Bec. It had all worked well, her dream come true to own such an amazing mare, until the accident. She'd lost her nerve, and her will to ride, and her beautiful mare had lost her life. The memory flash made her skin prickle. And then she'd lost her best friend, all in the course of a couple of months, as well as her dreams of making it big in the polo world. She'd never gotten over that period in her life, had always just pushed it from her mind, but her pain was still raw.

Ben let out a big breath of air and gave her a smile— a slow rise of his mouth, followed by a gentle wink. It was as if he had put his arm around her, comforted her, just by looking at her. No one else had ever made her feel quite like Ben could. Embraced, comforted, cared for, all in a single look. Pity it had taken her so many years to figure out that she was in love with him. When they'd finally taken that step, he was gone, and then she went from losing a friend to nursing a broken heart. Ben had never said anything, never told her that he thought of her as any more than a friend, and so she'd just kept her mouth shut and let him get on with his life.

"So what do you think?"

Rebecca raised her eyes. *What did she think?* Her mind was racing, took her a moment to remember what they were even talking about. And then she glanced at the filly before them.

Ben was watching her, waiting for her answer. But here, back on a horse again, after all this time?

"I, ah, don't think so."

Ben stepped up onto the railing and hauled himself into the corral. "If I persist long enough, she'll let me catch her, but she's wild when anyone tries to get near her."

"And you expect me to do what you guys can't?"

Ben walked backward until his back was pressed against the wooden rails, before climbing up to sit on the fence.

"You know you can do it, Bec."

Rebecca stayed on the other side of the fence, close to Ben but not quite touching. It was tempting, she could admit that, but there was no way she was up to it. No way she could summon the courage to climb on a spir-ited horse and stay calm enough and confident enough to be in control. Not after all this time.

"What's her name?"

Ben turned and smiled. "That mean you're ready to give it a go?"

She laughed, shaking her head as she looked back at the horse. No, all it meant was she was trying to change the subject.

"Missy," he told her. "Her name's Missy."

Rebecca kept watching the horse. *Missy.* She played the name through her mind. It was a pretty name, but it didn't make any difference. She wasn't going near her.

"What do you say?"

"Just give me some time." The words came out before she could think longer. And she wasn't even sure she was still talking about horses.

Ben jumped off the fence and landed on the hard packed dirt, his feet falling inches away from hers. Re-becca had a funny feeling she would live to regret that comment. There was no way he was going to let her leave at the end of this weekend without trying her luck with that horse, and the very idea terrified her. She didn't know if it was simply losing her nerve or just the years of not riding catching up on her, but she couldn't even comprehend climbing back into the saddle, with or without Ben egging her on.

He stood close to her, too close, and their eyes met for just a second. It was long enough to feel like one second too long, though. Neither of them knew what to say. Ben because he wasn't the type to just come out and say something, and her because she had too much to hide. Too much at stake. Just being with him was a risk, or at least it was until she was ready to come clean and tell him what she'd done. It wasn't that she was going to keep it from him, she just wanted to do it right, to break it to him the right way, if that was even possible.

Rebecca walked beside Ben. She was listening to him but her eyes were floating around their surroundings, drinking in the familiar sights she had gone so long without seeing.

"What do you think?"

She turned her attention back to Ben. She had no idea what he was talking about. *Again*.

Gus appeared ahead of them and saved her from having to answer. He leaned against the corner of the stable block, resting a leg, but he was smiling. Rebecca guessed that he was probably feeling worse than he let on, but this was his life. The alternative was to cart him off to hospital, or a rest home, and what good would that do him? He deserved to be here till his last day, doing what he loved.

"So when are you two going off for a ride?"

Rebecca laughed and glanced at Ben. She hoped that

he hadn't put his grandfather up to it. "I'm not sure I'll be riding at all this weekend. These days I prefer my feet firmly on the ground."

"Do you remember Willy?" Gus asked

She nodded. "Who could forget him?" Although as she said it, she was wondering if it was a trick question. "He must be, what? Twenty...twenty-two years old now?" He'd been Gus's horse when she was a teenager. The most reliable, safe, sweet horse she'd ever come across, and he'd been Gus's pride and joy.

"Sure is. I can't ride anymore and he's going to waste just sitting around. Thought he could do with a walk around the farm. What do you say?"

Rebecca took a step backward and walked straight smack bang into Ben. He must have stopped right behind her, his large frame preventing her from making a getaway. She lurched forward and felt trapped. Backward meant into Ben and forward meant the horse. She didn't know what scared her more. Her heart was hammering, although the idea of falling back into the warmth of Ben's body was sounding like the more attractive option right now.

"I, ah, I don't know, Gus. Really, I..."

"Are you telling me you came all the way here without your riding gear?"

Gulp. He had her there. Yes, she had brought it, but with no intention of actually *putting it on*. She eyed up the horse some more and felt a lump of genuine terror knot in her throat, but at least riding would give her a distraction aside from Ben.

"How about it, Bec?"

Ben placed his hands on either side of her arms, still standing behind her. It was nothing more than a gentle press of his skin against hers, but it sent a butterfly-soft shiver down her back. He was too close and it was only making her feel more guilty about everything, like a traitor for even being there.

Gus was watching her, Ben was touching her, even the horse seemed to be staring at her, waiting for her answer.

"Okay fine, I'll do it."

Maybe it was the pressure, the sun making her giddy, hell, it might have even been the way Ben was looking at her, but she felt her resolve buckle. But all of a sudden going for a trail ride didn't seem like the stupidest idea in the world.

"Okay?" Ben seemed doubtful, and Gus winked before leaving them to it.

"Don't sound so surprised," she muttered.

She knew this was only the start of it, or maybe it wasn't. Because once she told Ben the truth he'd never forgive her, and then she'd never be invited back ever again.

"Do you want to go get changed?" Ben asked.

He looked her up and down, and Rebecca tried not to laugh as a smile kicked the corners of her mouth up. "I've never ridden in a sundress and sandals before, and I'm not about to start."

She turned and headed back to the car as Ben laughed, wanting to look back at him but not letting herself. There was something about Ben, there always had been; a quiet strength about him that she'd been drawn to when they were both only at school, and that confidence had translated into a super sexy guy. There was nothing arrogant about him even though he'd played with the best polo players in the world, and his manner with animals? That had always set him apart from any man she'd ever met before. *And it was why he'd be such a darn good father.* She swallowed hard and tried not to think about what-ifs—Ben had made it clear he wasn't ever going to have a family of his own, that he wouldn't ever repeat the mistakes his own mom had made, and she knew that his hurt ran so deep that nothing, *nothing*, was capable of changing his mind. Which was why she'd kept her secret all this time. But now it was time for him to decide, for him to be the one to make that choice.

She tugged the car door open and grabbed her bag. All of her other belongings were in a small suitcase, but her riding clothes were in the same bag they'd always been in. She pulled back the zip and just looked at them for a moment, before sucking up all her jitters and swallowing them away.

She looked around to check she was alone, then took off her sandals and replaced them with socks and pulled her jodhpurs over her ankles and up her thighs. The material stretched tight, but she was pleased to be able to do the waist up. Years on, not to mention one child later, and she could still fit into the tight breeches—it was a good feeling.

Rebecca tugged her dress over her shoulders and placed it on the backseat, before grabbing her former favorite faded gray Pearl Jam T-shirt she had once worn on a daily basis. She searched for a tie in the glove box and then yanked her hair into a plait, before grabbing her helmet and gloves and closing the car door.

This was it. It was now or never.

Ben emerged from around the side of the stables, sitting astride a striking chestnut horse, and leading Willy on his left. She drew in a big breath of air and marched onward, trying hard to keep her smile from faltering.

"You look good."

His words made her smile, even if she didn't believe him for a second. "Liar liar pants on fire," she joked. "But thanks for the compliment."

"Need a hand getting on?" he asked.

"Nah, I'm fine." She was lying, but she'd rather struggle on without any assistance from Ben. His hands anywhere near her body right now was not a good idea.

She took the reins and lifted her left leg, hopping on one foot as she tried to get it high enough to get her left one through the stirrup.

"Not quite as flexible as you used to be, huh?"

Ben dismounted and moved to help her. Heat flooded Rebecca's face as he touched her shoulder, laughing softly.

"If it makes you feel any better, some of the guys I rode with in Argentina spent half their lives on horseback and could only mount if they were standing on a fence."

Rebecca grimaced. She hadn't realized that getting *on* the horse would be the tough part.

"Here."

Ben cupped his hands and indicated for her to put her knee up. She did, his strong palms closing around her leg, sending spasms of warmth through her body.

"Thanks," she said. "On three."

She bounced three times before Ben sprang her into the air, and straight on to Willy's back. She landed with a soft thump and felt that all too familiar turmoil in her stomach. The accident hit her memory bank like it was yesterday.

She was about to jump straight off when Ben placed a hand to her thigh, almost sending her flying off the other side. All those years they had touched, slept side by side in sleeping bags, sat close, and there had never been a reaction like that. It was as if that one night all those years ago was still pulling them together; their skin still reactive to the pressure of one another's touch. His hand felt hot, heating through the fabric of her jodhpurs, and she knew he felt it, too.

"You're okay," he soothed, never taking his eyes off her.

She swallowed a lump that felt as big as a rock and nodded. Suddenly the horse seemed like the safe bet.

Ben raised his other hand to shield his eyes from the sun, gave her one of his sexy-as-heck winks and then turned back to his horse.

"You'll be just fine."

All of a sudden she knew she was right. It wasn't the horse she needed to be scared of. Danger had just looked her straight in the eye and she'd managed to survive it. For now.

CHAPTER FIVE

REBECCA FINALLY STARTED to relax. Her back had been rigid, legs clammy and neck stiff. She wondered if she'd even been breathing for fear of falling off.

"I guess this is why they say to get straight back in the saddle after a fall."

Ben was riding slightly ahead of her but he reined back to match her horse's stride.

"Sometimes that's easier said than done," he said.

"I've kept something from you all this time, Ben," she admitted. It was almost impossible preparing to confess this, let alone telling him her big secret. *Baby steps*, she just needed to take baby steps.

He turned to watch her, eyebrows raised in question.

Rebecca sighed, looking away from him. She'd told him at the time that she'd turned down the offer she'd been made, that she'd decided she just didn't want to leave her family and live overseas anymore. "I lied to you," she said simply. "I was never offered a position on the women's team, but I didn't want to hold you back, and then after my fall, I didn't even know if I wanted to play anymore."

When he never replied, the only sound their horses' hooves echoing on the dirt, she braved a glance at him.

From side on his jaw looked like it was cut from steel, his entire face like stone.

"You shouldn't have done that." His voice was deep and gravelly. "I wouldn't have just left you like that if I'd…"

"And that's why I did it. I wasn't going to make you second-guess what you wanted. We were only friends, right?" Just saying it hurt her. "It wasn't like you were walking out on your girlfriend."

"So you lied and told me you couldn't leave your family? That staying behind was what you wanted? That we just didn't share the same dreams anymore?" He grunted. "And we might not have been dating, Bec, but we were damn good friends. We'd always planned on going together."

She knew he was angry, but she'd needed to tell him.

"I just wanted you to know the truth, Ben. It was a long time ago, but still."

He made a grunting noise again, his shoulders bunched. "You still shouldn't have lied to me."

"I was a mess after everything that happened," she said. "I was still dreaming of making a team when in reality I was terrified at the idea of even getting on a horse and playing a game again. And then you…" She let her voice trail off, not really wanting to open up to him about how she'd felt. "I lost everything. My confidence was shattered and I was a mess."

"I would have tried to help you, Bec. I wouldn't have just walked away if I'd known the truth."

And that's why she hadn't told him. She hadn't wanted to clip his wings, would never have done that to him, but there had also been a little voice in her head telling her that after everything that had happened, she hadn't been good enough for him anymore. That he wouldn't want her if she couldn't even muster the courage to get back in the saddle and try to make another team.

They rode in silence, Rebecca staring straight ahead, her nerves about being on horseback slowly disappearing. It was a strange feeling being nervous about a sport that had once been her life.

"So how do you feel right now?" Ben asked.

Bec relaxed her grip on the reins and sat deep in the saddle, actually loving how good it felt. The start of a smile was tugging at the corners of her mouth and she couldn't resist the pull. Maybe he was going to let bygones be bygones, which meant that she had to do the same.

"You know what?" She grinned over at him, trying to push the past out of her mind, at least for the afternoon. "Now that I'm not hanging on for dear life, it feels kinda good."

"How about a canter down to the creek?"

Ben was sitting straight-backed, comfortable in the saddle, his broad shoulders stretched wide. There was something about seeing him in his white T-shirt, jeans and baseball cap that sent her back years in her mind. He probably felt the same looking at her.

She sucked up her courage and shortened her reins. "Just remember that I'm not the rider I used to be."

She clucked Willy first into a trot and then into his rocking horse canter. Rebecca moved back and forth, feeling her legs stretch out, calf muscles groaning with the movement. There was nothing particularly easy about riding all over again, but it was a bit like the old bike theory. Once you knew how, it was something you never truly forgot.

"Doing good, *cowgirl*, doing good," called Ben with a cowboy drawl.

Rebecca stayed focused, still expecting Willy to do something out of the ordinary, but he behaved like a complete gentleman.

Ben pulled back to a walk and Rebecca followed his lead, her chest rising rapidly with the burst of exercise.

"It's just up there." He pointed.

"Uh-huh." Her lungs were screaming for more air— she wasn't capable of saying anything else.

They rode in silence the rest of the way, and Rebecca felt those darn butterflies ignite in her stomach again. Ben was gorgeous and charming and so easy to be around, and he hadn't even given her that much of a grilling over the whole lie. He deserved to know about Lexie, too, once she figured out how to break it to him, then her. She just needed to make sure he was certain about staying, that he wasn't going to end up sacrificing his life simply to act out of duty and stay for his daughter. *Or her.* That was why she'd let him go in the first place.

"You coming?"

Ben's voice from up ahead spurred her back in to action. She urged Willy into a trot and shook her head to rid her mind of its worries.

Ben chanced a glance over his shoulder. Rebecca was sitting so elegantly on the horse it looked as though she was right at home, but he knew it had taken a lot of courage for her to get back in the saddle and open up to him. It was a weird feeling, being back out here with Rebecca. He wasn't quite sure what to do, how to act, what to say. Did he behave like they were just old friends reunited, or was he meant to factor in *that* night? Maybe it was because he'd become used to casual relationships with women; women he'd meet after a polo game, drink champagne with and then realize he had absolutely zero things in common with them. Whereas with Bec…seeing her again was like finding a favorite something that he'd missed for years, then realizing it still fit like a glove. But they were only friends, had been *only* friends for years.

He stopped at the creek's edge, no more than a trickle of water flowing down beneath some overhanging trees. It had been their spot, the place they'd always come to talk, when they needed to be alone. Parent troubles, friends, horse issues—it had been their place to figure life out.

It didn't look any different now than it had then. Ben dismounted and tied his horse loosely to a blue gum tree. He turned back around to Rebecca. She had her feet out of the stirrups, stretching her ankles, and the grimace on her face was hard to ignore.

"Every single part of my body is protesting right now," she explained.

"Want a hand down?"

Rebecca looked at him gratefully. "Oh, yeah."

He tried his hardest not to look, not to feel, but it was impossible. She swung her far leg over and came down toward him, and Ben put both hands up, catching her around the waist and guiding her to the ground. She landed with a tiny thump.

His palms were pressed against the flimsy material of her T-shirt, he could feel her taut skin beneath his hands. Despite his best intentions he didn't let go, not straight away, their bodies only inches apart. It wasn't until Rebecca cleared her throat that he stepped back, hands falling away.

Ben was about to apologize, but she turned, her dark blue eyes smiling in his direction. There was nothing to be said. The attraction that had started the night before he'd left was still there, he knew it and she knew it. But things had changed. She was a mom now, and he couldn't be a dad, not even a stepdad. And with Bec? If anything happened between them, it wasn't going to be a casual night of sex again—she meant too much for him to treat her like that. Which left him wondering what the hell *could* happen between them. If he had to consider the possibility of getting close to someone's else's kid.

"I should be saying thank you, Bec," he said, searching for the right words. "You shouldn't have lied to me, but the fact that you let me follow my dreams? You were an awesome friend. It was the best thing I've ever done and I don't regret it for a second."

She nodded, her eyes leaving his as if she was nervous about something. "I wasn't that great a friend."

He chuckled. "Believe me, you were." She hadn't brought up that night and he wasn't going to, either, because the last thing he needed was for her to be embarrassed when things were starting to feel easy between them again. "When my mom left, there wasn't a day that went past that I didn't feel guilty. Knowing that she'd sacrificed everything she'd ever wanted to have me, it made me feel like crap. But then I guess you already know all that, right?"

Rebecca reached out, her fingers brushing his arm in the softest caress as she met his gaze again. "She had no right to make you feel that way."

Ben shrugged. "Maybe. But when you're eight years old and you find out that your mom never wanted you? It's not exactly an easy pill to swallow. No kid deserves that."

"Maybe she regretted telling you that," Rebecca said.

He ground his teeth together, trying to keep his anger at bay. "If she regretted it she'd have come back. She made it pretty clear that her career was more important than I was."

Rebecca's hand fell away, her smile sad. "You deserved better, Ben. We both know that."

"Hey, I'm a big boy now, the past is in the past and all that," he said, brushing it off as if it meant nothing to him, even though there wasn't a day that passed that he didn't wonder how a mother could do that to her son. "All I was trying to say was I'm not angry with you, for lying to me. You let me go, and I should be thanking you instead of being so angry. You were never the kind of person to hold someone back and that makes you special."

He saw a flicker of something in her face, something he couldn't put his finger on, but he didn't call her out on it. It'd been a long time since they'd been together, so maybe he was wrong.

"Just tell me it was worth it?" she asked. "That you had the time of your life."

He bumped shoulders with her, grinning. "It was incredible. You would have loved it over there."

She laughed. "You mean the playing and the horses, or the champagne and the parties?"

"Both. Although the latter was definitely the highlight." He laughed. "Seriously, the money over there is incredible. The champagne and top-shelf liquor flows like it's soda, and the clothes and the diamonds, the cars and horseflesh, it's like nothing I'd ever seen before. I never got used to it, even after all that time, and I'm sure as hell pleased I never tried to keep up with those lifestyles."

"Sounds tough. You must have been so miserable," she joked.

"Yeah, it was such a bore riding hundred-thousand-dollar horses and swilling Veuve Clicquot."

"Hmm, I'm sure."

This was what he'd missed, just hanging out with someone he actually had a connection with. Playing overseas had been fun, but this was real life, and it was reality that he'd yearned for. Telling stories about his time was fun, but in truth it had been superficial, and he was happy to have his feet back on Australian soil, even if he still missed his teammates like crazy.

"So tell me all about it. Was it as amazing as we always thought it would be? Parties aside?"

Rebecca toyed with the frayed hem of her T-shirt and watched Ben skim stones across the water. He was lying down, propped up by one elbow, while she sat cross-legged beside him. Telling him the truth had been tough, but after hearing him say she'd done the right thing, listening to him talk about his mom again, she was feeling better about what she'd kept from him. He was still going to be furious when she told him everything, but at least they'd made some headway.

"Yeah. But the guys are rough." He grimaced. "As in rough with their horses. It's just the way things are with polo, but you know how I am. I love the sport, but I missed home." Ben looked off into the distance. "I gotta say that it was the first time I'd ever felt like part of a real family, though, so that was good. I mean, Gus always remained the most important person in my life, but feeling like I had a whole team of brothers was pretty cool. We traveled in the owner's private jets around the world to play. He even jetted the horses rather than keep different stables. The money he had was surreal."

She wondered if he'd missed her, or if he was just referring to Gus. Or maybe he meant the red Australian dirt and she was being way too sentimental. Either way, what he'd experienced sounded incredible.

"You know, it was like, every day over there was a way to prove to myself that I was worth something. I wanted to show Gus that I could dream big and achieve what I'd always talked about, but maybe it was a way to prove to the rest of the world that I didn't deserve to be orphaned by my parents."

Rebecca nodded. "I get it." She'd always known he was running from demons, because she'd always been the one he opened up to.

"And how about you? You pleased you stayed behind in the end?" He shook his head. "Or did you regret what had happened?"

"I should have told you I didn't make the team."

"Yeah, but the question is did you actually want to go or not?" he asked, his expression serious. "Was it still what you wanted?"

"To start with, yes. But after my fall? It killed my confidence, Ben. I wanted to go away, but I couldn't just head off and expect to tag along with you if I wasn't playing or working. I needed to figure out what the hell I was going to do with my life, find something that I could actually make a go of." He kept flicking the stones, listening but not saying anything, so she continued. "I should have been better at emailing, but then I had Lexie and..." She didn't know what else to say.

"I get it. You were busy, times changed. It wasn't like we were together or anything." He angled his body so he was facing her, a frown dragging his mouth down. "But what happened that night, it was a long time coming, right?"

She sucked in a breath. "Um, yeah." Rebecca glanced at Ben, his expression serious. "But we always said we'd never ruin things, didn't we? That our friendship was what mattered."

A slow smile spread across Ben's face. "Maybe we were stupid. Maybe we should have just followed our instincts from the start."

"I thought our instincts were to be friends and not complicate things," she said drily.

"Yeah, well look how well that turned out." Ben reached out and touched her hand, a gesture that shouldn't have rattled her but did. "And then you went and met someone else and had a baby."

Her heart started to pound, as if it was about to beat right out of her chest.

"You okay?"

She nodded. "Just thinking about Lexie. I only ever leave her if I have to go to work, so I'm feeling a bit guilty."

"She's with your parents, though?"

"Yeah. They adore her and she has them wrapped around her little finger." Bec laughed. "She probably has more fun with them than she has with me, but I still don't like leaving her."

She looked across into a pair of deep brown eyes that were hauntingly, yet comfortingly, the exact same as her daughter's, the gold fleck unmistakable.

"You sure you're not going to tell me who the guy was? Because if he's someone I know..."

Rebecca gave Ben a smile that could have won her an

acting award, a practiced smile to stop him from worrying. She'd been using the same one on her dad for years. "How about we pretend like we've gone back in time for the rest of the afternoon?"

He grunted. "I just wish I'd been here for you, that's all. You shouldn't have had to go through that alone."

"As my friend?" she asked, pulse hammering again. "You wish you were here for me as my friend or something else?"

He looked confused. "Of course. That's what we were, right?"

His words hurt. Like a fist to her gut. He might not have thought they were together, that they'd become anything more than good friends, but that night they had spent together had changed everything for her. She'd fallen in love with him, and if she was honest, it wasn't as though she'd ever fallen back out of love. Not once in all these years, even after meeting plenty of nice guys through the restaurant. But even if he'd stayed, they may have just gone back to being friends, to nothing more. Unless of course she'd told him about her being pregnant, then he'd have probably proposed to her because of his sense of duty. And the only thing worse than wishing they were together would have been knowing they were together because he thought they had to be.

"We *were* friends," she said, sucking back a burst of emotion that he would probably never understand. "But I was fine, Ben. I was absolutely fine."

"I guess being a mom kept you pretty busy. I just hope you were happy and busy."

Ben said it with a smile but all Rebecca felt was a lump of dread knot in her throat. Lexie. Her daughter. *Their daughter.* She needed to change the subject before they broached into even more dangerous territory, or before Ben started to figure out the timeline.

"Bec?"

Ben looked worried. She closed her eyes for a moment and felt the sun trickle through the branches above her. Her feet were hot inside her boots, but the rest of her felt great. Bare arms in the sun, the sticky air brushing past her skin, and nothing but the sound of birds cawing in the trees. She owed it to herself to relax, and if she stopped worrying, then maybe it wouldn't be so hard to change the subject and just enjoy being with Ben as she tried to figure everything out.

"You know what?" she said, her eyes lazily popping open. "Let's just lie here a bit longer. I never get to sit and do nothing anymore."

A little part of her might feel like the world's worst mother for being here and leaving Lexie at home, but it was once in more than three years, and if she kept working at the pace she did every day for another year, she'd probably end up in hospital with exhaustion.

"Fine by me," said Ben, pulling his cap lower over his eyes and reclining back.

They were side by side now, so close to touching, but achingly far apart. Rebecca had closed her eyes again, but her body was far from relaxed. She wanted to tell Ben how good this felt, to be here with him again, to forget about everything else. She wanted to tell him she'd missed him, that she wanted to be part of his life again, but she knew it was impossible. She wished she could explain why she'd done what she'd done, how she hadn't felt worthy of him, how she hadn't wanted to hold him back from his dreams, but nothing sounded quite right when she practiced it in her mind.

If she was truly honest with herself, she knew that coming here had been a mistake. She had known it from the day Gus had asked her to make the trip. But if she hadn't come, she would always have been wondering what if. What if Ben wanted to see her for a reason? What if Gus died and she felt guilty forever for not making the effort to see him? The list in her mind just went on and on.

And now that she was here, it was intoxicating. The smell, feel, touch of horses beneath her hands and around her were enough to lull her back in time. The same with Ben. The house. Gus, too. It was like being transported back to enjoy a time where everything seemed fine, where anything she dreamed was possible, where being with Ben was a possibility.

As if he knew she was thinking about him, Ben nudged his hat back and propped himself up on his elbow again. Rebecca had opened her eyes as soon as he had moved, but she stayed lying on her back.

"You ever think what would have happened if I hadn't gone away?"

Rebecca let out a low lungful of air and looked over at him. He seemed to have moved closer but she knew he hadn't. Ben was plucking at some long shoots of grass, but she could tell he was off balance, that he wasn't entirely comfortable talking to her about the past, although she guessed he'd been sitting on that question awhile.

"Yeah, I do." She took a slow, deep breath. "Or at least I used to. A lot."

They stayed silent for a moment, both looking at his hands, watching his fingers pull at each blade. Rebecca's mouth was dry, as if she'd just consumed a ball of cotton wool. He had no idea how much she wished he'd stayed, how often she thought of how different life would be. For starters, she wouldn't be a single mom, because she'd have told him right from the start. The *only* reason she'd kept it from him was so she wasn't the one responsible for killing his dream because she hadn't wanted him to resent her or her child. *Especially not their child.*

"So what was your conclusion?"

Rebecca felt her cheeks flush hot. What had her thoughts been?

"I think we'd have made it," he said, not waiting for her to reply. "If we'd just admitted how we felt instead of pretending like it meant nothing. If we'd been together instead of pretending like we were only supposed to be friends when we both know that was crap."

Ben maneuvered the single blade of grass between forefinger and thumb, before lifting it to run it over her bare arm. She couldn't stop her eyes from closing, the tiny hairs on her arm rising with the touch, her breath coming in short pants. It felt as though he was caressing her, skin to skin, even though no part of him was actually touching her, the grass doing all the skimming across her arm.

Her eyes popped open again when he spoke, but she was feeling drowsy and excited all at once. Her mind roaring, stomach turning.

"Why did it take us so long to realize?" he asked, voice sexy and low.

She knew exactly what he meant. After all those years of being buddies, friends only, why had it taken an alcohol-fueled night and him leaving to draw them together? When they could have had so long having fun instead of pretending like they both just wanted to be platonic.

But the very next day they'd gone on like *nothing* had happened.

"We could have been great," she croaked, still entranced by the grass-to-skin thing he was doing to her.

He stopped then, and their eyes met. She leaned in, her gaze falling from his mouth back to his eyes. Was he trying to tell her he still wanted her? Was he trying to tell her that their night together hadn't been one big mistake?

"Rebecca, I…"

She watched him expectantly, desperate for him to close the gap between them and move forward. Aching to taste his kiss. After all this time of wishing he was with her, that he would come home for her, and now he was so close.

Ben looked at her long and hard before reaching one hand into her hair, cupping the back of her skull and drawing her close. He crushed her lips so softly against his, the light touch of his skin sending ripples of pleasure down her spine. It should have felt wrong, but if felt so, so right.

Ben ran his hand down the length of her hair, before pulling back and looking at her, his smile crinkling his eyes in that delicious way it always did. The Ben she'd said goodbye to had had no little fine wrinkles, hardly any stubble on his jaw, but she liked him ever better this way than before. There was a maturity there that she found achingly attractive, shorter hair and a covering of barely there facial hair.

How was it that some men just got more and more delicious with age? He'd been handsome as a teen, all the women had liked him in his early twenties, especially in his polo getup, but now he was a man. Grown-up. Strong. *Real.* The kind of man you knew could protect you and rescue you, like a modern-day warrior who looked after those close to him. She could look into those dark brown eyes all day long and never tire of the view. And those lips…*mmm*, she loved those lips.

"I've really missed you, Bec. And I don't just mean that I've missed my friend. I've wanted you ever since that night."

She nodded, biting down on her lower lip. And she could spend all day listening to words like that.

He gave her a heartbreaking smile, then lay back again, his eyes toward the sky. She loved that about him, too. The way he could say something like that and not worry about hearing the words back. Confident enough in himself to say what he thought and leave it at that.

She watched him lying there and wondered what he was thinking about. Things had changed from old friends reunited to something more, and despite loving every second of that kiss, she was terrified. Alarm bells she should have been listening to were trying their hardest to signal, but she pushed them away. The bubble was going to burst soon, she was only delaying the inevitable, because as much as Ben was saying he liked her a whole lot more than just friends now, when he found out what she'd kept from him he'd never forgive her. *Never.*

CHAPTER SIX

"How are you feeling?"

Rebecca cast her eye over Ben. She would be feeling a whole lot better if she wasn't staring at his lips and wishing he was kissing her all over again.

"I think I'll be stiff tomorrow."

He laughed, a deep chuckle that made Rebecca tingle all over.

"Maybe dinner will make you feel better?"

Dinner? "You mean just here?"

He adjusted his baseball cap, one hand on the reins. "Gus thought we'd go out for dinner, just somewhere local, nothing fancy."

She nodded. If it was the three of them, then she had nothing to worry about.

"I've missed good Australian food. Prawns, Moreton Bay bugs, baramundi…" Ben blew out a whistle. "Man, I'm starving just thinking about all that seafood."

"I eat at our restaurant all the time, but I'm usually just standing out back having a few mouthfuls when I get a chance."

"So you don't get out much?"

"Nope." She grinned. "My girl is my life, and unless

it's a burger or somewhere with a playground we tend to stay at home unless it's work."

Ben was riding close to her, but the horses didn't seem to mind. Rebecca was worried about bumping knees or stirrups. Kind of the same worry she remembered as a teen anticipating her first kiss, not wanting to knock teeth and knowing it was going to happen anyway.

"You're a great mom, Bec," Ben said with a smile. "But you deserve a night out and I need the company."

She could tell by the look on his face that he wasn't just saying it.

"How would you know that I'm any good as a mom?"

"Because I can see it in you. You've always been so caring, so gentle, I just know you'd be fantastic." He laughed. "Maybe that's why I knew we'd never work out, because I need to find some troubled woman who's as screwed up as me about kids. You were always going to make a great mom."

She looked down, but when she eventually raised her eyes he was still watching her. His eyes flickered from the track they were riding to sideways, catching her as they passed. Every time he said something like that, every little comment where he was trying to flatter her or just plain make up for the fact that nothing had happened between them, it just made her resolve to tell him waver.

"So you're still sure about that? That you'll never be a father?" The words were almost impossible to push out, but she did it. "I always thought you'd, I don't know, grow out of it or something."

"Hell yes, I'm still sure," he said straight back, not missing a beat. "I'm not dad material. Never have been, never will be."

"But you're so different to your mom, you're..."

"Not going to be a dad." His tone was final, determined. "I can't be. I like being around kids, but I can't be the dad."

Rebecca shrugged. "I just know you'd be amazing, that's all."

"Well don't eye me up as your next baby daddy, okay?" he said with a chuckle. "Because it's never gonna happen. I'll be the fun uncle to your little one and that's as close as I'll get."

Ben was laughing but Rebecca could hardly breathe, let alone joke back. Her head was pounding as loud as her heart now.

"Bec?"

She forced a smile.

"Man, I'm sorry. I didn't mean that, you know, like you'd want another baby with a different guy..."

"Ben, it's fine, you were just joking around," she said. "Now tell me where we're going for dinner."

"Everything okay at home?"

Ben reached out to touch Bec's arm, realizing he'd frightened her. She'd jumped the minute he'd spoken.

"Yeah, everything's fine."

"So you're not about to run off back to the city on me?" he asked.

"Ha, not yet. But I've never actually been away from her before, not properly, so I might bail on you in the night. I'm usually back from the restaurant by 1 a.m. and then I crash wherever she is."

They both laughed, but Ben guessed she was telling the truth. "So I have this crazy feeling that your dating pool must be pretty limited."

The shock on Bec's face was palpable. "Yeah, I guess you could say that."

"Sorry, none of my business. I just mean that between working the hours you do and being a mom…" He ran a hand through his hair, wishing he'd just kept his mouth shut. "Sorry, just forget I said anything. I seem to be getting pretty good at putting my foot in it."

Bec sighed, her chest visibly rising as she took a big breath to fill her lungs again. "Since I had Lexie, I haven't really dated at all. The last few years have just flown past, one blur to another."

Ben watched her face, tried to read whether he'd offended her or not, and got the feeling it was definitely the latter. "I guess what I'm trying to ask is whether you're seeing anyone right now."

The question hung between them, the silence almost painful as she stared at him, her mouth open but not moving.

"Ah, no. No I'm not," she stammered.

"Good." He grinned, moving closer to her, every part of him focused on every single part of her, her skin warm beneath his touch as he circled his fingers around her wrist, his other hand rising to her face. "Then you won't mind if I do this again."

Bec was still silent, but she hadn't tried to move away, either, so he followed his instincts and did what he should have done over a decade ago when they'd first met. He'd always been so conscious of not ruining their friendship, of not pushing her and waiting to let her make the first move if she wanted things to change between them, but not now. Now he knew exactly what he wanted, and tonight that something was Bec. All thoughts aside, he wanted Rebecca.

When they'd been together last time, they'd been drunk. Right now, it was still daylight, he could see every expression on her face. Ben didn't hesitate any longer; he cupped her cheek and kissed her, lips closing over hers gently at first, testing the waters, then more firmly as she leaned into him. He kissed her just like he'd wanted to kiss her the four years he'd been away, stroking her hair, inhaling the feminine scent of her perfume. Her lips were warm and pliable, so soft that he forced himself to slow down, to tease her and be gentle with her.

Ben stifled a groan as she placed her hands on his chest, pushing him back ever so slightly, but enough that their lips parted. He stared down into eyes the most beautiful shade of blue, watched as her breath came in short, ragged pants.

"Slow down, cowboy," she murmured.

"Slow down?" He chuckled and leaned in, pressing another kiss to her lips even as she tried to push him away. "I've been waiting a real long time to do that again, so I'm kinda keen to speed things up."

Rebecca laughed, eyes locked on his as they stood still. It was as though everything else had disappeared and it was just the two of them—Ben wanted her, he always had. The only trouble now was that he had to make it clear to her that he wasn't looking for a role as stepdad of the year.

"I'm not sure we should be doing this," she muttered.

Ben shrugged. "Why not?"

"Because we've already made this mistake once."

"Maybe it wasn't a mistake," he said simply. "Are you sure it wasn't the right thing, only we did it at the wrong time?"

Rebecca looked unsure. "I can't commit to anything, Ben. It's just not that simple for me anymore."

"Then let's just keep it simple," he said. The thought of being around her daughter wasn't something he was sure about, only because he didn't know what to do around kids, but he missed Bec, and he wanted his friend back.

"What are you suggesting?" she asked, eyes wide as she clutched the front of his T-shirt.

"How about we take it one night at a time." Ben wanted her so badly—in his arms, in his bed, hell, he just wanted Bec back in his life again. He knew things were never going to be the same, but still.

"What about if it was just for tonight?" she asked.

Ben hated the thought of only having her for one night, but one night might lead to more and…to hell with it. One night was better than nothing, and he had plenty of time to convince her otherwise.

"Whatever you want, Bec." Ben ran his hands up and down her arms, his body humming with anticipation. "You set the rules and I'll follow."

She smiled up at him. "Slow. Just keep it slow, and you won't hear any complaints from me."

He laughed. "Okay, well in the interests of keeping things slow, I'm gonna go do a few jobs before we head out. You okay here?"

Rebecca nodded, taking a step back, her arms folded across her chest. They stood, watching each other for a moment; a moment where Ben could have said to hell with it and stormed back toward her again, but he didn't. Because he didn't want to scare Bec off, not before their night together had even started.

Rebecca wasn't sure if she was being fobbed off, or if he actually had some things to do, but she didn't mind. Still obsessing about *the kiss*, but fine. She was bound to find something to keep her entertained for the next while. With foals to watch and horses being trained, there wasn't any shortage of things to do. And it would at least keep her thoughts pure. No more sizing Ben up as if he was a juicy steak waiting to be consumed. Or maybe that's exactly what she needed to do—get him out of her system once and for all. Although maybe that's essentially what she'd just agreed to.

"I'll take your bag up to the house and leave it just inside the door. Make yourself at home, okay?" Ben called over his shoulder.

"Sounds good. Thanks." It was as if they hadn't just had that whole awkward conversation, as if things were back to normal again.

She'd dropped her small case to the ground and Ben bent to retrieve it. Rebecca almost reached out to touch his hair—as thick as Lexie's and almost the same color.

"I'll see you soon."

Ben nodded, his mouth twisted into a smile, and turned, her bag in his hand. She just stood there, watching him go, and wondered what the hell she was doing playing along as if nothing had changed. But despite wanting to look away, Rebecca's eyes were locked on the way his jeans hung from his wry hips, his tanned arms seemingly chocolate against his white T, and the way his stride ate up the dirt as he walked.

She was in way over her head just being back at McFarlane's, but she was damned if she was going to do anything about it until at least the morning. Lexie was safe, she was enjoying herself, or at least trying to, and the surroundings were breathtaking. Not to mention she wanted a good catch-up with Gus, too. *And maybe a repeat evening with Ben.*

Once Ben disappeared around the corner, so she knew there was no chance of being caught, she wandered back over to the yards. It was as if the filly was beckoning her, only she knew it was plain stupid to even think like that. The horse was probably just grazing, minding her own business, but Rebecca felt a pull toward the yard. She reasoned with herself that it was perhaps just because she felt confident after the ride, but there was something else there. She wanted to prove that she still had it, that after submerging herself in motherhood, and everything else life had thrown her way, that she could still change, go back in time. Be the one person to make a difference and connect with an animal and develop their trust. The only problem was that she wanted to find out alone, without the pressure of anyone watching. She hadn't lied to Ben when she'd said her fall and everything that had happened had broken her—her confidence had been in tatters and it had taken a long time for her to claw back from her despair.

Her feet walked her over in the right direction but her mind was screaming out to just head back to the house and read a book. Anything but put herself in a position of potential danger with a half-wild horse. Something about being here was making her feel like the fifteen-year-old who'd first visited the farm, full of confidence and not planning on letting anything stop her from fulfilling her dreams.

Missy was watching her, although she was pretending not to. Her head was bent down, but one eye was focused on Rebecca's progress. She ignored the horse, keeping her gaze focused on a spot to the side, not wanting to threaten her. This was about the animal deciding to trust her, and direct eye contact established nothing but dominance.

Rebecca looked over each shoulder but no one was around. She walked slowly until she reached the corral, then cautiously bent to maneuver through the railings. She was still wondering what the hell she was doing but she was in there now.

The horse looked incredibly beautiful. The sunlight was bouncing off her shiny black coat, brown dapples ever so delicately showing through. Everything about the filly was immaculate, from her trimmed tail to her glossy mane, and it made Rebecca think she had to be pretty special. There was a reason Gus wanted to persist with her.

"Hey, girl," she called, keeping her voice soft. It was hard not to sound nervous but she was trying her best. She knew the horse would have already picked up on her heartbeat, and she needed to slow down.

The horse snorted but kept grazing, unworried. Rebecca felt a familiar static in her stomach but forced herself to keep on going. This was her chance to see if she still had it. She seriously doubted it.

"You and me," she half whispered, "we're going to be good friends."

Rebecca stopped and waited. The horse still didn't look up. She decided to change her tactic.

Missy was still watching her, but Rebecca didn't acknowledge it. Instead, she sat down, careful to move slowly, crossing her legs and keeping her head down. She kept her eyes focused on the ground. Looking up, even slightly, would break the connection, break the trust, and make the horse look at her as a predator rather than a nonthreatening being. Now it was time to wait.

Sure enough, it was only minutes before the horse decided to investigate. Rebecca stayed still. It seemed dangerous, but she knew that so long as she was non-threatening and didn't spook her, there was little chance of injury.

It was nerve-racking, sitting so still, but she did it. Missy had her head low to the ground, looking at Rebecca, snorting. She moved forward slowly, inquisitively, and soon her muzzle was touching Rebecca. Just gently, her whiskers skimming the very top of her head, moving her hair ever so, blowing through her nostrils close to Rebecca's skin.

And then she sniffed at her face, tentatively, and Rebecca couldn't help but smile. It had taken this incredibly untrusting horse just minutes to come close, and now she was standing, unworried, beside her. A horse Ben claimed hadn't developed a bond with any of the men, not even him.

Rebecca raised her eyes, still not making direct contact. A flutter ran through her veins. *She still had it.* Like clockwork, the horse stayed calm, brought her nose close to Rebecca's, and Bec slowly reached out one hand. It was magical, as if there was an element of witchcraft, but Rebecca knew that sometimes a horse just needed a gentle approach, and sometimes preferred a woman over a man.

She touched her gently, then drew her feet up beneath her, until she was in a squat position.

"You're a good girl, Missy," she clucked. "A real good girl."

The horse had her ears pricked, listening. But she was no longer nervous, or afraid.

Rebecca reluctantly pulled up to her full height, one hand still resting on Missy's shoulder.

"I think you and I are going to get along just fine."

Now she was standing beside the horse, running her hand rhythmically back and forward along her soft coat. Rebecca loved the senses of being back around horses. The smell, touch, feel, everything just took her on a path back in time. It didn't mean she felt confident about getting *on* them, but maybe handling them was different. She still felt an element of control that she hadn't realized she'd still have.

"Well done."

Gus's croaky tone took her by surprise. She stayed still, not letting it break her bond with the horse.

She eventually turned around, keeping one hand on Missy, and was surprised to see Gus and Ben both standing nearby, watching her. Her face flooded with heat, embarrassed that they'd been there when she'd thought she was alone.

"Nice work," said Ben.

Rebecca could tell from the look on his face that he was pleased with her. His eyes were shining, a big smile stretching his face wide.

"I knew you had it in you still," said Gus, his focus on the filly. "I knew."

Rebecca looked between the two men. Ben was like a replica of his granddad—just a young, stronger version. They both had the same magnetism, the same aura about them, and she loved them both dearly, no matter how much she tried to pretend otherwise.

"You set me up." She said her words in an even, calm voice to avoid alarming the horse. "You guys knew I wouldn't be able to resist her and I walked straight into the trap."

The two men looked at one another and smiled. The kind of coconspirator type of smile she remembered only too well. She had been prey to their duping plenty of times as a gullible teenager.

"Maybe," Ben called out. "But I bet you feel damn good for doing it."

She tried to look angry and failed miserably, not really caring what they'd done. They'd been right—it made her feel good for proving to herself that she could still do it, because lately all she did was work in the restaurant. And if she wasn't working she was caring for Lexie. It was nice to know she was still good at something else.

"I'd say you really owe me that dinner now," she said.

Gus hobbled off with his cane, whistling a familiar tune. She knew he was pleased with himself. He wouldn't have doubted for a moment that she could resist the filly, but then he hadn't known how low she'd been, what had really happened.

Ben grinned at her and Rebecca almost felt she'd be safer staying in the round pen than being beside him. He was definitely more mature than she remembered him, and with that came a certain confidence that she didn't recall. The way he looked at her, it made her feel wanted, that he appreciated her. For two people who were meant to be friends, it was most unnerving. But then hadn't they just agreed that they both wanted to be more than just platonic, for tonight anyway?

"I'm looking forward to it," she muttered, more to herself than for anyone else's ears.

She watched his eyes as they danced over her. A delicious, deep brown that was dangerous yet kind. This was a man she trusted, that she had loved and still did, but every time she looked at him, there was an echo of guilt that she couldn't truly shake. If he ever found out what she'd kept from him, she knew he'd never look at her that way again. Which was why she had to let herself have this one night with him before she sent everything into free fall. Her telling the truth wasn't just going to affect Ben, it was going to impact on her own family, and Gus. She'd lied to them all, and after keeping her secret for so long...it wasn't even worth thinking about what might happen.

Ben was still watching her and she shook away the worries and focused on the filly again. She could enjoy the next day and night; beyond that she had no idea what was going to happen.

CHAPTER SEVEN

BEN SAT ON the wide veranda that stretched around three sides of the big old house, beer in hand, mind a million miles away. The low early evening sun drifted in through the thick wisteria, and he closed his eyes, basking in the quiet peacefulness of his surroundings.

There was something about Australia, something he couldn't explain, but being back was better than good, it felt right. He thought he'd never come back, but after a few years it was all he'd wanted. He'd always craved a family; even though he had Gus it hadn't been like growing up with parents and siblings, and his polo family had given him a team load of brothers to live and travel with. But now…now he wanted to be home, was ready to be home. And the only thing he wanted more was Rebecca. His only trouble was exactly *what* he wanted from her. One second he thought he knew, and the next he was questioning himself all over again.

Ben took another pull of beer and lazily opened his eyes. Rebecca was upstairs getting ready for dinner and he was just biding his time waiting for her. His grandfather had told him with a big grin that he was tired and turning in early, which he knew was rubbish, but he wasn't going to argue with him. He wanted some time alone with Bec, just the two of them. He only wished he had his head in the right place first. All he knew was he wanted her, and beyond that he didn't have a clue what he was going to do.

He heard a noise and finished his beer, jumped up and opened the side door that led back into the house. And then he saw Rebecca, making her way down the stairs, wearing tight jeans that showed off every inch of her super long legs, and a sparkly sequined top that seemed to make her eyes shine an even brighter shade of blue when she came closer. She was a knockout, pure and simple. All the women put together from the fancy polo days couldn't hold a candle to her.

"Wow," said Ben, realizing she was staring at him. "You look great." *She looked better than great, she looked freaking amazing.*

Rebecca's cheeks flushed. "Thanks."

He glanced up and down her body again, quickly, hoping she wouldn't notice. All this time he'd wondered if he was imagining how beautiful she was, but his answer was right there in front of him.

"No, seriously, Bec, you look stunning."

She looked self-conscious, slipping her jacket on and covering up far too much skin for his liking.

"So where are we going? You still haven't told me."

Ben glanced down at his shirt with the sleeves rolled up and his worn pair of jeans. Maybe he should have gotten more dressed up.

"Somewhere good. Let's go."

"What about Gus?"

"He's missing in action." Ben laughed. "Looks like he set us both up. Crazy old fool made the booking the day you said you were coming, then scurried off to bed just before as if he had the whole thing planned from the beginning."

He liked the fact that Rebecca still blushed. She might be all grown-up and a mom, but she was still shy when it came to anything happening beyond friends between them and it was an endearing quality. Especially after how bold so many of the women he'd met overseas had been, how brazen they'd been about wanting to bed any of the guys in his team.

"So it's just the two of us, then?"

"That okay with you?" he asked.

"Just two old friends catching up, right?"

Ben caught her wink and gave her a quiet smile straight back. He owed Gus a huge thank-you for giving him some alone time with Bec, and he wasn't going to waste a minute.

"You ready?"

"As I'll ever be. Let's go."

Ben grabbed his keys off the hall stand and checked he had his wallet in his back pocket, before touching his hand to Rebecca's back and guiding her toward the front door.

They pulled up outside Ruby's restaurant and Rebecca ran her hands over her jeans and gave herself a mental pep talk. She only had a moment alone before Ben moved around to open her door. It was funny, she never expected men to be quite so chivalrous when it came to everyday things like that, but opening doors was just the kind of thing Ben had always done.

"Not quite like our old haunt."

Ben had laughter in his eyes and Bec grinned.

"Nothing like it," she affirmed. They'd had a favorite burger place back in the day, when they'd been able to eat as much grease as they wanted and still be skinny as racehorses.

"You sure you don't want to jump back in the car and get a burger? Maybe some fries drowned in ketchup?"

Rebecca shook her head and felt relieved that she'd loosened up a little. It had been silly worrying, there was nothing to feel concerned about. Whatever happened, happened. She could worry about everything else another day. She needed to give herself a break, even if it was for only a few hours.

"I think this place looks like exactly where we should be headed. It'll be nice to be waited on for once."

Ben walked beside her as they crossed the short distance to the restaurant. It was nothing too fancy, not like some of the Melbourne restaurants she encountered in the city, but it was fresh and modern, and the food smelled great. She liked that she could partially see into the kitchen at the other end of the restaurant—she loved seeing the hustle and bustle of where her food was being prepared.

There was a lovely community feeling in Geelong, and it was something Rebecca missed in the city. It wasn't for everyone, but she kind of liked that if you lived here you would more than likely know a handful of the people dining. That the waiters would know you by name because this was your favorite local dinner spot.

As if on cue a waiter appeared, dressed in black with a smart white half apron tied at his waist.

"Ben," said the man, nodding. "Nice to see you back again so soon."

Rebecca felt her back bristle and wished it away, wondering if Ben had been here with a date already since he'd been home.

"The food was too good to bother going anywhere else," Ben replied politely.

The waiter motioned for them to follow, menus in hand, and Ben placed his open palm lightly to her back again. It wasn't any less surprising than the first time he'd done it, but she managed to gulp down her nerves.

She glanced around the room, seeing mostly couples and a few bigger tables. It was nice—intimate but not fussy, just how she liked it. And it was only early so the place wasn't too busy yet.

The waiter stopped and placed the menus on a table overlooking the water, one of only a few in the restaurant. Either Ben had fluked a good spot, or that crafty old grandfather of his had planned the whole night! She was pretty sure there was no luck involved, which only made her nervous all over again.

"I'll be back to take your drink order soon."

Ben waited for Rebecca to sit before taking his jacket off and settling down across from her. He cleared his throat. Rebecca raised her eyes from the water glass she'd been focused on, trying to quell the nerves jingling like chimes in her belly. It was stupid to feel so unsure, they had way too much history for her to even think about being uncomfortable just chatting and sharing a meal with him, but she couldn't help the way she felt.

"I, ah, didn't exactly plan this," Ben said, eyebrows drawn together as if he was trying to figure out how to explain the fact they had the most romantic table in the house.

"Oh, don't worry!" Rebecca tried to take her voice down a decibel from the high-pitched soprano it had altered to. "This is fine. It's lovely. Maybe Gus did it just to embarrass you."

The waiter reappeared and Ben selected a white wine from the famous Barossa Valley. Rebecca felt like chugging a whole bottle just to calm herself, although thankfully she had the menu to scan now, which meant she had something to look at other than Ben or the gorgeous view.

"What are you going to have?" Ben had placed his down on the table and was watching her.

"Me, ah, well…maybe fish of the day. I love the sound of the king prawns that come with it."

He nodded. "Hmm, good choice. I've been hanging out for seafood so I'm thinking the Moreton Bay bugs and prawns."

They ordered and Rebecca was left with no other option but to look back at Ben. It terrified her. Apart from the similarity of those eyes to Lexie's, she was scared of the intensity of his stare, of the way his eyes looked at her as if they could see right to her soul. Maybe that was why she'd never been attracted to another man since Ben had left. Once she'd had those eyes on her, no other pair ever lived up to it.

"You never did tell me what your parents are up to. What about your brother?"

Phew, she was happy talking family. Safe topic. She was just pleased Ben hadn't run into her brother himself, because then they'd have bonded over their mutual desire to know who Lexie's father was, which would only make the whole situation worse when she did finally come clean.

"Mum and Dad are great, they're making the most of retirement," she said, gratefully taking a gulp of wine. "They spend a bit of time traveling, and I'm happy running the restaurant. It means I can spend lots of time with

Lexie, but it does make juggling things tough when they head away on one of their cruises."

Ben nodded and leaned back in his chair. Rebecca almost felt the tiny bit of extra distance made it easier for her to relax, and at least she knew Ben was genuinely interested in her family. It had almost broken her own mom's heart when he'd left—she'd absolutely loved him and the feeling had been mutual, even more so probably because Ben had zero relationship with his own mother.

"My brother, well, he's a dad now, another on the way. Met a great girl through work and they've been together and happy ever since. But they have twins, so Lexie is always trying to compete with them and keep up with their adventures."

"What about you?" Ben asked, leaning forward. "Have you been okay, really? I mean, I know you love your daughter, but it must have been pretty tough doing it alone. Growing up so quick like that, aside from all the other stuff you went through."

Rebecca felt a mist cloud her eyes but she expertly blinked it away. She didn't cry, it just wasn't what she did. And this was no exception, just because someone had actually asked her that question and genuinely cared about the answer. She wished she could just tell him, that she could open up about what had happened and he'd open his arms wide and tell her she had nothing to worry about, that everything would miraculously be okay. But she was a realist, and she knew there was no amount of wishing that could turn what had happened into them being a happy little white-picket-fence family. If that was the case, she'd have told him right at the start when she'd first found out; if she had even a niggle of doubt that he was interested in being with her and playing happy families, then she would have told him a thousand times over.

"It's been hard, I'm not going to lie," she admitted. "But honestly? I love my girl and I like being in the restaurant, so life's pretty good. I might have given you a different answer when I was sleep deprived and exhausted a year or so ago, but I've found my rhythm now."

She knew what he wanted to know, though. Whether she'd had a man in her life, if she'd been alone all this time. There was a steely glint in his eye, a determined edge to his smile that told her he wanted to dig deeper.

"And Lexie's dad? He's never helped you out? Never been a part of her life at all?"

Rebecca reached for her wine again. This was not a conversation that she wanted to have right now. Not saying anything was one thing, but lying was something entirely different and she wasn't comfortable with it, not for a second. If she could just find the words to tell him, the right way to break it to him…

"How about you?" she asked, drawing on all her strength, not ready, not prepared enough to come out and say it yet. "You sure you don't have some gorgeous Argentinian woman packing her things as we speak to come live the good life in Australia with you?"

Their dinner arrived then and Rebecca smiled her thanks at the waiter, pleased for the distraction. Any break in the intensity of talking like this with Ben was a welcome one.

"You know what? You're the only person I've seen since coming home, other than Gus really." Ben took a mouthful and waited till he'd finished before continuing. "I just feel like I've missed out on so much time with Gus, and any time I miss out on now seems wasted." He cleared his throat, glancing up at the same time as one side of his mouth kicked out into a smile. "And no, there's no special someone. You think I would have kissed you if there was?"

Rebecca was pleased she'd already swallowed, otherwise she'd have choked. "Ah, well…" Talk about stunning her into speechlessness. "I guess not."

"Which means we're both single."

"I guess you're right." She had control of her voice now, her nerves settling into a more sedate ball than the writhing one they'd leaped into before.

"So back to Gus," she said, refocusing on her food and cutting the fish into a more manageable bite. "Have the doctors said how long?" she asked gently.

Ben toyed with his fork, the humor that had been in his gaze fading. "Maybe six months, maybe longer, but there's nothing they can do for him. He kept it pretty quiet, but I knew when he finally came out and told me that we were on borrowed time."

"He was great to us, wasn't he?" said Rebecca, smiling at Ben even though she knew it probably hurt like hell for him to talk about his granddad like this. "I don't think either of us would have turned out the same without him. He's a one in a million kind of man."

Ben smiled back at her, his eyes locking on hers, not giving her a moment to look away. She knew he felt the same—hell, his granddad had been the only stable thing in his life, the one person who'd unconditionally loved him from the day he was born.

"He's definitely one in a million," Ben said, grinning as he watched her. "And I'm gonna spend every damn minute I can with him so he knows it."

"Well, good." She ate another mouthful, looking out

at the water as she chewed. It was a beautiful balmy Melbourne night, and with the water twinkling under the soft lights, she could have been anywhere in the world. Ben might terrify her, but she also felt a pull toward him that was impossible to deny.

"Rebecca, the way I left, the way things went down between us before…"

"Don't," she said softly, interrupting him. "We don't need to talk about it. We've already been there."

He shook his head and reached for her hand, his fingers closing over hers in a touch so gentle, so caring, it made the tiny hairs on her arm stand on end. He squeezed, forcing her to look up instead of stare at where their skin was connected, his brown eyes focused on hers.

"I don't want you to think it was because I didn't care about you," he said simply. "What happened between us was years of pent-up attraction I reckon, and maybe if I hadn't been about to fly out it would never have happened. Maybe we never would have made that leap into dangerous territory."

"Yeah," she agreed. "It was like as soon as we knew you were going, all bets were off."

He touched her cheek, his palm so soft to her face it made her sigh. "I wanted you for so long, Bec. You have no idea how hard it was for me to just keep things between us as friends. But I always knew I'd rather have you as my friend than lose you completely, so I never pushed it."

She laughed, shaking her head. "Oh, I know."

He arched an eyebrow and only made her laugh louder. "Then why the hell did we decide we weren't allowed to take things any further? That we had to remain platonic friends?"

Rebecca shrugged. "I think it was just an unwritten rule, neither of us wanting to ruin what we had. I felt the same." She was numb just having this conversation, knowing that if she'd only said something, if they'd only... *it isn't worth thinking about the past like that.* Her heart didn't need to be damaged any more than it already was.

"I say to hell with rules, then." Ben's voice was softer now, but it packed an even greater punch than before. "Whenever you want to take things further, how about you just tell me this time around, huh?"

She cleared her throat. "I can't deal with complications, Ben, which is why I've kind of avoided getting involved with anyone." It was a lie—she hadn't let anyone close because no one had ever measured up to him, and because she didn't want to introduce Lexie to a man.

"How about we take this one day at a time and don't put any labels on what we are?" he asked. "We're friends, nothing's going to change that, but if you want more, well, then, what'd be wrong with that?"

Rebecca opened her mouth to reply, needing to set the record straight and say something, when her phone sounded out, its shrill ring almost sending her off her chair.

"Shivers!" she gasped, grabbing it and pushing a side button to mute the loud volume.

Ben picked up his fork and started to eat again, as if they'd been having a conversation about food instead of sex.

"Oh, it's home," she said by way of explanation, reading the screen. "Sorry, I'll have to take it."

Rebecca put her hand over her mouth and spoke quietly into the mouthpiece.

"Hey, Mom. Don't tell me, she's trying to convince you to give her ice cream in bed?" She laughed into the phone but her smile faded when she was greeted with a big sob.

"Bec, oh, I..." Her mom sobbed down the line at her. "We're at the hospital."

Rebecca felt an ice-cold shiver pierce her spine. This could not be happening. *The hospital?*

"Slow down. Talk me through it. Tell me what's happened."

Ben dropped his fork to his plate, worried eyes meeting hers. She shook her head and reached for her purse.

"I thought she was just coming down with a cold, but then her temperature spiked. About an hour after going to bed she went all floppy and the alarm went off on the thermometer and..." Her mom sobbed again. "I'm so sorry to bother you, Bec, when you're finally taking some time to yourself."

Rebecca was trying to keep her voice calm but tears had welled in her eyes like huge stones, her voice choking at the thought of something happening to her little girl. "Is she okay now?" She stood and indicated to Ben with a nod of her head toward the door that they had to go. He jumped up straight away, throwing his napkin down and pulling out his wallet.

"She's doing fine, but she's asking for you."

"I'm coming now," she said, sounding more confident than she was. If there was one thing she'd always been good at it was staying calm in an emergency. "Just tell her I love her and that I'll be there soon."

She watched as Ben quickly paid the bill, racing back to her and walking with her to the door. When she hung up, she took a big, shuddering breath and pushed her phone into her pocket. Tears filled her eyes, burned like fire as she thought about Lexie without her.

"Bec?"

She glanced across at Ben, let him take her hand when he reached for it, linking their fingers. "It's Lexie," she managed, her breath coming in short pants as she tried to stay calm. She needed to tell him now but the words were choking her.

"Whatever it is, she'll be fine, okay?" Ben reassured, forcing her to stop and holding her hand tight as he looked down at her. "I'll drive you wherever we need to go, and we'll get there fast. So don't worry." His eyes were determined, strong, sexy all rolled into one.

"Thanks," Rebecca muttered, keeping hold of his hand. Her heart was hammering, mouth dry as she tried to swallow. All she cared about was getting to Lexie, but if Ben insisted on coming into the hospital with her? Then tonight was going to get a whole lot tougher than it already was.

He ran ahead of her when they were close to the car, unlocking it and flinging open her door before running around to the other side. She jumped in and fixed her seat belt.

"I know she'll be okay but…" Rebecca took a deep breath. "What if it's something more serious? What if it's…?"

"Let's just take this one step at a time, okay?"

Rebecca nodded and sunk as deep into the seat as she could, wishing she'd just stayed home. Wishing she'd never said yes to seeing Ben, wishing she'd just come straight out and told him the day he'd walked into her restaurant.

"We'll be there in less than an hour, Bec. Just hold tight and we'll be there before you know it."

"I'm sorry about dinner," she murmured, wondering how things had gone from seeming so perfect to being so, so awful in such a short time.

"Dinner? Are you kidding me?" Ben made a sort of grunting sound. "You have nothing to apologize for. This is your little girl we're talking about."

The car traveled fast, gravel spitting out behind them as they left the small side road and hit the main highway back to Melbourne city. Once they were cruising fast, the road dark except for a handful of cars up ahead or passing them, he reached for her, his hand clasping hers again and settling on her thigh.

Ben glanced at her, but she couldn't look back. Tears stung her eyes again, a pain in her chest that she'd only ever felt before when she'd waved Ben goodbye at the airport and believed she'd never see him again.

"Hey," he said softly.

She took a deep, shuddering breath, then angled her body slightly so she could see his face.

"Everything's going to be just fine, Bec. I promise."

She braved a smile, but she didn't believe him for a second. He had no idea whether everything was going to be okay or not. And even worse than that? She knew, in her heart, that she'd never stopped loving him. Not for a second. Only before, she'd imagined that when he did come home one day, he'd have a glamorous wife on his arm; a wife who was happy not having children, who just wanted to be the fun-loving, polo-wife party girl. In that scenario she believed they'd never have even had a chance to rekindle what they might have had. *Never* in a million years had she thought he'd come home single.

Instead, Ben had come back the same rugged, down-to-earth guy she'd always loved. Single, strong and even more handsome than ever. And so instead of resenting him or knowing she'd been right in not telling him what had happened after their night together, she was thinking all sorts of dangerous what-ifs. And those kinds of thoughts were capable of breaking a girl's heart, if the slow, painful shattering of hers was anything to go by.

And it wasn't *her* little girl she was worried about. *It was theirs.*

CHAPTER EIGHT

BEN FELT UTTERLY HELPLESS. He had no idea how to comfort Bec, didn't even know where to start, but what he could do was drive fast and get her into the hospital before her little girl had a chance to get really upset about her mom not being there. He slowed to turn into the hospital, gripping the steering wheel tight beneath his fingers.

"We're here," he said, scanning for the nearest park and pulling into the space.

He looked across at Bec; she was white as a sheet and her hands were trembling.

"Come on, I'll take you in." He hadn't planned on going in with her, thought she'd rather just be with her family, but she looked like she needed some help.

It was as though she'd been jolted from a dream then, lurching into action and pushing her door open, eyes suddenly flashing as she glanced over at him.

"You don't have to come," she said as she hurried toward the front entrance, breaking into a jog. "I'll be fine."

He grunted, catching up to her. "I'll get you to your daughter and then go." Ben didn't say anything, but just in case they were somehow at the wrong place or they'd already gone home, he wanted to be able to drive her.

Bec reached for him and he took her hand, both of them hurrying through the entrance.

"Thanks," she said as they waited at the elevator, her eyes meeting his.

"Bec, I'd never leave you when you needed me. It's no problem."

She gulped and took her hand back, folding them tight across her chest. He frowned as he watched her fidget, wondering if he'd somehow said the wrong thing. But that was being stupid. She was a mom scared about the health of her daughter; now was not the time to go reading into her body language.

They stepped into the elevator and headed to the right floor, with Bec checking her phone for the hundredth time to reread the text from her mom.

"We're here," Ben said as the doors opened and they rushed out. "I'll go find out where to…"

"Lexie!" Bec's high-pitched call echoed straight through his ear. "Lexie!"

Bec pushed past him, running fast in her heels and then dropping to her knees and throwing her arms around a little girl. Her hair was dark brown with streaks of blond through it, her arms wrapped tight around her mom's neck.

Ben stood back, not needing to be part of it. And then Bec's mom saw him and a smile broke out on her face, the worried frown lines disappearing when she locked eyes with him. He slowly made his way over, opened his arms and gave her a warm hug.

"Ben! What a lovely surprise."

He kissed her cheek before letting her go. "Sorry I stole your daughter away for the evening."

She pursed her lips. "Rebecca? Don't be silly. That

girl needed some time to herself. Between the restaurant and her little one, she doesn't exactly take any time off."

"Her daughter?" Ben asked.

"Is going to be fine. The doctor said there's some nasty viruses going around, probably something she picked up in preschool. They said she was better off going home and having a good sleep in her own bed now that her fever has broken. The worst has long passed."

Bec stood up then, her daughter in her arms. "Ben, you can't drive all the way back to Geelong again tonight."

He laughed. "It's only an hour. I'll be fine."

"Stay with Rebecca," her mom said, patting his shoulder before moving toward her daughter and kissing her granddaughter. "Granddad's gone to bring the car around front. Why don't you meet us at Rebecca's?"

Ben looked at Bec, didn't want to do anything that would make her uncomfortable, but all she seemed worried about was her daughter.

"Are you sure?" he asked, eyes never leaving Bec's.

"You drove me all this way and we ran out on dinner. Having you back to my place is the least I can do."

"Well that's settled, then," her mom said, looking pleased with herself and striding off ahead of them.

"If we just change Lexie's seat into your car, we can go straight to my place and let my folks go home."

He nodded and followed. It should have been awkward tagging along with her family, but they'd been part of each other's lives for so many years that it just didn't. He blew out a sigh of relief as the elevator dinged and they all stepped in, watching Bec with her girl tucked tight into her arms. It was a dose of reality seeing her in mom mode, told him that he had to tread carefully, but it didn't scare him. Not yet. Because he wanted Rebecca. *He needed Rebecca*. And he doubted anything was going to change that, little girl or not.

Rebecca shut the door and padded quietly back to the lounge. Ben was sitting back on the sofa, eyes shut, and she hoped he wasn't actually asleep.

"Ben?" she whispered once she was standing in front of him.

His eyes popped open, a slow smile breaking out on his face when he saw her.

"Hey. Is she asleep?"

"Snoring her little head off already," Rebecca said. "I was going to snuggle her up in my bed, but she went happily into her own. Her temperature's fine and she seemed happy enough."

He nodded, his eyes on hers. She took a deep breath, staring at him, wishing she could just ignore the way she felt for him and carry on like she had been these past few years. But she couldn't. The one man she'd ever loved was sitting on her sofa, looking back at her, and there was no way she could resist him, even if it was under false pretenses.

Rebecca moved fast, not wanting to give herself time to doubt; one moment she was standing in front of him, the next she was straddling him, her thighs on either side of his.

Ben didn't question, he just went with it, hands on her hips as she dipped her head and kissed him, lips over his, tasting him, doing what she'd only dreamed about doing for so long. His mouth was warm against hers, his hands skimming up her body, fingers tangling in her hair.

She pushed back for a second, trying to catch her

breath, wondering what the hell she was doing. She'd resisted him for so many years, always determined never to be the one to make the first move, but after the night they'd just had…

"You okay?" Ben asked, one hand stroking her face as he gazed up at her.

"You said to tell you if I wanted this," she murmured, moistening her dry lips with her tongue.

He chuckled. "I did."

"Well, this is what I want," she said, refusing to give in to her insecurities. "Just tonight. Just once."

He nodded, his palm cupped to her cheek as he guided her back forward. "Your wish," he muttered, "is my command."

Rebecca relaxed into his touch, sighed into his mouth as he kissed her so gently, his lips soft to start with, then rougher, more insistent as his hands explored under her top, skimming across her skin. Her body hummed, every part of her on edge, reactive to his fingertips, to his mouth, to *anything* he did to her. She should have made him a bed on the sofa and gone to her own room alone, but she couldn't. Because she needed Ben like she'd never needed anything in her life before.

She worked the buttons of his shirt, undoing them slowly one by one, moaning as he took his lips off hers and started plucking gentle kisses down her neck, inching toward her collarbone. There was an urgency to his touch, to the way she was touching him, just like their first and only ever night together.

Just one night. She just needed one night with Ben. No questions, no thinking about the past. Just one selfish night of being with him.

She could worry about the rest in the morning.

* * *

Ben cradled Bec in his arms, wishing he could just carry her to her room and keep her tight against him for the rest of the evening. But they weren't just two single people anymore; she had a daughter to worry about, which meant he couldn't exactly be naked in her bed come morning.

"I don't want you to think I'm running out on you, because I'd like nothing better than to spend the next twenty-four hours exploring every inch of you, but I think I'll head home."

Her eyes popped open. She'd been curled against him like a cat who couldn't get enough of being petted, and now she was pushed back and staring at him.

"You want to go already?"

He dropped a kiss to lips plump from all the attention his mouth had been giving them. "I don't want to, but it might be easier. You know, with Lexie."

She sighed and dropped her head to his chest again. "You're right. You're absolutely right."

"You going to the polo next weekend?" he asked.

Rebecca nodded against him. "Half for fun, half for work. I need to oversee catering to one of the corporate areas."

He stroked her hair, the golden blond strands like silk against his fingers. "It'll be the first time I've ever gone for fun, although I have offered to play if they need me."

She ran her hand down his arm. "We never missed a year, did we?"

"No, we didn't." He tucked his fingers under her chin, tilted her face up to him so he could kiss her again and look into her blue eyes. "So I'll see you on Saturday?"

She nodded. "Yes."

"It's a date, then."

Rebecca shook her head. "This was a one-time thing, Ben."

"So says you," he joked straight back.

"I'm serious. We can't do this again."

He laughed at her solemn expression. "We'll see."

She stayed silent, but she didn't pull away until a noise down the hall sent her scrambling for her clothes.

"I think that's my cue," he said.

Rebecca paused and bent down, her lips seeking out his in one long, slow kiss. "Drive safely."

He watched as she hurried toward her daughter's room, waiting until she'd disappeared from sight before reaching for his jeans. Their lives had changed, hell, everything had changed, but now that he'd had her once, he wasn't going to give her up again without a fight.

CHAPTER NINE

THE CROWD WAS BUZZING. Women dressed in tiny dresses and super-high heels were drinking champagne, most of them completely ignoring what was happening on the field, their male counterparts swilling imported beer and looking more interested in the horses galloping past toward the goalposts. It was amazing being part of the event here, but she could only imagine what it was like in the exclusive areas of the Argentinian or London polo scenes.

Bec wiggled her toes, wishing she hadn't worn brand-new shoes. They were bright yellow stilettos and they looked fabulous, but her feet were protesting big-time.

"Hey, gorgeous."

A shiver ran through her body. Suddenly her feet were the least of her worries. Rebecca slowly turned, recognizing Ben's deep, sexy voice. She'd avoided his calls during the week, not wanting to talk about their night together because then she'd have to feel guilty all over again. But she'd known he'd find her today; the only question had been when.

"Hey," she said, his gaze filled with enough heat to set her on fire.

"You enjoying the game?"

Bec laughed. "Probably more than you are. I bet you'd rather be playing than watching."

He shrugged. "Hey, what's one year watching? I'll be back on the team before I know it."

"Confident, much?" she said with a laugh.

He took a step closer to her and her resolve died. So much for telling him that she couldn't be anything more than friends with him, for swallowing her fears and breaking the news to him that she'd kept something from him and couldn't go on not telling him the truth today.

"Are you all done with work?" he asked, brushing back one of her curls that had separated from the others.

She swallowed, stuck in the web of his gaze. "Almost."

"You look beautiful today," he said, looking her up and down, his smile taking her breath away.

Rebecca stayed silent. She'd be lying if she said she hadn't made a massive effort on her appearance because she'd known he was going to be there, because she knew she'd end up spending time with him. She'd brought a new dress and heels to wear, showing off more skin than she ever usually would, her hair set in soft curls that made her feel all '50s pinup with her bright red lipstick.

"We have plenty of food if you're hungry and…"

Ben laughed and reached for her hand. "In case you haven't noticed I've been trying to get hold of you this week. It's not your food that I'm interested in."

Rebecca wanted to flirt with him, to let him tug her toward the polo field so they could watch the final chukker, hear more about his time away and what it was like, so they could reminisce and have fun. But she couldn't lie to him any longer, the weight of what she'd kept from him burning into her conscience.

"Ben, we need to talk."

He laughed, linking his fingers with hers. "How about we talk later and play now."

It broke her heart to see him like this. This was the old Ben, the Ben she'd had fun with all her life, the Ben she'd always remembered. She wanted to keep this version of him committed to memory, because when he heard what she had to say...

Ben frowned. "Okay, come on. Let's go sit by the field and you can tell me whatever's worrying you so much."

She grabbed a glass of champagne from a passing waiter, taking a few sips to calm her nerves. Ben kept hold of her other hand and she followed him through the crowd, wishing they were just two people having fun, that she could let her hair down and pretend like nothing had changed between them. But she'd already done that. Now it was time for the truth.

"So what is it that you're so desperate to tell me?" he asked, sitting down beside Bec and facing the field. He was reluctant to admit it but he was kind of enjoying being on the sidelines, for one day anyway. His granddad was out there somewhere, close to the action, watching horses he'd trained and sold thunder around the field, and Ben was just happy to be back at the famous Melbourne Polo in the City.

"Ben, I don't think there's an easy way to tell you this, so I'm just going to come out and say it."

He frowned. The expression on her face had him worried, her eyes filled with what looked to be...tears? What the hell was she upset about?

"Bec, what's wrong?"

"You're her father, Ben. I know I should have told you

sooner, that I shouldn't have kept it from you, but Lexie's your daughter."

Ben froze. No part of his body moved, not so much as a quiver as he stared at her. The smile had long disappeared from Bec's mouth, and now his did, too.

"*What*?" He must have misheard her. She'd said he was...

"I know it's probably hard for you to make sense of right now, but Lexie's your daughter. I just couldn't..."

"Hold on a minute." He pushed back his chair, needing to put distance between them, to just stare at Rebecca for a moment and try to figure out what the hell she was trying to explain to him. "You're saying that our one night together, that I..." Ben jumped up, running his hand hard through his hair and grinding his teeth together. "I'm her *father*?"

He turned back to Rebecca to see tears sliding down her cheeks. She wasn't making a noise, silently crying.

"I'm sorry."

"Damn right you should be sorry!" he hissed. "I've been back here all this time, we've been with each other, and you never thought this should be the first thing you tell me?" His head was pounding, fury building inside him. "You had no right to keep this from me."

She nodded but he didn't care how upset she was. He'd come back desperate to see her again, to spend time with the one and only woman he'd ever trusted, and she'd blindsided him with this. How the hell could he be a father? He'd thought she was different, that after all the fake women more interested in fame and money he'd been surrounded with, that Bec was different. That he'd never have to worry about her not being honest. And now—he swallowed. Hard.

"Ben, I..."

"Mommy!"

The high-pitched voice calling out shattered every thought in his mind. He turned slowly, seeing a blond-haired little girl running fast, arms pumping as she made her way toward Rebecca. She flew into her mother's arms as he just stared on, watching in disbelief.

"She was so excited about coming." Ben stayed still as he listened to Rebecca's mother calling out. "Is she okay with you now?"

"Yes, she's fine," Rebecca called back.

Ben couldn't take his eyes off the girl. *Off his daughter.* All this time he'd been furious that some jerk had left Rebecca to be a solo parent, without ever guessing that that someone could have been him. And now that he looked at her...every part of him ached, with anger or resentment or disbelief; he had no idea which.

And now that she was here, he had to suck up every bit of anger that he wanted to hurl at Rebecca and save it for later. Because he wouldn't lose his temper in front of a child, and he sure as hell wouldn't do it in front of *his* child.

It was time for them to leave, and he wasn't going to let Rebecca get away without explaining everything to him. He wanted answers now and he wasn't taking no for an answer.

CHAPTER TEN

"WE'RE GOING BACK to Geelong." His words were meant as a statement, not a question. He stood staring at her, his height advantage suddenly daunting as he stood too close. "And Lexie's coming with us."

Rebecca stood her ground, refusing to be intimidated. She might have done the wrong thing in lying to him all this time, but she'd done it to protect her daughter and she'd do anything to keep her protected and in her safe little cocoon forever if she had to. She folded her arms across her chest, not giving in to the tremor of fear running through her body.

"I think we're best to just head back to my place."

Ben smiled at Lexie, touching her shoulder before moving to stand closer to Rebecca, his eyes burning into her with none of the kindness in his gaze that he'd just shown Lexie.

"We've got a lot to talk about, Rebecca," he said. "We'll go by your place and get Lexie's things, then we're heading to Geelong."

"You need to understand why I…"

"Enough," he said, his voice so low it was only just audible. "There's nothing you can say right now, Rebecca, so just don't."

When Ben finally turned away she let out a big breath she hadn't even realized she was holding. He bent to say something to Lexie, made her smile, then walked off. His long legs ate up the ground as she watched him, at the same time as she almost collapsed from fear.

"Mommy?"

Lexie's little voice was like an injection of energy to her body. She picked herself up and fixed a smile, bending down and holding out an arm to her.

"We're going on an adventure tonight. What do you think about going to visit Ben's farm?"

"Yay!"

Rebecca scooped her up and waved goodbye to her staff as she passed by where they were still working. They were almost done packing up and there was nothing left for her to do, and besides, there was no point in delaying the inevitable.

"Can we go now?"

Rebecca nodded and pressed a kiss to Lexie's forehead. "We sure can."

A fresh wave of fear washed through her, but she forced it away. There was no point in fearing the unknown. Trouble was, when it involved her little girl's future, it was impossible not to worry.

Rebecca turned and looked back at her daughter. She'd fallen asleep. They weren't even ten minutes out of the city and she had already succumbed to slumber. Her get out of jail free card was snoozing, which meant the interrogation was just about to start.

"She's asleep," she said, moving back to her sitting position as far away from Ben as possible. If she could have put a bigger gap between them in the car then she would have—in fact she'd prefer him on a plane heading back to Argentina if she had a choice right now. It might be her car they were driving in, but it felt like she was a prisoner.

He didn't answer. Rebecca glanced over and saw the tight clench of his jaw. She wasn't looking forward to this at all.

"What were you even thinking keeping this from me?" he demanded, his voice low. "You've had every opportunity to tell me, Rebecca."

She sighed and looked out the window. At the buildings blurring past, the inky-black sky, other cars whizzing by. All this time she'd wondered how it would happen. Whether Lexie would be a child or an adult, and now here she was, about to explain why she'd kept a secret that was going to ruin their friendship forever.

"Well?"

He clearly wasn't going to let her get away with staying silent, not now that Lexie was asleep.

"I don't know where to begin," she said honestly, her thoughts a jumble.

"How about starting with the part where you forgot to tell me I was a father." His voice was like ice, so cold he could have turned her to stone.

Rebecca knew he had every right to hate her, to be angry with her, but the steel-edged ring to his tone scared her. She had acted how she thought best at the time. Yes, it was flawed, but if it were to happen all over again, she'd probably do the same. She hadn't done it to hurt him, she'd done it because she cared enough about him to let him go.

"I found out when I was two months pregnant," she started, digging her fingernails deep into her palm to force pain other than what she was feeling in her heart. It had hurt at the time; the hurt had been so bad she'd been curled into a ball on the floor, cradling her belly, wishing she could make everything right and go back in time, her tears a puddle on the bathroom tiles beneath her. But this pain was stabbing, relentlessly washing over her in thick waves. She'd been so broken, so damaged already over everything, and then there had been Lexie. And from the day she'd been born, everything had changed; she'd had someone to love and pour all her energy into, and she'd never wished her baby away or resented her for a moment.

There was silence as she waited for Ben to do the math. She knew he would.

"So when I came home for that week, before I flew back for my first pro game in Europe, you knew then?"

His voice was incredulous and she swallowed down tears. A show of emotion now would only make her look pathetic, and it was Ben who should be upset and angry, not her. This was his time to be hurt, not hers.

"I'd just found out. When you came home I was so pleased to see you but, damn it, Ben! You had your whole future planned and there was no way I was going to ruin your life, to clip your wings and hold you back. I wasn't going to let history repeat itself."

"Don't..." He lowered his voice. "Don't give me that. I had a right to know. You can't put this on me when I never had the chance to be a part of our child's life, when you never let it be my choice."

She took a deep, slow breath. "What's the one thing you've always told me? The one thing you were always so sure about your future?"

Rebecca could see how tight his grip on the steering

wheel was, his body rigid as he glowered at the road. "Don't you turn this around on me, don't you dare."

"You said you never wanted to be a dad," she continued, undeterred. Now she'd started she couldn't stop. "You said you never wanted to be a parent because of your mom, because of what she did to you. That you never wanted to have a child and ever let them think they'd held you back from doing what you wanted to do with your life." She shook her head and turned to stare at him. "Tell me I'm wrong, Ben. Tell me I'm not saying the exact words you said to me so many times, that that wouldn't have been exactly what would have happened."

He was silent. The only noise was the tires on the road and it only made her mouth dryer, the pounding in her head louder.

"Ben…"

"Don't you dare put words in my mouth," he growled out, slamming one palm against the steering wheel. "Whatever the hell I said had nothing to do with *our kid*. Hell, Bec, I know what it was like to grow up without my parents. I would never do that to a child, to our…" His voice trailed off, as if he had no idea what to say next.

"I didn't even know if I was going to go through with it when you were back," she said in a low voice. "I was alone, I knew my family would be devastated, and I just needed the time to get my head around it all. To deal with…*me*."

Ben looked over at her. "What changed your mind?"

"You." She said the word simply, without hesitation.

"Me?" His focus was entirely back on the road now, but his laugh was low and cynical. "You kept it from me, but somehow *I* helped to change your mind."

"I loved you, Ben. I couldn't terminate what we'd

made." She quickly brushed stray tears away as they trickled down her cheek. "You have to believe me, that I wanted to do right by you, that I would never have kept it from you if I hadn't known you would resent me or her. Because I know you, I knew you better than you probably even knew yourself back then, and that meant I knew you'd stay with me, *with us*, out of duty."

He didn't respond and she squirmed, wishing she could get out of the car. It was starting to feel very claustrophobic and if she didn't have Lexie curled up in the backseat she'd have demanded he stop the car and let her the hell out.

"I didn't want to hold you back. I knew you'd feel obliged to do the honorable thing, and I didn't want to stand in the way of your future." She bit back a sob. "Look at your mom, what that did to you knowing that she'd compromised her medical career to have you. You forget that I was there for you when you tried to reconnect with her, that I saw how much she hurt you. I didn't want you to end up making the same mistakes as she did, when you didn't even have a choice in the matter."

"I still had a right to know." He punched out each word. "No matter what you thought or what I'd said or what we'd been through, I still had a right to know."

"I know you did," she whispered. "I know."

Rebecca felt dreadful, but she deserved it.

"I'm sorry, Ben, but I did what seemed best at the time," she said, needing him to at least understand why she'd done what she'd done. "It may have been the wrong decision, but I was young, scared and alone."

"I would have been there for you, Bec," he responded, his voice back to his soft, understated tone. "I would have stood by you. *Damn it*! You know I would have."

She let out a heaving breath.

"And that's exactly why I didn't tell you."

Lexie moaned in her sleep as Ben pulled her up into his arms. It was the first time they'd touched, other than when he'd dropped his hand to her shoulder earlier in the day. Shadows played across the girl's face as he carried her up to the house, and Ben watched each one. The way the light fell over his daughter's skin did something to him, hurt him somehow, and it took all his strength not to pass her to Rebecca. The last thing he wanted was to hold her, to be close to her when...hell, he didn't even know what to think.

He could hear Rebecca following behind, but he didn't acknowledge her. She could follow them upstairs, and when they got to the guest room she could take over. As much as he wanted to not be close to Lexie, something else was making him want to keep her close forever, to know what it was like to hold a child that was his own flesh and blood.

"She can sleep in bed with me," Rebecca whispered to him.

Ben nodded and kept walking. Lexie stirred but didn't wake, and Ben waited until Rebecca had rearranged the bedding before placing her on the mattress. He pulled the sheet and covers up under her chin and watched her long and hard before turning away. Rebecca was staring at him but he went straight past her and back downstairs.

Only hours ago, he'd been ready to ask Rebecca for something more, to apologize for leaving her behind in the first place and ask if they could be something more. If he was honest with himself he knew something had been wrong, that there had been more going on than her simply not wanting to leave her family, but he'd been desperate to get away and he'd decided not to ask questions. It had been Argentina, playing polo for one of the best teams in the world, or staying home and hoping that the girl who'd been his best friend for years might want something more. By the time they'd spent the night together, he'd already signed on the dotted line and cashed his first check from the team, and his flight was booked to go. It had been too late to change his mind even if he'd wanted to.

He was so angry with her his blood was boiling, but as much as he wanted to hate her and put all the blame on her, it wasn't all her fault. Maybe he was just tired, shell-shocked, but he could barely wrap his head around the whole situation. *A daughter.* She looked like him— her eyes were the same deep shade of brown, beautiful against golden hair the same color as her mom's. And from the desperation, the anguish he'd seen on Rebecca's face earlier, he knew there was no point in asking if she was sure about the girl's paternity. She was his; as true as the fact the sun would rise every morning, Lexie was his daughter.

Ben tripped his way down the stairs, his brain on the verge of exploding. Just when he'd thought life was going to get simpler, that things were going to be easy back home and he might have a chance of connecting with the woman he'd left behind, he was faced with this. With a daughter. A child of his own when he'd never even considered the fact that he might be a father in his lifetime, when he'd just gotten his head around the idea of being a fun kind of uncle to the girl if he and Bec did finally become more permanently involved.

A noise upstairs told him that Rebecca was on her way

down, which meant this was all about to become very real, very fast. He stifled the bellow he felt like roaring and reasoned with himself that a drink was what he needed. A very, very strong one. Or two. *Or three.*

Rebecca found Ben sitting at the kitchen table. He had a tumbler in front of him and she watched as he took a sharp swig of the golden brown liquid as she walked into the room. Unless he'd changed his habits since leaving, Rebecca knew that Ben wasn't much of a drinker. He'd always liked the odd beer, but definitely not spirits and certainly not straight. It made her eyes water just looking at straight whiskey.

"Want one?" Ben asked, raising his eyes.

She nodded. Rebecca had never drunk straight spirits before, not once, but she didn't think that now was the right time to say no.

Ben downed what was left in his tumbler before going into the kitchen, dropping a few ice cubes into his glass and into a fresh one, then pouring a small portion of whiskey into each.

"Jack Daniel's on the rocks," he announced, his glare still cold as ice.

She took a tiny sip and felt her eyes well with tears as she swallowed. Her throat was on fire as the liquid traced a fiery path right to her belly, then ignited all over again.

"It gets better," he said, downing another quick gulp. "Just keep drinking."

Rebecca didn't recall ever feeling quite this awkward, and especially not with the one person in the world she'd always been able to be herself around. She took another hesitant sip. It still tasted awful but not as bad as the first, and if it helped her feel a bit less anxious about the whole situation, then maybe it would be worth it.

"So where to from here?" Ben asked. "What the hell are we going to do?"

He was staring at her, which was worse than just seeing his angry side profile in the car, although maybe the alcohol was starting to numb her system a little because he didn't seem quite as irate.

"I know you hate me for what I've done," she said. "But I am sorry, Ben, more sorry than you'll ever understand. And I need you to get that I didn't do this to hurt you. The last few years have been rough, but no matter how tough it got I didn't want to be the one to shatter your dreams. Then as time passed, I didn't want it to be Lexie you resented." She shrugged. "*Me*, sure, but the idea that you could blame my gorgeous little girl?"

"*Our*," he corrected. "*Our* gorgeous little girl, Bec. The fact that she's ours is why it wasn't your secret to keep. Why you should have let me decide if I wanted to come home for her, if she was more important to me than my career."

"I'm sorry. There's nothing more I can say." Rebecca wrapped one arm tight around herself. "I'm sorry a thousand times over, Ben, and I need you to believe me." She bit her lip hard to stop the tears from falling.

"What if I'd not come back for another few years, though? What if we'd never bumped into one another? Would you have ever told me? Would I still be walking around not knowing that I had a beautiful little girl out there in the world?"

Rebecca realized there was no point in lying, because she wasn't going to hold back now that Ben knew. "No. I wouldn't have sought you out to tell you, if that's what you're asking. Not if you hadn't come home of your own free will."

He glared at her and took another long sip of his drink, draining the glass.

"Just because you're her mom doesn't mean you have a right to keep your daughter's father from her," Ben snapped. "I could understand a mother protecting her child from a violent person, from a drug addict, from some lowlife they're better off not knowing. But hell, Rebecca, did you really think I'd be *that bad* a parent? That I couldn't man the hell up and deal with the consequences of what had happened between us, of what we'd made?"

"No!" she almost yelled the word. "I wanted you to live the life you wanted to live, not come back here for me. For a baby you didn't choose to have." She bit back a sob, a torrent of emotion that choked her. "Don't you see, Ben? I know what a great dad you'd be, but you didn't want a child. You wanted to travel the world playing polo with the best players in the world, and that's exactly what I wanted you to do."

"I would have, though," he said, his stare unrelenting. "I would have dropped everything to look after you. I would have stayed." Ben shook his head. "Or I would have taken you with me. Either way I wouldn't have just left you. If you'd even just told me how you felt about me, not insisted that you wanted us to just be friends, this all could have changed."

"If you came home for me, I wanted it to be because you loved me, wanted me, not because you felt obliged to." She forced a smile. "I have always wanted a family, Ben, you've always known that. There was no way I could ever see us working long term because we wanted different things, which is why I wanted to stay friends.

And that was before I knew I was pregnant. Loving you wasn't enough."

"But *I did love you*."

He said the words so softly, so honestly that it was like a sucker punch straight to her stomach. He was lying, he was… She bit back a sob, shaking her head as she balled her fists. She'd waited so long to hear those words, and now she had, it was too late. Because he already hated her. Because she'd already ruined everything. But it still didn't change the fact that they'd always wanted different things.

"But was I wrong? Did you want the same as me?"

"No." He shook his head. "I loved you because you were you, because I thought you would never lie to me, never betray me." He shook his head. "I thought I knew you."

"Ben, please don't…" His words were like a knife piercing her skin, the pain so intense she could hardly stand it.

Ben watched her long and hard before standing. "If you'd been honest with me, everything would have been different. *Everything*."

He walked his now-empty glass back into the kitchen and slammed his hand down hard on the counter, his fury so fierce her hands started to tremble just watching him. She stayed silent, watching, listening, waiting. Ben didn't talk until he returned to the room, his eyes finally meeting hers, the storm in his gaze like a cyclone. She watched as he leaned against the wall, his big frame rigid with tension. She saw her daughter in him as she studied his face, in the line of his mouth and the slant of his eyes. That was how Lexie looked when she was cross with her, when Rebecca didn't give her what she wanted. Only Lexie's minor temper tantrums had nothing on the fierce stare and angry-bear hulk facing her now who looked as though he was capable of crushing anything in his path with his bare hands.

"Do your parents know?" His voice was low and husky, so deep it tugged every single one of her heartstrings.

She swallowed and dipped her head. "Nobody knows. Just me."

He raised his eyebrows in question. She knew she'd just sunk even lower in his opinion than she already had.

"I told them that I had a one-night stand, that it was some jerk I never saw again." She paused and looked up at him before going back to picking at her nails. "They had no reason not to believe me, aside from the fact that I've always been Ms. Responsible. The difficult part would have been believing I'd actually had random sex, not the fact the guy had bailed."

"And you're telling me no one ever put two and two together?" His glare was cool again, his entire face frosty.

"I guess you see what you want to see. You'd been gone a long time before she started to look like you, and thankfully no one ever made the connection." She sighed. "It's one of the reasons I never came to see Gus again, because I didn't want to lie to his face. And besides, no one knew about what happened between us, did they? As far as everybody else was concerned we'd just parted as friends."

"What would have happened if I hadn't gone, Bec?"

"We would never have spent the night together," she said simply. "We would have stayed as friends, we wouldn't be having this conversation."

"You're sure about that?" he asked. "I never thought

I was good enough for you, Bec. I knew that I couldn't give you what you wanted, but maybe we still would have ended up in bed together eventually."

"*You* not good enough for *me*?" She almost laughed. "That's the stupidest thing I've ever heard."

"I'm going to bed," he announced.

Rebecca merely nodded and stayed seated. She watched as he walked away. His shoulders were slumped, head down, hands jammed into his pockets. This wasn't the Ben McFarlane she knew. There was anger seething through his veins, she knew that, but she also guessed he was heartbroken. He would have thought he could always trust her, with the history they had behind them, and she knew he was probably as upset about her deception as he was about what she'd kept from him.

A painful tickle of concern played down her back, leaving her aching and worried. She could go and get Lexie and run, head back to her place since it was her car they'd brought, but that would only be delaying the inevitable. Besides, Ben would find them wherever they were. There had been a look in his eyes that said he was not going to be giving his girl up, and that frightened her more than anything.

"Ben!" she called out, jumping up and chasing after him.

He stopped, his hand on the bannister, about to walk up the stairs. He didn't say anything, but he didn't move, either.

"Ben, I want you to know that I loved you, too," she told him. "I loved you so bad it hurt, and if there was any way I thought we could have made it work, as a family, I'd have made that choice in a heartbeat."

He turned, slowly, his stormy gaze catching hers as he

stared, jaw locked hard. "Yeah? Well that ship has sailed, Bec. A long, long time ago."

She swallowed a wave of emotion, a tide of hurt and sadness exploding through her body. "Ben," she whispered. He turned and started to walk again, his back like a brick wall between them. "Ben!" she begged, louder this time, her voice full of unshed tears.

But he never turned back. She'd lost him. From the moment she'd told him, she'd lost him, and he'd just made his intentions very, very clear. It was over. Any little dreams she'd ever entertained about them reuniting, any fantasies she'd had about a perfect little family...that's all they were. Broken dreams and fantasies.

Ben was right. They were done.

There was no chance of finding sleep. Ben kept his eyes trained on the ceiling. Even in the dark he didn't feel tired. Exhausted in plenty of ways but not tired enough for sleep to seek him out. After the day he'd had he should be shattered, but he wasn't.

He was so angry with Rebecca the fury was consuming him; his body was on fire with a rage he'd never felt before. Which is why he'd walked away from her before he said something he'd regret forever. His grandfather had more patience than a handful of men put together, and he'd remembered that when he'd left Bec standing downstairs alone. He would have rather yelled at her, called her all sorts of names and slammed his fist through a wall; but he hadn't.

He had a daughter. *A daughter.* A little girl who was probably too young yet to have worried about not having a father, but he knew those thoughts would come soon. By the time he'd started school and seen all the other kids with both parents visiting on sports day and at science fairs, he'd realized he was the odd one out. Hardly any of the other kids had come from single parent homes back then. Add to that a mother who resented the time she'd had to spend with him, and he'd had a pretty lousy time when it came to parents. If it hadn't been for his grand-dad... He shook his head. He didn't even want to think about it. And now here he was, finding out that he was a dad, and no matter how furious he was with Rebecca, nothing changed the fact that he had a kid.

Ben lay another few moments, eyes shut, before getting up and pulling on his jeans, leaving his chest bare. He needed to talk to someone about this, someone other than Rebecca. Gus would be sound asleep by now, having left the game before them, but considering they might only have months left together, he doubted the old man would mind being woken. This affected both of them. Gus was now officially a great-grandfather, and Ben needed his advice. *Fast.*

There was a part of him that wanted to listen to Rebecca, that wanted to forgive her, but it just didn't seem possible. Not now. After all they'd gone through together, all the ups and downs over so many years, nothing changed the fact that she'd lied to him. Or omitted to tell him—no matter how he put it the fact didn't change. But he'd asked her about Lexie's father, that first time at the restaurant and then when they were out riding, which meant she'd had every opportunity to tell him.

He still would have been angry, hell, nothing could change how he felt, but to wait all this time?

There was nothing to like about what had happened, or how he'd found out, but he had to deal with the fact that he did have a daughter. That there were consequences to the night he and Rebecca had shared. The trouble was, he'd never have shut his own flesh and blood out of his life, never would have walked away. He'd never wanted to repeat his own mother's mistakes, and then he'd gone and done exactly that without even knowing.

He walked straight past the room Rebecca and Lexie were in and resisted the urge to push it open, not to seek Rebecca out, but to catch a glimpse of his daughter. When he looked at her, he knew he was a dad, could feel that the child who looked back was part of him. But the thought of living up to the title terrified him, just the idea of being around her or touching her, talking to her even, scaring him now that he knew he was her dad.

Ben gritted his teeth and kept moving, not stopping until he reached the other end of the long hall, tapping on his grandfather's door. He might not have had a dad growing up, but he'd had a darn good male role model. All this time he'd been scared of being a father because he didn't have his own to show him the ropes, hadn't had a parent to depend on, but he'd had Gus, and now that he was faced with being a dad to Lexie, he realized that he would know instinctively what to do, if he let himself. Because everything good in him, he'd learned from Gus. And no one could ever take that away from him.

CHAPTER ELEVEN

THERE WAS NO way to explain how she felt. Her entire body was aching, Lexie was jammed up hard against her, one arm slung over her face, and she was dead tired. Rebecca guessed that being caught out after years of hiding the truth wasn't meant to be easy, but she was exhausted. All night she'd writhed around on the sheets, trying not to disturb Lexie but desperately craving sleep—anything to give her some relief from reliving the conversations she'd had with Ben. He probably felt the same, racked with guilt and anger for different reasons. *And coming to terms with the fact that he had a daughter.*

Rebecca listened out but could hear no noise in the house. Both men had always been early risers, but given that it was Sunday she expected they might be a little later out of bed. Besides, she was desperate for a coffee to kick-start the morning. Running into Ben was a risk she'd have to take, and at the end of the day she was going to have to face him sometime. They were going to have to sort things out one way or another. To think that the last time they'd been together had been like heaven on earth, and now they were barely talking.

Once she'd pried herself out from her daughter's octopus-like grasp, she ran a quick brush through her hair, pulled it up into a ponytail and rummaged for a T-shirt. She looked down at her legs and left them bare—the T was superlong and she didn't have anything on show.

A quick glance back at Lexie reassured her she wasn't going to wake up while her mother was gone, and she slipped out the door, stopping in the hallway to listen out. She couldn't hear a thing. She tiptoed down the stairs, cringing when she hit a squeaky board and hurrying the rest of the way down. She padded across the timber floor to the kitchen, smiled when she inhaled the faint smell of coffee wafting around her. Gus must have made a pot last night; unless Ben had gotten back up from bed, she guessed the old man had been up, unable to sleep. Rebecca deposited the remains into the bin and scooped fresh granules from the container, just like old times. She'd always tried to be up first when she'd stayed over, making coffee and gulping down her first cup before Ben was awake, buzzed about training the polo ponies with him. By sunrise they'd always been galloping down the beach—Geelong was famous for being horse country, and the proximity to the beach for training was one of the reasons it was so popular.

The smell of fresh coffee made her smile. She could almost taste the strong flavor of black, sugary syrup just from inhaling it. A complete contradiction to her usually obsessive compulsive healthy, organic choice in whatever she put into her body, but it was a habit she'd never been able to break. No tea, herbal concoction, *nothing* could make her feel like coffee did, particularly in the morning.

She took a slow sip, inhaled the aroma and shut her eyes for a second. With her eyes closed, she could be any-where, drinking coffee at home, at the restaurant—hell, she could be at a resort in Fiji. Then she opened them, and looked straight out the window to the yellowed green grass fields beyond the house. But she wasn't *anywhere*. She was at the McFarlanes' place, she was with Ben, and she was guessing that at some stage today she was going to have to tell Lexie that she had a dad.

Ben stopped dead. He smelled the coffee, it had lulled him down from his bedroom, but he thought Gus had just got down before him like usual, when reality couldn't have been farther from the truth. Nothing could prepare him for what he found.

Rebecca had her back turned. She was fussing over what he presumed was the coffee press, and as far as he was concerned, she could do it all morning. He couldn't see much of her upper half, with the exception of the nape of her neck, which was exposed from her hair being pulled back. But her lower half. *Wow*. He'd never seen anything so sexy.

He hoped she had nothing on at all beyond that T-shirt, but he remembered she had always been fond of boy shorts. He'd hassled her about it for years, when she'd always laughed at other girls' obsessions with G-strings, but he guessed the boy shorts had become rather brief from what he could see of her bent forward. Because all he could see was an endless expanse of tanned, toned, slim legs, stretching up to what was an incredibly firm bottom. Hmm. It was starting to be a rather uncomfortable viewing experience.

Every single piece of him was furious with her still, even after talking to Gus late into the night, but the woman looked like something out of a men's magazine and he couldn't take his eyes off her.

Then she turned around. He didn't know what to do so

he just stared back at her. The reality was, he wanted to shock her, take action instead of just standing there staring at her. He wanted to kiss the surprised pout straight off her lips. Rip her shirt off to take his mind off the fact that she'd completely thrown him.

But hell, her front profile was even more tempting than the rear. She clearly had nothing on beneath the T-shirt, and it clung gently to her breasts. With her face free from makeup she looked more like the teenage Rebecca. Lips pillowy from sleep still, eyes slightly puffy, cheeks flushed.

"Morning." He wished he'd just turned and gone back to bed the minute he'd seen her down there.

She gave him a tight smile. Hardly the come-hither look his male organs were wishing for, even if he was angry with her.

"Hey," she replied.

"You're up early." He kept his distance as he moved into the kitchen and reached for a cup, not wanting to get anywhere close to her bare skin.

Rebecca shrugged. "Didn't get much sleep. But then I'm guessing you probably had a rough night, too."

Ben poured himself coffee and went straight back out to the adjoining living room. He could still see her but it was far less arousing than being within a few feet of her. She even smelled amazing, which hadn't helped the fact that he was trying to ignore her.

They were both silent, sipping away soundlessly on their coffees, so much hanging between them that needed to be said. Had to be said. They shared a daughter, and that meant they had a lot to work out. No matter how he felt about her right now, they had to find a way to get past it enough to talk.

"Lexie's still asleep?"

Rebecca nodded. "She usually sleeps in a little after a late night."

Ben frowned and took another sip of his coffee. How the hell could they go from being strangers to friends again after so long, and then feel more like strangers than ever again, so fast? It made him furious and no matter how bad he wanted to be the better person here, he couldn't.

"Ben, I think we need—"

A noise stopped her midsentence and the same noise made Ben put down his coffee. Lexie's little voice echoed out down the hall just before a blur rushed past Ben, hurtling at high speed toward Rebecca.

"Oh. Hey, honey." He watched as Bec scooped her up for a cuddle, but the little girl was wriggling again soon, running back in the same direction she'd come from and reappearing with Gus by her side. He had his cane in one hand and the other resting on Lexie's shoulder.

"Mommy, this is Gus."

Once they were both in the room she sidled back over to her mom, grinning at Gus as she held on to Rebecca's leg.

No, he's your great-granddad. Ben was on the verge of exploding, angry all over again, but one look at the sweet, innocent expression on the little girl's face pacified him.

"You okay, sweetie?" He listened to Rebecca talk to her, watched as she kissed her cheek. There was no mistaking they were mother and daughter, and the way Lexie gazed at her? It told him that no matter how much he hated what she'd done to him, what she'd kept from him, his daughter had been cared for by someone who adored her. There was no way a child could look at a mother like that unless she meant the world to her.

Lexie tucked her head against her mom's chest, peeking over at him. "I didn't know where you were."

Rebecca kissed her again before putting her to her feet. "I shouldn't have left you. Sorry, sweetheart."

"Then *he* found me," Lexie said, sticking her thumb out at Gus. "And he told me all about the horses he has. *Horses*, Mommy. *Horses*."

Ben stifled a smile. He guessed the old saying was true—the apple never did fall far from the tree.

"Gus does have some pretty special horses."

Rebecca looked up at Gus as she spoke. He was smiling, but he was also giving her a look. She could feel Ben behind her, still keeping his distance, but close enough to know that he was there. *Gus knew.* It was obvious from the way he was looking at them, and from the way he was going back and forth with his eyes from father to daughter as if he was putting two and two together. She forced a smile. It was tough to see them like this, to know that she'd caused so much hurt, especially if it meant losing the love and respect of two men who'd always meant so much to her.

"Lexie, Gus is Ben's granddaddy," she continued, trying to stop her voice from shaking. "Mr. McFarlane was very special to me when I was…younger."

Lexie smiled coyly at Gus.

"None of this Mr. McFarlane business," said Gus, swatting his hand through the air. Lexie giggled and put her head hard against Rebecca's chest. "We had a good old chat on the way downstairs, didn't we?"

Rebecca turned her body around so Lexie was facing Ben.

"You remember Ben from last night? Mommy's friend?"

"Yup," she said, smiling as Ben held his hand up in hello, his grin all for his daughter, his eyes lighting up in a way they'd used to do for her.

"Well, let's go get us changed shall we, miss? Then we can have some breakfast."

She carried Lexie back toward the stairs, the little girl still light enough to carry on her hip.

"Who's G-Gus?" Lexie got a bit stuck on the "G" sound and made Rebecca laugh.

"I told you," she said, pulling a T-shirt over her daughter's arms and harder over her head once they were in the bedroom. When she tugged it past her ears, she shook her head and grinned up at her. "He's Ben's granddad," she repeated, just in case she had actually forgotten, despite having told her twice already.

"Where's his dad?"

She suddenly didn't like the way this conversation was heading at all. Any conversation right now that involved daddy talk seemed dangerous.

"Ben's daddy? I'm not sure."

"What about my daddy? Why don't I have a daddy?"

Rebecca had walked straight into that one.

"Let's go back down for breakfast, huh?"

She had talked about her dad before. Or at least made up a father figure and stuck with the story. He was a very busy man and might never come home, all sorts of things, but as Lexie got older she had known it wasn't a question that could be so easily shirked, especially when she was trying to make sure her daughter felt loved even if she did have only one parent. And the lies no longer sounded convincing, not as she became older and understood so much more.

Lexie jumped up and grabbed her hand and Rebecca followed her out the door. She would have liked to spend some more time on her makeup but if this got her out of talking about daddies, then she was up for it.

"So, do you go to kindergarten or anything?"

Lexie nodded, a mischievous smile on her face. Ben was all out of ideas—there was only so much he could think to talk about with a three-year-old, but school seemed like a safe topic. He watched as his daughter munched on rice bubbles. Lucky Rebecca had thought to bring a stash, because they didn't have anything like that here.

He noticed Rebecca was taking a painstakingly long time to eat her toast. She was staring at the marmalade as if it was dangerous, not taking her eyes from it, nibbling delicately around the edges. Gus had gone out to do his rounds; hell, they were like some dysfunctional family, sitting together but not communicating.

"So I'm guessing you like horses," Ben said, refusing to give up on the conversation stakes just yet, even though he was as good as terrified just sitting here with her.

Lexie's reaction told him he'd finally hit the jackpot. Her eyes were wide, bright, and she slurped milk down her chin in her excitement.

"Have you ever ridden a horse?" Ben asked

"No." Phew, for a while there he'd wondered if he was ever going to come up with something they could talk about.

"You want to go for a ride with me today, then?"

"Like on a real horse?" Lexie had knocked her bowl forward and sent milk sloshing, but Ben couldn't have cared less. He finally felt like he was making some headway.

He chuckled. "Yeah, on a real horse. What do you say?"

"Let's go!"

"Ahem." Rebecca cleared her throat and smiled tightly at Ben. "Mommy needs to talk to Ben for a second, Lexie. You go and find your shoes."

Lexie sprinted off back toward the stairs and Ben glared at Rebecca.

"I'm not so sure about her riding," she said.

"She's coming riding with me today." Even if he had no idea how to talk to her or what to do, she was his and he needed to deal with it in his own way.

There was no chance he was negotiating on this. He'd gone all Lexie's life without making decisions, without having the chance to do things with her, and today that was going to change. He was a father, and that meant manning up and taking responsibility.

"Ben..." she protested again.

"No!" He thumped his mug down and pushed to his feet. "*No*. You had it your way, now it's my turn."

She cast her eyes down and Ben wished he hadn't spoken to her so harshly. He'd never spoken to her like that before and he didn't need to start now, no matter what had gone on between them. She was *Rebecca*. They had way too much history for him to be acting like a complete idiot. And besides, even though she'd lied to him, he still wanted her.. No matter how he'd like to pretend otherwise, his desire for Rebecca went beyond anything he was capable of controlling.

He wanted to hate her for keeping this kind of secret from him. He thought deep down that part of him did hate her, but it wasn't something he was enjoying. He didn't want to feel like that about her. She'd betrayed him, *hurt him* like nothing in his life had before, and although he knew it would be almost impossible to completely trust her again, damn it but he wanted to try.

The urge to yell and curse had passed, Gus had seen to that when they'd talked, but anger wasn't something that could just be forgotten. But it was starting to fade, more a dull ache now than a bone-deep fury. And part of him knew that he had to take some of the blame. He *had* always made his thoughts on parenthood blatantly obvious. He had left her behind and moved on with his life, even though he'd known there was more between them than just friendship. But then deep down he'd never really thought he was good enough for her. He'd grown up since then, realized what kind of man he was and what he wanted, but back then he hadn't.

His mind was a jumble of thoughts and he needed to get outside. *Outside with my horses, and away from Rebecca.*

Lexie appeared behind her mother and Ben forced the smile back on his face. He didn't want their daughter to see them arguing, not when it was the first time he'd actually spent time with the kid.

"You ready?" Ben asked.

Lexie looked down at her feet and shrugged. Ben stifled a laugh and bent down, putting the girl's hand on his shoulder to balance her, then removing each shoe and putting it on the correct foot, hands shaking. He laced them up, wishing just the simple act of helping her on with her shoes didn't put the fear of God in him.

He knew Rebecca was watching them, and as Lexie reached for his hand, he closed his eyes. His daughter had just felt comfortable enough to put her small hand in his, and her skin was warm and sticky, probably still covered in some of her breakfast. Soft and innocent in a way that an adult's skin just wasn't anymore—hell, his probably felt rough as anything to her. It took every inch of his willpower not to tug his hand out, because nothing about holding on to her felt any kind of natural.

Ben turned back to Rebecca. Tears welled in her eyes that he didn't want to acknowledge. He didn't want to dig the knife deeper, he *wanted* to let go, but a familiar pool of anger was beginning to form behind his eyes again, and he just couldn't help himself.

"I don't know why you kept this from me, Rebecca," he said, voice low, barely more than a whisper. "Honestly, I just don't understand." Lexie wouldn't know what they were talking about, he wasn't saying anything that would upset the girl, but he needed Rebecca to know. She'd hurt him badly, and it wasn't something he could just take on board and move on from that easily.

Rebecca was watching them, tears soundlessly streaming down her cheeks as she stared at Lexie holding his hand. "I'm sorry," she said. "I'm sorry a thousand times over."

Something changed in Ben then, something that he hadn't even known he was capable of. Because he knew. He knew then, without a doubt, from the emotion written all over her face and the pain in her eyes, that it wasn't because she'd wanted to hurt him that she'd done what she'd done. That when she'd told him she was trying to protect him, and do the best for their daughter, that without a shadow of doubt she'd meant it. But he'd had a right to know, to make his own decision about being involved in Lexie's life, and what he wanted was his daughter, to be her dad. Right now it was the only clear thing in his seriously screwed-up thoughts. But then maybe if he hadn't had the time away, hadn't had the chance to grow and follow his dreams, he wouldn't be feeling like this.

Lexie must have heard the catch in her mother's voice and turned, dropping Ben's hand when she realized her mom was crying.

"Mommy, what's wrong?"

Rebecca wiped at her eyes and braved a smile. Lexie stood in front of her, her eyebrows pulled together, worried about her mom. Rebecca gave her a quick hug before pressing their foreheads together, eyes on hers as she gave her a look that seemed to reassure her that everything was okay.

"I'm just excited about you going out to see the horses, that's all."

"Really?" Lexie asked, clearly not entirely convinced.

"Yes, really. You go for it, cowgirl."

As Lexie scooted toward the door she squared her shoulders and stood, taking a few steps toward Ben. The look on her face was different now; she wiped her tears away and took a visibly deep breath as he watched her.

"I did what I thought was right, Ben," she said, wrapping her arms around herself as she stared straight into his eyes. "I know now that it wasn't, and when I said last night that I'd do the same thing all over again? That I wouldn't change anything? I was lying. I'd tell you in a heartbeat, Ben." She forced her lip to stop quivering. "As soon as I saw you with her, I knew it was the wrong thing. That you needed to be the one to make that decision. But at the time all I could think about was protecting her and not holding you back."

"You're a great mom," he said, staring straight at her, wanting to wrap her into a big hug and tug her hard against him. "But you're one hell of a lousy friend."

Rebecca sighed. "Yeah. I was. And for the record, you would have been a great dad."

He didn't like the past tense. "I'll make up for it," he said, surprised by how deep and raspy his voice was. "She ain't growing up without a dad, not anymore." What he needed was to know when they were going to tell her, but he didn't want to argue. They could take it one step at a time. *Starting now.* Which would give him the chance to figure out how to act naturally around her, how to just be himself and not be scared of her as if she was some fragile doll that he could break.

He was home, and now he had a daughter, and that meant he had to grow the hell up and accept his responsibilities. He wasn't ever going to make the same mistakes his mother had; his child was going to come first, there was no other option acceptable to him.

Ben walked out the door and found Lexie standing on the porch, her eyes trained on his, excitement just about bursting from her.

"Come on, Ben!"

He grinned and took her hand, letting her enthusiasm rub off on him. He'd always been terrified of being a dad, but suddenly being with Lexie, having her hand in his, was the most exhilarated he'd felt in ages. *Except for having Bec in his arms the other night.* He still had no idea what to do with her, how to act, but he was darn well going to try.

CHAPTER TWELVE

BEN PROPPED LEXIE up on the side of the corral and laughed at the serious look on her face. The kid was so excited she looked as if she could hardly breathe.

"You sit there, darlin'," he told her, putting one hand on either side of Lexie's legs and bending to look her in the eye. "I'm gonna bring Willy around so you can have a ride."

Lexie's eyes were open so wide they were about to pop. Ben gave her a wink and spun around to go get the horse.

"No running away, okay?" he called.

She was cute—shy but quietly determined. He liked that about her.

He caught Willy and gave the horse a scratch as they walked, watching Lexie as she kicked her legs against the timber she was sitting on.

"Lexie, I'd like you to meet Willy."

She looked nervous, her bottom lip grabbing under her top teeth. He hesitated then reached out for her when he saw her wobble, not sure how to touch her. She was so tiny and cute, he just didn't know what to do.

"Have you ever patted a horse before, Lexie?"

She shook her head and Ben tried not to freeze when

she looped an arm around his neck so he could swing her down, just tried to behave as naturally as she was. She kept her legs firmly locked around his hips so he couldn't let her go, taking the initiative. It was reassuring to know he could just follow her lead.

"He's a real sweetheart, this one. And he loves to be stroked just here," Ben said, laughing when she gave him a superfast touch to the nose. "You know, your mom rode Willy just the other day."

Lexie turned to look at Ben, her brown eyes so innocently turned upward in question, as though she didn't believe that her mom had ever ridden a horse, let alone this one. Then she went back to tentatively touching Willy's nose, before letting her hand drift a little higher to touch the horse on the forehead.

"I thought you and I could go for a ride together on Willy. You can sit up front and we can go for a wander around the farm."

"Okay." Her voice was so quiet it was almost a whisper.

Ben popped her back up on the fence, tied Willy up a little bit farther away and hurriedly put on the horse's saddle and bridle. He'd worry about brushing him down later. He gave him a quick pat and untied his rope, turning back to Lexie.

"So I'm gonna lift you up nice and slow, then I'll hop up behind you."

He went to scoop Lexie up but received a quivering-lipped look that told him he was about to have a crash course in how to deal with tears if he didn't do something fast. He stared at her, trying to figure out what the heck he was supposed to do.

"Ah, how about I hop on first then lift you up?"

Lexie nodded and Ben quickly did exactly that, mounting, then reaching down for her. He hauled her up so her tiny body fitted snugly against his. She tucked back tightly against him, resting her head against his chest as he kept one hand pressed firmly to her, the other looped through the reins.

"You okay, sweetheart?"

She nodded, the movement gentle against his chest. "Uh-huh."

Ben bent his head to talk into his daughter's ear, tried to just do what felt natural to him. He so desperately wanted to whisper to her, to tell her he was her dad, that she had a father who loved her, but he didn't. *Couldn't.* No matter how angry he was with Rebecca, he wanted it to be right. *He wanted to get this right.* Finding out she had a dad was special, and it wasn't something he wanted to muck up. Although finding out he had a dad who wanted him would have been a bonus no matter how it had happened where he was concerned. He'd spent the latter half of his teens desperate to find his father, and when he had finally tracked down the guy who was biologically related to him, it had been the worst thing he'd ever done. His mom was lousy, but his father didn't even want to acknowledge he existed.

"Lexie, riding's all about relaxing," he told her. "Sit back against me, feel every step the horse takes. I want you to feel safe up here. There's nothing to fear."

He felt Lexie's body soften slightly. Her head knocked back again to rest on Ben's chest, which sent his heart thumping overtime. They rode like that for a few minutes, just circling around the large round pen.

"You feeling it?"

"Yup."

"You sure?" he asked, starting to relax himself, no longer so worried about having her body against his, being in charge of someone so tiny.

"Yeah, Ben," she said, wriggling against him. "I'm feelin' it."

He chuckled and pulled her closer to him, before steering Willy out of the yard so they could ride out over the farm. He was pretty sure he'd just fallen head over heels in love.

Rebecca was shaking, her entire body as nervous as a bunch of keys jangling. She'd decided there was nothing more terrifying than seeing her daughter sit on a horse, followed very closely by the terror of knowing her little girl was sitting with her father. Would Ben tell her? How would Lexie react? She knew her daughter would be thrilled to have a dad, but what did it mean for them? Would Ben ever trust her or want to be around her again? Would he go for joint custody? Her body shuddered as she took a deep, worried breath.

She'd started out watching them from a distance, standing on the porch, on the one hand nostalgic about what could have been, on the other so scared of what was going to happen next. She and Ben had been so close, almost as if they were on the cusp of reuniting, living in a fantasy world where she didn't have some massive lie she was keeping from him. And the night they'd had? She groaned just thinking about it.

When she thought of Ben, her mind was full of memories, all of them good except for the way she'd hurt him the day before. Riding, yes, but so many other things, too. They'd had so many first times together: a stolen pack of cigarettes from Gus they'd smoked till they were blue in the face—to her knowledge neither of them had touched a cigarette since, but she remembered that day with a smile; they'd gotten drunk together for the first time; learned how to play polo, how to start a horse under saddle. The point was, they had been together every one of those times.

She and Ben went back so far. Sticky fingers from cola and hotdogs at the local fair, red faces from nasty sunburn, sitting out by the river talking, star-fished on the grass. There had been a time they'd shared everything, talked about everything, been everything to one another. *Been friends.*

And now she'd ruined it. But she had to think about it with no regrets. She was a mother now, her priority had been her daughter ever since she'd given birth to her. Losing out on a chance to be with Ben was a result of what she'd kept from him, and now Lexie had to be her number one. She might have thought Ben would never come home, not after all this time, but the past was the past. Lexie was her future, because she was fairly certain Ben would never forgive her enough for them to go back to where they'd been, to even be friends again, let alone the lovers they'd been only a week ago.

She heard the gentle clip-clop of hooves on the hard packed earth and raised her eyes again. Rebecca had become so engrossed in her thoughts she'd dropped her head and been gazing at her own toes. Willy was coming her way, and that meant she knew where Ben was heading. He was off toward the river, the place they'd always raced to on his crazy polo ponies.

Ben had his head dipped low, talking to Lexie, her little girl smiling with one of her hands on the reins, Ben's large ones covering hers. For a guy who hadn't known what the hell to do with the little girl a short time ago, he looked pretty at ease now.

She was on the bottom step of the porch now and Lexie saw her. She took one hand off the pommel and waved fiercely to her, a grin from one ear right to the other.

"Hey, honey," she called.

Her heart was screaming out, she wanted nothing more than to pull her down and protect her, but she knew Lexie was in good hands. Ben was one of the best horsemen she knew, and if her girl was safe on any horse, it was on a horse with Ben. *Lexie's dad*, she thought. It just didn't sound right. Even though she'd known all this time, it had seemed more like a dream. A fantasy. But Daddy was most certainly back in their lives.

As she waved Lexie on, with her so gleefully smiling and waving back, Rebecca sucked down her pride and glanced at Ben. The look she received in return sent prickles spiking over her entire body. They rode by, but Ben's eyes never left hers—a piercing gaze that conveyed everything. *His hurt, his disappointment, his distrust.* But there was something else; the anger she'd seen in his gaze earlier seemed to have softened somehow, a look that made her hope…she sucked in a big lungful of air. She wasn't even going to think it, because she'd only end up heartbroken all over again.

All that mattered was that Lexie was smiling, and that from this day on, she'd have a dad who loved her. Lexie had always had a mom who'd do anything for her and grandparents who thought the world of her, but nothing would beat adding a dad to the mix. *Nothing.*

* * *

They still weren't back. It had been two hours since they'd left, and still they hadn't returned. Lexie would be starving hungry, grumpy as hell probably, and Ben should have known better than to take so long. Rebecca knew only too well that something could have happened...a snake bite, a fall, *anything*!

"That's not doing you any favors."

Gus's no-nonsense voice snapped her out of it. She looked up from her seat on the edge of the porch. Eyes that had been trained on the direction they'd left in finally taking a break.

"That worrying. It's no good," Gus said.

"They've just been a long—"

"They're fine." He gave her a sharp look and sat down beside her.

Rebecca started to cry and Gus didn't even attempt to comfort her. She sat there with tears dripping steadily down her cheeks and he didn't say a word until she'd sucked all her sadness back and cleared her throat.

"What you did was wrong, girl," he said, his voice even deeper than she'd remembered it all these years.

She nodded. She'd had a feeling Ben would have confided in him, but knowing she'd let Gus down hurt, too. Seeing him again now, she knew he deserved to be a grandfather. He had been so great to her, and Lexie would have enjoyed spending time with him. It was all such a mess, and the worst part was that it was all her doing. She'd tried so desperately to do the right thing, and all she'd done was make everything a hundred times worse than it had to be.

"You were young, Ben was leaving," he said, before

making a deep grunting noise in his throat. "Bad choices, but I can understand. They weren't choices you'd have made if he'd been home or you'd been able to go with him. Not to mention the two of you needed your heads banged together for not seeing that you were supposed to be more than friends."

Rebecca looked up, hardly able to believe what he was saying.

"You can?"

"Yes, Rebecca. I can." He turned to face her. "But I'm not the one you have to convince."

As if on cue, the trio appeared. Willy plodding along, Ben sitting straight, and her girl, *their girl*, slumped back. Fast asleep.

She looked over at Gus but he was gone, the light tap of the door falling shut signaling that he'd headed back inside again. Part of her wanted to flee before facing another discussion with Ben, but another part of her knew she had to face up to her decision and meet the consequences. Once the weekend was over, she was going to have to admit her lie to her family, and some of her friends, so things weren't exactly going to get any easier.

There was an awfully strained feeling between them, despite them both trying their best for Lexie's sake. Rebecca watched Lexie as her eyes drooped slightly, despite continuing to munch on her sandwich. The kid was starving, but once her blood sugar levels were restored, she'd be bouncing off the walls again.

"You want a nap?" Rebecca asked, as Lexie stuffed the last piece into her mouth.

"Uh-uh," she managed, her cheeks bulging like a little chipmunk settling in for winter. "Ben told me I could meet the foals."

She looked his way and Ben just shrugged. Rebecca knew better than to say no without softening her response, especially when Lexie was having so much fun, so she tried her best to talk around it.

"Maybe later sweetheart."

"Why?"

"Because the foals need a midafternoon nap, too. They're only babies, remember."

That seemed to satisfy her, and she managed to get her upstairs and settled in for a sleep, tucking her up in bed with a blanket pulled up to her chin. She stroked her head and stared down at her, watching as she drifted off to sleep, before heading back to face Ben. He was thumbing through the paper, but she could tell he wasn't really interested. He was turning the pages too fast to actually be reading them.

"We'll be heading off later this afternoon."

Her words seemed to cut through the invisible barrier he'd erected between them.

"When?" he asked, looking up.

"Doesn't matter when, so long as we're home before dark. I have to work tomorrow."

Ben nodded and went back to flicking through the paper. It was so unlike him to be rude, to be so distant. She had no idea what to do. Rebecca felt more alone now somehow than ever before. Worse than being without a loving man by her side giving birth, worse than thinking Lexie would resent her for not giving her a two-parent family, just the pits. It was like watching from above, not actually being part of the scene unfolding before her.

Because in all the years she'd known Ben, all the times they'd been through, she'd never known him to be so resentful, so angry, so brooding.

"Lexie wanted to know when she could come here again. When she'd be able to stay for longer," Ben said, the fact that he was talking to her taking her by surprise.

"What did you say?" she asked.

"I said sometime soon." He met her gaze. "But what I should have said was all the time."

"You can't keep blaming me," she said, refusing to be the bad guy forever. "You know now, so the only thing left to do is figure out how we're going to make this work. I was wrong, I was stupid, but I can't take it back."

"The only reason I know, *Rebecca*, is because you were forced to tell me." Ben ground out his words.

He stood up and went to walk outside, his fists balled at his sides as he moved farther away from her.

"I loved you, Ben," she said to his back. "I loved you then and I love you now, and that's exactly why I didn't tell you. You want the truth? Well that's it. But the day you came back there was no doubt in my mind that I had to tell you, it was just a matter of when. *And how.*"

When he kept on walking, not stopping to look back, not acknowledging her words, not saying anything, she realized it was over. If he was going to forgive her, he would have done it by now.

Rebecca ran up the stairs to the bedroom. Lexie had her arms flung out, in deep sleep, but she couldn't wait for her to wake. Instead, she threw their things into the two bags she had, not stopping to fold, just getting everything of theirs packed and ready to go. It only took her one trip down to fill the car, then she was back upstairs, pulling Lexie into her arms.

She murmured, eyes half-open, and Rebecca smiled bravely down at her. It took her only a moment to put her in the car, fixed into her seat, and then she was behind the wheel. It was time for her to go home and give Ben some space.

CHAPTER THIRTEEN

REBECCA WATCHED LEXIE as she zoomed around with her cousins. Her brother, Ryan, and his wife, Lucy, had twin boys and they ran her girl ragged. They had a blast together all the time, and it wasn't as if she was planning on giving Lexie any siblings, so it was the perfect balance. She couldn't imagine letting anyone else close to them, let alone marrying a man and having more children. And now that she'd ruined everything with Ben... She shook her head, trying to push him from her mind. Being with him the other night had made her hope, *yearn*, for more, but she'd always known what the reality was going to be.

The atmosphere was relaxed and happy, as it always was when her family got together, and that's what she had to focus on. Now that her parents had retired and left her to the day-to-day running of the restaurant, they either enjoyed long days looking after their grandkids, putting on family lunches, or traveling around Australia. She wouldn't give up their Sundays together for anything—family meant everything to her, and if she hadn't had them she had no idea how she'd have pulled through the last few years.

And then she was back to Ben again. She took a deep breath, watching the kids as they ran around the backyard. Every second she had to herself, every moment of not doing something, was spent thinking about him. About the way she'd left, about the look on his face when he'd been teaching Lexie to ride—*everything*. He'd been so awkward with her at first, but it hadn't taken him long to look more at ease.

Her dad called out from the barbecue and she gathered herself up, cringing when she realized her bottom was wet from the grass.

"Meat's ready!" her father hollered, in case they hadn't heard him the first time.

Rebecca's mother appeared at the open door to the house, carrying a big salad bowl. She smiled at her daughter as she passed and Bec felt nervous all over again. Today was the day she was going to tell them. The secret was out and it was time she told her family. The only reason she had hidden Lexie's paternity anyway was to shield Ben, but the lies were over now and she wanted to start fresh. They were her family and they'd be shocked, but they'd forgive her. *Unlike Ben.* Her mother would probably be more upset about the fact she'd kept it from him than from them.

The twins and Lexie came hurtling from their playhouse, and Rebecca scooped up a plate and took a sausage from the grill. Her father swatted at her but she managed to steal it anyway.

"You going to dish out for your two?" she asked her sister-in-law.

Lucy nodded and hauled up from her seat. Rebecca's brother cast her a watchful stare from his spot near the table, and Rebecca followed his gaze, seeing that it was his wife he was keeping a close eye on. Lucy was heavily pregnant and from the look of it he was in full alpha protective mode. It was a look she'd never had cast in her direction before, and she wished she had.

She pushed the thoughts away, ones she'd long since forgotten about that were somehow rising to the surface again, and took a slice of bread, squirting tomato sauce over it before wrapping it around the sausage. Lexie stood at her side, waiting like a drooling Labrador for her lunch.

"Why don't you take this back to the playhouse?" she suggested.

Lexie nodded and reached for the plate, grinning up at her.

"What about Leo and Sammy?" Lexie asked.

Rebecca looked at her cousins and smiled. The boys were slightly older than Lexie, loved her to pieces and always included her in their games.

"Their mommy will get theirs," Rebecca said, licking some sauce from her finger that must have slipped from the bottle when she'd squeezed it "No running with food in your mouth!"

She skipped away anyway, Rebecca's words lost to the excitement of racing away from the adults.

Rebecca took her place at the table that covered the deck and fiddled with the edge of her napkin. This was going to be hard. Around her, the others were tucking in. Lucy was heaping her plate high with food, her mother was fussing over the salad and her dad was dishing steak on to everyone's plates, chargrilled just like always. Only her brother was actually looking at her. Ryan sat across the table, his eyes trained on her, eyebrows raised as he asked her a question without even saying anything.

"Did you have fun at the polo? Or was it all work and no play?" asked Lucy.

Bec smiled, digging her fingernails into her palm. It was now or never.

"It was busy, but good." She was conscious of all the faces now looking her way, everyone listening to her. "We served a lot of food and the crowd seemed to love it, and then I had a catch-up with, ah, Ben."

"Sorry we couldn't help out," Lucy continued, still serving herself food. "Next time you can count on me." She patted her stomach and made them all laugh. "Next year I'll be begging for a day at the polo! I'll just have to leave your brother behind with the kids."

"Must have been nice catching up with Ben again." Her mom made that clucking sound she did whenever Ben's name was mentioned, and Rebecca stifled a groan. They'd loved him like a son, which was why telling them was going to be even harder.

"Bec, are you okay? You seem kind of…" Ryan was staring at her, the question still on his lips. When she glanced at his plate and saw he hadn't touched his food, she knew he wasn't going to let it go. He knew something was up.

She took a deep breath and ran her tongue lightly over her lips. Her mouth was so dry it was like it was full of cotton candy. But here she was, surrounded by the people who loved her most, and she needed desperately to get this off her chest.

Rebecca looked over to make sure Lexie wasn't near, but she could hear their excited shrieks from the back fence. She turned back to see everyone waiting, watching her. It wasn't as if she was often the center of attention and she hated it.

"I, ah, well…" She hesitated.

Her mother placed her fork back on the table. Every

sound, every look, was sending Rebecca's pulse rate higher. She closed her eyes for a moment and drew on all the courage she had.

"As you all know, I've been spending some time with Ben. He's back in Australia for good."

"Oh, that's wonderful news." Her mother beamed at her. "It'll be so nice for you two to reconnect some more."

At least Rebecca could count on her brother for picking up on her feelings—he was giving her a weird look again.

"Anyway, what I'm trying to say is that while I was there, I had to tell Ben something that I've kept from him and from all of you."

That stopped her mother from saying anything else. Rebecca blinked away tears, refusing to break down.

"Ben is Lexie's father." She said it so fast she wondered if they'd heard. But a glance around each face saw there was no mistaking it. They'd heard all right. Only no one was saying anything.

"*What?*" Ryan's face had turned a deep red and he thumped his fist down hard on the table, the first to react.

The clatter of cutlery made Rebecca jump. Her brother hadn't taken the news of her having a baby on her own well back then, so hearing that it was Ben's would have come as a shock. Probably a bigger shock to him than to her parents.

"Before you all jump to conclusions," she said, looking firmly at Ryan, "I want you to know that Ben didn't know. I only just told him, so there's no need to make him out to be the bad guy. If anyone is to blame, it's me."

Her mother looked as if she might cry, her father was back to fussing with the meat, and Ryan was still glaring at her.

"You're telling me that Ben McFarlane left you when you were pregnant?"

Rebecca looked sideways, not wanting to deal with her brother all hot under the collar. Lucy had her lips pursed, and she at least hoped her sister-in-law would be able to keep her brother calm.

"Ben had no idea I was pregnant when he left," she told him. "Had he known, he would have stayed. I can promise you that."

"So when are you getting married?" Ryan asked.

That made her laugh, although the noise died in her mouth when she saw the serious look on her brother's face.

"Ryan, I'm not marrying him!" she insisted. "We haven't even told Lexie yet. It's kind of difficult." She shook her head. "And that's why I didn't tell him in the first place, because he *would* have married me, out of a sense of duty, and the last thing I wanted was Ben giving up his dreams for me and resenting me for having to be tied to us." Not to mention the fact that she'd never really believed she deserved him, that she was worthy of him when she couldn't even face her own fears of getting back on a horse, of trying harder to make the team she'd dreamed about for years.

"I guess she does look like Ben, when you think about it," her mother said, as if she was having a conversation with herself.

"I can't believe you lied to us all this time. All that garbage you spun about…"

Rebecca shook her head and stood up from the table, interrupting her brother.

"You know what? I shouldn't have lied, but I don't owe any of you an apology. The only person I need to say sorry to is Ben, and God only knows I've said that to him a hundred times over these past few days. But Lexie is my daughter, and who her father is, was my business. *Is* my business."

She stormed past the table and fled into the house, rushed into the bathroom and burst into tears. She had never spoken to her family like that, *never*, and she hated that she just had. The truth was, she *was* sorry. Sorry to everyone she'd hurt for not telling them the truth. But was she so bad to have wanted to protect her own daughter? To protect Ben and her own heart, too? Was she that terrible to want to let Ben go and live out his dreams? Because once upon a time they'd been her dreams, too.

A light knock on the door made her haul in a big sob and dab at her eyes.

"Honey, let me in. *Please*." Her mother's soft voice made the urge to cry even greater.

She swung open the door and fell into her mother's arms, holding on tight and sobbing, her body shaking as she cried and cried. Rebecca felt like a child again, enveloped in her mother's comforting embrace.

"It's okay, honey. No one's angry with you. It's okay."

She knew Ryan wouldn't take long to forgive her, but her mother was wrong. There was someone angry with her, and the way her heart was slowly shattering, piece by piece, told her she'd blown it. Anything that might have been between her and Ben was well and truly over. She'd hurt him so badly and she just wanted to make it right. She wanted *him*. Not just as a friend, but as her something more, as the loving father of her child and as her lover.

Her mother held her tight in her arms, rocked her back and forward like Rebecca did to her own daughter to comfort her. It was not something she'd ever thought her mom would have to do to her again.

"It's going to be okay," her mother soothed.

"I love him," Rebecca choked. "I love him so bad."

"I know, sweetie," she said, and sighed. "I know. You loved him then, you always did."

"But I love him now, too. I never stopped."

Rebecca squeezed her eyes shut and willed Ben's face, his touch, his scent, to disappear from her memories. She'd never stopped loving him, and now, when she had almost had him back, she'd lost him forever. And it was all her fault.

The sun was beating down hard on Ben's bare arms, but he wasn't going to give up. He was sweltering from the heat, sweat pouring from his skin, and he was determined to keep going.

"Ben!"

He heard Gus call out to him, but he refused to listen. He only needed a few more minutes, another half hour maybe, and he'd have cracked the filly. She was still dancing around him, snorting in that arrogant little way of hers, teasing him before skipping away. But if there was one thing he was, it was determined.

"Ben!"

The voice was closer this time. He still ignored it, until a firm hand fell on his shoulder.

"Enough."

The word took a moment to filter through his senses, but the continued pressure on his shoulder made him stop.

"I said, enough,' the slow, steady voice was unrelenting.

Ben turned slowly and looked at his grandfather.

"I want you to get out of here, and don't work with another horse until you've cleared your head."

He bit back a retort, and he was pleased he had. Gus didn't need to be on the sharp end of his tongue, just because he felt lousy. And besides, his grandfather was right. He should never have come out here expecting to work with the young filly in this frame of mind. He knew better, and Gus shouldn't have had to remind him.

Ben gave the filly a look he hoped conveyed his remorse, and exited through the wooden rails. Gus went the long way, walking through the gate. It wasn't that he'd been too hard on her, but he wasn't being patient enough, soft enough to a horse that needed gentle coaxing.

"What do you want, son?"

Ben closed his eyes for a second before turning to watch his grandfather. What he needed was a way to push all the thoughts running through his head away, to just inhale the fresh air out on the farm and give himself a break.

"I said, what do you want?" his grandfather repeated.

Clearly the old man wasn't in one of his chilled out moods. He was asking a question and he expected an answer.

"I don't know."

"Yes, you do," Gus replied. "You know exactly what you want, son. You just need to admit it."

He watched Ben, the two of them looking at one another for a long moment, before walking off with the assistance of his cane. Gus called over his shoulder.

"I'm going to get us a beer. Think about your answer."

Ben sat on the veranda and held the beer bottle against his forehead. The wet, cool feel was helping to reduce his body temperature, but it wasn't helping his thoughts any. He could sense his grandfather's eyes on him, and he knew he had to say something. If he couldn't tell Gus, who could he tell?

"I want Lexie to know I'm her father. I want my daughter." He sucked back a breath, then blew it out slowly. "I want to know how to act around her, just figure out how to be her dad."

Gus nodded. He took a slow swig of his beer, his eyes not leaving Ben's.

"What else do you want?"

Ben shrugged, but his aloofness wasn't fooling Gus. They sat in silence, the only noise the whinny of horses in the distance, and the odd chirp of a bird in the big trees surrounding the house.

"I want Rebecca, okay? I bloody darn well want Rebecca." Ben pushed up to his feet and stormed the length of the veranda, before rounding on his grandfather. "Is that what you wanted to hear?"

Gus just smiled at him.

"You're an idiot, you know that?" Ben glowered at Gus's words. "Get in that car and don't come back until you've told her."

Ben put his beer down and walked toward his grand-dad. He suddenly had this feeling that he wouldn't know what to do without Gus around, that he couldn't bear the thought of life without him. His age had caught up to him fast, and it scared the hell out of Ben.

"Come here you old pain in the neck."

Gus stood and they embraced. The kind of firm, strong hug that men shared when it really meant something. The kind of hug Ben had always been able to count on, when he was a little boy to right now as a fully grown man. The type of support every human being needed in life.

"Call *me* a pain in the neck?" Gus chuckled. "You've been like a bear with a thorn, boy."

Ben grinned.

"You know that little pony we talked about?"

"I'm on it," said Gus.

"Great. I'm gonna head into town and see if I can't get them both back here."

CHAPTER FOURTEEN

THE RESTAURANT WAS BUZZING, which made it easier for Ben to slip in unnoticed. He'd gone straight to Rebecca's house, but then figured she'd be working.

It had always been busy, but it felt different now. He wondered if it was Rebecca's touch, making it that much more special, more intimate, than it had been previously. It had always been one of inner-city Melbourne's busiest Italian restaurants, but the subtle changes made it even more appealing.

Ben kept his head down and sat at a vacant table. He was a bundle of nerves and he hated it. He toyed with the menu but his eyes just skimmed over the words. He didn't care what he ate. For the first time in as long as he could remember he wasn't even interested in food. All he cared about was the woman he'd come here to see.

"Would you like to hear the specials?"

He looked up into pretty blue eyes. *Not Rebecca.* He didn't want to offend the young woman, so he politely said no and just ordered the spaghetti Bolognese. If Rebecca wasn't the one to bring his lunch over, he'd just eat and drink coffee until the rush had died down.

Ben watched the hum of people, coming and going, listening to laughter and conversation, but all he wanted was to see Rebecca. His eyes danced over each table, then out to the kitchen, scanning for her. *And then he saw her.*

Rebecca emerged, holding two steaming plates of food, held high out to each side. Her golden blond hair was pulled back into a loose ponytail, and it swished behind her as she moved. Her mouth was tipped up at each corner into a smile, and she looked happy. He hoped she'd still have that sweet look on her face when she saw him.

He let his eyes follow her as she hurried to a table and placed the two plates down, before saying a few words and heading back to the kitchen. Ben exercised all his willpower to stay seated, when all he wanted to do was take off after her.

His gaze stayed trained on the kitchen, and this time he was rewarded more quickly when she appeared again almost straight away, this time holding only one plate. Ben sat back, trying to look relaxed. She was heading his way. Ten steps, eight, six... She saw him.

Rebecca locked eyes with him, her mouth turning heart shaped with surprise. She looked over one shoulder, and then at the plate, as if wanting it to be a mistake. She hesitated. Ben rose to his feet.

"I think that's my spaghetti."

She still looked stunned, so he walked the few steps to meet her and took the plate for himself.

"Can you sit a minute?" he asked.

She shook her head, looking as though she was about to take off in the other direction.

"Please."

"I can't," she stammered. "We're so busy and I need to get more orders to tables."

He watched her, eyes bonded on hers, and then nodded.

"Okay. I'll wait."

Rebecca took a few steps backward before rushing off in the direction of the kitchen. Ben sat down and tried to approach his meal with interest, but his stomach was growling with a different type of hunger. Now that he'd seen her again, he wanted her. Badly. And this time he wasn't going to let anything get in their way. She'd apologized to him enough and it was time to put the past in the past and claim his family. He'd wasted enough time without wasting even more behaving like an idiot.

He'd left her once, walked away when he knew in his heart that he shouldn't have gone without telling her how he truly felt, but now he was back. For good. And there was nothing, *nothing*, going to stand in his way.

There were only a handful of patrons left. Ben pushed his coffee cup away. It was his third and he had enough caffeine in his system to keep him alert for days.

He'd watched Rebecca walk back and forth from the kitchen, smiling her way around each table, and now he was waiting for her to reappear. She'd disappeared out back a few minutes ago and not reemerged. Part of him was worried that she'd done a runner out the fire exit, but he believed in her more than that. Hoped he could trust that she wouldn't just leave him.

But even if she did bolt, he'd track her down and make her hear him out. If she was worried about listening to him fume at her again, she was wrong—he was a big enough man to admit he hadn't dealt with finding out well, but he was going to make up for it now. He was going to be a great dad even if it terrified him; and if she let him, he was going to make up for lost time with her, too.

He smiled as Rebecca finally reappeared and walked toward him—she hadn't bailed after all. She was fiddling with her apron, playing with the edge, and when she got closer she held her hands behind her back and untied it. She was wearing dark denim jeans, ballet flats and a plain black T-shirt, and she looked great.

"Hey," she said.

Ben hadn't seen Bec blush in a long time, but her cheeks were as pink and flushed as he'd ever seen them.

"Hey," he said back.

He stood and pulled out a chair. She sat down, her hands still busy on the cotton of her apron, obviously trying to distract herself from the fact that he was there.

"I had to see you, Bec," he started, pleased when she finally looked up. "When you left like that the other day, I didn't know what to think."

She at least gave him a reaction then.

"What did you expect, Ben?" She kept her voice low but she was clearly angry. "You made it pretty clear you didn't want me around."

"Bec…"

This wasn't going well. He'd come in here knowing exactly what he wanted to say, had practiced the entire conversation while he was waiting for her, and now he could hardly get his words out.

"No, Ben, let me," she said. "I'm not going to say sorry again because you've made it pretty clear there's no chance of me being forgiven. So why are you here?"

He stayed quiet. She was wrong, but he could tell now wasn't the time to tell her otherwise. She had something to say and he was going to sit tight and let her say it.

"Lexie's your daughter, and you have every right to be part of her life. We can work out some sort of an arrangement, something that works for both of us. My family knows now, so it's all out in the open."

Ben nodded. "Where is she now?"

"At my parent's place. She had a little cold, so I let her hang out there all day instead of going to preschool."

"She's okay, though?"

Rebecca nodded and stood up. "Sorry if you came all the way in just to see her, but I've really got to help tidy up. I'm off tonight and I want everything ready for dinner service before I leave."

Ben stood, too. There was so much he wanted to say but clearly now was the wrong time. Wrong place. At least he'd been able to observe these past few hours. If he'd been unsure to start with, he was positive now.

He just needed to figure out how to show her how he felt, so she believed him when he told her that he loved her. It wasn't just because they had a daughter together, or because he wanted to be part of Lexie's life. He wanted Rebecca, whether they had a child or not. And by the end of the day there was no way she wouldn't know exactly what he wanted. *Her.*

Ben pulled his car up outside the Stewarts' place. He hadn't come here that much as a kid, he and Rebecca tended to spend all their time at the stables when they hung out, but he still knew it well.

There was a car he didn't recognize out front, but he could hardly wait until the guest had gone. He didn't have long before Rebecca arrived back, and he needed to talk to her parents before she came home. And he wanted to spend some time with his girl.

He crossed the road and took a deep breath. It was odd knowing that Lexie had no idea he was her father, but he was still desperate to see her. His mind had done nothing other than flick between Rebecca and Lexie for the past few days, and even thought it sounded stupid even in his own head, he'd missed her.

Ben pushed the doorbell and waited. It was only a few minutes before a heavily pregnant woman flung open the door.

"Hi," she said.

"Ah, hi," he said back. "This still the Stewarts' place?"

A scream and a thunder of feet took him by surprise. The woman laughed as three kids, all in various states of undress, ran down the hall toward them.

"Sorry," she said.

"Ben!"

He recognized Lexie straightaway when she slid on the timber floorboards and screeched to a halt. At least he knew he had the right place.

"Hey, Lexie."

Lexie shot straight forward and grabbed his leg, her wet hair colliding with his chest when he bent down.

"What have you been doing?"

"Water fights," she said, shrugging. "I'm supposed to be sick, but I'm fine."

"You're Ben?"

The woman who'd answered the door had a warm expression on her face, smiling as she stared down at him.

"Sorry, Ben McFarlane," he said, standing and holding out his free hand. "And you are?"

"Lucy," she said, letting go and resting her hand on top of her belly. "Ryan's wife."

Ben nodded. "Can I come in?"

Rebecca turned the radio up loud and sung along. Badly. Seeing Ben today had been worse than when he'd first come back. She still felt such a fool for telling him she loved him, couldn't stop playing that day over and over in her mind. She'd managed to keep her feelings for him hidden for years, but now she seemed incapable of not making a mess of everything.

She pulled up outside her parents' place and noticed the black Holden next to the curb. The car looked a little too familiar. It only took a second before her heart hit the footpath. What was he doing here? Had he come for Lexie?

Rebecca rushed up the drive and pushed open the front door. He might only want their daughter, not her, but he couldn't just barge in like this and expect to take her!

"Mom!" she called. "Lexie!"

There was no one in the house. She rushed through the lounge and into the kitchen, worried something had happened. Where were they?

And then she saw the open doors leading out to the backyard and she was greeted with her worst nightmare. Ben was sitting beside her mother, both with chairs they had pulled out onto the grass. Lucy was fanning herself beneath a big tree, and her father was standing beside the water tap. Lexie was squealing with delight as she ran and then slid down some slippery, green, plastic water thing, and the twins were running back and forward with her. One would run and belly flop onto the plastic, then slide to the end, before the next child would start.

Rebecca looked at Ben. He'd obviously just said something funny, because he had her mother with her head thrown back in laughter. She felt physically sick. It was like some sort of weird setup.

"Mommy!"

Lexie was the first to notice her standing there. She

gave her a wave and then shooed her away as she shook out water from her hair.

Ben jumped up and headed her way. Rebecca felt the urge to run, but forced her feet to stay rooted to the spot. He obviously hadn't come here to steal Lexie away, so what on earth was he doing?

"What are you doing here?" she asked, not wasting any time.

He gave her a big smile and shrugged.

"Not quite the welcome I was hoping for." He reached for her arm but she angled herself so he didn't quite connect.

"Look, I get that you want to make up for lost time, but this is kind of hard for me," she told him.

"Rebecca…"

"No, Ben, don't bother. I shouldn't have lied. I know it's Lexie you want, not me, and I should have just kept my mouth shut."

"Rebecca."

She looked up and into his chocolate-colored eyes; eyes she'd dreamed about for months after he'd left, before she was able to just gaze into her daughter's.

"I need you to come with me. I've organized for your dad to run the restaurant tomorrow. I need you and Lexie to join me."

That knocked the wind out of her as if she'd been sucker punched.

"You have no right to come here and change my life around," she whispered, conscious that all eyes were on them. "I can't believe you think you can just rearrange me and tell me what to do."

"You know what, Bec?"

"What?" she fired back.

"Just shut up and do what I say for once. Okay?" He laughed. "And has anyone ever told you that you look damn gorgeous when you're all mad?"

She looked past him to see her mother grinning. She'd probably never heard anyone boss her daughter around like that before. Rebecca glared at her and turned her back. Just when she needed someone on her team her own family was swapping sides. She gave Ben what she hoped was an unimpressed stare, hands on her hips, but she had to admit it was nice seeing him joke around, laugh like that. It reminded her of the Ben of old.

"Fine," she snapped, although her anger was quickly dissipating.

Ben grinned and turned back to the kids.

"Lexie, last round, sweetheart. I've got a surprise for you," Ben called out, as if he was suddenly at ease with spending time with her, hanging out with the child he'd looked as good as terrified of when she'd first told him.

Rebecca shook her head and received only a shrug of the shoulders from her mother. Conveniently her dad was still busying himself with the children's game. Lucy just gave her a thumbs-up and Bec glowered back at her. It was as if everybody but her knew what was going on and she didn't like it at all. She was always the one in control, planning to the last detail, organizing everybody else. Ben had no right to barge in here, into her family's home, and tell her what to do!

She looked back at her mother and her sister-in-law, then to Ben. They were all grinning like dummies.

This was definitely an ambush. She knew when she'd been outnumbered, and right now she was guessing those numbers were at least one hundred to one.

CHAPTER FIFTEEN

REBECCA DIDN'T LIKE SURPRISES, and she wasn't particularly pleased that Ben had spent time with her parents without discussing it with her first.

The car slowed and Rebecca refocused. She could hardly believe they were at McFarlane's all ready.

"Are we here?"

Lexie's sleepy voice broke the silence.

"Yup, we're here," Ben told her.

Was she the only one not happy? Ben had grinned the entire trip here, Lexie had chirped excitedly before falling asleep and was clearly back to her perky self again already, and she felt nothing but miserable. A wave of dread kept looping through her stomach, telling her something was wrong, but there was little she could do. Ben had made it clear he expected her to comply, and she was sick of arguing with him. Of feeling like everything was her fault. She simply couldn't be bothered fighting, saying no, especially with Lexie around. And the way she felt around him even though she knew nothing could happen? *Ugh*. Being in such close proximity to him wasn't doing her any favors.

When the car stopped she got out and helped Lexie, but her daughter made a beeline straight for Ben, trotting along beside him like a loyal puppy dog. So much for her clingy girl, she thought. Someone better came along and she was gone in a flash.

Rebecca wanted to feel happy that Lexie was going to have a dad in her life, she knew it was petty to think otherwise, but she couldn't help it. Ben was so clearly besotted with his child, and so appalled by her, she felt torn. It had been wrong not to tell him, she could see that now, but what more could she do than say sorry? If there was anything that could make things right between them, she'd do it.

"You coming, Bec?"

Ben calling out spurred her into action and she hurried after them.

"Come on, Mommy!" Lexie called.

She had soon caught up with them, catching a glimpse of Gus waving out, then disappearing into the stable. Something was definitely up. She had that feeling like everything was just too quiet, like some sort of set up.

"Are you ready for a surprise?"

Lexie nodded fiercely. If she'd nodded any harder her head would have fallen off.

Ben looked around to Rebecca. He gave her a look and pointed at Lexie. They stared at one another a long while, before she nodded. There was nothing else she could do, the message was conveyed so clearly in his eyes, his desperation clear for anyone to see.

She got it. He was going to tell Lexie that he was her dad. It upset her that they hadn't talked about it first, but she was Ben's daughter, and she guessed it was up to him to decide how and when he wanted her to find out. Ben walked toward her and she felt guilty for wanting to keep it from their little girl.

"You okay with me telling her?" Ben asked in a low tone, his mouth achingly close to her ear when he moved over, his hand closing over her forearm.

"Yes." What else could she say?

Ben beamed at her and whipped Lexie off her feet and up into his arms, as if he'd done it a million times before. He'd obviously decided he wanted to make a huge effort with her, and it showed.

"Lexie, today's a very special day. Do you know why?"

"'Coz I didn't have to go to preschool?"

Lexie squinted up at Ben, the sun in her eyes. Ben laughed and swung her, before hoisting her up onto his shoulders. Rebecca kept her distance. Her entire body was numb, her eyes wet, hands clammy. All she could do was watch, and feel her heart crumble into piece after piece. To an outsider, this would have looked happy, idyllic even. But the reality was Lexie had gained a father and she'd lost a friend. There was no chance for her and Ben to be anything other than civil parents, with no chance of a reconciliation. His feelings toward her had made that clear.

"Today's a special day because today you get to meet your dad." Rebecca listened to Ben's gruff, deep words as Lexie screwed her face up.

"Where is he?" Lexie asked.

Ben smiled. Rebecca didn't think she'd ever seen him look so happy. Not when they used to gallop down the beach, racing side by side on horseback; not when they used to sneak out and sit on the roof, talking for hours well into the night; *not ever*. She had never since she'd known him ever seen him look like that.

"I'm your dad, Lexie," Ben said simply. "It's me."

Lexie looked confused and Rebecca worried she didn't understand.

"How can you be my dad? You're Ben," Lexie asked.

"I know it's hard to understand, kiddo, but I promise you that I'm your dad, and I'm always going to be. I'm your father, sweetheart."

Lexie wriggled and he pulled her down from where she was perched on his shoulders, putting her on his hip so she could look at both of them. Rebecca had tears in her eyes but she tried so hard to stop them from falling.

"Mommy, do you know that Ben is my dad?"

That made them both laugh. Rebecca just smiled, trying to look happy, watching as little Lexie sat back in Ben's arms to look up at him some more. Children were so innocent, she thought. Her darling wee girl was so kind, so sweet and loving, and looking at her in her father's arms did make her happy. She only wished that same man wanted them both in his arms, not just his daughter. That they could be the family she had secretly dreamed of all these years. It broke her heart to think that Ben would meet someone, someday, and that Lexie would be with her daddy and another woman.

"There's one more surprise."

Rebecca looked up. What else was going on?

Lexie was wriggling so much that Ben had to put her down. Just as he did so, Gus came slowly around the corner, leading the cutest, tubbiest little pony Rebecca had ever seen.

Lexie was dead still now. She was holding on to Ben but she wasn't moving.

"This, Lexie, is a present from your dad."

Rebecca watched as Lexie looked from the pony to Ben.

"Since you love horses so much, I thought you deserved your own pony. Especially if you're going to be spending time here."

Lexie zoomed forward. Thankfully the pint-size pony wasn't worried, and just stood as Lexie inspected every inch of him, touching, patting, talking to him all the while.

Ben left her to it, under Gus's watchful eye, and turned to Rebecca. His grandfather was grinning ear to ear.

"We need to talk," Ben said in a low voice. "Keen for a ride?"

Rebecca nodded, still numb.

"Come on, then."

She followed after him, hardly able to process what was going on. She had no idea what to expect, only for the first time all afternoon, she was starting to believe it might be something good. Something so good she didn't even want to admit it.

They rode in silence for a while. Rebecca had no idea where they were going, why she was here, or what Ben wanted to talk about. If he just wanted to talk custody arrangements? She swallowed hard. Surely he wouldn't be making such an effort if it wasn't something more… Rebecca shook her head, as if it would somehow make the thoughts disappear. What she needed to do was just stop thinking.

Ben stopped then. She halted behind him and waited for his lead.

"Let's get off here," he said before dismounting.

She was pleased at least that she had her old riding mojo back. Her brain might have been working overtime, but her body had been loving the easy motion of the horse's walk.

Rebecca followed his lead, wishing Ben had been guiding her down, like he'd helped her mount that first time she'd ridden with him again after he'd arrived home. She craved his hands on her body, palms firm at her hips, the steadiness of his hold on her. They were dangerous wishes, she knew that, but she couldn't help it and it was worse knowing it was never going to happen again. Besides, she didn't need his assistance now. She wasn't the same timid rider she'd been that first day back on the farm.

Ben took the reins from her and tied the horses to a low fallen tree trunk in the shade. The day was hot, but the sun was sitting lower now, a late afternoon breeze keeping the temperature bearable.

He sat down on the same big trunk and beckoned her over. Rebecca complied, keeping her distance from him. She still didn't know why they were here, what they were doing, and the last thing she needed was to be within touching distance to him.

"I hope you didn't mind me telling her back there?"

She shook her head. "She'll have a lot of questions later, once she's had time to process, but that's okay."

"So you're all right with it?"

"She's your daughter, Ben. You had every right to tell her."

"Not too extravagant with the pony?"

Ben was smiling and she smiled back. He was obviously very proud of the cute pony he'd bought, and he deserved to enjoy the moment.

"It was the best present a kid could wish for. It was very kind of you."

They sat a few more minutes. Rebecca was feeling incredibly uncomfortable. This might not be hard for him, but she'd thought about him every day since he'd left. Thought about him double as much since she'd stormed out the other day. Wishing things were different; wishing she'd just told him before ending up confessing the way she had. She just wished she could go back in time and change everything, but she couldn't and she just had to suck it up and get on with her life.

"You don't want to go for full custody or anything, do you?" The thought made her feel worse than sick. "I love her so much, Ben, and I just couldn't deal with…" She bit down hard on her lip, shaking her head. "I just want to protect her."

Ben didn't answer, but he did shuffle closer to her along the rough wood of the tree trunk.

"I didn't bring you out here to talk about Lexie. And I sure as hell don't want to take her away from you."

She looked up. "You didn't? *Wait, you don't?*"

Ben shook his head, his eyes looking straight ahead toward endless parched yellow grass.

"I wanted to tell you that I understand. I know why you did what you did, and I need you to know that I forgive you."

She went to answer but snapped her mouth back closed. *He forgave her?*

"I've had time to think these past few days, and it made me realize that I was a jerk. I was hurt, but I still should have listened to you, heard you out." He shrugged. "We were best friends, Bec. You were the one person in the world who always knew me as well as I knew myself, and I guess it was hard hearing what you had to say the other day, the fact that you knew how scared I was of ever being a parent, of what I'd been through. You were right, I just didn't want to admit to it."

"You had every right to treat me like that, Ben," she answered. "I never should have kept it from you. It was wrong, I know that."

Ben took her hand, and she fought not to pull it away. She didn't want his touch, his pity. Didn't want him to feel sorry for her. She just wanted to figure out how they were going to make this parenting thing work then get on with it. Hoping for something more was stupid, dangerous.

Ben held her hand tighter so she couldn't pull it away. "Did you mean it when you said you still loved me?"

Rebecca's heart collapsed, then kick-started again. She didn't trust her voice, didn't know if she could even force a word out.

"Did you?" Ben asked again.

"Yes," she stammered. There was no point in lying—she'd told him how she felt the other day and it wasn't as if anything had changed.

"Bec," he said, standing and pacing a few steps before coming back to stand in front of her, casting a shadow over her as he blocked out the dappled sun coming through the leaves.

"I'm sorry, Ben," she said, wanting nothing more than to fall to the ground and cry, to shatter into pieces and not have to re-form until he'd gone. "I wish I didn't but I do. I wish I could just want to be friends with you, but it'd be a lie."

"You've said sorry enough," he whispered, dropping to his knees. "I forgive you, Rebecca. *I forgive you.*"

She looked up, warmth slowly trickling back into her veins as she met his gaze.

Ben dropped to his knees and grasped her hands between his. She didn't know where to look. *What was he doing?*

"Bec, will you marry me?"

CHAPTER SIXTEEN

REBECCA SUCKED IN a sharp lungful of air. Marry him? *Was he kidding?*

"Ben, you can't be serious!"

His eyes didn't leave hers, his hands steady as he clasped hers, fingers linked together.

"I'm serious, Bec." He smiled, then repeated his question. "Will you marry me?"

She snatched her hands away from him, hating how desperately she wanted him, how badly she just wanted to throw herself into his arms.

"No," she whispered.

Ben stared at her, long and hard.

"What do you mean, *no*?"

She blinked back a gasp of unshed tears and jumped up, made her way to her horse. Willy stood patiently, but when she made a grab for his reins a heavy, firm grip stopped her. Ben's fingers dug into her arm, not letting her move another inch.

"Let me go." She tried to sound forceful but it came out as little more than a whisper.

"*No*." Ben kept hold, his grip firm on her arm as he reached for her other wrist. His gaze made his intentions clear: there was no chance of him letting her go.

"You're not going anywhere."

"Let go of me, Ben." She fought hard, struggling to release herself. "Ben, you're hurting me!"

He let go of her wrist, his other hand softening over her arm.

"Why?" he asked.

Rebecca slumped against the horse, her resolve long gone. She turned sad eyes in Ben's direction.

"Same reason I didn't tell you about Lexie in the first place," she said sadly.

Ben looked confused, folding his arms across his chest as he stared at her.

"I didn't want you to propose back then just because you thought it was the right thing to do, and I don't want you to have to do it now. You don't owe me anything, Ben. You don't need to marry me out of some sense of, I don't know, duty."

"*Duty*? Is that honestly what you think?"

"Oh, I don't know," she said, trying hard not to cry. "Pity, then, whatever you want to call it. But you don't need to propose to me because you feel you have to."

Ben stepped toward her and placed a hand softly on each arm. She closed her eyes and tried to ignore the fact that he was touching her, of how good it felt to have his skin over hers. The man of her dreams had just asked her to marry him, was touching her, holding her, but it wasn't real, she knew that. She'd always known that he would step up if he knew, and here he was trying to make an honest woman of her.

"Rebecca, look at me."

When she didn't reply, he hooked one finger under her chin, forcing her to look at him. She swallowed, finally returning his gaze.

Ben didn't give her any warning. He crushed his lips hard against hers, taking her mouth with force. Rebecca tried to pull away, halfheartedly, before giving in and kissing him back. His hands were all over her, up and down her back, touching her hair, cupping her face. They stayed like that for what felt like hours, lost to one another's touch, lips locked, hands exploring, skin alight.

It was Ben who pulled back. He still had his hands around her waist, encircling her, keeping her locked in his cocoon.

"Did that feel like a man who pities you?" he asked. "Who thinks he has to marry you just because it's the right thing to do?"

She caught her lower lip beneath her teeth, still not wanting to hope that maybe she'd been wrong all this time.

"No," she managed to whisper in reply.

"I love you, Rebecca. I always have." He leaned in and pressed a soft, barely there kiss to her lips, his mouth hovering over hers. "And I always will. I should have told you years ago."

She let her eyes flutter shut for a moment, fighting the feeling that it was a dream. When she opened them again he was still there, his warm brown gaze locked on hers.

"I have always loved you, Rebecca. You have to believe me when I say I want you to marry me because I *still* love you, not because it's the right thing to do."

She nodded. It was all she could do. Her own voice had been taken captive in her throat.

"I want you to be my wife. I want to be Lexie's dad. And I want us all to be together." He sighed. "No pity.

No sense of duty. Just because I damn well love you, Bec."

She looked up at him. His gaze was unwavering, hands strong on her hips as he held her gently in place.

"So, will you have me?" he asked.

"Yes," she murmured, the word drawing them closer together, her arms looping around his neck, letting herself believe that he actually did want her just for her. "Yes, Ben. Yes a million times over."

Ben pulled her in tight against him then, his lips falling to hers once more. She sighed into his mouth as he kissed her, before he trailed butterfly-soft kisses down her throat.

Rebecca moaned, her legs close to buckling beneath her. Ben didn't stop. He scooped her into his arms, his mouth back on hers. She shuddered as his tongue teased her lips, groaned as he dropped slowly to the ground and put her carefully on the grass.

He tugged his T-shirt off in between long, languid kisses, and Rebecca ran her hands over his strong back, felt his hard muscles coil and tense beneath her touch.

"I've been waiting to do this again for so long," he muttered against her lips.

Rebecca moaned beneath his touch. *So had she.*

"You are so beautiful," said Ben, holding her close.

She looked away, shy at being the object of his words but not wanting him to stop touching her, kissing her.

Rebecca closed her eyes and let Ben caress her. She had dreamed of this for so long, never thinking that one day she would be back in his arms. Back with the man she loved. She had gone all this time alone, with no other human being to keep her warm at night, to be her mate in life, to love, and now she had Ben, and she was never, ever going to let him go. Not if she could help it.

Ben traced a fingertip over Rebecca's skin, starting at her wrist then all the way up to her neck, and to her lips. Rebecca giggled and he dropped another kiss to her mouth.

"You are going to marry me, aren't you?"

She smiled at him, her mouth stretched wide, her face mirroring how he felt.

"Yes, I'm going to marry you, Ben McFarlane. A hundred times *yes*."

"Good."

"Good?" she repeated. "Is that all you think of me? *Good*."

He pinned her back on the grass, his mouth inches from her face, trying to be serious when all he wanted to do was laugh.

"Do you need me to show you again what I really think of you?" he growled.

Rebecca burst out laughing as he held her down.

"Okay, okay," she said, giggling.

Ben let her go and lay back down beside her, their bodies side by side. He kept hold of her hand, fingers interlinked.

"What do you think Lexie will make of us being together? Of me marrying her mom?"

"She already loves you, Ben," she said, squeezing his fingers. "I think she fell in love with you from the moment she met you, like she knew there was some sort of connection there."

Ben propped up on one elbow again, looking down at her. Her golden hair was fanned out around her over the grass and he stared down into eyes that had haunted him for years.

"You know what?" she asked.

"What?" He smiled as she stroked his arm, her touch featherlight.

"I think Lexie would have been happy with you in our lives even if you weren't her biological dad."

Ben opened his eyes. For all his worrying about being a father, of not wanting to screw up like his own mom had, he suddenly wasn't scared of being in Lexie's life. Maybe Bec had been right in letting him go at the time, even though it hurt like hell to admit it. He wanted to be Lexie's father—it was a belly-deep feeling that would be impossible to fight, but if he'd been faced with this before he'd been away, maybe it would have been harder to accept, to man up to. Maybe he wouldn't have realized how badly he wanted Bec as his partner instead of his friend, to be back on home soil, to make a life for himself on the land he'd grown up on.

"She's a great kid, you know?" His voice was hoarse with emotion.

Rebecca nodded her agreement. "Yeah, and you're going to be just as good a dad."

He hoped so. Man, did he hope so. "If I can be half as good a dad as Gus has been a granddad to me, then I guess I'll be fine." He blew out a breath. "I was so scared of her that first day, I didn't know what to do or how to even talk around her, but once I thought about how Gus was with me, it started to come more naturally."

She leaned up and kissed his jaw. Rebecca crawled up into his arms and he tugged her tight, holding her close.

"I was so scared of being close to anyone, and in the process I somehow forgot that I was already close to you.

I pushed you away when I should have kept you at my side. Made you a part of my life."

She sighed, head to his chest. "Does any of that matter now?"

"No," he whispered, kissing the top of her head. "Because I'm going to spend every day from this day forward making it up to you."

CHAPTER SEVENTEEN

REBECCA EYED THE beautiful black filly and bit down a lump of fear threatening to constrict her throat. She had been psyching herself up for this moment for days, but it didn't make it any easier.

She knew Ben was watching her but she didn't turn. He had offered countless times to help her, but this was something she had to do alone. There was no point becoming the first Mrs. McFarlane to take residence here since Ben's grandmother, without proving she could conquer her fear. Ben had been man enough to forgive her, to make her realize that she deserved his love, and that he was acting from his own feelings and not from duty. And now she owed it to herself to step up, take ownership of her past and believe in her own abilities. As a rider, as a woman and as an equal to him on the farm.

"Hey, Missy," she soothed, leaving her fear on the other side of the corral. "How's my girl today, huh?"

As if understanding her, the horse nickered and reached out her nose to run it over Rebecca's forearm, tickling her bare skin.

Rebecca brushed Missy's back, her hands moving along the indent of her shoulder, then down around her belly. Next she softly rubbed her face, before moving to place the saddle on her back. The horse didn't move, and Rebecca gradually tightened the girth. When she moved to tease the bit into her mouth there was no hesitation, and she slipped the bridle over her head.

She glanced over her shoulder at her support crew and smiled. It was nice to see Gus and Ben standing there, but some of the polo guys who'd arrived were a little intimidating.

Rebecca talked in her low singsong voice to Missy and led her out to the center of the corral. A few strokes of the neck and tug of each stirrup later, and she was settling into the saddle.

Missy jumped and quivered, but Rebecca stayed calmed. She kept talking, a running commentary of nonsense that made the horse relax and listen, ears flicking back and forth. Rebecca squeezed her legs and they moved forward at a slow walk. That was all she wanted from today, didn't want to push things too far.

It wasn't the most relaxing of rides, but Rebecca was proud of herself. A few weeks ago, she'd been scared of going near a horse again. Now? She couldn't deny having a belly full of nerves, but she was finding her way back to her past in the best possible way. She was a mom, she ran a restaurant, and now she was going to be Ben's wife, a wife who'd be confident back in the saddle with him, training for polo matches and having fun. She finally felt like *her* again.

Missy jumped beneath her but she just kept on talking, keeping a firm contact with the reins. Rebecca circled her and then pulled to a halt, before swinging her feet out from the stirrups. She praised the horse.

Nothing had turned out the way she'd expected, but she couldn't be happier. She looked across and met Ben's strong, unwavering gaze. When he grinned she blew him a kiss. She was finally with the man she loved, and nothing, *nothing*, could take that away from her.

Ben gave his grandfather a nudge, not even trying to wipe the beamer of a smile from his face. He'd always known she had it in her. There was something exciting about seeing his girl, his wife-to-be, sitting proud on a horse. Gus had known she could do it, he'd hoped she could do it, and eventually Rebecca had believed enough in herself to trust her instincts and give it a go again.

Nobody could have blamed her for being scared, for not wanting to try again, but she had, and he was pleased. He loved Bec, he loved his daughter, and he loved horses. Just thinking about training with her again, playing polo side by side with her, made him grin.

Ben jumped to his feet and moved toward his fiancée. It gave him a buzz just thinking about marrying her.

"Son?"

He turned and looked at his grandfather. Gus looked as proud of his granddaughter-in-law-to-be as he was himself.

"I think it's time Rebecca had a horse of her own again."

Ben gave him a nod and they both walked toward her. She was making a fuss over the adoring horse she had just made look like a quiet donkey, when in fact she was the only one to connect with her at all.

A patter of hooves and a squeal of delight made them all turn. Ben laughed as he watched his daughter come running, as fast as her little legs would carry her, her placid pony in tow. Lexie was holding the end of the lead rope and the pony trotted beside her.

"I thought I told you to wait for us?" Ben said, trying to sound angry and failing. He'd been the same as a kid and he wasn't going to deny Lexie the fun of playing with her pony. That's why he had spent so much getting a kind old horse to teach Lexie the ropes, so he didn't have to worry every time his daughter was out in the field. They were a cute pair, and the pony had been well worth the money.

"You said not to *ride* him on my own," called a breathless Lexie. "See, Mommy? I'm just playing with him, not riding him."

Ben looked at Rebecca and saw her try to hide a smile behind her hand. She had them there; they *had* only said no riding.

"What do you say, *Mommy*?" asked Ben.

Rebecca put one hand on her hip, then burst into laughter as Lexie and the podgy pony ran past.

"Just stay close," Ben called after their adventurous daughter. "And remember she's a horse, not a dog. You need to be careful."

Ben leaned on the rails and watched as Gus approached Rebecca and Missy. He committed to memory the way his grandfather's weathered hand moved in slow circles over the horse's muzzle, then up her neck. The filly certainly responded to Rebecca, but she was partial to Gus, too.

"You did good out there," he heard his granddad say.

Rebecca looked up from grooming. "Thanks."

She gave the filly a final swoop with the brush then untied her lead rope, ready to walk her back out.

"She'd make a great polo pony if we had anyone decent to ride her, you know," said Gus.

"I know," agreed Rebecca.

Gus pushed his hat up higher to look her in the eye as Ben watched on.

"You never should have lost your horse in that accident, Rebecca." He waited till she looked up before continuing. "You're a great rider and you always will be, which is why I want you to have her."

"No! Gus, she's worth too much and I don't even know if I'd make it through a whole chukker now..."

"I've made my mind up. Don't deny an old man a gift."

"Ben, did you hear that?" Rebecca called out. "Tell him I can't take her."

Ben just grinned and shrugged. "Sorry, but I'm not taking your side on this one."

"Rebecca, she's yours. Make me proud. Just promise me that you'll have fun, and look after that grandson of mine when I'm gone. Okay?"

Ben wiped away a tear as he watched Rebecca walk the horse out into the yard and give Gus an impromptu kiss on the cheek, her arm slung around his shoulders.

"You're the best granddad in the world, you know that?"

"No, love, you're the best granddaughter, and I've waited a long time to have you. So if I want to spoil you, then so be it."

Ben jogged the distance to catch up with them, arms looping around Rebecca's waist once she'd let the horse go.

"We *are* going to have fun, you know that, right?" He kissed her neck, holding her tight. "I love you."

She turned in his arms, eyes shining with tears. "I love you, too."

EPILOGUE

BEN SMILED OVER at Rebecca's parents before giving his grandfather a nudge. Gus was standing next to him, dapper in a dark suit and soft pink tie, matching his grandson. He hadn't expected Gus to be on his feet for the ceremony, but the old man was tough as nails and had managed to surprise them all.

A noise from behind stole his attention and Ben laughed when he saw the commotion. Rebecca's brother was trying to coax Lexie down from her pony and wasn't having much luck. From the day he'd given his daughter the friendly little gray gelding, Lexie had hardly given the poor horse a second to relax. It had been love at first sight; his daughter had fallen for the pony as fast as Ben had fallen for his little girl.

There was a whisper through the crowd as the string quartet started to play, and the soft lull of music made Ben stare at the house, at the door where Rebecca was going to enter from. He held his breath and closed his eyes for a second. When he opened them she was walking toward him. Not on her father's arm, not flanked by a gaggle of bridesmaids, just Rebecca walking toward him, a smile on her face that mirrored his own.

For the first time in his life Ben almost cried in public, but he checked his emotion, swallowed hard and just
focused on Bec. Her eyes were shining as she held out
her hands to him once she reached him, and he clasped
them as tightly as he could before pulling her in for a
kiss, just a gentle touch of his mouth to hers to tell her
how much he loved her.

Rebecca pressed into him and sighed into his mouth.

"We're meant to wait until after we're married," she
whispered, throwing her head back to laugh as he kept
her encircled in his arms.

Not the guests behind them, the celebrant clearing her
throat, even Lexie standing with her pony and a huge
smile, could distract Ben. He had the woman he loved
in his arms, and he didn't ever want to let go.

Rebecca squeezed her husband's hand and shook her head
as she watched Lexie. She'd refused to come in for the
party, preferring instead to race around with her pony,
and neither she nor Ben had any intention of forcing her
to come in. She was sitting under the shade of the big
blue gum tree, sharing food from her paper plate with
her four-legged best friend, and there was nothing she'd
rather see her little girl doing.

"I love you, baby," Ben murmured in her ear.

Rebecca turned to smile at him and press a kiss to
his lips.

The small group of guests were all looking up as metal
sounded out on glass. There were no planned speeches
but...Rebecca smiled. Gus was standing with his wine-
glass in hand, clearing his throat. If anyone was going
to speak, she was pleased it was him.

"I don't want to talk all night or anything like that, but someone needs to say a few words about our lovebirds over there," said Gus.

There was a murmur of laughter until his still-strong, deep voice rang out again.

"You probably all know that I haven't got much longer, but what you might not know is just how much I love these two."

He gestured at Rebecca and Ben and she dabbed at the corners of her eyes with her napkin, trying hard not to let any tears spill. To even think about Gus not being around was heartbreaking, especially when she'd gone so many years without seeing him.

"I always knew these two would find a way to be together. As kids, they were inseparable, as young adults, it was obvious to anyone but them that they were in love, and as full-grown adults they were even more stubborn! All I ever heard was nonsense about how they were just friends."

Ben squeezed Rebecca's hand and she laughed. There was no denying how stupid they'd been.

"What I want to say, though, is that these two deserve to be happy, and I know they'll be together for as long as they're living. Which is why I want to present them with the deed to McFarlane Stables."

Rebecca gasped and Ben dropped his glass with a thump to the table. *He what?*

"Before you two protest," continued Gus, waving them away, "I want you to know that I've thought long and hard about this, and the paperwork's already done." He paused, his eyes meeting first hers then Ben's, his smile wide. "So please join with me in raising your glasses in toast to the new Mr. and Mrs. McFarlane, custodians of McFarlane Stables."

Rebecca leaned into Ben and he dropped a kiss to her head. If life couldn't get any more perfect, it just had.

* * * * *

HER PLAYBOY'S PROPOSAL

KATE HARDY

To my fellow Medical authors – because you're
a really lovely bunch and I'm proud to
be one of you. xxx

CHAPTER ONE

Isla took a deep breath outside the staffroom door. Today was her second day at the emergency department of the London Victoria Hospital, and she was still finding her place in the team. She'd liked the colleagues she'd met yesterday, and hopefully today would go just as well—with new people who didn't know her past and wouldn't judge her. She pushed the door open, then smiled at the nurse who was checking the roster on the pinboard. 'Morning, Lorraine.'

'Morning, Isla. You're on cubicles with Josie and Harry the Heartbreaker this morning,' Lorraine said.

'Harry the Heartbreaker?' Isla asked.

Lorraine wrinkled her nose. 'I guess that's a bit of a mean nickname—Harry's a good doctor and he's great with patients. He listens to them and gives them a chance to talk.'

'So he's very charming, but he's a bit careless with women?' Isla knew the type. Only too well.

'Harry dates a lot,' Lorraine said. 'He doesn't lead his girlfriends on, exactly, but hardly anyone makes it past a third date with him.'

And lots of women saw him as a challenge and tried to be the exception to his rule, Isla guessed. 'Uh-huh,' she said. She certainly wouldn't be one of them. After what had happened with Stewart, she had no intention of dating anyone ever again. She was better off on her own.

'OK, so he'd be a nightmare to date,' Lorraine said with a wry smile, 'but he's a good colleague. I'm sure you'll get on well with him.'

So professionally their relationship would be just fine; but it would be safer to keep Harry the Heartbreaker at a distance on a personal level. Isla appreciated the heads-up. 'Everyone else in the department has been lovely so far,' she said, smiling back. 'I'm sure it will be fine.'

Though she hadn't been prepared for quite how gorgeous Harry the Heartbreaker was when she actually saw him. The expression 'tall, dark and handsome' didn't even begin to do him justice. He would've been perfectly cast as one of the brooding heroes of a television costume drama, with dark curly hair that was a little too long and flopped over his forehead, dark eyes, a strong jaw and the most sensual mouth she'd ever seen. On horseback, wearing a white shirt, breeches and tailcoat, he'd be irresistible.

Harry the Heart-throb.

Harry the *Heartbreaker*, she reminded herself.

Luckily Josie had already triaged the first patient and was ready to assist Harry, which meant that Isla had enough time to compose herself and see the next patient on the list.

Harry was a colleague and that was all. Isla had no intention of getting involved with anyone again, no matter how gorgeous the man looked. Stewart had destroyed her trust completely, and that wasn't something she'd be able to put behind her easily.

* * *

Harry finished writing up his notes and walked into the corridor to call the next patient through. He knew that Josie had gone to triage her next patient, so he'd be working with the newest member of the team, Isla McKenna. He'd been on leave yesterday when she'd started at the London Victoria and knew nothing about her, other than that she was a senior nurse.

He eyed the nurse in the corridor with interest. Even without the double giveaways of her name and her accent, he would've guessed that Isla McKenna was a Scot. She had that fine porcelain skin, a dusting of freckles across her nose, sharp blue eyes and, beneath her white nurse's cap, dark red hair that he'd just bet looked amazing in the sunlight. Pure Celt. It was a long time since he'd found someone so instantly attractive. Not that he was going to act on it. For all he knew, she could already be involved with someone; the lack of a ring on her left hand meant nothing. 'Isla McKenna, I presume?' he asked.

She nodded.

'Harry Gardiner. Nice to meet you. How are you settling in to the ward?' he asked as they walked down to the cubicles together.

'Fine, thanks. The team seems very nice.'

'They're a good bunch,' he said. 'So where were you before you moved here?'

'Scotland,' she said, her face suddenly shuttering.

Clearly she thought he was prying and she'd given him as vague an answer as she could without being openly rude. 'Uh-huh,' he said, lightly. 'Just making polite conversation—as you would with any new colleague.'

She blushed, and her skin clashed spectacularly with her hair. 'Sorry. I didn't mean to be rude,' she muttered.

'Then let's pretend we've never spoken and start again.' He held out his hand. 'Harry Gardiner, special reg. Nice to meet you, and welcome to the London Victoria.'

'Isla McKenna, sister. Thank you, and nice to meet you, too,' she said.

Her handshake was firm, and Harry was surprised to discover that his skin actually tingled where it touched hers.

Not good.

He normally tried not to date colleagues within his own department. It made things less complicated if his date turned out to have greater expectations than he wanted to fulfil—which they usually did. And instant attraction to the newest member of their team definitely wasn't a good idea.

'So who's next?' he asked. Hopefully focussing on work would get his common sense back to where it should be—firmly in control of his libido.

'Arthur Kemp, aged seventy-three, suspected stroke,' Isla said, filling him in. 'The paramedics did a FAST assessment—' the Face Arm Speech Test was used in cases of suspected stroke to check whether the patient's face seemed to fall on one side or if they could smile, whether they could hold both arms above their head, or if their speech was slurred '—and they gave him some aspirin on the way here. I've done an initial assessment.'

'ROSIER?' Harry asked. Recognition of Stroke in the Emergency Room was a standard protocol.

She nodded. 'His score pretty much confirms it's a stroke. I checked ABCD2 as well, and the good news is that his score is nil on the D—he's not diabetic. His blood sugar is fine.'

Harry picked up immediately what she was telling him—there was only one section of the test with a nil score. 'So the rest of it's a full house?'

'I'm afraid so,' she said. 'He's over sixty, he has high blood pressure and residual weakness on his left side, and the incident happened over an hour ago now.'

'Which puts him at higher risk of having a second stroke in the next two days,' Harry said. 'OK. Does he live on his own, or is he in any kind of residential care?'

'He has a flat where there's a warden on duty three days a week, and a care team comes in three times a day to sort out his meals and medication,' Isla told him. 'They're the ones who called the ambulance for him this morning.'

'So if he did have a second stroke and the warden wasn't on duty or it happened between the care team's visits, the chances are he wouldn't be found for a few hours, or maybe not even overnight.' Harry wrinkled his nose. 'I'm really not happy with that. I think we need to admit him to the acute unit for the next couple of days, so we can keep an eye on him.'

'I agree with you. His speech is a little bit slurred and I'm not happy about his ability to swallow,' Isla added. 'He said he was thirsty and I gave him a couple of sips of water, but I'd recommend putting him on a drip to prevent dehydration, and keep him nil by mouth for the next two or three hours. Nobody's going to be able to sit with him while he drinks and then for a few minutes afterwards to make sure he's OK—there just won't be the time.'

'Good points, and noted.'

Mr Kemp was sitting on a bed, waiting to be seen.

Isla introduced him quickly. 'Mr Kemp, this is Dr Gardiner.'

'Everyone calls me Harry,' Harry said with a smile. 'So can you tell me about what happened this morning, Mr Kemp?'

'I had a bit of a headache, then I tripped and fell and I couldn't get up again,' Mr Kemp said. 'My carer found me when she came in to give me my tablets and my breakfast.'

Isla noticed that Harry sat on the chair and held the old man's hand, encouraging him to talk. He was kind and waited for an answer, rather than rushing the patient or pressuring him to stop rambling and hurry up. Lorraine had been spot on about his skills as a doctor, she thought. 'Can you remember, either before or after you fell, did you black out at all?' Harry asked. 'Or did you hit your head?'

Arthur looked confused. 'I'm not sure. I don't think I blacked out and I don't remember hitting my head. It's hard to say.' He grimaced. 'Sorry, Doctor. I'm not much use. My daughter's husband says I'm an old fool.'

So there were family tensions, too. The chances were, if they suggested that he went to stay with his family for a few days, the answer would be no—even if they had the room to let the old man stay. 'Don't worry, it's fine,' Harry reassured him. 'I'm just going to do a couple of checks now to see how you're doing. Is that OK?'

'Yes, Doctor. And I'm sorry I'm such a nuisance.'

Either the old man was used to being made to feel as if he was a problem, or he was habitually anxious. Or maybe a bit of both, Harry thought. He checked Mr Kemp's visual fields and encouraged him to raise his arms; the residual weakness on Mr Kemp's left side that

Isla had mentioned early was very clear. And there was a walking frame next to the bed, he noticed. 'Do you normally walk with a frame?'

'Yes, though I hate the wretched thing.' Arthur grimaced. 'It always trips me up. It did that this morning. That's why I fell. Useless thing.'

Harry guessed that Mr Kemp did what a lot of elderly people did with a walking frame—he lifted it and carried it a couple of centimetres above the ground, rather than leaving the feet on the floor and pushing it along and letting it support him. Maybe he could arrange some support to help the old man use the frame properly, so it helped him rather than hindered him.

'Can you see if you can walk a little bit with me?' he asked.

He helped Mr Kemp to his feet, then walked into the corridor with him, encouraged him to turn round and then walk back to the cubicle. Harry noticed that his patient was shuffling. He was also leaning slightly to the left—the same as when he was sitting up—and leaning back slightly when he walked. Harry would need to put that on Mr Kemp's notes to be passed on to any carers, so they could help guide him with a hand resting just behind his back, and stop him as soon as he started shuffling and encourage him to take bigger steps.

Once Mr Kemp was seated safely again, Harry said, 'I'm going to send you for an MRI scan, because you had a headache and I want to rule out anything nasty, but I think Sister McKenna here is right and you've had a small stroke.'

'A stroke?' Arthur looked as if he couldn't quite take it in. 'How could I have had a stroke?'

'The most likely cause is a blood clot that stopped the blood supply to your brain for a little while,' Harry explained. 'It should be cleared by now because you're able to walk and talk and move your arms, but I'm going to admit you to the acute medical unit so we can keep an eye on you for a day or two.' He decided not to tell Mr Kemp that his risk of a second stroke was higher over the next day or two; there was no point in worrying the poor man sick. Though his family would definitely need to know. 'Has anyone been in touch with your family?'

'Sharon, my carer—she should have rung my daughter, but Becky'll be at work and won't be able to come right away.' He grimaced. 'I feel bad about taking her away from her job. Her work is so important.'

'And I bet she'll think her dad is just as important as her job,' Isla said reassuringly.

'Too right,' Harry said. Even though he didn't quite feel that about his own father. Then again, Bertie Gardiner was more than capable of looking after himself— that, or his wife-to-be Trixie, who was a couple of years younger than Harry, could look out for him.

He shook himself. Not now. He wasn't going to think about the upcoming wedding. Or the fact that his father was still trying to talk him into being his best man, and Harry had done that job twice already—did he really need to do it all over again for his father's *seventh* wedding? 'We'll have had your scan done by the time your daughter comes to see you,' Harry said, 'and we'll be able to give her a better idea of your treatment plan.'

'Treatment?' Mr Kemp asked.

'The stroke has affected your left side, so you'll need a little bit of help from a physiotherapist to get you back to how you were before the stroke,' Harry said. 'I'm also going to write you up for some medication which you can take after your scan.'

'Is there anything you'd like to ask us?' Isla asked.

'Well, I'd really like a nice cup of tea,' Mr Kemp said wistfully. 'If it wouldn't be too much trouble.'

'We can sort that out in a few minutes, after you've had your scan,' Isla said. 'At the moment you're finding it hard to swallow and I don't want you to choke or burn yourself on a hot drink, but we'll try again in half an hour and you might be able to swallow better by then. And I'll make sure you get your cup of tea, even if I have to make it myself.'

'Seconded,' Harry said, 'though I'll admit my tea isn't the best and you'd be better off with coffee if I'm the one who ends up making it.' He smiled at the old man. 'We'll get things sorted out and make sure your daughter finds you.' He shook the old man's hand and stood up. 'Try not to worry. We'll make sure you get looked after properly.'

'I'll be back with you in a second, Mr Kemp,' Isla said, and followed Harry out of the cubicles.

'Can you organise a scan and then transfer him to the acute unit?' he asked quietly when they were outside the cubicle.

She smiled at him. 'Sure, no problem.'

Her smile transformed her face completely. Harry felt the lick of desire deep inside his gut and had to remind himself that his new colleague might be gorgeous, but she was also off limits. 'Thanks,' he said. 'I'll write everything up.'

It was a busy morning, with the usual falls and sprains and strains, and a six-month-old baby with a temperature that wouldn't go down and had then started having a fit. The baby's mother had panicked and asked a neighbour to drive them in rather than waiting for an ambulance, and the triage team had rushed her straight into the department.

The baby's jaws were clenched firmly together, so Harry looked at Isla and said quietly, 'Naso-pharyngeal, I think.'

Almost as soon as he'd finished talking, she had an appropriately sized tube in her hand and was lubricating the end. Between them, they secured the baby's airway and gave her oxygen, and Isla was already drawing up a phial of diazepam.

Clearly she'd come across convulsions in babies before.

Between them, they checked the baby's blood glucose and temperature.

'Pyrexia,' Harry said softly. 'I'm pretty sure this is a febrile convulsion.'

'So we need to cool her down and check for infection,' Isla said. At his nod, Isla deftly took off the baby's sleep-suit and sponged her skin with tepid water while Harry checked with the baby's distraught mother when she'd last given the baby liquid paracetamol. Once the fit had stopped and the baby's temperature spike had cooled, Isla prepared everything for an infection screen.

'I've never seen anything like that before. Is Erin going to be all right?' the baby's mother asked.

'She's in the best place and you did the right thing to bring her in,' Harry reassured her. 'I think the fit was caused by her high temperature, but we need to find out what's causing that—if it's a virus or a bacterial infection—and then we can treat her properly.'

'Will she have any more fits?' Erin's mother asked.

'Very possibly,' Isla said, 'but that doesn't mean that she'll develop epilepsy. Having a high temperature is the most common cause of fits in children between

Erin's age and school age. We see this sort of thing a lot, so try not to worry.'

Worry, Harry thought. Parents always worried themselves sick over small children. And so did their older siblings—especially when they were supposed to be taking care of them and things went badly wrong.

He pushed the thought away. It was years ago, now, and he was older and wiser. Plus nowadays Tasha would give him very short shrift if he fussed over her too much; she was fiercely independent. And you couldn't change the past; all you could do was learn from it. Harry had most definitely learned. He never, ever wanted to be responsible for a child in that way again.

'I'm going to admit her,' Harry said, 'purely because she's so young and it's the first time she's had a fit. Plus I want to find out what's causing the infection. We'll keep an eye on her in case she has more convulsions. But you can stay with her.'

'I'll take you both up to the ward and introduce you to the team,' Isla said.

'And she's going to be all right?' the baby's mother asked again.

'Yes,' Harry said, and patted her arm. 'I know it's scary, but try not to worry.'

Ha. And what a hypocrite he was. He knew that panicky feeling all too well. *Would the baby be all right?* The overwhelming relief when you knew that the baby would survive. And then the guilt later on when you discovered that, actually, there was a problem after all… Harry's mistake had come back to haunt him big time.

'Is there anyone we can call for you?' Isla asked.

'My mum.' Erin's mother dragged in a breath. 'My husband's working away.'

'OK. As soon as Erin's settled on the ward, we'll get in touch with your mum,' Isla promised.

Harry worked with Isla on most of his list of patients that morning, and he liked the fact that his new colleague was incredibly calm, had a sharp eye, and her quiet and gentle manner stopped patients or their parents panicking. The perfect emergency nurse. He had no idea where she'd trained or where she'd worked before—Scotland was a pretty big area—but he'd just bet that she was sorely missed. She'd certainly be appreciated at the London Victoria.

They hadn't had time for a coffee break all morning and Harry was thirsty and ravenous by the time he took his lunch break—late, and he knew he'd end up grabbing something fast in the canteen so he could be back on the ward in time. When he walked into the staffroom, Isla was there.

'Hi, there. Do you want to come and grab some lunch with me?' he asked.

She gave him a cool smile. 'Thanks, but I don't think so.'

He frowned. 'Why not?'

Her expression said quite clearly, *do you really have to ask?* But she was polite as she said, 'It's nice of you to ask me, but I don't think we're each other's type.'

He blinked, not quite following. 'What?'

She looked uncomfortable. 'I, um, might be new here, but that doesn't make me an instant addition to a little black book.'

Then the penny dropped. She thought he was asking her out? Some of the other staff teased him about being a heartbreaker and a serial dater, but that was far from true. He always made sure that whoever he dated knew it was for fun, not for ever. And he hadn't been asking her out on a date anyway. Obviously someone had been gossiping about him and she'd listened to the tittle-tattle rather than waiting to see for herself. 'Actually,' he said quietly, 'as you're new to the team, I was guessing that you hadn't had time to find your way around the hospital that well yet and you might not have anyone to sit with at lunchtime, that's all.'

Her face flamed, clashing with that spectacular hair. 'I—um—sorry. I'd just heard…' She broke off. 'Sorry. I'm putting my foot in it even more.'

'Heard what?' The words were out before he could stop them.

'You have, um, a bit of a reputation for, um, dating a lot.'

He sighed. 'Honestly, where the hospital grapevine's concerned, you can't win. If you don't date, then either you're gay or you've got some tragic past; and if you do date but make it clear you're not looking for a serious relationship, then you're at the mercy of everyone who wants to be the exception to the rule and you get called a heartbreaker. Not everyone's desperate to pair off and settle down.'

'I know.' She bit her lip. 'Sorry.'

But he noticed that she still hadn't accepted his invitation to join him for lunch. Which stung. Was his reputation really that bad?

Pushing down his exasperation at the hospital grapevine, Harry gave Isla his sweetest smile. 'OK, but I give you fair warning—if you try and eat a sandwich in here, you'll be lucky to finish half of it before someone calls you to help out with something.'

'I guess it's all part of working in a hospital environment,' she said lightly.

OK. He could take a hint. 'See you later,' he said.

In the canteen, Harry saw a crowd he recognised from the maternity ward and joined them. But all the while he was thinking about Isla. Why had their new nurse been so guarded? Was it just because of whatever nonsense she'd heard about him on the hospital grapevine? Or was she like that with everyone?

Just as Harry had predicted, Isla was halfway through her sandwich when someone came into the rest room and asked her to help out.

She didn't mind—it was all part and parcel of being part of a team on the busiest department in the hospital.

But she did feel bad about the way she'd reacted to Harry the Heartbreaker. Especially after he'd explained why he'd asked her to lunch; it was just what she would've done herself if a new team member had joined the practice where she'd worked on the island. She'd been unfair to him. And, even though she'd apologised, she'd felt too awkward to join him and ended up making things worse. He probably thought she was standoffish and rude. But how could she explain without telling him about the past she was trying to put well and truly behind her?

It didn't help that she found him so attractive.

Common sense told Isla that she needed to keep her distance. Apart from the fact that she'd seen a few working relationships turn really awkward and sour after the personal relationship had ended, she wasn't in the market for a relationship anyway. Particularly with someone who had the reputation of being a charmer.

Professional only, she reminded herself. She'd apologise again for the sake for their working relationship. And that would be that.

* * *

Isla was rostered on cubicles again with Josie and Harry in the afternoon. Harry had just finished with a patient who'd been brought in with a degloving injury; when he came out of the cubicle, she asked quietly, 'Can we have a quick word?'

'Sure.'

Isla took a deep breath. 'I wanted to apologise about earlier.'

He looked blank. 'About what?'

'I was rude and standoffish when you asked me to go to lunch with you.'

His eyes crinkled at the corners. 'Oh, that. Don't worry about it. Blame it on the hospital grapevine blowing everything out of proportion.'

She felt the betraying colour seep into her face. This would be the easy option because there was some truth in it, but he'd been kind and he didn't deserve it. 'Should've known better because hospital gossip likes to embroider things,' she said. Not just hospitals: any small community. Like an island off the coast of Scotland where everybody knew practically everything about everyone. And she of all people knew how it felt to be gossiped about unfairly. 'I was rude. And I apologise. And maybe I can buy you a cup of tea later to make up for being so horrible.'

'You weren't horrible, just a bit...well, offish. Apology and offer of tea accepted. We can have Mr Kemp as our chaperone, if you like,' he suggested.

How could he be so good-natured about it? It made her feel even more guilty. 'I guess it's a good excuse to see how he's getting on.'

'Great. It's a non-date,' Harry said.

And oh, that smile. It could light up a room. He really was gorgeous. And nice with it. And he had a sense of humour.

It would be all too easy to let Harry Gardiner tempt her.

But this nurse wasn't for tempting.

They spent their afternoon break in the Acute Medical Unit with Mr Kemp.

'Thank you for the tea,' he said.

'Our pleasure,' Isla told him with a smile.

'You won't get into trouble for being here, will you?' he checked.

This time, Harry smiled. 'It's our afternoon break. We're allowed to take it outside our own ward if we want to.'

'I'm such a trouble to you,' Mr Kemp said.

'It's fine,' Isla reassured him. 'Has your daughter been able to visit, yet?'

'She's coming straight after work. I do feel bad about it. She's had to get someone to pick up the kids.'

'All the working mums I know are great at juggling,' Harry said. 'I bet you she's picked up her friend's children before now. It won't be a problem. Everyone mucks in to help their friends. How are you feeling?'

'Well enough to go home,' Mr Kemp said. 'If I was home, I wouldn't be a burden to everyone.'

He was able to swallow again, Isla thought, but he definitely wasn't quite ready to go home. And he'd be far more of a worry to his family if he was on his own in his flat. 'I'm sure the team here will sort things out for you,' she said brightly.

And she discovered that Lorraine had been absolutely on the ball about Harry being great with patients, because he somehow managed to find out that Mr Kemp loved dogs and got him chatting about that, distracting him from his worries about being a burden.

'You were brilliant with Mr Kemp,' she said on their way back to the Emergency Department.

Harry gave a dismissive wave of his hand. 'Just chatting. And I noticed you were watching him drinking and assessing him.'

She nodded. 'I'm happier with his swallowing, but I think he'll be in for a couple more days yet. They'll want to assess him for a water infection or a chest infection, in case that contributed to the fall as well as the stroke. And they'll need to get social services in to look at his care plan as well as talk to his family. I'm guessing that he's not so good with accepting help, and from what he said to us earlier it sounded as if his son-in-law doesn't have much patience.'

'Very true.' Harry gave her a sidelong look. 'Though I know a few people caught between caring for their kids and caring for their elderly parents. It can be hard to juggle, and—well, not all parents are easy.'

'And some are brilliant.' Isla's own parents had been wonderful—they'd never believed Andrew's accusations right from the start, and they'd encouraged her to retrain in Glasgow and then move to London and start again.

'Yes, some are brilliant.' Harry was looking curiously at her.

'It takes all sorts to make a world,' she said brightly. Why on earth hadn't she moved him away from the subject of parents? Why had she had to open her mouth? 'And we have patients to see.'

'Yes, we do. Well, Sister McKenna.' He opened the door for her. 'Shall we?'

CHAPTER TWO

'Is Isla not coming tonight?' Harry asked Lorraine at the bowling alley, keeping his tone casual.

'No.'

Lorraine wasn't forthcoming with a reason and Harry knew better than to ask, because it would be the quickest way to fuel gossip. Not that Lorraine was one to promote the hospital rumour mill, but she might let slip to Isla that she thought Harry might be interested in her, and that would make things awkward between them at work. She'd already got the wrong idea about him.

All the same, this was the third team night out in a fortnight that Isla had missed. On the ward, she was an excellent colleague; she was good with patients and relatives, quick to offer sensible suggestions to clinical problems, and she got on well with everyone. The fact that she didn't come to any of the team nights out seemed odd, especially as she was new to the department and going out with the team would be a good chance for her to get to know her colleagues better.

Maybe Isla was a single parent or caring for an elderly relative, and it was difficult for her to arrange someone to sit with her child or whoever in the evenings. But he could hardly ask her about it without it seeming as if he was prying.

And he wasn't; though he was intrigued by her. Then again, if it turned out that she was a single parent, that'd be a deal-breaker for him. He really didn't want to be back in the position of having parental type responsibilities for a child. OK, so lightning rarely struck twice—but he didn't want to take the risk.

'Shame,' he said lightly, and switched the conversation round to who was going to be in which team.

Two days later, it was one of the worst days in the department Harry had had in months. He, Isla and Josie were in Resus together, trying to save a motorcyclist who'd been involved in a head-on crash—but the man's injuries were just too severe. Just when Harry had thought they were getting somewhere and the outcome might be bearable after all, the man had arrested and they just hadn't been able to get him back.

'I'm calling it,' Harry said when his last attempt with the defibrillator produced no change. 'It's been twenty minutes now. He's not responding. Is everyone agreed that we should stop?'

Isla and Josie both looked miserable, but voiced their agreement.

'OK. Time of death, one fifty-three,' he said softly, and pulled the sheet up to cover their patient's face. 'Thank you, team. You all worked really well.'

But it hadn't been enough, and they all knew it.

'OK. Once we've moved him out of Resus and cleaned him up, I'll go and find out if Reception managed to get hold of a next of kin and if anyone's here,' he said.

'If they have, I'll come with you, if you like,' Isla offered.

'Thank you.' He hated breaking bad news. Having

someone there would make it a little easier. And maybe she'd know what to say when he ran out of words.

The motorcyclist, Jonathan Pryor, was only twenty-seven, and his next of kin were his parents. The receptionist had already sent a message to Resus that Jonathan's mum was waiting in the relatives' room.

'I hate this bit so much,' he said softly as he and Isla walked towards the relatives' room.

'We did everything we possibly could,' she reminded him.

'I know.' It didn't make him feel any better. But the sympathy in her blue, blue eyes made his heart feel just a fraction less empty.

Mrs Pryor looked up hopefully as they knocked on the door and walked in. 'Jonathan? He's all right? He's out of Theatre or whatever and I can go and see him?'

Harry could see the very second that she realised the horrible truth—that her son was very far from being all right—and her face crumpled.

'I'm so sorry, Mrs Pryor,' he said softly, taking her hand. 'We did everything we could to save him, but he arrested on the table—he had a heart attack, and we just couldn't get him back.'

Sobs racked her body. 'I always hated him riding that wretched motorcycle. I worried myself sick every time he went out on it because I *knew* that something like this would happen. I can't bear it.' Her voice was a wail of distress. 'And now I'll never see him again. My boy. My little boy.'

Harry knew there was nothing he could do or say to make this better. He just sat down next to Mrs Pryor and kept holding her hand, letting her talk about her son.

Isla went to the vending machine. Harry knew without having to ask that she was making a cup of hot, sweet tea for Mrs Pryor. He could've done with one himself, but he wasn't going to be that selfish. The only thing he could do now for his patient was to comfort his grieving mother.

'Thank you, but I don't want it,' Mrs Pryor said when Isla offered her the paper cup. 'It won't bring my son back.'

'I know,' Isla said gently, 'but you've just had a horrible shock and this will help. Just a little bit, but it will help.'

Mrs Pryor looked as if she didn't believe the nurse, but she took the paper cup and sipped from it.

'Is there anyone we can call for you?' Harry asked.

'My—my husband.' She shook her head blankly. 'Oh, God. How am I going to tell him?'

'I can do that for you,' Harry said gently. 'It might be easier on both of you if I tell him.' Even though he hated breaking bad news.

Mrs Pryor dragged in a breath. 'All right—thank you.'

'And you can come and see Jonathan whenever you feel ready,' Isla said. 'I'll come with you, and you can spend some time alone with him, too. I can call the hospital chaplain to come and see you, if you'd like me to.'

Mrs Pryor shook her head. 'I've never been the religious type. Talking to the chaplain's not going to help. It's not going to bring Jonathan back, is it?''

'I understand,' Isla said, 'but if you change your mind just tell me. Anything we can do to help, we will.'

'He was only twenty-seven. That's way too young to die.' Mrs Pryor shut her eyes very tightly. 'And that's a stupid thing to say. I know children younger than that get killed in accidents every day.'

Yeah, Harry thought. Or, if not killed, left with life-changing injuries, even if they weren't picked up at first. His own little sister was proof of that. He pushed the thought and the guilt away. *Not now.* He needed to concentrate on his patient's bereaved mother.

'It's just...you never think it's going to happen to your own. You hope and you pray it never will.' She sighed. 'I know he was a grown man, but he'll always be my little boy.'

Harry went out to his office to call Mr Pryor to break the bad news, while Isla took over his job of holding Mrs Pryor's hand and letting her talk. On the way to his office, Harry asked one of the team to clean Jonathan's face and prepare him so his parents wouldn't have to see the full damage caused to their son by the crash. And then he went back to the relatives' room to join Isla and Mrs Pryor, staying there until Mr Pryor arrived, twenty minutes later. The Pryors clung together in their grief, clearly having trouble taking it all in. But finally, Mr Pryor asked brokenly, 'Can we see him?'

'Of course,' Harry said.

He and Isla took the Pryors through to the side room where Jonathan's body had been taken so they could see their son in private. They stayed for a few minutes in case the Pryors had any questions; then Isla caught Harry's eye and he gave the tiniest nod of agreement, knowing what she was going to say.

Then Isla said gently to the Pryors, 'We'll be just outside if you need us for anything.'

'Thank you,' Mrs Pryor said, her voice full of tears.

Outside the side room, Isla said to Harry, 'I'll finish up here—you'll be needed back in Resus.'

'Are you sure?' he asked. He was needed back in Resus; but at the same time he didn't think it was fair to leave Isla to deal with grieving parents all on her own.

She nodded. 'I'm sure.'

He reached out and squeezed her hand, trying to ignore the tingle that spread through his skin at her touch—now really wasn't an appropriate time. 'Thank you. You were brilliant. And even though I know you're more than capable of answering any questions the Pryors might have, if you need backup or want me to come and talk to them about anything, you know where to find me.'

'Yes. Those poor people,' she said softly.

'This is the bit of our job I really wish didn't exist,' Harry said.

'I know. But it does, and we have to do our best.' She squeezed his hand back, and loosened it. 'Off you go.'

He wrote up the paperwork, and headed back to Resus. To his relief, the next case was one that he could actually fix. The patient had collapsed, and all the tests showed Harry that it was a case of undiagnosed diabetes. The patient was in diabetic ketoacidosis; Harry was able to start treatment, and then explain to the patient's very relieved wife that her husband would be fine but they'd need to see a specialist about diabetes and learn how to monitor his blood sugar, plus in future they'd have to keep an eye on his diet to suit his medical condition.

Mid-afternoon, Harry actually had a chance to take his break. He hadn't seen Isla back in Resus since leaving her with the Pryors, so he went in search of her; he discovered that she was doing paperwork.

'Hey. I'm pulling rank,' he said.

She looked up. 'What?'

'Right now, I really need some cake. And I think, after the day you've had, so do you. So I prescribe the hospital canteen for both of us.'

'What about Josie?'

Harry smiled. 'She's already had her break and is in cubicles right now, but I'm going to bring her some cake back. You can help me pick what she'd like.'

For a moment, he thought Isla was going to balk at being alone with him; then she smiled. 'Thanks. I'd like that.'

'Let's go,' he said. 'We have fifteen minutes. Which is just about enough time to walk to the canteen, grab cake, and chuck back a mug of coffee.'

She rolled her eyes, but stood up to join him.

'How were the Pryors?' he asked softly when they were sitting at the table in the canteen with a massive slice of carrot cake and a mug of good, strong coffee each.

'Devastated,' she said. 'But they got to spend time with their son and I explained that he didn't suffer in Resus—that the end was quick.'

'Yeah,' he said with a sigh. 'I hate cases like that. The guy still had his whole life before him.' And something else had been bugging him. 'He was only five years younger than I am.' The exact same age as one of his siblings. And he'd had to fight the urge to text every single one of his siblings who was old enough to drive to say that they were never, ever, *ever* to ride a motorbike.

'He was three years younger than me,' Isla said.

It was first time she'd offered any personal information, and it encouraged him enough to say, 'You were brilliant with the Pryors and I really appreciate it. I assume you had a fair bit of experience with bereaved relatives when you worked in your last emergency department?'

'Actually, no.'

He blinked at her. 'How come?'

'I wasn't in an emergency department, as such—I was a nurse practitioner in a GP surgery. I retrained in Glasgow and then came here,' she said.

Something else he hadn't known about her. 'You retrained to give you better opportunities for promotion?' he asked.

'Something like that.'

She was clearly regretting sharing as much as she had, and he could tell that she was giving him back-off signals. OK. He'd take the hint. He smiled at her. 'Sorry. We're a nosey bunch at the London Victoria—and I talk way too much. Blame it on the sugar rush from the cake.'

'And on having a rough day,' she added. 'So you've always worked in the emergency department?'

'Pretty much. I trained in London; I did my foundation years here, with stints in Paediatrics and Gastroenterology.' Because of what had happened to Tasha, his first choice had been Paediatrics. He'd been so sure that it was his future. 'But, as soon as I started in the Emergency Department, I knew I'd found the right place for me. So I stayed and I worked my way up,' he said.

'Thirty-two's not that old for a special reg,' she said thoughtfully. 'Though I've already seen for myself that you're good at what you do.'

Funny how much her words warmed him. He inclined his head briefly. 'Thank you, kind madam.'

'It wasn't meant to be a compliment. It was a statement of fact,' she said crisply.

He grinned. 'I like you, Isla. You're good for my ego. Keeping it in check.'

She actually smiled back, and his heart missed a beat. When she smiled, she really was beautiful.

'I've known worse egos in my time,' she said.

'And you gave them just as short shrift?'

'Something like that.'

He looked at her. 'Can I ask you something?'

'That depends,' she said.

'Why haven't you come to any of the departmental nights out?'

'Because they're not really my thing,' she said.

'So you don't like ten-pin bowling, pub quizzes or pizza.' He paused. 'What kind of things do you like, Isla?'

'Why?'

'Because you've only been at the London Victoria for a couple of weeks, you've told me that you retrained to come here, and I'm assuming that you don't really know anyone around here. It must be a bit lonely.'

Yes, she was lonely. She still missed her family and her friends in the Western Isles hugely. And, even though she was trying to put her past behind her, part of her worried about socialising with her new colleagues. It would be too easy to let something slip. And then their reaction to her might change. Some would pity her; others would think there was no smoke without fire. And neither reaction was one she wanted to face.

She didn't think Harry was asking her out—he'd already made it clear he thought his reputation wasn't deserved—but it wouldn't hurt to make things clear. 'You're right—I don't know many people in London,' she said softly. 'And I could use a friend. *Just* a friend,' she added. 'Because I'm concentrating on my career right now.'

'That works for me,' Harry said. 'So can we be friends?'

'I'd like that,' she said. Even if his smile did make

her weak at the knees. Friendship was all she was prepared to offer.

'Friends,' he said, and reached over to shake her
hand.

And Isla really had to ignore the tingle that went
through her at the touch of his skin. Nothing was going
to happen between them. They were colleagues—about
to be friends—and that was all.

CHAPTER THREE

WHEN ISLA WENT into the staffroom that morning for a mug of tea, Harry was the only one there. He was staring into his mug of coffee as if he was trying to lose himself in it. She knew that feeling well—she'd been there herself only a few months ago, when her life had turned into a living nightmare—and her heart went out to him.

'Tough shift so far?' she asked, gently placing her hand on his arm for a moment.

'No—yes,' he admitted. Then he grimaced. 'Never mind. Forget I said anything.'

It wasn't like Harry Gardiner to be brusque. The doctor she'd got to know over the last month was full of smiles, always seeing the good in the world.

He also hadn't quite lived up to his heartbreaker reputation, because since Isla had known Harry he hadn't actually dated anyone. He'd even turned down a couple of offers, which was hardly the act of the Lothario that the hospital rumour mill made him out to be. Maybe he'd told her the truth when he'd said he wasn't a heartbreaker.

Right now, something had clearly upset him. Though she understood about keeping things to yourself. Since the day that Andrew Gillespie had made that awful accusation and her fiancé had actually believed him, she'd done the same. Keeping your feelings to yourself was the safest way. 'OK,' she said. 'But if you want to talk, you know where I am.'

'Thanks.' But Harry still seemed sunk in the depths of gloom. He was still serious when he was working in minors with her, not even summoning up his store of terrible jokes to distract a little boy whose knee he had to suture after Isla had cleaned up the bad cut.

By mid-afternoon, she was really worried about him. To the point of being bossy. 'Right. I'm pulling rank,' she said. 'You need cake, so I'm dragging you off to the canteen.'

'Yes, Sister McKenna,' he said. But his eyes were dull rather than gleaming with amusement. And that worried her even more.

Once they were sitting in the canteen—where she'd insisted on buying lemon cake for him—she asked, 'So are you going to tell me what's wrong?'

He said nothing; but she waited, knowing that if you gave someone enough space and time they'd start talking.

Except he didn't.

'Harry, either you've suddenly become a monk and taken a vow of silence as well as chastity, or something's wrong.'

He looked at her. 'How do you know I'm chaste?'

She met his gaze. 'According to the hospital rumour mill, you haven't dated in a month and everyone thinks you must be ill.'

'They ought to mind their own business.' He scowled. 'I'm not ill. I just don't want to date.'

Fair enough. She could understand that; it was how she felt, too.

'And the silence?' she asked.

He sighed. 'I don't want to talk about it here.'

So there *was* something wrong. And she liked Harry. She hated to think of him being miserable. And maybe talking to her would help him. 'After work, then? Somewhere else, somewhere that people from round here aren't likely to be hanging round to overhear what you're saying?'

There was a gleam of interest in his eyes. 'Are you asking me on a date, Sister McKenna?'

'That I'm most definitely not,' she said crisply. But then she softened. 'We're friends, Harry, and friends support each other. You look upset about something and you've been a bit serious at work lately, so something's obviously wrong. If you want to go for a drink with me after work or something and talk, then the offer's there.'

'I could use a friend,' he said. 'But you never socialise outside work, Isla. And isn't someone waiting at home for you?'

'I'm single, as well you know.'

He wrinkled his nose. 'I didn't mean that.'

'I don't follow.'

'Maybe you have a child,' he explained, 'or a relative you're caring for.'

'Is that what people are saying about me? That because I don't go on team nights out, I must be a single parent with babysitting problems?'

He winced. 'People get curious. But I haven't been gossiping about you.'

Given what he'd said about the hospital rumour mill, she believed him. 'Just for the record, I don't have a child, and I don't look after anyone. There's just me. And that's fine.'

'Not even a goldfish or a cat?'

'No.' She would've loved a dog, but it wouldn't be fair to leave a dog alone all day. Hospital shifts and pets didn't mix that well, unless you were in a family where you could share the care. Not to mention the clause in the lease of her flat saying that she couldn't have pets. 'You know what the old song says about not being able to take a goldfish for a walk.'

'I guess.' He paused. 'Thank you, Isla. I'll think of somewhere and text you. Shall we meet there?'

She knew exactly what he wasn't saying. Because, if they travelled to the pub or café together, someone was likely to see them and start speculating about whether they were seeing each other. Harry obviously didn't want to be the centre of gossip, and neither did she. 'Deal,' she said.

After his shift finished, Harry texted Isla the address of the wine bar and directions on how to find it.

Funny, she was the last person he'd expected to take him under her wing. She didn't date, whereas he had the not-quite-deserved reputation of dating hundreds of women and breaking their hearts. He'd been at the London Victoria for years and she'd been working there for just under a month. And yet she'd been the only one in the department who'd picked up his dark mood; and she'd been the only one who'd offered him a listening ear.

Harry didn't tend to talk about his family.

But maybe talking to someone who didn't know him that well—and most certainly didn't know any of the other people involved—might help. A fresh pair of eyes to help him see the right course of action. Because this wedding was really getting under his skin and Harry didn't have a clue why it was upsetting him so much.

It wasn't as if his father hadn't got remarried before. So why, why, *why* had it got to him so much this time?

Harry was already halfway through his glass of Merlot when Isla walked into the wine bar, looked round and came over to his table. 'Hi.'

'Hi. You look lovely. I've never seen you wearing normal clothes instead of your nurse's uniform.' The words were out before he could stop them and he grimaced. 'Sorry. I wasn't hitting on you.'

Much.

Because he had to admit that he was attracted to Isla McKenna. That gorgeous creamy skin, her dark red hair, the curve of her mouth that made her look like the proverbial princess just waiting to be woken from her sleep by love's first kiss...

He shook himself mentally.

Not now.

If he told Isla what was going through his head right now, she'd walk straight out of the bar. And it would take God knew how long to get their easy working relationship back in place. He didn't want that to happen.

'You look odd without a white coat, too,' she said, to his relief; clearly she hadn't picked up on his attraction to her and was just responding to his words at face value.

'Let me get you a drink. What would you like?' he asked.

'I'll join you in whatever you're having.' She gestured to his glass.

'Australian Merlot. OK. Back in a tick.'

Ordering a drink gave him enough time to compose himself. He bought her a glass of wine and walked back to their table, where she looked as if she was checking messages on her phone. 'Everything OK?' he asked.

'Yes.' She smiled at him. 'I'm just texting my mum, my sister and my brother to tell them I've had a good day.'

'You miss your family?' he asked.

She nodded. 'Sometimes the islands feel as far away as Australia.'

'The islands?' he asked, not sure what she meant.

'The Western Isles,' she said.

So she was from the Outer Hebrides? You couldn't get much more different from London, he thought: mountains, pretty little villages and the sea, compared to the capital's urban sprawl and the constant noise of traffic.

'It isn't that bad really,' she said. 'I can fly from here to Glasgow and then get a flight to Lewis, or get the train from Glasgow to Oban and catch the ferry home.'

But the wistfulness in her tone told him how much she missed her family. Something he couldn't quite get his head round, because he often felt so disconnected from his own. And how ironic that was, considering the size of his family. Eight siblings, with another one on the way. OK, so he didn't have much in common with his two youngest half-brothers; but he wasn't that close to the ones nearest his own age, either. And he always seemed to clash with his middle sister. Guilt made him overprotective, and she ended up rowing with him.

'But we're not talking about me,' she said before he could ask anything else. 'What's wrong?'

'You're very direct,' he said, playing for time.

'I find direct is the best way.'

He sighed. 'Considering how much you clearly miss your family, if I tell you what's bugging me you're going to think I'm the most selfish person in the universe.'

She smiled. 'Apart from the fact that there are usually two sides to every story, I very much doubt you're the most selfish person I've ever met.'

There was a tiny flicker in her expression, as if she was remembering something truly painful. And that made Harry feel bad about bringing those memories back to her.

'I'm sorry,' he said. 'Look, never mind. Let's just have a drink and talk about—oh, I dunno, the weather.' Something very English, and very safe.

She laughed. 'Nice try. Iain—my brother—squirms just like you do if we talk about anything remotely personal.'

'I guess it's a guy thing,' he said, trying to make light of it and wishing he hadn't started this.

'But sometimes,' she said gently, 'it's better out than in. A problem shared is a problem halved. And—' she wrinkled her nose. 'No, I can't think of any more clichés right now. Over to you.'

Despite his dark mood, Harry found himself smiling. He liked this woman. Really, really liked her. Which was another reason why he had to suppress his attraction to her. He wanted to keep her in his life instead of having to put up barriers, the way he normally did. 'I can't, either.' He blew out a breath. 'I hate talking about emotional stuff. And it's easier to talk when you're stuffed with carbs. They do fantastic pies here, and the butteriest, loveliest mashed potato in the world. Can we talk over dinner?'

'Pie and mash.' She groaned. 'Don't tell me you're planning to make me eat jellied eels or mushy peas as well.'

'Traditional London fare?' He laughed. 'No. For vegetables here I'd recommend the spinach. It's gloriously garlicky.'

'Provided we go halves,' she said, 'then yes. Let's have dinner. As friends, not as a date.'

Why was she so adamant about not dating? He guessed that maybe someone had hurt her. But he also had the strongest feeling that if he tried to focus on her or asked about her past, she'd shut the conversation down. 'Deal.'

Ordering food gave him a little more wriggle room.

But, once their food had been served and she'd agreed with him that the pie was to die for, he was back on the spot.

Eventually, he gave in and told her. Because hadn't that been the point of meeting her this evening, anyway? 'My dad's getting remarried,' he said.

'Uh-huh. And it's a problem why exactly?'

'Speaking like that makes you sound like Yoda.'

She gave him a narrow-eyed look. 'Don't try to change the subject.'

'You're a bossy lot, north of the border,' he muttered.

'And you Sassenachs have no staying power,' she said with a grin. 'Seriously, Harry, what's wrong? Don't you like his new wife-to-be?'

Harry shrugged. 'I don't really know her that well.'

'So what is it?'

'This is going to stay with you?' he checked.

She rolled her eyes. 'Of course it is.'

'Sorry. I didn't mean to accuse you of being a gossip. I know you're not. I don't...' He blew out a breath. 'Well, I don't tend to talk about my personal life.'

'And I appreciate that you're talking to me about it now,' she said softly.

He sighed. 'Dad wants me to be his best man.'

'And you don't want to do it?'

'No. It'd be for the third time,' Harry said. 'And I

really don't see the point of making such a big song and dance about the wedding, considering that in five years' time we'll be going through the exactly same thing all over again.'

She said nothing, just waited for him to finish.

He sighed again. 'My father—I don't know. Maybe it's a triumph of hope over experience. But this will be his seventh marriage, and this time his fiancée is younger than I am.'

His father's seventh marriage? Seeing that many relationships go wrong would make anyone wary of settling down, Isla thought. 'Maybe,' she said softly, 'your father hasn't found the right woman for him yet.'

'So this will be seventh time lucky? That'd go down really well in my best man's speech. Not.' He blew out a breath. 'Sorry. I didn't mean to be rude to you or take it out on you.' He grimaced. 'My father's charming—that is, he can be when it suits him. He can be great company. But he has a seriously low boredom threshold. And I can't understand why none of his wives has ever been able to see the pattern before she actually married him. Well, obviously not my mum, because she was the first. But every single one after that. Get married, have a baby, get bored, have an affair, move on. Nothing lasts for Dad for more than five years—well, his last one was almost seven years, but I think Julie was the one to end it instead of Dad. Or maybe he's slowing down a bit now he's in his mid-fifties.' Harry sighed. 'I really liked Fliss, his third wife. Considering she had to deal with me as a teenager...' He shrugged. 'She was really patient.'

'Did you live with your dad when you were growing up?' Isla asked.

Harry shook his head. 'I stayed with him for the occasional weekends, plus a week or so in the long school
holidays. I lived with my mum and my three half-sisters.
My mum also has a marriage habit, though at least she's
kept husband number four.' He paused. 'Maybe that's it.
Dad only has sons—six of us. Maybe he's hoping that
his new wife is carrying his daughter.'

Isla added it up swiftly. Harry was one of nine children, soon about to be ten? And he'd said something
about his mum being his father's first wife. 'I take it
you're the oldest?'

He nodded. 'Don't get me wrong. I like my brothers
and sisters well enough, but there's a whole generation
between me and the littlest ones, so we have absolutely
nothing in common. I feel more like an uncle than a
brother.' He gave her a thin smile. 'And let's just say the
best contraception ever is to get a teenager babysitting
for their younger siblings. I definitely don't want kids
of my own. Ever.'

'Remind me to tell my brother Iain how lucky he
is that he only had me and Mags tagging around after
him,' she said.

'You're the baby of the family?' he asked.

'Yes, and I'm thoroughly spoiled.'

He scoffed. 'You're far too sensible to be spoiled.'

'Thank you. I think.' She paused. 'Right. So you
don't want to be the best man and you don't want to go
to the wedding. I'm assuming you're trying not to hurt
anyone's feelings, so you could always say you can't
make the wedding due to pressure of work. That we're
really short-staffed and you just can't get the time off.'

'I've already tried that one,' Harry said. 'Dad says
my annual leave is part of my contract—he's a lawyer,
by the way, so I can't flannel him—and he says they

can always find a locum or call in an agency worker to fill in for me. Plus he gave me enough notice that I should've been able to swap off-duty with someone months ago to make sure I could be there.'

'How about a last-minute illness? Say we had noro-virus on the ward and you came down with it?' she suggested.

'Norovirus in the middle of summer?' He wrinkled his nose. 'Nope. That one's not going to fly.'

'You have other medics in your family, then?' she asked.

'One of my sisters is a trainee audiologist. But every-one knows that norovirus tends to be at its worst in the winter. All the newspapers make a big song and dance about emergency departments being on black alert at the peak of the winter vomiting virus season.' He sighed. 'I've thought about practically nothing else for weeks, and there just isn't a nice way to let everyone down.'

'So the kind approach isn't going to work. Have you tried telling any of your brothers that you don't want to go?'

He nodded. 'Jack—he's the next one down from me.'

'What did he say?'

'He thinks I should be there to support the old man. So does Fin—he's the next one down from Jack.'

'And how old are they?'

'Dad's kids are all spaced five years apart. So Jack and Fin are twenty-seven and twenty-two, respectively,' he explained. 'The odd one out will be the new baby, who'll be seven years younger than Evan—he's the youngest.'

'OK. So you have to go to the wedding. But what about this best man business? Isn't there anyone else who could do it? Does your dad have a best friend, a brother—or, hey, he could always be different and have a woman as his best man if he has a sister,' she suggested.

To her relief, that actually made Harry crack a smile. 'Best woman? I can't see Auntie Val agreeing to that. She says Dad's the male equivalent of a serial Bridezilla.' He took another sip of Merlot. 'Uncle Jeff—Dad's brother—has done the duty twice, and so has Marty, his best friend.'

'So if the three of you have all done it twice, what about your next brother down? Or the youngest one? Could it be their turn?'

'I could suggest it.' He paused. 'But even if I can be just a normal wedding guest instead of the best man, it still means running the gauntlet of everyone asking me how come I'm not married yet, and saying how I ought to get a move on and settle down because I'm ten years older now than Dad was when he got married the first time, and that means I'm totally on the shelf.'

'Apart from the fact that men are never described as being on the shelf, you would still've been a student medic at twenty-two,' Isla pointed out. 'And, with the crazy hours that junior doctors work, you wouldn't have had the time to get married or even spend that much time with your new wife back then.'

'But I'm not a student or a junior doctor now. In their view, I have no excuses not to settle down.'

'Maybe you could take a date to the wedding?' she suggested.

That would be Harry's worst nightmare. Taking a date to a family wedding implied that you were serious about taking the relationship further; then, when it was clear you didn't want to do that, someone would get hurt. But

Isla clearly meant well. 'I guess it would be a start—but it wouldn't stop the questions for long. They'd want to know how we met, how long we'd been dating, how serious it was, when we were planning to get engaged...' He rolled his eyes. 'They never stop.'

'So what would stop the questions?' she asked. 'What if you told them you're gay?'

'Nope. They'd still want to meet my partner. It's not the gender of my partner that's the issue—it's the non-existence.' He sighed. 'What would stop them? A hurricane, if it started raining fishes and frogs... No, that still wouldn't stop the questions for more than five minutes.' He blew out a breath. 'Or maybe I could invent a fiancée. And she isn't coming to the wedding with me because...' He wrinkled his nose. 'Why wouldn't she be with me?'

'She's working?' Isla suggested.

He shook his head. 'They'd never believe it. Same as the norovirus idea. The only way they'd believe I was engaged was if I turned up with my fiancée in tow.'

'And I'm assuming that you don't have anyone in your life who's even close to being a fiancée?'

No.

But, now he thought of it, that wasn't such a bad idea. If there was someone he could convince to go with him. Someone safe. Someone who wouldn't get the wrong idea. Someone *sensible*.

'That's a good point,' he said. 'She wouldn't have to be a real fiancée.' He smiled as he warmed to his theme. 'Just someone who'd go to the wedding with me and stop all the endless questions. Enough to keep everyone happy and nobody gets hurt.'

'Lying is never a good idea,' Isla said, grimacing.

'Hey—you suggested it.'

'Forget it. I was being flippant. It's a stupid idea.'

'Actually, I think it's a great one. And it won't be a lie. Just a teensy, tiny fib to shut everyone up. Not even a fib, really: it'd be more of an exaggeration,' Harry said. 'And if anyone asks me afterwards about setting a date, I can say that my fiancée and I realised we were making a mistake, had a long talk about it and agreed to call it all off.' He smiled. 'And my fake fiancée will know all this up front, so it'll be just fine. She won't be expecting me to marry her.'

'Do you have someone in mind?'

Someone safe. Who wouldn't get the wrong idea. Who didn't have a partner to make things complicated. And the person who ticked all those boxes just so happened to be sitting right opposite him.

Would she do it?

There was only one way to find out.

He looked straight at her. 'What are you doing, the weekend after next?'

CHAPTER FOUR

'LET ME GET this straight.' Isla's eyes were the most piercing shade of blue Harry had ever seen. 'You want me to go to this wedding with you—as your fake fiancée?'

It was the perfect solution to his problem. And she'd sort of suggested it in the first place. 'Yes.'

'No.'

'Why not? Because you're on duty and it'd be awkward to swap shifts with someone without explaining why and setting the hospital rumour mill going?'

'No, actually, I'm off duty that weekend.'

'Then what's the problem?' He frowned. 'You're exactly the right person to ask.'

'How?' she scoffed.

'Because if I ask anyone else to come to the wedding and meet my family, they'll have expectations,' he explained. 'They'll think that meeting my family means that I want a relationship with them. But you—you're different. You don't date. So you'll understand that I'm only asking you to come with me to the wedding to take the heat off me and stop my family nagging me to death about settling down, not because I'm secretly in love with you and want to spend the rest of my life with you.'

'That's crazy, Harry.' She shook her head. 'As I said, I was being flippant when I suggested it. You can't possibly go to a wedding and pretend you're with someone when you're not.'

'Why not?'

'Because you'll be lying to your family.'

'No, I'll just be distracting them a little,' he corrected. 'Isla, I'm asking you because I'm desperate.'

'Did you hear what you just said?' Her voice was so soft; and yet at the same time there was an edge to it.

And he could see why. He could've phrased it a lot better. He winced. 'I don't mean desperate as in...' He shook his head to clear it. 'I'm digging myself an even deeper hole, here. What I mean, Isla, is that I need a friend to support me through a day I'm really not looking forward to. A friend I can trust not to misinterpret my intentions.'

'We barely know each other,' she pointed out. 'For all you know, I could be a psychopath.'

'Ah, now that I *am* clear about,' he said. 'I've spent a month working with you. I've seen you with patients. You're kind—you're tough when you need to be and you don't shy away from difficult situations, but overall you're kind and you're sensible and you're...' He floundered for the right word. 'Well, you're nice.'

'Nice.' She sounded as if he'd just insulted her.

'I like you. Enormously. Which is why I'm asking you—because I can trust you,' he said. 'You're safe.'

'We'd still be lying to your family.'

'A white lie. Something to keep them all happy, so their attention stays on the wedding instead of on me.'

'Nobody's ever going to believe I'm your fiancée.'

'Of course they are. If we keep the story to as near the truth as possible, it'll be convincing. We work together—

and as far as they're concerned I fell in love with you as soon as I met you. You're a...what's the Scottish equivalent of an English rose?'

'I have no idea. A thistle?'

Hmm. She definitely sounded prickly right now.

'They won't buy it.' She rolled her eyes. 'I bet you normally date glamorous women. And I'm hardly the type who'd be scouted for a modelling agency.'

'You're a bit too short to be a model,' he agreed. 'But if you were six inches taller, you could be.'

She scoffed. 'It's not just my height. I'm not thin enough, either.'

'You're not fat by any stretch of the imagination. You have curves. Which isn't a bad thing.' Apart from the fact that now he was wondering what it would be like to touch said curves. How soft her skin would be under his fingertips. And she was strictly off limits, so he couldn't allow himself to think about that. 'Any of my family would take one look at you and think, yes, she's exactly the type Harry would fall for. Beautiful hair, beautiful skin, beautiful eyes, a kissable mouth.'

And now he'd said way too much. She was looking thoroughly insulted.

'It's not just about looks,' he said, guessing that was the problem—he knew his sisters hated being judged on what they looked like rather than who they were. 'As soon as they talked to you they'd think, yes, she's bright and sparky and not afraid to speak her mind, so she's perfect for Harry. He's not going to get bored with her. You've got the whole package, so it's totally believable that I'd fall for you.'

She lifted her chin. 'I'm not looking for a relationship.'

'I know, and neither am I. What I'm looking for right

now is a friend who'll help me out of a hole and humour my family for a weekend.'

'So it's suddenly gone from a day to a weekend?' she asked, sounding horrified.

'It's in Cornwall, which means it's a five-hour drive from here—and that's provided we don't get any hold-ups on the motorway. The wedding's on Saturday afternoon. We can drive up first thing in the morning, stay overnight in the hotel, and then drive back on Sunday at our leisure. Which is far better than spending at least ten hours stuck in a car, as well as going to a wedding.' He blew out a breath. 'And I know it's a bit of a cheek, asking you for two days of your precious off-duty. I wouldn't ask unless I was...'

'Desperate?' Her voice was very crisp and her accent was pronounced.

'Unless I could think of any other way out of it,' he corrected. 'Or if I could think of someone else who was single but who wouldn't misunderstand my motivation for asking her to be my plus-one for the wedding.' He sighed. 'Look, forget I asked. I don't want to ruin our working relationship. I like you and respect you too much for that, and I haven't meant to insult you. This whole thing about the wedding has temporarily scrambled my brains. You're right. It's crazy. Let's pretend we never had this conversation.' He gave her a grim smile. 'I'll just man up, go to the wedding, and do what I always do about the nagging—ignore it.' He looked away. 'My next brother down is married, and the brother below him is engaged. Maybe that'll be enough to distract them all.' Though, more likely, it would give everyone more ammunition. If Jack and Fin could find someone and settle down, why couldn't he?

Though he knew the answer to that. He didn't believe

in love. Not with the number of divorces he'd seen. The first one had been his parents, when he was five; then two more for his mum, and five more for his dad. That was all the proof Harry needed that marriage and settling down didn't work out for his family.

Isla looked at Harry. He'd said he didn't want to go to his father's wedding. Was it really that unreasonable of him to want someone to go with him—someone who wouldn't give him a hard time about his marital status? And to ask someone who he knew wouldn't misinterpret the request as his way of suggesting a serious relationship?

Then again, he was asking her to lie. Something she really didn't agree with. But she hadn't told Harry why she had such a thing about lying. About what had happened on the island: that her fiancé's stepfather ruined her life. He'd made a totally untrue complaint about her to her boss, which of course had been investigated. Any complaint against a member of the practice—even if it wasn't true—had to be considered seriously.

Even though she'd been completely exonerated of any wrong-doing, half the island had still believed that it must've been a cover-up. Andrew Gillespie was charming, popular, and employed a lot of people locally. What possible reason would he have had to lie?

She knew the answer to that. And if she'd told the full truth it would've blown his life apart—and there would've been collateral damage, too. People she really cared about would've been badly hurt. The gossip would have spread like wildfire, and done just as much damage.

But what had really hurt her was that Stewart had believed Andrew's lie. The one man she'd expected to be on her side… And he'd let her down. He hadn't backed her. At all.

She took a deep breath. 'Let me think about it.'

Harry's face brightened. 'You'll do it?'

'I said I'll *think* about it,' she corrected. And maybe she could find a compromise. Something that meant Harry could have her company at the wedding but without lying about it.

'Thank you. I appreciate it. And, if you do decide to go with me, I'd be more than happy to buy you a dress or whatever.'

'That's nice of you,' she said, 'but it really won't be necessary. Apart from the fact that I can afford to buy my own clothes, thank you very much, my wardrobe consists of a wee bit more than just my uniform and jeans.'

He laughed. 'That's what I like about you. You always tell it straight.'

'There's no point in doing otherwise.'

He smiled. 'Agreed.'

'So now can we change the subject?'

Isla thought about it late into the evening when she got home to her flat. She liked Harry's company; and weddings usually meant good food, good company and dancing, all of which she enjoyed. She was seriously tempted to go with him.

And that was exactly the reason why she should say no.

It would be all too easy to get involved with Harry, and she didn't want a relationship. Neither did he. And she really felt for him. Why did his family put so much pressure on him to settle down? Why couldn't they see him for who he was—a gifted doctor who was fantastic with patients?

Her own family had always supported her and valued her. They'd stuck up for her and done their best to squash the rumours that Andrew Gillespie had started. And, when it was clear that the whispers weren't going to go away and she was going to have to leave, they'd backed her. So Isla found it hard to understand why Harry's family didn't support him.

Or was it that he didn't let them close enough to support him? Had his determination to avoid his parents' mistakes and string of broken marriages made him push them away?

She decided to sleep on it.

And she was still mulling it over on her way to work, the next morning.

Not that she had a chance to discuss it with Harry during the day. He was rostered on cubicles while she was busy in Resus, spending the morning helping to stabilise a teenage girl who'd been knocked over crossing the road while she was so busy texting her boyfriend that she didn't see the car coming. The girl had a broken pelvis, her left leg and arm were broken in several places, she had internal bleeding, and the team had to fight hard to control it before she was able to go up to the operating theatre and have the bones fixed by the orthopaedics team. The afternoon was equally busy, with two heart attacks and a suspected stroke, though Isla was really glad that in all three cases there was a positive outcome and the patients were all admitted to the wards to recover.

By the time her shift was over, Harry had already left the hospital, though he'd also left a text message on her phone asking her to call him or text him when she'd come to a decision.

If she said no, she'd feel guilty about tossing him to the wolves.

If she said yes, she'd be lying. Something she didn't want to do. Someone else's lies had wrecked her engagement, and then she'd ended up leaving the job she loved and moving hundreds of miles away to make a new start.

But Harry was trying to keep his family happy, not trying to get his own way and prove how much power he had. Which was a very different category of lying from Andrew Gillespie's. It still wasn't good, but it wasn't meant maliciously. It meant Harry could let his family down gently.

Or maybe just having someone go with him to the wedding would be enough. They didn't necessarily have to pretend to be a couple, did they?

She picked up her phone and called him.

The line rang once, twice, three times—and then the voicemail message kicked in. Not even a personalised one, she noticed: Harry had left it as the standard bland recorded message saying that his number was unavailable right now, so please leave a message or send a text.

'It's Isla,' she said. 'Call me when you're free.'

It was another hour and a half before he returned the call.

'Hi. Sorry I didn't pick up—I was playing squash,' he said. 'How was Resus today?'

She liked the fact that he'd thought enough to ask her about her day rather than going straight in to asking whether she'd made a decision. 'Full-on,' she said, 'but all my patients survived, so it was a good day. How was cubicles?'

'Good, thanks.' He paused. 'I take it you were calling about my message?'

'Yes.' She took a deep breath. 'I've thought about it. A lot. I don't like lying, Harry. I can't go to the wedding with you as your fiancée.'

'Uh-huh.' His tone was perfectly composed and so bland that she didn't have a clue what he was thinking. 'I understand. And thank you for at least considering it. I appreciate that.'

Then she realised he thought she was turning him down. 'No, I'll go with you, Harry,' she said.

'So you've just changed your mind?' He sounded confused.

'No. I mean I'll go to the wedding with you, but as your friend—not as your fiancée.' She paused. 'That'll be enough to keep the heat off you, without us having to lie.'

'You'll actually go with me? Really?' He sounded faintly shocked, and then thrilled. 'Isla—thank you. I really appreciate it. And if there's ever a favour you want from me in return, just name it and it's yours.'

'It's fine,' she said.

'And I meant what I said about buying you an outfit for the wedding.'

'Really, there's no need. Though I could do with knowing the dress code.'

'The usual wedding stuff,' he said. 'It's a civil do. Just wear something pretty. Oh, and comfortable shoes.'

'Comfortable shoes don't normally go with pretty dresses,' she pointed out.

'They need to, in this case. The reception involves a barn dance.'

'A barn dance?'

'Don't worry if you've never done that kind of thing

before—they have a guy who calls out the steps. Actually, it's a good idea because it makes everyone mix, and you get to dance with absolutely everyone in the room.'

Did he really think she'd never been to that sort of thing before? 'I'm Scottish,' she reminded him with a smile. 'In the village where I lived back on the island, we used to have a ceilidh every third Friday of the month.'

'That,' he said, 'sounds like enormous fun.'

'It was.' And she'd missed it. But the last couple she'd gone to had been miserable, with people staring at her and whispering. In the end she'd made excuses not to go. 'Is there anything else I need to know? What about a wedding present?'

'I've already got that sorted,' he said. 'So I guess it's just timing. I thought we could wear something comfortable for the journey—just in case we get stuck in traffic, with it being a summer Saturday—and get changed at the hotel.'

And that was another issue. If he'd been expecting to take her to the wedding as his fake fiancée, did that mean he expected her to share a room with him? 'Won't all the rooms already be booked? So I might have to stay at a different hotel.'

'Dad block-booked the hotel. You'll have your own room,' he said.

'Thank you.' So at least there wouldn't be any misunderstandings there. That was a relief. She'd had enough misunderstandings to last her a lifetime.

'All I need now is your address, so I know where to pick you up,' he said.

She gave him the address to her flat.

'Excellent. And thank you for coming with me, Isla. I really appreciate it,' he said.

The next evening, just as Isla got home from work, her neighbour's door opened.

'There was a delivery for you while you were at work,' she said, handing Isla the most gorgeous bouquet. 'Is it your birthday or a special occasion?'

Isla smiled and shook her head. 'They're probably from my family in Scotland.'

'Because you've been in London for over a month now and they're missing you? I know how they feel.' The neighbour smiled ruefully. 'I really miss my daughter, now she's moved to Oxford. I send her a parcel every week so she knows I'm thinking of her. She works so hard and it's nice to be able to spoil her, even if it is at a distance.'

'And I bet she appreciates it just as much as I appreciate these,' Isla said. 'Thanks for taking them in for me.'

'Any time, love.' The neighbour smiled at her and went back to her own flat.

Once Isla had unlocked the door and put the flowers on the table, she looked at the card. The flowers weren't from her family; they were from Harry. His message was short, to the point, and written in handwriting she didn't recognise, so clearly he'd ordered them online or by phone.

I just wanted to say thank you for helping me. H x.

How lovely. She couldn't even remember the last time she'd had flowers delivered to her. And these were utterly beautiful—roses, gerberas, irises and gypsophila.

She called him. 'Thank you for the flowers, Harry.

They're lovely. You didn't need to do that, but they're gorgeous.'

'My pleasure. I hope it was OK to send them to your flat? I didn't want to give them to you at work in case it started any gossip.'

Which was really thoughtful of him. 'It's fine. My neighbour took them in for me.'

'And thank you about the best man stuff, too,' he said. 'I spoke to Dad at lunchtime and he loves the idea of Evan being his best man. Julie—Evan's mum—called me to say she thinks it's a good idea, too. It makes him feel important and that his dad isn't going to forget him, even though he no longer lives with him and Julie.'

'That's good. I'm glad.' She paused. 'That sounds like personal experience.'

'I guess it is,' he said. 'I was a bit younger than Evan when my parents split up, but I can still remember worrying that Dad would forget me if he didn't live with me, because he'd have a new family to look after.' He gave a wry chuckle. 'To Dad's credit, though, he tried to keep seeing us. Even when he was going through the screaming row stage of his marriages, Saturday mornings were reserved for his boys.'

'All of you? Or did you take turns?' she asked.

'All of us, until we'd pretty much flown the nest and were off at uni somewhere.' He gave a small huff of laughter. 'Though when I look back I was always in charge of getting us all to play football at the park, because Dad would be busy flirting with someone on the sidelines. That's how he is. Be warned, he'll probably flirt with you at the wedding.'

A cold shiver ran down Isla's spine. Andrew had flirted with her, too.

Almost as if Harry was reading her thoughts—which

was ridiculous, because of course he couldn't do that—he added, 'Just take it with a pinch of salt. He doesn't mean any harm by it. He just likes flirting.'

'Right.'

'Anyway. Thanks again,' Harry said. 'See you tomorrow.'

'See you tomorrow,' she said.

CHAPTER FIVE

THE NEXT WEEK and a bit flew by. At the crack of dawn on Saturday morning, Isla packed a small overnight case; she was glad she'd kept her packing to a minimum when Harry arrived, because she discovered that there wasn't much room for luggage in his bright red sports car.

'Do they know about this car on the ward?' she asked.

'Oh, yes.' He grinned. 'And they're torn between teasing me about it and pure envy because it's such a beautiful car.' He paused. 'Do you drive?'

'Yes, though I don't have a car in London because there's no point, not with the Tube being so good.'

His grin broadened. 'I'd never drive this to work because it's much more sensible to use the Tube, but on days off… Sometimes it's nice just to go wherever the mood takes you without having to worry about changing Tube lines or how far away the train station is from wherever you want to go.' He indicated the car. 'Do you want to drive?'

'Me?' She was faintly shocked. Weren't men usually possessive about their cars? And Stewart had always hated being driven by anyone else, so she'd always been the passenger when she'd been in the car with him.

'If you'd rather not drive through London, I'll do the first bit; but, if you'd like to get behind the wheel at any point, all you have to do is tell me,' Harry said. 'She's a dream to drive.'

'You're a walking cliché, Harry Gardiner,' she said, laughing. 'The hospital heartbreaker with his little red sports car.'

He just laughed back. 'Wait until you've driven her and then tell me I'm a cliché. Come on, let's go.'

The car was surprisingly comfortable. And Isla was highly amused to discover that the stereo system in the car was voice controlled. 'Boys and their toys,' she teased.

'It's so much better than faffing around trying to find what you want to listen to, or sitting through songs you're not in the mood for,' he said. 'By the way, if you'd rather connect your phone to the stereo and play something you prefer, that's fine by me.'

'Actually, I quite like this sort of stuff,' she admitted.

'Classic rock you can sing along to.' He gave her a sidelong glance. 'Now, Sister McKenna, that begs a question—can you sing?'

'You'd never get me doing karaoke,' she prevaricated.

'I won't tell anyone at work if you sing out of key,' he promised with a grin. 'Let's do it.'

'Seriously?'

'It'll take my mind off the wedding,' he said.

'So you're still dreading it?'

'A bit,' he admitted. 'Though I guess it'll be nice to see all my brothers. We don't get together that often nowadays.' He shrugged. 'Obviously the girls won't be there, because they're not Dad's, so you'll be saved from Maisie interrogating you.'

'Maisie?'

'My oldest sister,' he explained. 'Then there's Tasha and Bibi.' He gave her a wry smile. 'There are rather a lot of us, altogether.'

'It's nice that you all get on.'

'The siblings do, though the ex-wives are all a bit wary with each other,' he said. 'Obviously there have been some seriously sticky patches around all the divorces, but things settled down again after a while. The only one of his ex-wives coming to the wedding is Julie, and that's only because Evan's too little to come on his own.'

'Uh-huh,' she said. 'OK. Put on something we can sing to.'

'A girl after my own heart,' he said with a smile, and did exactly that.

Isla thoroughly enjoyed the journey; and, after they'd stopped for a rest break at a motorway service station, she actually drove his car for a while.

'Well?' he asked when they'd stopped and he'd taken the wheel again for the final bit of the journey.

'It's great,' she said. 'I can see why you love it.'

'Told you so,' he said with a grin.

Though he stopped singing along to the music as they drew nearer to the hotel where the wedding was being held. By the time he parked the car, he looked positively grim.

She reached over and squeezed his hand. 'Hey. It's going to be fine. The sun's shining and it's going to be better than you think.'

'Uh-huh.' He didn't sound convinced, but he returned the squeeze of her hand and gave her a half-smile. 'Thank you, Isla.'

'That's what friends are for. You'd do the same for me.' And she tried to ignore the fact that her skin was tingling where it touched his. It was a completely inappropriate reaction. Even if she wanted to start a relationship with someone—which she didn't—this definitely wasn't the place or the time. 'Let's do this,' she said.

He nodded, climbed out of the car, and insisted on carrying her luggage into the hotel as well as his own.

When they reached the desk to book in, the receptionist smiled at them. 'Dr Harry Gardiner? Welcome to Pentremain Hotel. Here's your key. You're in room 217. Second floor, then turn left when you get out of the lift.'

'There should be two rooms,' Harry said. 'Harry Gardiner and Isla McKenna.'

'I'm afraid there's only one room booked,' the receptionist said. 'But it *is* a double.'

'There must be a mistake,' Harry said. 'Dad definitely said we had two rooms.'

'I'm afraid there's only one.' The receptionist bit her lip. 'I'm so sorry. We're fully booked, so I can't offer you an alternative.'

'It's fine,' Isla said, seeing how awkward the receptionist looked and not wanting to make a fuss. 'We can sort this out later. Thank you for your help.' She forced a smile she didn't feel.

Going to the wedding with Harry was one thing; sharing a room with him was quite another. And he didn't look exactly thrilled about the situation, either.

They went to the lift and found their room in silence.

'I'm so sorry about this. I did say that we were just friends and we needed two rooms. I hope my father isn't making assumptions,' Harry said. 'Look, I'll ring round and see if I can find myself a room somewhere nearby.'

'Harry, this is your family. You ought to be the one to stay here,' Isla pointed out.

'I'm really sorry about this. Dad definitely said we

had two rooms. Give me a moment and I'll find an alternative,' he said, grabbing his phone to check the Internet for numbers of nearby hotels and guest houses.

Several phone calls later, he'd established that there were no rooms available anywhere near. 'Absolutely everywhere is fully booked with holidaymakers. Which I guess you'd expect on a weekend at this time of year.' He sighed. 'OK. I'll sleep in the car.'

'You can't possibly do that!' Isla frowned at him. 'Look, it's just for one night. We can share the room.'

'In that case, I'll take the couch.'

'You're too tall, your back will feel like murder tomorrow morning.' She took a deep breath. 'Look, we're adults. We can share a bed without...' She stopped before she said the words. Even thinking them made a slow burn start at the base of her spine. *Making love. With Harry.*

Any woman with a pulse would find Harry Gardiner attractive, and of course it would cross her mind to wonder what it would be like to be in his arms. She'd just have to make sure she didn't act on that impulse. 'Well,' she finished lamely.

'You're right. It's not as if we're teenagers,' he said. And at least he hadn't seemed to pick up on what was going through her head.

'Exactly. Now, we need to get changed,' she said briskly. 'Do you want to change in here or in the bathroom?'

'You pick,' he said.

'Bathroom,' she said, and escaped there with her dress and make-up bag.

Sharing a room with Isla McKenna.

It was the sensible solution, Harry knew.

The problem was, he didn't feel sensible. He was already on edge about the wedding, and if they shared a bed it would be all too easy to seek comfort in her.

She's your colleague, he reminded himself. Off limits. She wants a relationship just as little as you do. Keep your distance.

He'd just about got himself under control by the time he'd changed into the tailcoat, wing-collared shirt and cravat his father had asked him to wear. He left the top hat on the bed for the time being, took a deep breath and knocked on the bathroom door. 'Isla, I'm ready whenever you are,' he said, 'but don't take that as me rushing you. There's plenty of time. I just didn't want you to feel that you had to be stuck in there while I was faffing about in the other room.'

She opened the door. 'I'm ready,' she said softly.

Harry had never seen Isla dressed up before. He'd seen her wearing jeans and a T-shirt, and he'd seen her in her uniform at the hospital. On every occasion she'd worn her hair pinned back and no make-up, not even a touch of lipstick.

Today, she was wearing a simple blue dress that emphasised the colour of her eyes, a touch of mascara, the lightest shimmer of lipstick—and she looked stunning. Desire rushed through him, taking his breath away. How had he ever thought that Isla would be *safe*? He needed to get himself under control. Now.

'You look lovely,' he said, hearing the slight croak in his voice and feeling cross with himself for letting his emotions show.

'Thank you. You don't scrub up so badly yourself, Dr Gardiner,' she said.

Exactly the right words to help him keep his burgeoning feelings under control, and he was grateful for them. 'Shall we?' he asked and gestured to the door.

'Sure.' She gave him a cheeky grin. 'Don't forget your hat.'

'No.' He glanced at her high-heeled shoes and did a double-take. 'Isla, are you going to be able to dance in those?'

'I'm Scottish. Of course I can.' She grinned. 'And if I can't I'll just take them off.'

He really, really wished she hadn't said those words. Because now there was a picture on his head that he couldn't shift. Isla, all barefoot and beguiling, standing before him and looking up with her eyes full of laughter. And himself taking off every piece of her clothing, one by one...

Get a grip, Harry Gardiner, and keep your hands and your eyes to yourself, he warned himself. He pinned his best smile to his face, and opened the door.

'Isla, this is my father, Robert Gardiner,' Harry said formally when they joined the wedding party in the hotel gardens. 'Dad, this is my friend Isla McKenna.'

Isla could see the family resemblance. Although Bertie's hair was liberally streaked with grey, clearly once it had been as dark as Harry's, and if it hadn't been cut so short it would've been as curly as Harry's, too. Bertie had the same dark eyes and same sweet smile as his son, though Harry hadn't inherited his dimples.

'It's lovely to meet you, Mr Gardiner,' she said.

'Everyone calls me Bertie,' he corrected with a smile. 'It's lovely to meet you, too, Isla—I can call you Isla?'

'Yes, of course.'

'Good.' His eyes twinkled at her. 'I believe I have

you to thank for persuading Harry to be here at all, and I hear it was your idea for Evan to be my best man.'

She winced. 'Sorry, that sounds horribly like interference on my part.'

He smiled and clapped her shoulder. 'Sweetheart, it was an inspired suggestion, and you talked Harry into coming so I most definitely owe you champagne.'

For a moment, she froze. Andrew Gillespie had been just as charming and flirtatious, but he'd hidden a serpent under the smile. Then she remembered Harry's warning that his father would flirt with her but meant nothing by it. And he was right. There was nothing remotely assessing in the way Bertie looked at her. No hidden agendas. He wasn't a carbon copy of Andrew.

'Now, has my boy here introduced you to everyone?' Bertie asked.

'We've hardly had time, Dad—remember, we drove up this morning from London and we had to get changed.'

'You could've come last night and had dinner with us,' Bertie pointed out. 'But you said you were on a late shift and couldn't get anyone to swap with you.'

'Exactly.' Harry gave him a tight smile. 'I happen to work in the busiest department at the hospital, you know.'

'Hmm.' Bertie rolled his eyes. 'Come with me, sweetheart, and I'll introduce you.'

'Where's Trixie?' Harry asked.

Bertie smiled. 'Now, son, you've been to enough of my weddings to know that it's bad luck for the groom to see the bride before the ceremony.'

And then Isla finally relaxed, liking the way Harry's father was able to poke fun at himself.

The next thing she knew, she'd been introduced to a dozen or more of Harry's family, including most of his brothers. The twelve-year-old looked as if he'd rather not be there and she made a mental note to go and chat to him later; the seventeen-year-old looked a little awkward. The two oldest, Jack and Fin, seemed to be assessing her suitability for Harry.

'Sorry about that,' Harry said softly as soon as they were alone again. 'Clearly they were under instructions from Maisie. Jack's only a year and a bit older than her, and they see things pretty much the same way.'

'It's fine,' Isla said with a smile.

The wedding ceremony was held under a canopy on the clifftop, and the views were breathtaking. And seeing the sea made Isla feel suddenly homesick.

'Are you OK?' Harry asked.

'Sure. It's just been a while since I've seen the sea properly.'

'Before we go back to London,' he promised, 'we'll go for a walk on the beach.'

'I'll hold you to that. It's the one thing I regret about London—there's no sea. And I miss walking by the waves.'

'There's a beach of sorts on the Thames. I'll show you some time, if you like.'

'Thank you.'

The wedding itself was lovely. Harry's youngest brother was indeed the best man, and he handed the rings to Bertie at the altar.

Trixie and Bertie's vows were very simple and heartfelt. Isla guessed that Harry was going to find this bit the hardest, so she slipped her hand into his and squeezed his fingers. He squeezed back and then didn't let her hand go.

* * *

After the wedding, the photographer had everyone clustering together in groups. Isla particularly liked the one of Bertie with his six sons, all of them wearing top hats and then a second shot with them all throwing their hats into the air. She took a couple of snaps on her phone for posterity.

And then the photographer called her and Harry over. 'Now, you two. Stand together here.' He posed them, then shook his head. 'I want you closer than that,' he said.

Oh, help. He was clearly under the misapprehension that she and Harry were a proper couple. Just as she had a nasty feeling that Harry's family thought that, too—even though Harry had made it clear they were just friends.

'That's it. Arms round each other,' the photographer said.

They'd have to go along with it. Making a fuss now would make everything awkward and embarrassing.

'Look into each other's eyes,' the photographer said. 'That's it. I want to see the love. As if you're just about to kiss each other.'

Isla's mouth went dry.

Kissing Harry.

The worst thing was, she could just imagine it. Putting her hand up to stroke his cheek, then sliding her hand round his neck and drawing his head down to hers. Parting her lips. Seeing his pupils widen with desire. Feeling his lips brush against hers, all light and teasing and promising; and then he'd pull her closer, jam his mouth properly against hers and deepen the kiss...

'That's *exactly* what I'm talking about!' the photographer crowed.

Isla focussed again and saw the shock in Harry's eyes.

Had she given herself away? Or was he shocked because the same feelings had been coursing through him?

She didn't dare ask, but she made some excuse to dive back into the crowd. And please, please, let her libido be back under control before Harry could guess what she'd been thinking.

Trixie—who turned out to be a primary school teacher—clearly understood how bored the younger members of the family would find things, so she'd arranged a duck race on the stream running through the hotel grounds for them. Evan insisted on making a team with Harry, and made their duck into a pirate.

Harry was such a sweetheart, Isla thought; he was as patient with all the children here as he was in the emergency department. And yet he'd been so adamant about not wanting children of his own. She couldn't quite work it out.

'He's very good with children,' Bertie said, joining her.

'They love him at work—he has this stock of terrible jokes to distract them,' Isla said with a smile.

'I can imagine. Half of them come from his brothers.' Bertie paused. 'So you met when you started working together?'

Isla had half expected an inquisition. And the best way to stop the misconception being uncovered and making things really awkward would be to stick as closely to the truth as possible. 'Yes—a couple of months ago.'

'And you're a doctor, too?'

'No, I'm a nurse,' Isla said.

'Senior nurse, actually.' Harry came up and slung one arm casually around Isla's shoulders, clearly having worked out what was going on. 'Let's have the inquisition over now, please, Dad.'

'If you actually told me things, Harry,' Bertie grumbled good-naturedly, 'then I wouldn't have to pump other people for information, would I?'

'I'm a doctor. I'm used to keeping things confidential,' Harry said with a grin.

'You're impossible,' Bertie said with a sigh.

'Like father, like son,' Harry said with a broad wink. 'Isla's my friend. End of story. Come on, Isla—it's time for food and I'm starving,' he added, and shepherded her into the large marquee on the lawn.

The food was wonderful: Cornish crab terrine followed by roast beef and all the trimmings, then a rich pavlova with clotted cream and raspberries, and finally a selection of traditional Cornish cheeses and crackers.

The waiters topped up everyone's glasses with champagne, ready for the speeches.

The father of the bride gave the first speech. Sticking with tradition, he welcomed the guests, thanked everyone for coming, spoke a little bit about Bertie and Trixie, and then toasted the bride and groom.

Harry murmured in her ear, 'Excuse me—I'm going to have to leave you for a minute or two.'

She realised why when little Evan stood up on his chair, with Harry crouched beside him.

'I'm Evan and I'm my daddy's best man,' Evan said proudly. 'My big brother Harry says my speech has to be funny, so I'm going to tell you my favourite joke. What did the banana say to the monkey?' He waited for a moment before delivering the punchline. 'Nothing—bananas can't talk!'

Everyone laughed.

'Harry says the speech has got to be short as well as funny, so I'll stop now. Happy wedding day, Daddy and Trixie.'

Everyone echoed, 'Bertie and Trixie.'

Harry whispered something in Evan's ear and the little boy's eyes went wide. 'Harry, I forgot!'

Harry smiled at him and patted his shoulder, and mouthed, 'Go on.'

'Um, I'm sorry, everyone, I forgot the other bit. The bridesmaids look really pretty and they did a good job. You have to drink to the bridesmaids now.'

There were amused and indulgent laughs, and everyone chorused, 'The bridesmaids.'

Bertie stood up last. 'And I must say thank you to my best man, who did a fabulous job.'

'And Harry,' Evan chipped in.

Bertie grinned. 'I gather it was a bit of a team effort between my youngest and my oldest sons. But that's what family's all about. Pitching in together.' He raised his glass. 'I'd like to make a toast to my beautiful bride, Trixie, and to my wonderful family—thank you all for coming here to celebrate with us.'

Harry quietly came back to join their table at that point. Isla reached for his hand under the table and squeezed it.

After the speeches, it was time to cut the cake. 'The middle layer is chocolate,' Trixie said, 'so that should make all the men in my new family happy.'

'As sweet as you are,' Bertie said, and kissed her. 'And I believe the band is ready for us. Perhaps we could all move in to the other marquee?'

The band was set up at one end, and there were chairs lining the edges of the floor. For the first dance, the band played a slow dance; Bertie and Trixie started things off, followed by the bride and groom's parents, and then the bridesmaids and best man.

Isla wondered if Harry was going to suggest dancing with her, but at the end of the song the singer announced, 'And now it's time for you all you to dance off that cake—I want everybody up on the floor, and there's no excuse for not dancing because we're going to call the steps for you.'

There were protests from the younger members of the wedding party, but they were roundly ignored—and, by the middle of the first dance, everyone was laughing and thoroughly enjoying themselves. Isla knew most of the steps from the ceilidhs she'd been to back on the island. Her own wedding reception would've been just like this. But she pushed away the sadness; now wasn't the time or place, and she wasn't going to let the shadow of Andrew Gillespie spoil this weekend.

Harry watched Isla dancing while he was on the other side of the room. Her glorious hair flew out behind her, and she'd been telling the truth about being able to dance in high heels. Before today, he hadn't had a clue how well his colleague could dance. If the rest of the staff could see their quiet, capable, almost shy senior nurse right now...

She was sparkling, and she fitted in well with everyone. And he noticed that Isla had even managed to get his two middle brothers to join in the dancing, rather than sitting on the edge of the room, mired in teenage awkwardness. She'd actually got them laughing as they danced together. Harry already knew from working with her that she had great people skills, but this was something else. She wasn't just coping with his extended family, she was actually joining in with them.

He had a nasty feeling that Isla McKenna was the one woman who could tempt him to break his 'no serious relationships' rule. So much for asking her to come here with him because she was safe: she was nothing of the kind. And he would need to be careful, especially as they were sharing a room tonight.

And almost everyone in his family had something to say about her to him. Fin said it was about time he found someone like her; Jack pointed out how well she was getting on with everyone and how nice she was with the teenagers; Julie came over to say how much little Evan liked her and so did she.

If his family had their way, they'd be getting married next week, Harry thought moodily. And he hoped Isla wouldn't take any of it to heart. He'd told them the truth. They just didn't want to believe it, and wanted him to have the happy-ever-after.

Marriage wasn't an option he would ever seriously consider. In his world, the happiness from marriage was brief and the heartache lasted an awful lot longer.

The band had a break when the canapés and sandwiches appeared, and he managed to snatch some time with Isla.

'Oh, look at this—miniature Cornish pasties, and miniature scones with clotted cream and strawberry jam!' she exclaimed in delight. She tried a scone. 'Oh, you really have to try this, Harry,' she said, and popped a bite of scone into his mouth.

His lips tingled where her fingers had touched them.

Oh, help. He was going to have to keep himself under strict control. It would be all too easy to do something stupid—like catch her hand and kiss the back of her fingers, and then turn her hand over so his mouth could linger over the pulse at her wrist.

'This is one of the nicest weddings I've been to,' she said.

Harry pulled himself together with an effort. 'I guess it's better than I thought it would be.' The real reason that it was better for him was because she was there, but he was wary of telling her that because he didn't want her to take it the wrong way. Especially as he had a nasty feeling that it meant more to him than just the support of a friend—and, despite the fact they'd just celebrated a wedding, he knew this wouldn't last. It never did.

But he pushed the thoughts away and forced himself to smile and be sociable.

After the break, the band switched from the barn dance to more traditional wedding music. Isla danced with his two oldest brothers and Bertie, and then Harry reclaimed her.

Just as the band segued into a slow dance.

It was too late to back out now, because she was already in his arms.

Now he knew what it was like to hold her close. She was warm and soft and sweet. And it scared him, how right this felt—like the perfect fit.

He could see his father smiling approval at him. His brothers did likewise.

Oh, help. They all thought that he and Isla had been fibbing about their relationship and were a real couple— and, even though he'd originally intended that they believe that, he realised now that Isla had been right and it made things way too complicated.

They really ought to sit out the next dance. Go and talk to other people. Distract his family.

But he couldn't let her go. The next song was another slow dance, and he ended up drawing her closer and dancing cheek to cheek with her instead. He could smell her perfume, all soft and beguiling—much like Isla herself. He closed his eyes. All he had to do was turn his head towards her, just the tiniest fraction, and he'd be able to kiss the corner of her mouth. And then he'd find out if her lips were as sweet as the rest of her.

He felt almost giddy with need. It had been a long time since he'd wanted to kiss someone as much as he wanted to kiss Isla McKenna.

Giddy was about right. The mood of the wedding had clearly got to him and he needed to start being sensible, and that meant right now, before he did something they'd both regret.

He pulled away from her slightly.

'Are you OK?' she asked, her blue eyes dark with concern.

He nodded. 'I just need some fresh air.'

'I'll come with you if you like.'

He ought to say no. He really, really ought to make an excuse to put some distance between them. Not walk outside with her in the gardens under the light of a full moon.

But, despite his best intentions, he found himself saying yes, holding her hand and walking out of the marquee with her.

CHAPTER SIX

THE SKY WAS darkening and the first stars were appearing; they were so much brighter out here in the countryside than they were in London. Harry could hear the gentle, regular swish of the waves against the sand at the bottom of the cliffs and it was hypnotic, soothing his soul. He sat down on the grass next to Isla, looking out at the sea, and slid his arm round her shoulders. For a moment he felt the tiniest bit of resistance from her; then she leaned into him and slid her arm round his waist.

Funny how right it felt. Not that he was going to let himself think about that. Because he didn't do serious relationships and he valued Isla too much to mess things up between them.

They sat in companionable silence together for a while. Eventually, she was the one to break it. 'So are you really OK, Harry?' she asked softly.

'Yeah. I'm OK.' He blew out a breath. 'It's just… This whole wedding thing. It's good to see my brothers, but when I look at them I can't help remembering the times they've cried on my shoulder, convinced it was the end of the world because their mum and dad were fighting all the time, or had just split up and they had to move house and start at a new school. Every divorce caused so much damage. It uprooted the kids and made them so miserable.'

'They all seem pretty well adjusted now.'

Except him, perhaps. Not that he intended to discuss that. 'But they've still been hurt.' He sighed. 'Ten marriages between my parents. It's a bit excessive.'

'Your dad seems happy.'

'For the moment—but you can see the pattern, Isla. It's meant to be a seven-year itch, but Dad only seems to make it to four or five years before he's had enough and misses the thrill of the chase.' He shook his head. 'And I don't want to be like that, Isla. If I'm like my parents and I can't settle down... I don't want to hurt anyone.'

'And that's why you isolate yourself?' she asked.

He'd never thought about it in that way. He'd always thought about it as saving others from him repeating his parents' mistakes. 'I guess.'

She rubbed her thumb in a comforting movement against his back. 'You're pretty hard on yourself, Harry. From what I've seen today, your family loves you. Your brothers all look up to you.'

He gave her a wry smile. 'Maybe.'

She twisted her head to kiss his cheek, and heat zinged through him at the touch of her mouth against his skin. Just as much as it had when the photographer had suggested they should look in love with each other, as if they were just about to kiss.

Right at that moment he'd really wanted to kiss Isla, to see if her mouth was as soft and as sweet as it looked. Her eyes had been wide and dark, and it would've been oh, so easy to lean forward and do it. Just as he wanted to kiss her, right now.

This was a bad idea.

He knew he ought to take his arm from her shoulders, move away from her, and suggest that they go back to the marquee and join the dancing.

But he couldn't move. It felt as if they were held together by some magnetic force. Something he couldn't break—and, if he was honest with himself, something he didn't want to break.

'You're a good man, Harry Gardiner,' Isla said. 'I can understand why you avoid connecting with anyone—but you're really not being fair to yourself. You're loyal and you're kind, and I think you more than have the capacity within you to make a relationship work. To really love someone.'

He groaned. 'You sound like my mother. And my sisters.'

'If that's what they say, then I agree with them,' she said.

'Can we change the subject?' he asked plaintively.

'Because you're too chicken?'

Yes. 'No, because the sky's beautiful and I don't want to talk about something that makes me antsy.'

'Fair enough,' she said.

'You looked as if you were enjoying the dancing earlier.'

'The barn dance? Yes—it's very similar to the ceilidhs we had on the island. That's what we were going to have for our wedding.'

Wedding?

Isla had been going to get married?

The fact that she was single—and had made it clear she intended to stay that way—meant that something must have gone badly wrong. Was that the reason that had made her leave the island? And why she'd reacted so badly to the idea of being a fake fiancée—because she'd once been a real one?

'Were?' he asked softly.

She shook her head. 'Don't worry about it. It's a long story.'

'Right now I have all the time in the world.' His arm tightened round her shoulders. 'It's not going any further than me—you've kept my confidence and I'll keep yours. Plus someone very wise once told me it's good to talk because it's better out than in. A problem shared is a problem halved, and all that.'

'Before I ran out of clichés, you mean?' she asked wryly, clearly remembering that conversation.

'What happened? Your fiancé died?' he asked quietly. It was the only reason he could think of why Isla hadn't got married.

'Stewart? No. He's still alive and perfectly healthy, as far as I know.' She blew out a breath. 'We'd known each other since we were children. I guess it all goes with the territory of living in a small community. You end up settling down with someone you've known for ever.'

He waited, giving her the space to talk.

'We started dating a couple of years ago. He asked me to marry him and I said yes. My family liked him and I thought his liked me.'

So that had been the problem? Her ex's family hadn't liked her? And yet she'd still been prepared to meet his own family today. His respect for her went up another notch.

'But then Stewart's mum asked me for a favour,' she said softly. 'According to Bridie, Andrew—Stewart's stepfather—had bit of a drink problem. She wanted me to talk to him and see if I could persuade him to get some help to stop drinking, before he ended up with cirrhosis of the liver.' She looked away. 'I was trying to help.'

'And he didn't like you interfering?'

'Partly, but Andrew got the wrong end of the stick when I asked to talk to him privately. He assumed I was interested in him and he made a pass at me.' She sighed. 'I should've handled it better. I just hadn't expected him to react in that way. I always thought his marriage to Bridie was rock-solid and he would never even think about looking at another woman.'

'It wasn't your fault, Isla. Besides, any decent man understands that if a woman says no, it means no.' Harry had a nasty feeling where this might be going. 'So he wouldn't take no for an answer?'

'Oh, he did,' she said grimly. 'But Andrew Gillespie was used to getting his own way. He really didn't like the fact that I'd said no to him. So he called the head of the practice and said that I'd behaved unprofessionally. He claimed that I'd asked to see him privately under the guise of talking about his health, and then made a pass at him.'

'What? That's appalling. I hope your boss sent him away with a flea in his ear.'

'My boss,' she said, 'had to investigate. Exactly as he was bound to do if any patient made a complaint about any of the staff at the practice.'

'But it obviously wasn't true.'

'And I was exonerated.' She blew out a breath. 'But you know all the clichés. There's no smoke without fire. Mud sticks.'

He blinked. 'Other people believed him?'

She nodded. 'I lived in a village. Everyone knew me; but everyone also knew Andrew. He was popular with the locals—partly because he employed a lot of them, and partly because he could be very charming indeed.'

'But surely your fiancé and his mum knew the truth?'

'Andrew could be persuasive as well as charming.'

Harry really didn't get this. 'But his wife asked you to have a quiet word with him and help him with his drinking problem. She knew there was more to him than met the eye. Surely she must've known that he wasn't telling the truth?'

'And there's another cliché for you: stand by your man. Even if it means upholding a lie.'

'That's…that's…' He didn't have the words. 'I don't know what to say.' But there was one thing he could do. He shifted her on to his lap and held her close. 'Best I can do right now is give you a hug.'

'Gratefully accepted.'

And, oh, he wanted to kiss her. Except that would be totally inappropriate. He couldn't suggest that they lose their worries in each other. Much as he felt that it might help them both tonight, tomorrow they'd have to face up to their actions and it would all get way too messy. So he just held her. 'I'm really sorry that you had to go through something so horrible. And I don't see how anyone who'd known you for more than ten minutes could believe that you'd ever be unprofessional, much less try it on with your fiancé's stepfather.'

'Thank you for the vote of confidence,' she said.

'I still can't get over the fact that people you'd lived with and worked with and treated thought that you were capable of that kind of behaviour. Much less your ex. And right now I don't know what to say,' he said. 'Other than wanting to punch this Andrew Gillespie guy very hard—and I know exactly where to hit him to do the most damage—and wanting to shake your ex until his teeth rattle for being such an idiot and not seeing straight away that you weren't the one telling lies.'

'Violence doesn't solve anything,' she pointed out.

'Look at all the drunks we have to patch up on a Friday and Saturday night.'

'I know, but it would make me feel better,' he said.

She smiled. 'You're not a caveman, Harry.'

'Right now I'd quite like to be. Being civilised can be overrated.'

She stroked his cheek. 'Thank you for taking my part.'

'Isla, anybody who knows you would realise the truth without having to be told. You're honest, dependable and sincere.'

'Thank you. Though I wasn't fishing for compliments.'

'I know. I'm just telling you, that's all. And I'm sorry that you had to go through such a horrible situation. Though I'm glad you chose to work at the London Victoria. And I'm also very glad you're here with me right now.' And he really understood now why she wasn't in the market for a relationship—why she'd been wary even of joining in with the team outside work. She'd been let down so badly. It would be hard to take the risk of trusting someone again.

If anyone had told Isla a month ago that she'd be sitting on Harry's lap with their arms wrapped round each other, she would've scoffed.

And yet here they were. Doing exactly that.

And she'd just spilled her heart out to him.

Odd that Stewart had known her for years and years, and yet he'd got her totally wrong; whereas Harry had known her only a few weeks and he knew her for exactly who she was. *Honest, dependable and sincere.* It warmed her heart to know that was what he thought of her.

'I'm glad I'm here, too,' she said. And, even though she knew she was skating on very thin ice indeed, she gave in to the impulse to lean forward and kiss his cheek. 'Thank you for believing in me.'

His eyes went even darker. 'Isla.' He was looking at her mouth.

Just as she was looking at his.

Was he wondering the same as she was, right now? What it would be like if their lips actually touched? Did his mouth tingle with longing, the same way that hers did—the same way she'd felt when the photographer had posed them, except this time it was just the two of them in the starlight, and it felt so much more intense?

Clearly yes, because he leaned forward and touched his mouth to hers. And it felt as if the sky had lit up with a meteor shower. His mouth was warm and soft and sweet, promising and enticing rather than demanding, and she wanted more.

She slid her hands into his hair; his curls were silky under her fingertips. And he drew her closer so he could deepen the kiss.

'We wondered if you two lovebirds would be out here,' a voice said, and they broke apart.

She felt colour flare through her cheeks as she looked up at Harry's father and new stepmother. What on earth did she think she was doing, kissing Harry like that in the middle of the garden where anyone could see them?

'Don't say a single word,' Harry said, dragging a hand through his hair and looking as guilty as Isla felt.

'It's my wedding day and it's Cornwall, so it's meant to be romantic,' Bertie said. 'Though you weren't quite telling the truth about being just friends, were you?'

Harry groaned. 'Dad. Not now.'

'We came out to find you because Evan is supposed

to be going to bed and he refuses to go without saying goodnight to you—and that's both of you, actually,' Trixie said, including Isla. She grinned. 'He likes you. We all do, Isla.'

'OK, OK, we're coming,' Harry said, and exchanged a glance with Isla. She climbed off his lap and they headed in to the marquee to say goodnight to Evan. The little boy did his best to persuade them to read him a couple of stories each, but Julie whisked him away with a promise of 'later'.

'You're a natural with kids, Isla,' Harry remarked when Evan had gone.

'Because of my job,' she said. 'And so are you.'

He laughed. 'It's my job—and probably because I have so many siblings.'

'And yet you say you don't want kids of your own, even though you're so good with them. I don't get it.'

'I just don't,' Harry said. 'And I'd rather not talk about it.'

'Fair enough.' And she hadn't told him everything about Stewart, so she was hardly in a position to nag about keeping secrets.

'Come on—they're playing your song,' Harry said as the band started playing Abba's 'Dancing Queen'.

It was a deliberate distraction, and Isla knew it, but at the same time she didn't want to push him. He'd looked as if he'd had enough soul-baring for today.

'I'm a little bit older than seventeen, you know.'

'You can still dance,' he said, and led her onto the floor.

What else could she do but join in? Especially as this part of the band's set was cover versions of all the kind of songs that got everyone on the floor at weddings, from the youngest to the oldest.

Though Harry avoided the slow dances that were played every so often to change the mood and the tempo, she noticed. Which was probably just as well, given what had happened outside in the garden. If they'd been in each other's arms again, holding each other close, the temptation to repeat that kiss might've been too much for both of them.

At the end of the evening, they headed for their room.

'I really ought to take the couch,' Harry said.

'Because we kissed in the garden?' She took a deep breath. 'Let's blame it on the moonlight and Cornwall being romantic.'

'I guess.'

'Harry, we're adults. We've got a long drive back to London tomorrow. We both need sleep. It's not as if I'm planning to pounce on you.' Even though part of her really wanted to.

'Of course. And you're right.' He gave her a smile, but she could see that he had to make the effort. 'Do you want to use the bathroom first?'

'Thank you.'

She lingered as long as she dared, hoping to give herself a little time to calm down. Once she'd cleaned her teeth and changed into her pyjamas, she went back into the bedroom. Harry was still dressed. 'Do you have a preferred side of the bed?' she asked.

'Whichever you don't want,' he said.

'Thanks. I like to sleep by the window,' she said. 'See you in a bit.'

When Harry came out of the bathroom, he was wearing pyjamas and Isla was in bed. It was all very civilised and proper, but underneath everything there was an undercurrent. Her mouth was still tingling in memory of that kiss. Plus this was the first time she'd shared a bed with anyone since she'd broken up with Stewart. Even though they'd both made it clear that this was going to be completely chaste, it still felt unnerving.

Particularly as part of her didn't want this to be chaste at all. And, from the way Harry had kissed her under the stars, she had a feeling that it was the same for him. Wanting the ultimate closeness—but scared it would all go wrong, and not wanting to have to deal with the resultant carnage.

'Goodnight,' he said, climbed in beside her and turned his back.

Which was the most sensible way of dealing with it, she thought. Keeping temptation well at bay. 'Goodnight,' she echoed, and turned her own back.

Isla was very aware of his closeness and it took her a while before she could relax enough to sleep. She woke briefly in the night to discover that Harry was spooned against her, one arm wrapped round her waist and holding her close. She'd really missed this kind of closeness. It would be oh, so easy to turn round and kiss him awake; but that would change everything and it wouldn't be fair to either of them. She knew he didn't want a relationship; she didn't want one either.

Even if Harry Gardiner did kiss like an angel.

She'd just have to put it out of her mind. They were colleagues and friends, and that was that.

The next morning, Harry woke to find himself spooned against Isla, with his arm wrapped round her. Her hand was resting lightly over his, as if she welcomed the closeness.

He could tell from her slow, even breathing that she was still asleep.

Oh, help.

She was all warm and soft and sweet. It would be so easy to brush that glorious hair away from her shoulder and kiss the nape of her neck, his mouth brushing against her bare skin until she woke.

And he knew she'd respond to him, the way she'd responded to his kiss in the garden last night. If his father hadn't interrupted them, he had a nasty feeling that he might've carried Isla to the bed they shared right now and taken things a whole lot further.

As in all the way further.

He took a deep breath. She'd told him about what had happened to her in Scotland, though he had a feeling that she'd left a fair bit out. Why on earth hadn't her fiancé believed in her? Surely he'd realised that his stepfather hadn't been telling the truth? Although Isla hadn't said which of them had broken off the engagement, Harry knew it had shattered her faith in relationships.

So he needed to ignore his body's urging. He had to do the right thing.

Carefully, he disentangled himself from her without waking her, took a shower and dressed. It was still relatively early for a Sunday morning after a wedding reception, but they had a long way to drive and it would be sensible to leave earlier rather than later. He made them both a cup of tea from the hospitality tray on the dresser, set hers on the table next to her side of the bed, and touched her shoulder. 'Isla.'

Her eyes fluttered open. For a moment, she looked confused, as if she wasn't sure where she was or why someone was sharing her bedroom. Then her eyes widened. 'Oh. Harry.'

'Good morning. I made you a cup of tea.'

'Thank you,' she said, sounding almost shy. 'What time is it?'

'Eight. I know it's a bit early.'

'But we have a long drive.'

He was relieved that she understood. 'I thought I might go for a walk before breakfast. It'll give you a chance to shower and get changed.'

She looked grateful. 'I appreciate that.'

'See you in half an hour?'

'I'll be ready and packed,' she promised.

'Yeah.' He smiled at her. So there wasn't any collateral damage from last night, then—either from the kiss or from her telling him about her past. She still looked a little shy with him, but he knew she'd won her trust. Just as she'd won his.

And, back in London, everything would be just fine.

CHAPTER SEVEN

AT BREAKFAST, LITTLE Evan was there and insisted that they join him and his mother. Isla was amused to note that he copied Harry exactly in everything he ate; clearly the little boy had a serious case of hero-worship where his big brother was concerned.

When they'd finished, they said goodbye to Harry's family, then drove back to London. It was much quieter on the way back; there wasn't quite an awkward silence between them, but this time Harry was playing classical music rather than something they could both sing along to, and Isla didn't really know what to say. They probably ought to discuss what had happened yesterday and reset the ground rules, but she had the distinct impression that Harry didn't want to discuss it and would change the subject if she raised it.

Although they stopped for lunch, Harry suggested that they grabbed a burger at the motorway service station—and she noticed that this time he didn't offer to let her drive.

She'd always been good with people, but the way Harry was stonewalling her was unlike anything she'd ever known.

'Are you OK?' she asked.

'Sure. Just thinking about work.'

And there wasn't really an answer to that.

'Do you want to come in for coffee?' she asked when he parked outside her flat, even though she was pretty sure he'd say no.

'Thanks, but I've already taken up enough of your time this weekend,' he said, equally politely.

Isla felt as if somehow she'd done something wrong; but, if she tried to clear the air, would it make things even worse between them?

She was beginning to see what the hospital grapevine meant about Harry the Heartbreaker. He was already withdrawing from her and they'd gone to the wedding just as friends, not as part of a date. Was he really that wary of emotional involvement?

'Thank you for coming with me this weekend,' he said.

'Hey, that's what friends are for,' she said lightly. Though she had a nasty feeling that their burgeoning friendship had just hit an iceberg, one that could totally sink it.

Harry was still in scrupulously polite mode as he took her bag from the car and saw her to her door. 'See you at work tomorrow, then,' he said.

'Yes, see you tomorrow.'

And he really couldn't escape fast enough, she noticed. Back inside her flat, she kept herself busy by catching up with her chores, but it wasn't quite enough to occupy her full attention. She couldn't help wondering if what had almost happened between them in the moonlit garden would affect their relationship at work. Tomorrow, would Harry be his usual self with her, or would he have withdrawn even further?

She had no answer the next morning, because they

weren't rostered on together; he was in Resus and she was on triage duty.

But, in the middle of the morning, a woman came in carrying a toddler who rested limply against her. She sounded utterly distraught as she begged, 'Please help me—it's my grandson. I think he's dying!'

Isla signalled to the receptionist that she'd take the case.

She swiftly introduced herself. 'I can see that you're worried, but I need you to take a deep breath and answer some questions for me so I can help your grandson,' she said gently. 'What's his name and how old is he?'

The woman's voice was quavery but her answers were clear. 'Peter Jacobs, and he's two.'

'Can you tell me what's happened, Mrs Jacobs?'

'He started being sick and his vomit was a weird colour, a kind of greyish-black. And he's drowsy—at this time of the morning he's usually really lively. I called the ambulance, but they said they'd be a while before they could get to us, so I asked my neighbour to drive us in.'

Greyish-black vomit. It flagged up alarm signals in Isla's brain. 'Do you know if he's eaten anything he shouldn't have?' she asked.

'He said something about sweeties and tasting nasty. I couldn't think what he might have eaten, at first— I always keep any tablets in the medicine cabinet on the wall in the bathroom, and it has a child lock on it even though he can't reach it yet—but my husband's been taking iron tablets. He has arthritis in his hands so he can't use a childproof cap on his tablets. I didn't realise he'd left them in our bedroom instead of putting them back in the medicine cabinet. It has to be those—Peter hasn't been in the garden, so I can't think of anything else.'

'Do you have any idea how many tablets he might have eaten?'

Mrs Jacobs shook her head, and rummaged in her bag to produce a packet of iron supplement tablets. 'I brought these in case they'd help you. My husband can't remember how many he's taken, but it wasn't completely full. Please help us.' Her face was anguished. 'My son's never going to forgive me if anything happens to Peter.' She swallowed hard. 'If he—if he dies. I can't...'

'He's not going to die,' Isla soothed, though she knew that iron poisoning could be fatal in children. 'You did the right thing by bringing him straight here. Do you have any idea how long ago he might have taken the tablets?'

'It must have been in the last hour or two.' She bit her lip. 'Lee dropped him off just before he went to work. My daughter-in-law's away on business and Lee had to go in. I was only supposed to be minding Peter for the morning. And now...' She broke off, shuddering.

Isla squeezed her hand. 'Try not to worry. Let's go in to the department now because I need to discuss something very quickly with the doctor and then we'll treat your grandson.' She took Mrs Jacobs into Resus and beckoned Harry over.

'This is Mrs Jacobs and her grandson Peter, who's two and we think he might have accidentally eaten some iron tablets,' she said. 'Mrs Jacobs, would you like to sit here and give Peter a cuddle while I fill Dr Gardiner in on all the details?'

Mrs Jacobs looked grey with anxiety, but she did as Isla directed and sat on the bed with Peter on her lap.

'Mrs Jacobs doesn't know how many tablets he took, but she thinks it happened in the last couple of hours. The symptoms sound like iron poisoning.' She gave him a rundown of what Mrs Jacobs had told her.

'I agree—it sounds like iron poisoning.' Harry said. 'OK, we need serum iron, full blood count and glucose. Iron tablets are radio-opaque, so let's do an X-ray to find out how many tablets he took, and then we'll do gastric lavage or even whole bowel irrigation.'

Isla knew that activated charcoal couldn't absorb iron, so bowel irrigation was the most effective treatment, but it was going to be an unpleasant experience for the little boy and even worse for his grandmother. 'I know she's going to be worried about her grandson, but I think we should advise her to stay in the relatives' room while we treat him.'

'Agreed. Let her go with you to the X-ray,' Harry said, 'but then it's hot sweet tea and wait for us to finish.'

They went over to the bed where Mrs Jacobs was sitting with her grandson. 'Peter, I'm Dr Harry and I'm going to try and make you better,' Harry said.

The little boy clearly felt too ill to smile, let alone respond verbally.

Harry turned to the boy's grandmother. 'Mrs Jacobs, we're going to run some blood tests and give him an X-ray to see if we can get a better idea of how many iron tablets he's taken; then we'll be able to treat him. I know this is going to be hard for you, but while we're treating him I'd like you to wait in the relatives' room.'

'Why can't I stay with him? He doesn't know anyone here and he'll be frightened,' Mrs Jacobs said.

'It'll upset you more to see the treatment than it'll upset Peter to be with us, especially as he's quite groggy,'

Harry explained. 'I promise we'll do our best for him, and we'll come and get you so you can be with him again as soon as he's stable.'

She looked distraught. 'My son's never going to forgive me.'

Forgiveness. Yeah. Harry knew all about that. His mother and Tasha had forgiven him for that awful afternoon, but he'd never been able to forgive himself. Even now he still woke up in a cold sweat, having relived the whole thing in his dreams. Seeing his little sister tumble all the way down the stairs, and everything felt as if it was in super-slow motion—and, whatever he did, he just couldn't stop it happening. And then she lay there on the floor, not moving...

Except his dream was always that bit worse than real life. The worst and ultimate might-have-been. In his dream, Tasha never woke up. In real life, thank God, she had.

Mrs Jacobs bit her lip. 'I thought I'd been so careful. I've got cupboard locks and those things you put on the door to stop it slamming on their little fingers. I never thought he'd go into our bedroom and take those tablets.'

Just as Harry had never thought that Tasha would follow him up the stairs. He gave her a rueful smile. 'You can never predict anything with toddlers—and I'm sure your son will forgive you. You'd be surprised what children will forgive their parents.' *And their brothers.*

Mrs Jacobs didn't look convinced.

'You made a mistake, and you'll know in future to keep everything locked away,' Isla said. 'We'll do our best to make sure he's going to be absolutely fine. Do you want someone in the department to call your son for you?'

Mrs Jacobs shook her head. 'No, that wouldn't be fair on him. I'll do it.'

'OK,' Harry said, and squeezed her hand. 'Try not to worry too much, and this will take a while.'

'You can come with me to the X-ray department, so he won't be scared,' Isla said, 'and then I'll show you to the waiting room. Peter, sweetheart, I'm Nurse Isla, and I'm going to help Dr Harry look after you and make you better.'

She took Peter and Mrs Jacobs to the X-ray department, then showed the older woman where to wait. By the time Isla came back to Resus, Harry already had the X-ray up on his screen.

'There seem to be a dozen tablets,' he said. 'So we'll need to do a whole bowel irrigation.'

It was an unpleasant and lengthy procedure, but between them they managed to get rid of the iron tablets and stabilise Peter's condition.

'Shall I go and fetch his grandmother now?' Isla asked as they transferred the little boy to the recovery room.

'Good idea,' Harry said. 'The poor woman must be worried sick.'

Isla went into the relatives' room to see Mrs Jacobs. There was a man with her who bore enough family resemblance for Isla to guess that he was Peter's father.

They both looked up as she walked in. 'Is he all right?' they asked in unison.

'He's going to be absolutely fine,' Isla said, 'and you can come in to the recovery room to see him and have a word with Dr Gardiner.' She looked at the man. 'I assume you're Peter's father?'

'Yes. I couldn't believe it when Mum called me.'

'I'm sorry,' Mrs Jacobs said. 'And I promise you

nothing like this will ever happen again while I'm looking after him.'

'He could've *died*,' Mr Jacobs said, his voice cracking.

'But he didn't,' Isla said gently, resting her hand on his arm for a moment in sympathy, 'and accidents happen. The most important thing is that Peter's all right—and the scariest part is over now.'

She took them through to the recovery room, where Mr Jacobs put his arms round his son and held him tightly. The little boy was still groggy, but mumbled, 'Daddy, Peter got poorly tummy.'

'I know, baby. I love you,' Mr Jacobs said, 'and you're going to be all right.'

'Want Mummy,' Peter said tearfully.

'Mummy will be home soon,' Mr Jacobs said, 'and I'm not going to leave you until she's back. You're safe.'

The little boy snuggled against his father. And oh, how Harry never wanted to be in that position again. Worried sick about a small child whose injuries could've been fatal.

'Mr Jacobs, this is Dr Gardiner,' Isla said.

'Peter's going to be fine,' Harry said. 'I assume your mum already told you that he accidentally ate some iron tablets.'

'Dad should never have left his tablets where Peter could see them,' Mr Jacobs said, his voice tight. 'I can't believe he was so stupid.'

'Peter isn't the first toddler who's eaten tablets thinking that they were sweets and he won't be the last,' Harry said calmly. 'No matter how careful you are, accidents happen, and your mother did exactly the right thing in getting Peter straight here.'

What a hypocrite he was, telling this man that accidents happened and to forgive his mother. Because Harry had never been able to forgive himself for Tash's accident. Not after they discovered that the damage was more permanent than concussion and a broken arm. 'We irrigated his bowel to get rid of the tablets.'

'Oh, my God—that sounds horrific!' Mr Jacobs said, looking shocked.

'It's more effective at getting rid of the tablets than giving him an emetic, and it's also less risky,' Isla said.

'But he'll have nightmares about it.' Mr Jacobs bit his lip. 'My poor boy, having to go through all that.'

'He probably won't remember any of it. He's very young and was quite groggy when he came in,' Harry reassured him.

'So can I take him home now?' Mr Jacobs asked.

'No—because he's so young we want to admit him to the children's ward for the next twenty-four hours, so we can keep an eye on him,' Isla explained.

'So he could get worse?' Mrs Jacobs asked, her face full of fear.

'The early symptoms have settled now, but they sometimes come back the day after, so we always play it safe with young children and keep an eye on them,' Harry said. 'We can take you up to the children's ward and introduce you to the team, and they have facilities for parents or grandparents to stay overnight.'

'I can't believe…' Mr Jacobs shook his head as if to clear it. 'Oh, my God. If I'd lost him…'

'He's going to be fine,' Isla reassured him. 'I know it's easy for me to say, but try not to worry.'

Harry was glad she'd been the one to say it. Those particular words always felt like ashes in his mouth when the patient was a child.

She took the Jacobs family up to the children's ward

and helped them settle in, then headed back down to the Emergency Department. She'd missed her lunch break, so she grabbed a coffee in the staff kitchen and topped it up with cold water so she could drink it more quickly. She knew she could grab a chocolate bar from the vending machine on the way back to the triage team, and that would keep her going to the end of her shift.

Isla was halfway through her coffee when Harry walked in, holding two packets of sandwiches and two cans of fizzy drink. 'I guessed you wouldn't have time for lunch, either, so I nipped out to the sandwich stall by the hospital shop and grabbed these for us. They didn't have a huge choice but there's tuna mayo or chicken salad. You get first pick.'

'Thank you,' she said, feeling a huge surge of relief. Harry was behaving just as he had before they'd gone to Cornwall—which meant that the weekend hadn't damaged their working relationship after all. She hadn't realised quite how worried she'd been about it until she felt the weight leaving her shoulders. 'Why don't we split them and have one of each?'

'Sounds good to me,' he said.

'The kettle's hot. Do you want a coffee?'

He indicated the drinks. 'I'll get a quicker caffeine hit from this. I bet you put cold water in that coffee, didn't you?'

'Yes,' she admitted.

He grimaced. 'I prefer my coffee hot, thanks all the same. Do you want one of these cold drinks?'

'I'll stick with my half-cold coffee, but thanks for thinking of me,' she said. 'How much do I owe you for the sandwich?'

He flapped a dismissive hand. 'It's your shout, next time. That was a good call with young Peter.'

'I feel for his grandmother,' Isla said. 'She was trying her best, and accidents happen. Her son was so angry with her.'

'His dad probably feels guilty because he wasn't there to stop it happening, and that's why he was so angry,' Harry said. He blew out a breath. 'And that's another reason why I don't ever want to settle down and have children. You can't do a job like this and give enough attention to your kids.'

Plenty of other hospital staff managed it, Isla thought. Harry was letting his family background colour his judgement. But it wasn't her place to argue with him. 'Mmm,' she said noncommittally, and ate her sandwich. 'I'd better get back to the triage team.'

'And me to Resus. See you later.'

'Yeah.' She smiled at him. 'Thanks again for the sandwich.'

It was a busy week in the department. Isla wasn't looking forward to being rostered on cubicles on Saturday night; she hated having to pacify the more aggressive drunks, who seemed to take the hospital's zero tolerance policy personally and it made them even more aggressive with the staff.

She knew that having to deal with aggressive patients was par for the course for the shift, but her heart sank when she saw her patient at one o'clock in the morning; the guy had clearly been in a fight. As well as the black eye and lacerations to his face, there was what looked like a bite on his hand; either he'd hit the other man very hard on the mouth, in which case there might well be a tooth embedded within the bite, or the other guy had just bitten him anyway.

Damping down her dismay, she reminded herself that she was a professional.

'How long ago did this happen, Mr Bourne?' she asked.

'I've been waiting here for hours, so you tell me,' he asked, curling his lip.

Great. Drunk and aggressive, and not in the mood for giving information. She suppressed a sigh.

'I thought you lot had to see us within a certain time?'

'We have targets,' she said, 'but we have to treat the more urgent cases first. That's why we explain to patients that they might have to wait, and someone who came in after them might be seen first because their condition is more urgent.'

'Huh.' He swore enough to make his opinions about that very clear.

'I need to examine your hand, Mr Bourne. May I?'

He held his hand out for her to take a look. Thankfully, she couldn't see any foreign bodies in the wound. 'The good news is your hand isn't broken,' she said when she'd finished examining his hand, 'and there doesn't seem to be any joint involvement. As it's a puncture wound, there's more risk of it developing a bacterial infection, so I need to clean it thoroughly before you go. But it won't hurt because I'll do it under local anaesthetic. Can you remember the last time you had a tetanus injection?'

He shrugged and pulled a face. 'Dunno. Maybe when I was at school.'

'OK. I'll play it safe and give you a tetanus shot as well.'

He took one look at the needle before she anaesthetised his hand and was promptly sick.

''S not the drink. 'M not good with needles,' he slurred.

'It's OK,' she said. 'I'll clean it up when I've finished treating you.' She numbed the skin around the bite, irrigated it thoroughly, and had just turned away to get scalpel from the trolley to debride the ragged edges of the wound when she felt her bottom being roughly squeezed.

Unbelievable.

She turned round and glared at him. 'That's not appropriate behaviour, Mr Bourne. Don't do it again. And may I remind you that we have a zero tolerance policy here?'

'Oh, come on, love.' He leered at her. 'Everyone knows what you naughty nurses are like beneath that starched uniform.'

'You're here as my patient,' she said firmly, 'and nothing else. Just to make it very clear, Mr Bourne, I'm not interested, and I don't want you to touch me like that again. Got it?'

'You don't mean that. You know you want—'

But the man broke off his blustering when the curtain suddenly swished open.

Harry stood there, his arms folded and his face grim. 'Problem, Sister McKenna?'

She just nodded towards the patient.

'There's no problem, Doc,' Mr Bourne slurred. 'She's just being a tease, that's all. Playing hard to get.'

Isla had been here before, thanks to Andrew Gillespie. Another drunk, though he'd had more of a civilised veneer. Anger flashed through her; she was half tempted to be totally unprofessional and smack the guy over the head with one of the stainless steel bowls on the trolley.

But then she went ice cold. She'd told Harry some of what had happened with Andrew back on the island. And this case was oh, so similar. Would he think that Isla had been lying to him, and her two accusers were telling the truth after all? That she was a tease and she'd asked for it? Would he, like Stewart, refuse to back her?

'Playing hard to get? Absolutely not,' Harry said, his voice filled with contempt. 'That's complete and utter rubbish.'

Relief flooded through her. It wasn't going to be like before, then. Harry was going to back her. And she was shocked by how much she'd wanted him to believe her.

'We have a zero tolerance policy in this department,' Harry said, 'and that includes both verbal and physical abuse of the staff. Sister McKenna is here to treat you—and if you continue abusing her and touching her without her consent, then you'll leave the hospital without any treatment.'

Mr Bourne clenched his fists. 'And you'll make me, will you?'

'You're drunk,' Harry said. 'You've thrown up everywhere and you're barely capable of standing, so it wouldn't be hard for security to escort you out.'

'Too scared to do it yourself?' Mr Bourne taunted.

'No, too busy tending to people who need help,' Harry said. 'Don't try and play the tough nut, because I'm not interested. I'm here to do a job, not to bolster your ego. By the look of your hand, if we don't treat you, it'll be infected by the morning and it's going to hurt like hell—so it's your choice. You can apologise and let us do our job, or you can leave now and risk a serious infection. Your call.'

'I could sue you.'

'You could try,' Harry said, 'but who is a judge going to believe? Two professional medics, or someone who's too drunk to use his judgement?'

This could escalate very quickly, Isla thought. And if that comment about needles had been the truth rather than bravado, maybe there was a quick way of stopping Mr Bourne in his tracks. 'You'll need antibiotics,' she said, and took the largest syringe from the trolley.

The drunk went white when he saw it.

She quickly put a bowl into his hands. 'If you're going to throw up again, please try and aim for this. If you're sick over your hand, I'll have to clean it out again.'

He retched, but thankfully the bowl remained empty.

'Is there something you'd like to say to Sister Mc-Kenna?' Harry asked coolly.

'Sorry,' Mr Bourne mumbled.

'Good. And I don't want another word out of you unless it's to answer a question.' Harry turned to Isla. 'Sister McKenna, I'll stay with you to make sure this man doesn't make a nuisance of himself.'

'Thank you,' she said. 'And now I can get on with my job.' She finished debriding the wound. 'Because this is a bite wound, Mr Bourne,' she said, 'I can't put stitches in it straight away as there's a greater risk of infection. You'll need to go and see your family doctor or come back here in three or four days and we'll stitch it—then.' She put a sterile non-sticky dressing over it and looked at Harry. 'Given that it's a hand wound involving a human bite, should we use prophylactic antibiotics?'

'Good idea,' he said. 'I'll prepare the syringe for you.'

'And a tetanus shot, please,' she said.

'But you're the doctor,' the drunk man mumbled, staring at Harry as he drew up the medication. 'Not supposed to take orders from a nurse.'

'I told you I didn't want another word out of you,' Harry reminded him, 'and for your information Sister McKenna is a senior nurse and is more than qualified to do all of this. I'm only here as a chaperone because you were behaving like an idiot. I suggest you treat the staff here with the respect they deserve.'

'Sharp scratch,' Isla said cheerfully, and administered the tetanus shot.

Mr Bourne whimpered.

'And another,' she said, and gave him the antibiotics. 'I don't expect you'll remember what I say to you right now,' she said, 'so I'll give you a leaflet to back it up. Go to your family doctor or come back here in three or four days to have that wound stitched. If the skin around the wound goes red, swollen and tender, or you get a temperature, then you need to see someone straight away as it means you have an infection. But hopefully the antibiotics should prevent that happening in the first place.' She handed him the leaflet. 'Is anyone waiting for you outside?'

'Nah. The mate who brought me here will've gone home by now or his missis'll be in a snit with him, snotty cow that she is.'

'Then I'll leave you to make your own way out of the department,' she said.

He grimaced, got to his feet and lumbered off.

'I'm pulling rank,' Harry said. 'Staff kitchen, right now.'

Isla shook her head. 'I need to clean this place up first.'

'Then I'll help you,' he said, and did exactly as he promised.

When all the vomit had been cleaned up and the cubicle was fit for use again, he said softly, 'No more arguments. Staff kitchen.'

She nodded and went with him in silence.

He put the kettle on. 'I'm making you some hot, sweet tea. Are you all right?' he asked.

'Thanks, but I really don't need tea. I'm fine.'

'Sure? Apart from the fact that his behaviour was totally unacceptable, that must've brought back—'

'I'm fine,' she cut in, not wanting to hear the rest of it. Memories. Yeah. It had brought them back. But she wasn't going to let it throw her. 'And thank you for coming to the rescue.'

'Which any of us would do if any colleague was dealing with a difficult patient. You don't have to put up with behaviour like that.'

'Not just that,' she said softly, 'you believed me. You backed me.'

He smiled. 'Isla, apart from the fact that I know you well enough to be absolutely sure you'd never do anything unprofessional or encourage patients to grope you, the guy stank of stale booze and vomit—not exactly female fantasy material, was he?'

'I guess.'

Harry grimaced. 'And his attitude to women stank even more.'

She nodded. 'Just a bit.'

'Are you really sure you're OK?' he asked.

'Yes. But thank you for asking.'

He patted her shoulder. 'Any time.'

Heat zinged through her at his touch; and how inappropriate was that? Especially given that he'd just had to rescue her, and he'd said that she would never do anything unprofessional.

She could do with a cold shower.

Or an injection of common sense.

'I really don't need any tea, and it's heaving out there. We'd better get back to work. See you later,' she said. And she walked away before she said something needy or stupid. Harry Gardiner had made it very clear that he was off limits, and she'd promised herself she wouldn't get involved with anyone again.

And that was non-negotiable.

CHAPTER EIGHT

HARRY WAS WAITING for Isla when she came off duty after the handover.

'I'm seeing you home,' he said.

'Thank you, but there's no need,' she said.

'Actually, there is. You had a rotten shift.' He paused. 'And I'd just feel a bit happier if I saw you home and made you a bacon sandwich.'

'Tough. I don't have any bacon.'

'Then we'll do plan B,' he said. 'I know a very nice café not far from here where they do the best bacon sandwiches ever. And a bacon sandwich with a mug of tea is the best answer to a rubbish shift.'

'You're not going to give up, are you?' she asked.

He smiled. 'Nope.'

'A bacon sandwich would be nice,' she admitted, 'but I'm buying. To say thanks for rescuing me earlier.'

'Am I allowed to buy us a mug of tea, then?'

'I guess so.' She smiled at him.

They walked to the café together, where they ordered bacon sandwiches and a large pot of tea with two mugs.

'Thanks again for rescuing me,' she said.

'I'd do the same for any colleague who was being hassled by a patient,' he said.

'I don't mean just that—we'd all step in—but the fact that you believed me.'

'Of course I did,' he said softly. 'But that's why I wanted to have breakfast with you this morning. Because I don't want the behaviour of a stupid, thoughtless patient ripping open some fairly recent scars.'

'It did, a bit,' she admitted. 'It made me remember the look on Andrew's face when I turned him down, and then how my life suddenly went into quicksand mode.' And it was still her biggest fear: that someone would make another false accusation against her, that even though she was exonerated people would still think she'd done something wrong, and she'd have to pick up the wreckage of her life all over again.

Harry reached across the table and squeezed her hand. 'I know you had a tough time on the island, but that's not going to be repeated here,' he reassured her. 'Apart from the fact that every single person in our department knows you're totally professional, the guy was drunk and obnoxious.' He paused. 'There's more to it than that, isn't there?'

She sighed, suddenly too tired to hold it in any more. 'I was so scared you wouldn't back me.'

'Of course I'd back you! You're my colleague and my friend.' He frowned, as if remembering something. 'But you said your ex didn't back you when his stepfather lied about you. Why not?'

She sighed. 'I guess for him there were only two possibilities. One was that I was a faithless liar who was trying to cheat on him with his stepfather and was lying even more about it to save my own skin when I'd been found out. The other was that I was telling the truth, and the man who'd brought him up since he was two and treated him as if Stewart was his biological son rather than his adopted son was capable of cheating on Stewart's mother.'

'But surely he knew you well enough to know that you'd never cheat on him—that you weren't the liar?'

'That's what I'd hoped, but I was wrong,' she said sadly. 'I suppose he went for the lesser of two evils. For him, it was better to think that he'd made a mistake and picked the wrong person than to think that his mother had made a bad choice and could end up being hurt. Bridie had already had enough unhappiness in her life, with Stewart's dad being killed at sea when Stewart was only six months old. Andrew had made everything all right again. Stewart needed to believe that it was still going to be all right.'

'Even though that meant not believing you?'

'As I said, it was the lesser of two evils.' She bit her lip. 'I had hoped that, once he'd got over the shock, he'd see I was telling the truth and we'd work it out. But it was obvious he didn't want to see it. Then again, even if he had seen it, I'm not sure I would ever have managed to get past the feelings of being betrayed. How could I spend the rest of my life with someone who didn't believe me? What would happen the next time we had a difference of opinion—would he take my part, or would he assume that I was lying?' She looked away. 'So I broke it off.'

'Did Stewart know that Andrew had a drink problem?'

'I don't know. I guess Andrew could be very plausible and, if Bridie was colluding with him to keep the situation from everyone...' She sighed. 'Probably not.

'And you didn't tell Stewart the truth?'

'How could I? Breaching patient confidentiality is totally unprofessional—and doing that would've meant that Andrew's accusations were true, at least in part. Plus Bridie and Andrew could've denied that he had a drink problem. And that in turn would make Stewart and everyone else think that either I was lying to save myself, or that I was perfectly happy to gossip about something that a patient had told me in strictest confidence.'

'So whatever you did, you couldn't fix the situation—someone would end up being hurt. That's a horrible situation to be in.'

'It wasn't much fun at the time,' she said wryly. 'At least my family and close friends believed me.'

'But the gossip still drove you away from the island?'

'I was going to tough it out. But every day I had to face the same kind of speculation. Every day I had patients who didn't want to see me because they'd lost their trust in me. Every day I found I couldn't do my job properly because all the lies and the gossip were getting in the way. After three months of it, I wasn't sleeping or eating properly because I was so miserable. Which is when my parents, my brother and my sister sat me down, told me they loved me and they believed in me. They said basically I could stay on the island and let my soul wither away a little more every day, or I could leave and retrain and recapture the joy in what I did for a living.'

'And that's why you chose to work in the emergency department? Because you'd still be helping people, but they wouldn't know you and you wouldn't know them, and there wouldn't be any cradle-to-the-grave stuff?'

'Which is ironically why I became a nurse practitioner in the first place,' she said. 'But yes. And I like my job in the emergency department. I do.'

'But you miss your family.'

'I'm a big girl. I'll cope. And,' she added sadly, 'you might want to have it all, but in the end I guess you have to make some sacrifices and learn to compromise. That's life.'

'I guess,' he said. 'But in your shoes I'd be really angry about it.'

'I was,' she said, 'but I'm pretty much over the anger now. I'm just sad it worked out that way.'

'And then some idiot who's drunk out of their mind starts behaving in the same way towards you.'

'There is that,' she admitted.

'And because the guy had beer goggles on, he clearly assumed everyone else did, too.'

'Beer goggles?' She wasn't with him.

'When you've drunk enough beer to think that who-ever you see is more attractive than they are. Except in this case he was right about you and wrong about him-self,' Harry explained.

'Even sober and not covered in his own vomit, he wouldn't have been my type,' Isla said with a grimace.

'That's a cue to ask what your type is,' Harry said, 'except I wouldn't quite dare.'

'And I wouldn't answer,' Isla said crisply. Because she wouldn't dare tell Harry Gardiner that he was ex-actly her type. Not just because he was easy on the eyes, but because he was a genuinely nice guy and she liked the way he treated other people. She just wished he'd be a bit kinder to himself.

He laughed. 'And that's my cue to top up our mugs of tea.' He released her hand. 'Seriously, though, I was worried about you. We all have things in our career that make us flinch when we come across a similar case later on.' He always hated dealing with toddler falls. Especially serious ones. Not that he planned to tell Isla about that. Instead, he said, 'For me, it's a ruptured abdominal aortic aneurysm.'

'You lost the patient?' she asked.

'Yup. On my very first day in the emergency department. It was very nearly my last,' Harry said. 'I mean, I know statistically we lose more patients in our department than any other, simply because of the nature of the job. But I wasn't prepared to lose someone on my first day. She was the same age as my grandmother—in fact, she even looked like my grandmother. Masses of fluffy grey curls, carrying a little bit too much weight. She came in with back pain.' He blew out a breath. 'She was sweating, tachycardic and hypotensive. I thought it might be a ruptured abdominal aortic aneurysm, but she didn't have any mottled skin on her lower body and, because she was overweight, when I examined her I couldn't be sure that there was a pulsatile abdominal mass. I went to see my special reg to ask for a second opinion and some advice on what I should do next, but by the time we got back to my patient she'd collapsed and the nurse was calling for the crash team. And then we lost her. I went home after my shift and cried my eyes out, then I rang my grandmother and begged her to get herself checked out properly and go on a diet.'

'Oh, Harry.' Her sympathy showed in her expression, too.

'Going in to work the next day was awful. How did I know I wouldn't kill off any more patients?' He shrugged. 'I seriously thought about giving up medicine.'

'Harry, you didn't kill your patient. You were young and inexperienced, and you did the right thing—you knew you were in over your head and you went to get help rather than blundering on.'

'I still should've thought harder about what I was doing. I should've had a much lower threshold of suspicion and got the portable ultrasound.'

'Even then, you probably couldn't have saved her,' Isla pointed out. 'You know as well as I do that a ruptured aortic aneurysm has a really high mortality rate and a lot of patients don't even make it to hospital.'

'I knew that with my head,' Harry said, 'but my heart told me otherwise.'

'But you got through your next shift?'

'Yes. Actually, the senior sister on the ward was a real sweetheart. She gave me a hug when I came in, told me that I'd been unlucky to have such a bad first day in the department, and that I was to put it out of my head. And then she said I was rostered in Resus.' He blew out a breath. 'I was terrified that I'd kill another patient. But I saved someone. A toddler who'd had a severe allergic reaction to eggs. The paramedics had already given her adrenaline, but she got worse on the way to the emergency department and I had to intubate her and stabilise her. And that's when I realised what our job was all about. You do your very best to save someone. Sometimes you can't, and some patients are very difficult to help—but as long as you know you've done your very best then that's enough.'

That was true. But he hadn't done his best with Tasha, had he? He'd left the stair gate open and assumed she wouldn't follow him. And he wasn't going to put himself back in a situation where so much would be at risk—not ever, ever again.

When they'd finished their breakfast, Harry insisted on walking Isla home.

She paused at her front door. 'I guess that bacon

sandwich revived me a bit. Would you like to come in for a coffee?'

Part of Harry wanted to back away. After all, he'd told Isla some pretty personal stuff in the café. Plus he had a nasty feeling that this thing between them was drawing nearer and nearer towards a proper relationship, the one thing he'd always sworn to avoid—and actually going in to her flat was another step towards that.

But his mouth clearly wasn't working in sync with his brain, because he found himself saying, 'Thanks, I'd like that.'

'Come and sit down and I'll put the kettle on. Decaf?'

'If I'm to get any sleep this morning, then yes please,' he said with a smile.

She ushered him into her living room and bustled off to the kitchen. Her flat was neat and tidy, just as he'd expected.

The mantelpiece in her living room was full of framed photographs. There was one of Isla on her graduation day with two people who were obviously her parents, as he could see the resemblance to both of them; a couple of weddings that he guessed were her older sister and her brother, given that Isla was the bridesmaid and again he could see a resemblance; and others which were obviously christening photographs.

And the look of sheer love on her face as she was holding the babies told him everything: Isla was the sort who wanted to settle down and have a family. Right now she was still getting over the way her ex had let her down, but Harry thought that these photos were a warning sign that he really shouldn't start anything with her because they wanted completely different things out of life. Things that weren't compatible.

They'd talked about compromising, but this was one

area where he just couldn't compromise. He didn't want to be responsible for a child. Given his genes, if he tried to make a go of it with Isla and actually got married, there was a fair chance they'd end up divorced—and if they'd had a child, that would mean shattering another life. He didn't want to put a child through the kind of hurt he'd been through when he was smaller. And he didn't want to hurt Isla, either.

So he needed to back off.

Right now.

Which was exactly what he'd been doing since the wedding…until that drunk had groped Isla and claimed that she'd started it. Harry really couldn't have left her to deal with that on her own, especially because he knew it had happened to her before. And he'd been thinking with his heart rather than his head when he'd taken her for breakfast and seen her safely back here.

He was just about to stand up, go to the kitchen and make some excuse to leave when Isla came through with two mugs of coffee and a tin of biscuits, which she put down on the small coffee table in the centre of the room.

Too late.

He'd have to stay long enough to drink his coffee, or it'd be rude and he'd upset her. And he wanted to let her down *gently*.

Small talk. That was what would save the situation. 'Nice flat,' he said.

'I like it,' she said. 'It's light and airy, and although it's a bit on the small side it's convenient for work.'

He managed to keep the small talk going for just long enough to let him gulp down his coffee. Then he yawned and said, 'I really ought to leave and let you get some sleep. I need some myself or I'll be nodding off all through my shift tonight.'

'I know what you mean,' she said with a smile. 'See you later. And thanks again.'

'No problem,' he said.

And when he left her flat, he gave himself a pep talk all the way home. Back off. Keep your distance. And stop wanting something you definitely can't have.

CHAPTER NINE

HARRY WAS DISTANT with Isla that night at work; she would've put it down to them both being busy, but he didn't ask her to eat with him or have coffee together at their break.

They didn't see each other while they were off duty on Monday and Tuesday, but he was distant with her for the next couple shifts they worked together.

Something had obviously happened, but Isla couldn't work out what she'd said or done to upset him. He'd been so lovely with her when the drunk had upset her; he'd backed her on the ward, and then he'd made her feel safe and secure by having breakfast with her and walking her home. But, now she thought about it, he'd started going distant on her when she'd made him a mug of coffee, back at her flat.

She really needed to clear the air and find out what she'd done so she didn't repeat it. She valued him as a friend and a colleague and she didn't want anything spoiling that.

Was it the shadow of Andrew Gillespie? Harry had said he believed her, but was he having second thoughts now, the way so many people on the island had back then?

At the end of their shift on Friday, Isla waited to

catch Harry. 'Hey. I was thinking, maybe we could go for a drink somewhere.'

'Sorry, I can't.' He gave her an apologetic smile. 'I'm supposed to be playing squash. League match.'

Why did that feel like a made-up excuse? she wondered. 'Harry, I think we need to talk,' she said quietly. 'I've obviously done something to upset you and I'd like to clear the air. Can we meet after your squash game, maybe?'

He didn't look her in the eye and his tone was a little too breezy for her liking when he said, 'You haven't upset me at all.'

'So why have you been keeping as much distance as you can between us, this last week?' she asked.

Harry looked away. 'Have I?'

She sighed. He still couldn't look her in the eye? Oh, this was bad. 'Yes, and we both know it. I thought we were friends.'

'We are.'

'So what's happening?' she asked.

He shrugged. 'I've no idea what you mean.'

'Then come round for a drink when you've finished your squash match.'

'Sorry, I can't. We're all going out for a pizza afterwards.'

She gave up. 'OK, have it your way. Clearly I'm making a massive fuss over nothing. Enjoy your squash match.'

Harry watched her walk away, feeling guilty. After all, she was right: he had been lying to her. He wasn't playing squash at all this evening, much less going out for a meal afterwards with friends.

He lasted another two hours before the guilt got the better of him and he texted her. Isla, are you at home?

It was a while before she replied. Why? I thought you were playing squash. League match, you said.

He squirmed, practically hearing the tones of Scottish disdain and knowing he deserved it. But she had been right earlier: they did need to clear the air. Is that offer of a drink still open?

For a nasty five minutes, he thought she was going to say no. And he'd deserve that, too.

Then his phone pinged. Sure.

Relief flooded through him. See you in an hour?

He stopped off at the supermarket and bought an armful of the nicest flowers he could find, a mix of sweet-smelling white and lilac stocks. By the time he stood on her doorstep after ringing the bell, he felt ridiculously nervous.

'For you,' he said, thrusting the flowers at her when she opened the door.

'Thank you—that's very kind of you. But what's the occasion?' she asked.

She deserved the truth. 'No occasion. It's guilt and an apology,' he said.

She looked puzzled. 'I'm not with you, but come in. Do you prefer red or white wine?'

'Whatever you've got open.'

'There's a bottle of pinot grigio in the fridge. Perhaps you'd like to open it for me while I put these gorgeous flowers in water,' she suggested. 'The glasses are in the cupboard above the kettle.'

He found the glasses and the wine, opened the bottle, and poured them both a drink while she arranged the flowers in a vase, then put the bottle back in the fridge.

She ushered him through to the living room and he put the glasses down on the coffee table.

'So what's all this about, Harry?'

'You're right,' he said, 'about all of it. I *have* been avoiding you all week.'

'Why?'

He took a deep breath. 'Because we're supposed to be friends.'

She frowned. 'I thought we were.'

'We are.'

'Then...' Her frown deepened. 'Harry, you're not making any sense at all.'

'I know,' he said miserably. 'You were supposed to be safe.'

'And I'm not?'

'Far from it,' he said.

'Why?'

He sighed. 'Because I kissed you in Cornwall. Every time I see you, I want to do it again. And I know I'm rubbish at relationships and you've been hurt before, so the only thing I could do was stay out of your way,' he finished. 'Give me a few more days to get my head straight, and then hopefully I can look at you again without wanting to...' His mouth went dry as his imagination supplied the rest of it. Without wanting to pick her up, carry her to bed, and make love with her until they both saw stars.

'Without wanting to what, Harry?' she persisted.

'It doesn't matter,' he said, 'and I'm not going to make a nuisance of myself. But I thought you deserved an explanation and an apology.'

'Thank you.' She paused. 'But just supposing,' she asked softly, 'I've been thinking about Cornwall, too?'

'Then you're as crazy as I am,' he said, equally softly,

'because we can't do this. You've been badly hurt, and the last thing you need is to get mixed up with someone like me.'

'And how would you define someone like you?'

'You know what they call me at the hospital.' He shrugged. 'Harry the Heartbreaker. The man who won't date you more than three or four times because he doesn't do commitment.'

'That isn't the man I see,' she said. 'The man I see is kind, decent and caring. He notices the little things and he does his best to make everything right without making a huge song and dance about it all.'

'They're right about one thing. I don't do commitment,' he repeated. 'Come on, Isla. You've met my family.'

'And they're lovely.'

'They're lovely,' he agreed, 'but they're no good at commitment. My parents have ten marriages between them, including the one to each other. *Ten*. So it's in my genes to make a mess of things.'

'Or maybe,' she said, 'you could learn from your parents' mistakes.'

'I already have,' he said, 'and for me that means not getting involved in a serious relationship.' He looked at the glass of wine he hadn't even touched. 'I'd better go.'

'Why?'

'You know why, Isla. Because I don't want to give in to temptation and do something that'll hurt us both.'

'You curled around me in your sleep,' she said.

Yeah. He knew. He'd woken with her in his arms, all warm and soft and sweet. It had taken every single bit of his strength to climb out of that bed instead of waking her with a kiss. 'So?' he asked, trying his best to drawl the word and sound totally uninterested.

'So,' she said, 'maybe I woke before you did and I didn't move away.'

'Seriously?' That had never occurred to him. And now she'd said it, he could hardly breathe.

'Seriously,' she said. 'And maybe I've been thinking about it every single morning since when I've woken up. And maybe the bed's felt way too big.'

He went very still. 'Are you saying…?' He couldn't get the words out. Couldn't think straight. Was this really possible? Could they…?

'Maybe,' she said, 'I've been remembering how it felt when you kissed me.' She paused. 'And maybe I'd like you to do that again.'

'You'd actually risk a relationship with me?' he asked, wanting to make it clear.

'My head says no, that I should be sensible.'

'Fair enough.' He agreed with her completely.

'But there's another bit of me that thinks, maybe I shouldn't let what happened with Stewart wreck the rest of my life. Maybe it's time I was brave and took the risk.'

He could hardly breathe. She was choosing him? 'With me? But I'm about as high-risk as you could get.'

'I like you, Harry,' she said softly, 'and I think you like me, too. And I don't mean just as friends.'

'But what if it all goes wrong?' he asked. 'I can't promise you that this is going to work out. I can't promise you for ever.'

'I'm not expecting for ever. We're both adults. If it doesn't work out, then we'll be sensible about it and put our patients and the team first at work, just as we do now,' she said. 'But consider this, Harry—what if it goes right?'

His mouth went dry at the thought.

Risking a relationship with Isla McKenna.

Dating her.

Kissing her.

Making love with her.

He knew she'd been hurt. But if she was prepared to take the risk, then he'd have to step up to the plate and be brave, too.

'We need to set some ground rules,' he said.

She nodded. 'Ground rules sound fine to me.'

'Firstly, this is between you and me—as far as work is concerned, we're just colleagues.'

'That's sensible,' she said. 'Agreed.'

'Secondly, we're honest with each other—if we're uncomfortable with anything, then we say so.'

'Again, I don't have a problem with that.'

'Thirdly...' He couldn't think of anything else because his brain had turned to mush.

'Thirdly,' she said softly, 'why don't you just shut up and kiss me, Harry?'

Something he'd been aching to do ever since Cornwall—ever since he'd first found out how sweet and soft her mouth was.

'That,' he said, 'is the best idea I've heard all day.' He took her hand and drew it to his lips.

He could feel the shiver run through her as he kissed the back of each finger in turn, keeping his gaze firmly fixed on hers. Yeah. Me, too, he thought. He ached with wanting her. He turned her hand over and brushed his mouth against her wrist, and she shivered again. Still keeping eye contact, he found her pulse point with his lips; he could feel it beating strong and hard.

And then he drew her into his arms and kissed her properly.

And it felt as if the sun had just come out and made everything shimmery and sparkling.

He ended up sitting on her sofa, with Isla on his lap, her head pillowed against his shoulder and their arms wrapped round each other.

'OK?' he asked softly.

'Very OK,' she said, stroked his face.

'I'm on an early shift tomorrow. You?'

'Same,' she said.

'Are you busy afterwards? Or can I see you?'

'I'm not busy. I'd like to see you,' she said.

'Dinner,' he said. 'And dress up. Because we're actually going to go on a proper date.'

She laughed. 'Why does that make me feel as if I'm eighteen years old again?'

'Me, too. Which is crazy.' He kissed her lightly. 'Right now I want to do all kinds of things, but I'm going to keep myself in check because I think we need to take this slowly. Get used to the idea.' He stole another kiss. 'I don't date. But for you I'm going to try to change. I don't know if I can,' he warned, 'but I'm going to try. That's the best I can promise.'

'And that's enough for me,' she said.

'Hmm.' He kissed her again. 'I'll see you at work tomorrow. And then I'll meet you here at seven.'

'Sounds perfect.' She wriggled off his lap, letting him stand up, then walked him to the door and stole a kiss. 'Good night, Harry. Sweet dreams.'

'They will be,' he said softly. 'You, too.'

Isla managed to concentrate on her patients for the whole of Saturday—it helped that she and Harry were rostered on different sections of the departments and their breaks didn't coincide—but anticipation prickled through her once she was back at her flat.

A proper date.

And he wanted her to dress up.

So it ought to be a little black dress.

She dug out her favourite dress from her wardrobe, and took time with her hair and make-up. Her efforts were rewarded when she opened the door to Harry and his eyes widened.

'You look stunning,' he said.

'Thank you. And so do you.' She'd seen him wearing a suit before, but she was so used to seeing him in a white coat at work that she'd forgotten how sexy he looked in formal dress.

He reached out to twirl the end of her hair round one forefinger. 'Your hair is glorious,' he said, his voice catching.

'Thank you.' She smiled. 'It gets in the way at work. That's why I wear it pinned back.'

'I like it both ways—when you're being a starchy matron and when you're being a siren.'

She laughed. 'I'm not a matron—and I am so not starchy.'

'No, but you don't put up with any nonsense. Which is a good thing.'

'And I'm not a siren.'

'I beg to differ,' he said. 'You're the walking definition of sexy.'

She laughed again. 'Flatterer.'

'Nope. Statement of fact. And I can't wait to take you to dinner, Ms McKenna.' He glanced at her high heels. 'Can you walk in those?'

She rolled her eyes. 'I'm a nurse. I walk miles every day.'

'In flats.'

She took pity on him. 'Yes.'

'Good. Because it's a nice evening and I wanted to stroll hand in hand with you.'

'Works for me,' she said with a smile, and locked the door behind her.

They walked hand in hand to the tube station. Harry didn't say where they were going, but she also noted that he didn't have to stop and look up directions. Was it because he usually took his dates to wherever he'd booked a table, or did he just know London really well?

'This might be a bit cheesy,' he warned when they got to the West End. 'I've never been to this place before, but it's always on the list of the most romantic restaurants in London and the reviews are good. And I wanted to take you somewhere a bit special for our first date.'

So there she had her answers: he knew London well, and he'd never taken anyone else to this particular restaurant. Warmth spread through her and she found herself relaxing. And she fell in love with the restaurant on sight: the ceiling had been made into a canopy covered in white blossom and fairy lights, there were tealight candles on the tables casting a soft glow, the seats were all covered in red velvet, and the tablecloths were pure white damask.

'I can see exactly why this place tops the list,' she said. 'It's lovely.'

And the menu was equally good; she couldn't resist the hand-dived Scottish scallops, then corn-fed spring chicken with potato gnocchi, green beans and baby carrots. Harry joined her; it tasted every bit as good as it sounded, and he insisted on sharing a bottle of champagne.

'This is fabulous,' she said, 'but remember we're going halves.'

'Absolutely not,' he told her, his dark eyes sincere.

'This is our first official date, so I am most definitely picking up the bill, but...'

Anticipation tightened in her stomach. Was he saying there were strings attached to dinner?

'If you want to buy me lunch tomorrow, I won't be offended,' he finished. 'Or just a chocolate brownie and some coffee in the hospital canteen, if you're working.'

'I'm off duty tomorrow. If you are, too, then it's a date for lunch,' she said.

'And a walk first,' he said. 'There's something I want to show you.'

'What?' she asked, intrigued.

'If I tell you now, it won't be a surprise tomorrow,' he said, tapping his nose and laughing.

She liked this side of Harry—the fun, charming, relaxed man.

And she enjoyed sharing a pudding with him, even if he did eat more of the chocolate mille-feuille than she did.

'I've had a really lovely evening,' she said when he walked her back to her front door. 'Thank you.'

'My pleasure.'

'Do you want to come in?'

He stole a kiss. 'Yes. But I'm not going to. We're going to take this slowly.'

So neither of them would get afraid and back away? 'Works for me,' she said softly, and kissed him goodnight. 'I'll see you tomorrow.'

CHAPTER TEN

ON SUNDAY MORNING Harry woke, smiling, because he knew he was seeing Isla. He texted her to let her know he was on the way to meet her.

'So where are we going?' she asked when they left her flat.

'I thought we'd have a wander through the city.'

She smiled. 'Sounds good.'

When they emerged from the Tube station, Isla looked around and said, 'Isn't that Big Ben? So we're doing the touristy places?'

'Not especially,' he said, 'though if you want me to take a picture of you with Big Ben or the statue of Boudicca in the background, we can go up to the bridge.'

'No, I'm happy to go wherever you had in mind.'

He took her along the south bank, then groaned when they stopped. 'Sorry, I should've checked the tides.'

'Tides?' she asked.

'The Thames is a tidal river, so sometimes you see the beach just here and I thought you might like that. I guess it's the nearest you'll get to the sea in London.'

'Maybe another time,' she said.

They walked over the Millennium Bridge to St Paul's; then Harry led her through little side streets and a park to a part of Clerkenwell that was full of upscale clothes shops, jewellers, art shops and cafés.

'I thought we could have lunch here,' he said.

'This is lovely.' Most of the cafés had tables outside with umbrellas to shield their patrons from the sun; it made the place feel almost Mediterranean. 'Do you recommend anywhere in particular?' she asked.

'I haven't been here before,' Harry admitted. 'So pick one that takes your fancy.'

They browsed the menus on the boards outside; Isla chose a café with a French influence and they ordered a croque monsieur with freshly squeezed orange juice, then shared a brownie.

'Good choice,' Harry said. 'The food's great here.'

'And it's really nice exploring London with someone who actually knows the place,' Isla said.

'I've lived in London since I was eighteen. Obviously I don't know every single street, but I know a few nice out-of-the-way places,' he said, 'and it's always good to find somewhere new. I saw a write-up of this area in a magazine.' And he couldn't think of anyone he wanted to share this with more.

Funny, now he'd actually made the decision to start a proper relationship, it felt easy. Natural. The wariness he usually felt when dating someone had gone.

Or maybe it was because he'd found the right person.

Not that he was going to pressure Isla by telling her that. It was way too soon even to be thinking about it. They'd keep this low-key and fun, and see where it took them both.

At work, Harry and Isla managed to be professional with each other and treated each other strictly as colleagues. They were careful never to leave the hospital together unless it was as part of a group. Harry had persuaded Isla to open up a little more and come to one of the team nights out. He noticed that she thoroughly enjoyed the ten pin bowling, and went pink when one of the others told her they were all glad she'd come along because it was nice to get to know her outside work.

Later that evening, she told him, 'I'm glad you made me go. I really feel part of the team now.'

'Good. Welcome to London,' he said, and kissed her.

He saw Isla most days after work; one of them would cook, or they'd grab a takeaway, or if they'd gone into the city they'd find some nice little bistro. He felt they were getting closer, more and more in tune; the more he got to know her, the more he discovered they had in common. He actually felt in tune with her. There wasn't that antsy feeling that she'd expect more than he could give and it would all go spectacularly wrong. With her, he could relax and be himself—something he'd never experienced before. At the end of the evening it was getting harder to kiss her goodbye on her doorstep.

And it was harder to keep everything to himself at work, too. Whenever he saw Isla, it made him feel as if the sun had just come out. He found himself making excuses just so that their paths would cross in the department. And surely someone at the hospital would notice that he smiled more when she was around and start asking questions?

One Wednesday night when he'd walked her home after the cinema, she said to him, 'How brave are you feeling?'

'Why?' he asked.

'As we've made it way past your proverbial fourth

date,' she said, 'I thought maybe we could, um, run a repeat of a certain garden in Cornwall. Except it won't be in a garden and we're not going to be interrupted. And this time we don't have to stop and be sensible.'

Heat rose through him. 'Are you saying...?'

'Yes.' She lifted her chin. 'I'm ready.'

The heat turned up a notch. 'Me, too,' he said softly. 'You have no idea how much I want you.'

'I think, Dr Gardiner, that might be mutual.' And the huskiness in her tone told him that she meant it.

Once she'd closed the front door behind them, he pulled her into his arms and kissed her. He nibbled her lower lip until she opened her mouth, letting him deepen the kiss. It was intoxicating; but it still wasn't enough. He needed the ultimate closeness.

He broke the kiss, whispering her name, and drew a trail of open-mouthed kisses all the way down her throat. She tipped her head back and gave a breathy little moan.

So she was as turned on as he was? Good—though he had no intention of stopping yet.

The thin strap of her top was no obstacle to him. He nuzzled along her shoulder, then along the line of her collarbones. 'I want you so much, Isla,' he whispered. 'Your skin's so soft, and I want to touch you. See you.'

'Do it,' she said, her voice shaky.

'Not here.' He picked her up.

'Troglodyte,' she teased.

'Yeah.' He stole another kiss. 'So where am I going?'

'Harry, my flat has four rooms and you've seen three of them. I hardly think you need directions or a map.'

He laughed. 'Sister McKenna, with her scathing Scottish common sense.' He carried her across the hallway to the one doorway he hadn't walked through. 'Are you sure about this, Isla?' he asked.

'Very sure.' She paused. 'Though do you have protection?'

'Yes.' He stole a kiss. 'And that's not because I'm taking you for granted or because I sleep around.'

'I know. You're being practical.'

'Exactly.' He wanted to make love with her but he didn't want to make a baby with her. He didn't want children. Ever. He'd already had that responsibility way too young in his life, and it had gone badly wrong. He wanted to keep life simple. *Safe*. None of that gut-wrenching fear.

He pushed the thoughts away, opened the door while balancing Isla in his arms, carried her over to the bed and then set her on her feet again. He let her slide down his body so she could feel how much she turned him on.

'Well, now, Dr Gardiner,' she said, but her voice was all breathy and her face was all pink and her eyes were all wide.

'Well, now, Sister McKenna,' he said, and his voice was as husky as hers. 'What next?'

'Your move,' she said.

'Good.' He slid his fingers under the hem of her top, stroked along the flat planes of her abdomen. 'May I?' he asked softly.

She nodded, and let him peel the soft jersey material over her head.

She was wearing a strapless bra; he traced the edges of the material with his fingertips, then slid one hand behind her back, stroked along her spine and unhooked her bra.

'You're beautiful,' he whispered as the garment fell to the floor.

Colour heated her face. 'And I feel very overdressed.'

'Your move,' he said.

She was almost shy in the way she undid his shirt and slid the soft cotton off his shoulders. 'Very nice pectorals, Dr Gardiner.' She smiled and slid her hands across his chest, then down over his abdomen. 'And that's a proper six-pack.'

'So we're touching as well as looking now, are we?' He cupped her breasts and rubbed the pad of his thumbs across her hardening nipples.

She shivered. 'Oh, yes, we're touching.'

'Touching isn't enough. I want to taste you, Isla. Explore you.' He dropped to his knees and took one nipple into his mouth. She slid her hands into his hair; he could feel the slight tremor in her hands as he teased her with his lips and his tongue.

She followed his lead, dropping to her knees and undoing the button of his jeans.

He did the same with hers, then leaned his forehead against her bare shoulder and chuckled.

'What's so funny?' she asked.

'We didn't think this through.' He gestured to their positions. 'Right now I'll be able to pull your jeans down as far as your knees, and that's about it.'

She looked at him. 'And we're on the floor, when there's a nice soft bed right next to us. How old are we, sixteen?'

He stole a kiss. 'You make me feel like a teenager. In a good way, though; there's none of the angst and fear that the first time's going to be a disaster instead of perfect.' He nibbled her earlobe. 'Because we're both old enough to know it's not going to be perfect or a disaster.'

'What is it going to be, then?' she asked.

'An exploration. Discovering what each other likes. Where and how we like to be touched. Kissed.' He punctuated his words with kisses, then got to his feet, took her hands and drew her to her feet beside him.

'Starting here,' he said, and finished undoing her jeans. He stooped to slide the denim down over her curves and helped her step out of them. 'Your move, I think.'

She did the same with him, then grinned. 'You're wearing odd socks.'

'It's a London thing. A trend. The ultimate in sophistication,' he said.

She laughed. 'Is it, hell.'

'Busted.' He kissed her. 'I wasn't paying attention last time I did my laundry. I was thinking of you. Fantasising.'

'Oh, yes?'

'Definitely yes.'

He got rid of the rest of their clothes, pushed the duvet to one side, then picked her up and laid her against the pillows. 'You look like a mermaid,' he said, kneeling down beside her.

'A mermaid?'

'With that glorious hair spread out like that—definitely a mermaid. Or maybe a Victorian model for some super-sultry goddess,' he mused.

'Compliment accepted.' She reached up to stroke his face. 'And you're as beautiful as a Michelangelo statue.'

'Why, thank you.' He leaned forward to steal a kiss. 'And your skin's like alabaster, except you're warm and you smell of peaches.'

He nuzzled his way down her sternum, then paid attention to the soft underside of her breasts. 'You're incredibly lovely,' he said.

'Just like you fantasised when you were doing your laundry?'

'Way better,' he said. He rocked back on his haunches. 'I want to explore you,' he said softly.

Colour bloomed again in her cheeks. 'I'm all yours.'

He started at the hollows of her anklebones, stroking and kissing his way up to the back of her knees. Her breathing had grown shallow by the time he parted her thighs, and she slid her hands into his hair to urge him on. She shivered when he drew his tongue along her sex, dragged in a breathy moan when he did it again, and when he started teasing her clitoris he heard her murmured 'oh' of pleasure.

Harry was really looking forward to watching Isla fall apart under his touch. He loved the idea that he could turn all that sharp common sense to mush, just for a little while.

Her body tensed, and he felt the moment that her climax hit.

'Harry,' she whispered, and he shifted up the bed so he could hold her tightly.

'OK?' he asked when she'd stopped shaking.

'Very OK—I wasn't expecting that,' she said. 'I thought you said this wasn't going to be perfect?'

He smiled and stroked her face. 'I'm not finished yet, not by a long way.'

'No—I think it's my turn to make you fall apart,' she said. Her hands were warm and sure as she explored him.

Harry loved the way she made him feel, the way his blood heated with desire as she stroked and caressed him. Then she dipped her head so that glorious hair brushed against his skin, and desire surged through him.

'Isla,' he said softly, 'I love what you're doing to me and you feel like heaven—but right now I really, *really* need to be inside you.'

'Your wish is my command,' she teased. 'Condom?'

'In my wallet—in my jeans pocket.'

She climbed off the bed, fished his wallet out of his jeans and threw it to him. He caught it and took out the condom. 'Are you really sure about this?'

'Really sure,' she said, her voice husky, and took the little foil packet from him. She opened it, rolled it over his shaft and leaned over him to kiss him. 'Do you have any idea how sexy you look, lying there on my bed?'

'Not as sexy as you'll look with your hair spread over the pillow like a mermaid,' he replied.

'Hmm, so the man has a thing about mermaids?'

He drew her down to him, shifted so that she was lying beneath him and knelt between her thighs. 'Yeah,' he said, and eased into her.

It was very far from the first time that he'd ever made love, but it was the first time that Harry had ever felt this kind of completeness, this kind of bond.

Which made Isla McKenna dangerous to his peace of mind.

But she drew him so much that he couldn't resist her. Didn't want to resist her.

She held him tightly as his climax burst through him.

CHAPTER ELEVEN

WHEN HARRY HAD floated back to earth, he moved carefully. 'Help yourself to anything you need in the bathroom,' Isla said. 'The linen cupboard's in there with fresh towels.'

'Thanks.'

Isla lay curled in bed while Harry was in the bathroom, feeling warm and comfortable and that all was right with the world. She didn't bother getting up and dressing; Harry hadn't taken his clothes with him to the bathroom, and she was pretty sure that he'd come back to bed with her. Like Cornwall all over again, except this time they wouldn't be falling asleep on opposite sides of the bed, trying to keep a careful distance between them. This time, they'd fall asleep in each other's arms.

When Harry came back, his skin was still damp from the shower and he looked utterly gorgeous.

'I'm afraid I smell of flowers,' he said. 'Your shower gel's a bit, um, girly.'

She laughed. 'Actually, in Regency times, there was very little difference between the scents men and women used. Lots of them were floral—based on rose, lavender or orange flower water.'

He looked intrigued. 'How do you know that?'

'I read a lot of Regency romances,' she said, 'and I

was interested in all the social history side of things. I looked up a few things on the Internet—according to one of the really long-established London perfume houses, Beau Brummell's favourite scent involved lavender.'

'Beau Brummell? Hmm. So you like Regency dandies, do you?'

'And Scottish lairds—and I dare you to say it's girly for a man to wear a kilt.'

He laughed. 'Can you imagine me in a kilt?'

'Oh yes—especially if you let your hair grow a bit.'

'My hair?'

'You know your mermaid thing? Well, that's me and period drama. It's the sort of thing I love watching on telly. And you'd be the perfect period drama hero,' she said. 'I can imagine you riding horseback and wearing a tricorn hat.'

'We could always play the lady and the highwayman,' he said with a grin. 'I think I'd like that. Hands up, my lady.'

'Now, you need a domino mask to do that properly, and maybe a white silk scarf over your face, otherwise I could tell the local magistrate what you look like and you'd get arrested.' She laughed. 'Come back to bed.'

He shook his head. 'Sorry, I really need to go. I'm on an early shift tomorrow.'

'I have an alarm clock.'

'Even so. I don't have a change of clothes or a toothbrush.'

'I can always put your stuff through the washing machine, and I'm pretty sure I have a spare toothbrush in the bathroom cabinet.'

But he wouldn't be swayed. And the carefree, laughing man who'd just teased her about her highwayman fantasy had suddenly gone distant on her.

He got dressed in about ten seconds flat.

And Isla felt wrong-footed, unsure what to do next. Should she get dressed and see him out? Or just grab her dressing gown?

But when she moved to get out of bed, he said, 'Stay there. You look comfortable. I'll see myself out.'

'OK.'

'See you tomorrow,' he said.

'Sure,' she said, masking the flood of hurt that he could walk away so easily. And she noticed that he didn't even kiss her goodbye before he left. How could he switch from being so sexy and dishevelled to so cool and dispassionate, so very fast?

She'd thought they were both ready for the next step, but had this been an intimacy too far? Was Harry having second thoughts about their relationship? And would he revert to being the heartbreaker that the hospital grapevine said he was? Was he right when he said he wasn't capable of committing to a relationship?

Bottom line: had she just made a really, really stupid mistake?

The questions went round and round in her head. And she had no answers at all.

Harry knew he'd behaved badly.

He'd seen the hurt in Isla's face, even though she'd masked it quickly.

And he'd bet right now that she was feeling used. That he'd basically had his way with her and walked away.

Ah, hell.

This was a mess.

Maybe he needed to be honest with her and tell her that he was running scared. Panicking. But that would mean admitting that his feelings about her were changing. That he thought he might be falling in love with her—her warmth, shot through with common sense and humour that he found irresistible.

He didn't get involved. He'd never wanted to get involved. He'd seen the carnage it left behind every time his parents divorced their current partner—and, even though everyone eventually managed to be civil for the children's sake, he knew from first-hand experience what it felt like in the early days. When your world crumbled round you and you thought it was your fault, that you'd done something bad that made it impossible for your parents to live together. When you didn't understand what was going on.

And so he'd always kept his relationships light. Walked away before things started getting serious.

Except this time it was too late. It was already serious between him and Isla. And he didn't know when or how that had happened. They'd started off as friends; then, little by little, he'd fallen in love with her. Everything from her dry, slightly scathing sense of humour through to the way she smiled. From the cool, capable way she handled every crisis at work through to her sensual delight in eating out.

The blood seemed to rush out of his head as it hit home: he was in love with her.

Which left him stuck between a rock and a hard place.

Either he walked away from Isla—which would hurt; or he let their relationship move forward, risking being hurt even more when it went wrong. Because it *would* go wrong: he'd learned that from his parents. Love didn't last.

Isla had said at his father's wedding that she thought he had the capacity to make a relationship work—that he was isolating himself, and it was wrong because he was loyal and kind and loving.

But he wasn't so sure. Did he really have that capacity?

He'd already hurt her. Guilt prickled at him. He knew she'd wanted him to stay, and yet he'd walked away. Rejected her. Let his own fears get in the way. He hadn't been fair to her. At all.

And he slept badly enough that night that he texted her first thing in the morning.

I'm sorry. I was an idiot last night.

Her reply was suitably crisp: Yes, you were.

I don't have any excuses.

But he wasn't quite ready to admit the truth—that he'd never felt like this about anyone before and it left him in a flat spin.

But can you forgive me?

It was a big ask, and he knew it.

I'll think about it, she replied. See you at work.

Would things have changed between them at work? It was the one constant in his life, the place where he was sure of himself and knew he belonged. He didn't want that to change. And he was antsy all the way to the hospital.

But Sister McKenna was as calm and professional as she always was, treating Harry just like she treated every other member of the team. It helped that they weren't rostered on together; and Harry was able to relax and sort out his patients' problems.

Isla didn't reply to his text suggesting dinner. She also hadn't said anything about any other arrangements, so he bought flowers and chocolates and headed over to her flat. If she wasn't in, then he'd leave his apology with a neighbour.

Thankfully, she was in.

And she frowned when she saw the flowers and chocolates. 'Harry, what is this?'

'An apology,' he said.

She raised an eyebrow. 'Would you be repeating your father's mistakes, by any chance?'

It had never occurred to him before: but, yes, he was. Now he thought about it, Bertie was always sending flowers or chocolates to apologise for behaving badly. 'Ah,' he said, and grimaced. 'I think the penny might just have dropped.'

'I don't want you to give me flowers or chocolates when we fall out,' she said.

No. He knew that she wanted something that would cost him far more. She wanted him to talk to her. To open his heart.

He blew out a breath. 'I'm really not good at this sort of stuff, Isla.'

'Would a mug of tea help?'

Even though he knew it had strings attached, he nodded. Because he knew she was making more of a concession than he deserved.

'Come in. And thank you for the flowers. Though

if you ever buy me flowers again,' she warned, 'then I might hit you over the head with them.'

'Noted. Though I guess at least they'd be soft,' he said, trying for humour.

To his relief, she laughed.

Taking heart from her reaction, he walked forward and put his arms round her. 'I'm sorry. It's just…'

'You don't do relationships, and I asked you to stay the night. Which is tantamount to proposing to you with a megaphone while standing on a table in the middle of the hospital canteen.'

'In a nutshell,' he agreed. 'Isla—I did warn you I was rubbish at relationships.'

'And you're using your parents as an excuse,' she said.

He winced. 'You don't pull your punches.'

'You're the one who set the ground rules,' she reminded him. 'Honesty.'

'You want honesty?' He leaned his forehead against hers. 'OK. I want to be with you. I want to make a go of this. The way I feel… I…' He blew out a breath. 'I'm never this inarticulate. Sorry. I'm making a mess of this. But I don't want to hurt you, and I don't want to end up hurt either.'

'Then you need to make a leap of faith. Is it really so hard to stay the night?'

'Last time I did that…' His voice faded. 'Actually, the last time I spent the night with anyone was with you. But the time before that—my girlfriend assumed that our relationship meant more to me than it did. And it got messy.'

'Spending the night,' she said, 'means both of us get

a little more sleep before work, the next day. But I guess you didn't bring a change of clothes or a toothbrush.'

'No. Can you be a little bit patient with me?' he asked.

'I can, but there's a string attached.'

He wasn't sure he wanted to know the answer, but he knew he had to ask the question. 'Which is?'

'As long as you promise to talk to me in future,' she said.

He remembered something that gave him a way out. 'I thought you liked brooding Regency rakes?'

'In period dramas on screen or in books, yes,' she said. 'In real life, they'd be a pain in the neck. I'd rather have openness and the truth, even if it hurts.' She gave him a wry smile. 'Because the alternative is leaving me to guess what's in your head. And I'm not a mind-reader. What I imagine can hurt me far more than the truth.'

'I'm sorry,' he said. 'I…have feelings for you.' There, it was out. The best he could say for now, anyway. He wasn't ready to say the L-word; he was still trying to come to terms with his feelings.

Odd. At work, he could always find the right words. Here, when it really mattered, he found himself silent. He couldn't even quote a song or poetry at her. His mind had gone completely blank. He felt numb and stupid and awkward.

She stroked his face. 'I have feelings for you, too, Harry. One of them's exasperation.'

He knew he deserved it. But he took a tiny risk and stole a kiss. 'I'm trying, Isla. This isn't easy for me.'

'I know.' She kissed him back. 'But we'll get there. We'll just have to work on it a bit harder. Together.'

She had more faith in him that than he did, he thought wryly.

* * *

Harry still hadn't quite managed to spend the whole night with Isla when she went back to the Western Isles to see her family for four days, the week before her birthday. She didn't ask him to go with her, and he wasn't sure if he was more relieved or disappointed.

He was shocked to discover just how much he missed her during those four days. Even though there was a team night out and a squash match to keep him busy on two of those evenings, he still missed her. The odd text and snatched phone call just weren't enough.

And if he put it all together, it was obvious. He was ready to move on. To take the next step. To take a risk. With her.

Surreptitiously, he checked out her off-duty for the week of her birthday and changed his own off-duty to match. He didn't want to take the next step in London; it would be better on neutral ground. If he took her away for her birthday, he'd be able to relax instead of panicking that it was all going to go wrong. He spent the evening researching, and found what he hoped would be the perfect place.

He knew which flight she was catching back to London, and met her at the airport with an armful of flowers.

'They're soft ones,' he said, 'because I remember what you said you'd do next time I bought you flowers.' Hit him over the head with them.

She laughed, clearly remembering. 'I meant if you gave me apology flowers instead of talking things through,' she said. 'These are different. They're romantic. Welcome-home flowers. I love them.'

He knew she wanted the words. And he was half-surprised that he was ready to say them. 'I missed you,' he said. 'A lot.'

'I missed you, too.'

'Did you have a good time?'

She nodded. 'It was lovely. It made me realise how much I miss the island. The sky and the mountains and the freshness of the air. And most of all, the sea.'

Then there was a fair chance that she'd really love what he'd arranged for her birthday. Though a nasty thought struck him. If she was homesick... 'Do you miss it enough to want to go back?'

'I've moved on,' she said softly, 'and they replaced me at the practice, so if I went back now...' She shrugged. 'I wouldn't have a place, really.'

'But you've retrained. You're an emergency nurse. I assume there are hospitals on the islands?'

'I could work in the emergency department in Benbecula, or in the GP acute department in Stornoway,' she said.

'But?'

She shook her head. 'Not right now. Maybe some time in the future.'

So she did want to go back. Then what was stopping her? He remembered what she'd told him about the way people had behaved towards her after the whole thing blew up with her fiancé's stepfather. 'Are people still giving you a hard time about Gillespie?'

'No, but I did see Stewart while I was there.'

He went cold. That night after their fight and he'd admitted to his feelings... She'd said she had feelings for him, too. But had seeing her ex again changed that? Maybe the surprise he'd planned for her birthday was a bad idea after all.

'He's engaged to another lass,' she said, 'someone we both went to school with, and I wish them both well.'

'And you're OK about that?' he asked softly.

She nodded. 'I've moved on. I've met someone else. Someone I really like.'

He smiled and kissed her. 'I like you, too.' More than liked, if he was honest about it, but he wasn't quite ready to say it yet. 'So it's your birthday on Monday.'

'Yes. I assume it's standard practice to bring in cake for everyone in the department?'

'And chocolate bars for those off duty,' he confirmed. 'And birthdays are always celebrated at the local pizza place with the team, so I'm afraid I can't take you out to dinner on your actual birthday.'

'Because otherwise people will work it out that we're an item.'

He knew that hurt her, but he still wasn't quite ready to go public. 'However,' he said, 'you're off duty two days later—that's when I'm taking you out to dinner.' He paused. 'And you'll need to pack.'

'Pack?' She looked surprised, then wary.

Did she think that he was asking her to stay at his place? 'For two days,' he said. 'It's part of your birthday present. You'll need casual stuff for walking, and something nice to dress up in. I'll pick you up at your place after your shift.'

It was good to be back in London. Isla had a feeling that Harry had missed her as much as she'd missed him—his lovemaking that evening was even more tender—but she noticed that he still didn't stay overnight.

Though he was planning to take her away for her birthday, the following week. But then a nasty thought struck her: were they sharing a room, or had he booked separate rooms?

On her birthday, she was touched to discover that banners and balloons had been put up in the staffroom, and the team had clubbed together to buy her some gorgeous earrings. She thoroughly enjoyed the team night out at the pizza place, especially as someone had arranged for a birthday cake with candles and everyone sang 'Happy birthday' to her.

Harry saw her home afterwards, and gave her a beautifully wrapped parcel. 'It's the first bit of your present,' he said. It was a beautiful bangle, inlaid with precious stones, and he'd clearly paid attention to the kind of things she liked. But again, he didn't stay the night. Not even on her birthday. And it hurt. Would he ever be ready to spend the night with her—to make a move towards a greater commitment?

Isla was rushed off her feet on the early shift on the Tuesday. Harry still hadn't told her where they were going, but after their shift he picked her up in his little red sports car and drove her down to the Dorset coast, down a tiny track to a lighthouse.

'We're staying here?' she asked, surprised. 'That's just lovely.'

'For two nights,' he said. 'I know you miss the sea and I thought you'd like it here.'

It was incredibly romantic; there was a four-poster bed against one wall, opposite picture windows that overlooking the sea. She walked over to the window and gazed out. 'Harry, this is so perfect. Thank you.'

And he'd booked only one room. She knew that for him spending the whole night together was a huge turning point. For the first time, she really started to hope that he could get past his fear of falling in love and they had a future.

'I got it right, then?' For a moment, he looked really vulnerable.

'More than right,' she said, kissing him. 'However did you find this place?'

'Just did a bit of research,' he said. 'Luckily, because it's midweek, they had a vacancy.'

Dinner was fabulous: locally caught fish, followed by local ice cream on Dorset apple cake. But better still was afterwards, when Harry carried her over the threshold to the four-poster bed. It felt almost like a honeymoon, Isla thought.

In the next morning, she woke in his arms. And, unlike their trip to Cornwall, Harry made love with her before breakfast.

The morning was bright; they went to Lyme Regis and walked along the famous harbour wall of the Cobb, then headed for the cliffs and looked among the loose stones for fossils. Harry was the first one to find an ammonite and presented it to Isla with a bow. Then they headed for the boulders; they were marvelling over the massive ammonites embedded in the rock bed when they heard a scream from the shallows.

A small girl was holding her foot up and crying, while her mother was clearly trying to calm her down and find out what had just happened.

'Maybe the poor kid's trodden on something sharp,' Harry suggested.

'Do you think we ought to go and offer to help?' Isla asked.

'Yes,' Harry said, and took her hand.

'We're medics,' he said to the little girl's mum, who

was sitting on the sand next to her daughter, looking at the little girl's foot. 'Can we help?'

'Abbie said she trod on something and it hurt—I can't see anything but I wondered if she'd trodden on some glass,' the mum said.

'Abbie, I'm Dr Harry,' he said to the little girl, 'and this is Nurse Isla. Can we look at your foot?'

The little girl was still crying, but nodded shyly.

'I can't see any glass or any blood like you'd get with a cut,' Harry said, 'but I think she might have stood on a weever fish. They bury themselves in the sand under shallow water; the spines on their back and gills are laced with venom, and it feels like a sting if you step on them.' He showed the woman the swollen and reddening spot on Abbie's foot. 'We'd better get her over to the lifeguards' hut. We need some tweezers so we can take the spine out, clean the area with soap and water and rinse it with fresh water, then put Abbie's foot in hot water so it'll "cook" the protein in the venom and stop it hurting. And hopefully they'll have some infant paracetamol.'

'I've got the paracetamol,' Abbie's mum said.

'Good. I'll carry her over for you,' he said.

'I'll go ahead and talk to them so they can put the kettle on and get the first aid kit out,' Isla said.

Harry carried Abbie to the hut where the lifeguards were working. Isla had already explained their theory, and the first aid kit was out already.

He set Abbie gently on the bed so he could crouch down and examine her foot again, this time with a torch illuminating the area. 'I can get one of the spines out, but there's another one near the joint of her big toe, so I'd like that one looked at in the nearest emergency department,' he said.

One of the lifeguards called the ambulance while Harry took out the weever fish spine he could see easily, and the other provided a deep bowl of hot water.

'Ow, it's hot!' Abbie said, crying again.

'I know, sweetheart, but you need to put your foot in to stop it hurting,' Harry said. 'If you can do that for me, I'll tell you a story.'

'All right,' Abbie said bravely.

He'd just finished telling her a long-drawn-out version of the Three Little Pigs—where he had everyone in the lifeguards' hut booming out the wolf's threat to huff and puff and blow the house down—when the ambulance arrived. Harry gave a quick rundown to the paramedics.

'Thank you so much for looking after us,' Abbie's mum said. 'And I'm so sorry we took up your time on your holiday.'

'It's fine,' he said with a smile. 'Hope Abbie feels better soon.'

He was so good with children, Isla thought. So why was he so adamant he didn't want children of his own? What had happened in his past? Had he dated someone with a child and it had all gone wrong? But she couldn't think of a way to ask him without it seeming like prying. She'd have to wait until he was ready to open up to her and talk about it. But Harry was stubborn. Would he ever be ready?

'Well, Dr Gardiner, I think you earned a pot of tea and a scone with jam and clotted cream,' she said lightly.

'Sounds good to me,' Harry said, and looped his arm round her shoulders.

They ended up spending the rest of the day at the coast, eating fish and chips on the cliff-top and watching the setting sun. The spectacular flares of red and orange faded to yellow at the horizon, and the colours were reflected across the sea.

'Definitely a selfie moment,' Harry said, and took a picture of them on his phone with the sunset behind them.

This was perfect, Isla thought. It couldn't have been a nicer day.

The next day, they went exploring again; they stopped to walk up the hill and view the famous natural limestone arch of Durdle Door, and discovered the enormous chalk-cut figure of the Cerne Giant looming across another hill. And just being together was so good.

Back in London, this time Harry stayed overnight at Isla's flat.

They'd definitely taken a step forward, she thought. And maybe, just maybe, this was going to work out.

CHAPTER TWELVE

OVER THE NEXT couple of months, Harry and Isla grew closer still. They both kept a change of clothes and toiletries at each other's flat, though they were careful not to arrive at work together when they were on the same shift, and they hadn't made a big deal of letting people know that they were an item.

But one morning Isla felt really rough when she got out of bed.

'Are you all right?' Harry asked.

'I feel a bit queasy,' Isla admitted. 'I think maybe I'm coming down with that bug that's hit the department.' Which probably explained why she seemed to have gone off coffee, the last few days.

'Maybe you ought to stay home and call in sick,' Harry said. 'If you've got the lurgy, you don't want to spread it to the rest of the team or the patients.'

Normally it took a lot more than a bug to stop Isla working her shift, but right at that moment she felt absolutely terrible. 'Yes, I think you're right,' she said.

Harry made her some toast and a mug of hot lemon and honey; he also brought a jug of iced water in to the bedroom and put it by her bedside. 'Can I get you anything else to make you comfortable? A book or a magazine?'

'I'll be fine. But thank you.' She smiled. 'You have a lovely bedside manner. Anyone would think you were a doctor.'

'Yeah, yeah.' He grinned back. 'Text me later to let me know how you're feeling, OK?'

'Yes—though I was thinking, maybe you'd better not come back here after work today. I don't want you to pick it up.'

'I've got the constitution of an ox,' he claimed. 'Look, I'll call you when I leave work and see how you're doing, and then you can tell me if you want me to pick up anything from the shops for you.' He kissed her forehead. 'For now, get some rest.'

Isla lay curled up in bed with a magazine for the rest of the morning. She was feeling considerably better by lunchtime, and she felt a bit guilty about being off sick when she was clearly fine. Or maybe she'd been lucky and had the super-mild version of the bug and it was over now. She texted Harry to say she felt better and was just going out to get a bit of fresh air. But, when she went to the corner shop to buy some milk, the woman in the queue in front of Isla was wearing some really strong perfume which made her feel queasy again; and the smell of greasy food wafting from the fast food place next door to the corner shop made her feel even worse.

When she got back home, it slammed into her. Nausea first thing, a heightened sense of smell, an aversion to coffee... If a patient had described those symptoms to her, she would've suggested doing a pregnancy test. But she couldn't be pregnant—could she?

They'd always been really careful to use condoms.

Although, the night of her birthday, they'd got carried away with the sheer romance of having a bedroom in a lighthouse, and maybe that night they hadn't been as careful then as they should've been.

She thought back. Her last period had been really light, and she knew that women sometimes had break-through bleeding during early pregnancy. Could she be pregnant?

It niggled at her for the next hour.

In the end, she went to the local supermarket and picked up a pregnancy test. This would prove once and for all that she was making a fuss about nothing.

She did the test and stared at the little window, willing the words 'not pregnant' to appear. Although she hoped that Harry was revising his views on the 'never settling down' question, she was pretty sure that his stance on never having children of his own hadn't changed. She knew he was dead set against it.

She kept staring at the window. Then, to her horror, the word 'pregnant' appeared. Followed by '3+'—meaning that she was more than three weeks pregnant.

What?

She couldn't be.

Maybe the test was faulty. Maybe there was a problem with the pixels or something in the area on the screen that should've said 'not', and that was why it was blank. Just as well there were two kits in the box.

She did the second one, just to reassure herself that the first one was a mistake.

Except the result was the same: Pregnant. More than three weeks.

Oh, no. She was going to have to tell Harry.

But how? How, when she knew that he didn't want children? When he was practically phobic about it?

She still hadn't found the words by the time he called her.

'I've just finished my shift now, so I'm on my way to see you,' he said. 'Do you want me to pick up anything from the shops?'

'No, thanks—it's fine.'

'How are you feeling?' he asked.

Panicky. 'Better,' she lied. 'But I think maybe it'd be best if you didn't come over, just in case I'm still incubating this bug.'

And that would give her time to work out how to tell him the news, wouldn't it?

Except she still hadn't come up with anything by the next morning. She felt even queasier than she had the previous morning and only just made it to the bathroom before she was sick.

Grimly, she washed her face and cleaned her teeth.

She definitely couldn't let Harry stay over—or stay with him—until she'd told him the news, because she didn't want him to work it out for himself. Which of course he would, if she dashed out of bed and threw up every morning.

She just hoped that none of her patients that day would be wearing particularly strong perfume or aftershave, and that she could either avoid the hospital canteen completely or they'd have totally bland foods on the menu with no smell.

Thankfully, she wasn't rostered on with Harry. But he caught up with her at her break. 'Are you sure you should be in? How are you feeling?' he asked, his dark eyes filled with concern.

'Fine,' she fibbed, and sipped her glass of water in the hope that it would stop her reacting to the smell of his coffee. 'How was your morning?'

'Rushed off my feet.' He grimaced. 'I had one mum bringing in a sick baby, but she had two more children with her under school age, both of them with rotten colds. Clearly she hadn't been able to get anyone to babysit them while she brought the baby in to us. It was total chaos, with both of the toddlers wanting their mum's attention, and she was trying to explain the baby's symptoms to me at the same time. I couldn't hear myself think.'

'Was the baby OK?'

'She had bronchiolitis,' he said. 'Classic intercostal recession. I sent her up to the children's ward. I took a sample of mucus from her nose, but I'm pretty sure it'll be RSV positive. It's the beginning of the RSV season,' he said with a sigh, 'where they'll have two bays of the children's ward full of babies on oxygen therapy, and every single member of staff up there will have the cold from hell.' He rolled his eyes. 'And people wonder why I never want to have kids.'

She flinched inwardly, knowing that he was just exaggerating a bit to make his morning sound dramatic— or was he? He was always brilliant with any sick children who came into the department, and at the wedding he'd been so good with his youngest brother. Yet he'd always been adamant that he didn't want kids of his own and he'd never really explained why. When she'd tried to ask him, he'd simply changed the subject.

So she really wasn't looking forward to telling him the news that, actually, he was going to be a dad. She had to find a way to soften the blow for him, but she had no idea how.

'Do you want to come over for dinner tonight?' he asked.

'I'm still feeling a bit fragile, so I think I'd better pass and have an early night with a hot water bottle,' she said. She knew she was being a coward, but she really needed to work out the right way to tell him. A way that wouldn't hurt him. Just... How?

Was it his imagination, Harry wondered a couple of days later, or was Isla trying to avoid him? Ever since she'd gone down with that bug, she'd been acting strangely. Had she changed her mind about their relationship? He'd been seriously thinking about it himself; he'd never felt like this about anyone else before in his life. And she made him feel that the world was a better place. Just being with her made his heart feel lighter. He'd started to think about asking her to move in with him, maybe even take the next step and get engaged. Take the risk he'd always avoided in the past, so sure it would go wrong because he'd seen it go wrong so often for both his parents.

But now Isla seemed to be going distant on him, he was having doubts about it again. Did he have it all wrong? Did she not feel the same as he did, any more? Or was he so messed up about the idea of commitment that he couldn't see straight?

By the end of the week he was really concerned. They hadn't spent any time together for more than a week, so something was definitely wrong. All he could do was persuade Isla to go somewhere quiet with him, and then maybe he could talk to her and find out what the problem was. And then he could solve it. He hoped.

They had a busy shift in Resus that morning, and Harry was about to suggest that they went for a break between patients when the paramedics brought in in a woman who'd been in an RTA.

'Mrs Paulette Freeman,' the paramedic said. 'A bicycle courier cut in front of her; she had to swerve to avoid him, and crashed into the car on her right-hand side, which made her air bag go off. She's thirty years old, and twelve weeks pregnant with her first baby. There haven't been any problems so far in the pregnancy, and when we examined her there was no sign of bleeding. Her blood group is A positive.'

Harry and Isla exchanged a glance of relief at the news about the blood group. At least there wouldn't be a risk to the fetus from rhesus antibodies.

'Can you remember, did you bang your head at all, Mrs Freeman?' Harry asked.

'No, but the airbag went straight into my stomach.' Mrs Freeman looked anxious. 'Is my baby all right? Maybe I shouldn't have worn my seat belt.'

'Seat belts really do reduce the risk of serious injury in pregnancy,' Harry reassured her, 'so you did the right thing. Now, I'm going to examine you—just let me know if any area feels a bit tender.'

'My stomach's a bit sore,' she said, 'but that's probably from the airbag. It doesn't matter about me. What about the baby?'

'The baby's pretty well cushioned in there but of course you're worried. My job now is to see how you both are,' Harry said. 'Try and relax for me.' He added quietly to Isla, 'Call the maternity department and get Theo Petrakis down here, please. I always play it supersafe with pregnant patients.' He turned back to Mrs Freeman. 'Is there someone we can call for you?'

'My husband,' she said.

'I'll do that. Can you tell me his number?' Isla asked, then wrote the number down as Mrs Freeman said it. 'I'll call him straight away and ask him to come in,' she said.

'I'm going to examine your stomach now, Mrs Freeman,' Harry said. 'Tell me if anything hurts.'

She was white-faced and tight-lipped, and didn't say a word. He couldn't feel any uterine contractions, but the uterus felt firmer than he'd like.

A pelvic examination showed no sign of bleeding, which he hoped was a good thing. But he was starting to get a bad feeling about this case.

'I'm just going to listen to the baby's heartbeat,' he said, and set up the Doppler probe. But instead of the nice fast clop-clop he was expecting to hear, there was silence. He couldn't pick up the baby's heartbeat.

'What's wrong?' Mrs Freeman asked. 'Why can't we hear the baby's heartbeat?'

'I'm sure there's nothing to worry about,' Harry reassured her. 'Often this particular machine doesn't work very well in the first trimester. I'll try the old-fashioned way—obviously you won't be able to hear it, but I will.' He picked up a horn-shaped Pinard stethoscope; but, to his dismay, he still couldn't hear anything.

Isla came back in. 'I've spoken to your husband, Mrs Freeman, and he's on his way in. Dr Gardiner, Mr Petrakis is on his way down right now.'

'Good. I just want to get the portable ultrasound. I'll be back in a tick,' Harry said, doing his best to sound calm and breezy.

Isla had clearly seen the Doppler and the Pinard next to the bed and obviously worked out that he hadn't been able to pick up the baby's heartbeat, because when he brought the machine back she was sitting next to the bed, holding Mrs Freeman's hand.

Harry's bad feeling suddenly got a whole lot worse.

He knew that pregnant women could lose a lot of blood before they started showing any sign of hypovolaemic shock. In a case like this, with blunt force trauma, there was a high risk of placental abruption—

where the placenta separated from the uterus before the baby was born—and the fetus was likely to suffer. Worst-case scenario, the baby wouldn't survive. Although there was no sign of bleeding, with a concealed placental abruption the blood remained in the uterus. It was the more severe form of abruption and if his fears were correct the baby had already died.

'I'm going to do an ultrasound now to see what's going on,' he said. 'It's very like the machine they used when they did your dating scan, Mrs Freeman. Can you bare your stomach again for me so I can put some gel on it? I'm afraid our gel down here tends to be a bit cold.'

'I don't care if it's like ice, as long as my baby's OK,' she said, and pulled the hem of her top up so he could smear the radio-conductive gel over her abdomen.

He ran the transceiver head over her abdomen and begged silently, oh, please let the baby be kicking away.

The ultrasound didn't show any sign of a blood clot, but it did show him the thing he'd been dreading: the baby wasn't moving and there was no heartbeat.

Oh, hell. He was going to have to deliver the worst possible news. This was the bit of his job he really, really hated.

Theo arrived just before Harry could open his mouth. 'You asked to see me, Dr Gardiner?'

'Yes. Thank you for coming. Excuse me a second,' Harry said to Mrs Freeman. 'I just want to have a quick word with Mr Petrakis, our senior obstetric consultant. I'll introduce you properly in a moment.'

He walked away and said to Theo in a low voice, 'I couldn't pick up the fetal heartbeat. I know that's common in the first trimester, but also there's no movement or heartbeat showing on the ultrasound. The mum's not bleeding and I couldn't see a clot, and there's no sign right at this moment of hypovolaemic shock—but, given that it was blunt trauma and what's happened to the fetus, I think we're looking at a concealed placental abruption.'

'Sounds like it,' Theo said. 'Poor woman. In that case we need to restore her blood volume before she goes into shock and we'll have to deliver the baby PV—it's the only way to stop the bleeding from the abruption. And I'll want to admit her to the ward for monitoring in case she goes into DIC.'

Harry went back over to Mrs Freeman with Theo and introduced the specialist to her. Theo looked at the ultrasound and from the expression in the consultant's eyes Harry could tell that his original diagnosis was indeed correct. They wouldn't have time to wait for her husband to arrive to break the news; they needed to treat her now, before she went into shock.

He sat down beside her on the opposite side from Isla and held her other hand. 'Mrs Freeman, I'm so sorry. There is no nice way to tell you this, but I'm afraid the accident caused what we call a placental abruption. Basically it means that the force of the accident made your placenta detach from the uterus.'

'What about my baby?'

'I'm so sorry,' he said. 'We still need to treat you, but I'm afraid there's nothing we can do for the baby.'

She stared at him in horror. 'My baby's dead?' she whispered.

'I'm so sorry,' he said again. If only he could make this right. But there was nothing that anyone could do.

Mrs Freeman was shaking. Fat tears were rolling down her cheeks, but she made no sound. What he was seeing was total desolation. And it wasn't fixable.

Isla had her arm round Mrs Freeman's shoulders, doing her best to comfort her.

Feeling helpless, Harry explained what they were going to do next and that they needed to keep her in for a little while to keep an eye on her.

Halfway through treatment her husband arrived and Harry had to break the bad news all over again.

'I'm so sorry, Mr Freeman,' he finished.

Mr Freeman looked dazed. 'Our baby's dead? And Paulette?'

'We're treating her now, but we want to keep her in for monitoring. Would you like to come and be with her?'

'Yes—I— Is she going to be all right?'

'She's going to be fine,' Harry reassured him. 'I'm just so sorry I can't give you better news.'

By the time Harry's shift finished, he was completely drained. The last thing he felt like doing was talking to Isla to find out what was wrong, but he knew it had to be done. Maybe he could arrange to see her tomorrow and they could sort it out then. When they'd both had time to recover from their rough day.

But when he saw her outside the staff kitchen, he could see that she'd been crying.

'Are you all right?' he asked softly, even though he knew it was a stupid question; it was obvious that she wasn't OK at all.

'Rough shift,' she said. 'You should know. You were there.'

'Yeah.' He closed his eyes for a moment. 'I hate breaking that kind of news to people. I hate seeing their dreams shatter like that.' He opened his eyes again. 'I don't know about you, but I can't face going anywhere and talking tonight. Shall we just get a pizza and go back to my place?'

'I...' She dragged in a breath. 'Harry, we really need to talk.'

He went cold. The way she was talking sounded horribly final. Just like the way he'd always broken the news to whoever he was dating that it wasn't really working and he'd rather they just stayed as friends.

Was Isla going to end it between them?

But surely not right now—not after the day they'd both had.

Not feeling up to talking, he asked, 'Can this wait until tomorrow?'

She shook her head. 'It's already been dragging on too long.'

He really didn't like the sound of that. He had a nasty feeling that he knew why she'd been distant, these last few days: because she was ending it.

'Is that café round the corner still open?' she asked.

He guessed that she meant the one where he'd taken her for a bacon sandwich, the morning after the night shift where the drunk had come on to her. 'We can take a look,' he said. 'Is that where you want to go?'

'It'll be a lot more private than the hospital canteen. It means we can talk.'

'OK.'

They walked to the café in silence. Harry could feel himself getting more and more tense, the nearer they got to the café; and, even though he was trying to prepare himself for being dumped, it just hurt too damn much. He didn't want it to end between them. He wanted to take it forward. Take the risk.

'Tea and a bacon sandwich?' he asked outside the door to the café.

She shook her head. 'Just a glass of water for me, thanks.'

'OK. If you find us a table, I'll sort out the drinks.' He ordered himself a mug of tea, to put off the moment that little bit longer.

When the waitress sorted out the drinks, Harry discovered that Isla had found them a quiet table out of the way. Good.

Well, he wasn't going to be weak and wait to be dumped. He was going to initiate the discussion and ask up front. 'So are you going to tell me what I've done wrong?' he asked as he sat down.

'Wrong? What do you mean, wrong?'

'It feels as if you've been avoiding me for the last few days,' he said. And he was aware how ironic it was that they'd had this conversation before—except, last time, he'd been the one doing the avoiding.

'That's because I have,' she said softly.

Pain lanced through him. He hadn't been imagining it, then. She was going to end it—and she'd been working out how to tell him, the last few days. While he, being a fool, had been thinking about moving their relationship on to the next step.

'So what did I do wrong?' he repeated.

'Nothing.'

He didn't get it. 'So why were you avoiding me?'

She took a deep breath. 'There isn't an easy way to say this.'

So she was definitely ending it—and he was shocked to realise how much it hurt. How much she meant to him and how empty his life was going to be without her.

* * *

This was one of the hardest things Isla had ever done. She hated the fact that her words were going to blow Harry's world apart. She was just about to make his worst nightmare come true.

But he'd clearly already worked out that something wasn't right.

Even though her timing wasn't brilliant—he was already feeling low after a rotten shift—she couldn't keep it from him any longer.

'I'm pregnant,' she said.

He looked at her, saying absolutely nothing—and she couldn't tell a thing from his expression. How he was feeling, what he was thinking...nothing.

'With our baby,' she clarified. Not that there could be any mistake. They'd both been faithful to each other.

Still he said nothing. He just stared at her as if he couldn't believe what he was hearing. He looked shocked to the core.

Well, what had she expected? That he'd throw his arms round her and tell her how thrilled he was?

He'd made it clear enough that he never wanted children, and she was telling him that he was going to be a father—exactly what he didn't want.

The fact that he'd said nothing at all made it very obvious that he hadn't changed his mind. He just didn't know how to tell her without hurting her.

So she was going to have to be brave and be the one to walk away.

'It's all right,' she said, even though it wasn't and it left her feeling bone-deep tired and unutterably sad. 'I know you don't want children. I'm not expecting anything from you, and I understand that it's the end between us.'

And it was clear what she needed to do next. This was Harry's patch. He'd lived in London since he was a student; he'd trained and worked in the same hospital for twelve years. She'd been in the emergency department at the London Victoria for only a few months. It was obvious which of the two of them would have to leave.

'I'm going home to Scotland,' she said. 'To the island. But I didn't want to leave without telling you why. I'm sorry, Harry.'

And she got up to leave.

CHAPTER THIRTEEN

SHOCK RADIATED THROUGH HARRY.

He couldn't believe what he was hearing.

Isla was pregnant?

With his baby?

Well, of *course* his baby—she wasn't the sort to have an affair. He knew that without having to ask.

But he couldn't quite process the idea of being a father. He couldn't say a word. It felt as if his mouth had been filled with glue. And someone had glued him to his seat, too, because Isla was walking away from him and he was still stuck here, watching her leave.

This had to be a nightmare. One of those hyper-real dreams where the situation was so close to real life that it could really be happening, but there was something out of kilter that would tell you it was all a figment of your imagination.

Like being stuck to your seat. Like there being no sound at all, even though they were in a café and there would usually be the hiss of steam from a coffee machine and the sound of a spoon clinking against a mug as sugar was stirred in, the low buzz of other people talking.

He'd wake up in a second. It'd be stupid o'clock in the morning, and he'd be in either his own bed or Isla's, spooned round her body. He'd hear her soft, regular breathing and he'd know that this was just a dream and all was right with the world.

Any second now.

Any second now.

But then the door closed behind her and the sound all seemed to rush back in—like the moment when a tube train arrived at the station, and all the noise echoed everywhere. Hissing steam, clinking spoons and mugs, the hum of conversation.

Oh, dear God.

This wasn't a nightmare.

Isla was pregnant, she was planning to leave London, and…

No, no, no.

He couldn't let her leave.

He needed to talk to her. Tell her how he felt about her. Ask her to stay. Beg her to stay. On his knees, if he had to.

He could do with someone tipping a bucket of ice-cold water over him to shock his brain back into working again, so he could find the right words to ask her to stay. Failing that, he'd just have to hope that he could muddle his way through it.

Ignoring the startled looks of the other customers in the café, he left his unfinished mug of tea where it was and rushed out after Isla.

He looked out either side of the door in the street. He thought he caught sight of her walking away and called out, 'Isla, wait!'

Either she hadn't heard him or the woman wasn't actually Isla. Inwardly praying that it was the former, he ran after her and finally caught up with her.

Thank God. It was her.

'Isla, wait,' he said again.

She stopped and stared at him. 'Why? You made it perfectly clear just now that you didn't want to know.'

'Did I, hell.'

'I told you the news and you didn't say a word.'

'You didn't exactly give me a chance!' he protested.

'I did,' she said. 'I sat there like a lemon, staring at you and waiting for you to say something.'

'I was too shocked to think straight, let alone for my mouth to work. I needed a few seconds for the news to sink in. And now it has. I think.'

She blinked back the tears. 'Harry, you've told me often enough that you don't want kids and you don't want to settle down. I'm not expecting you to change for me.'

'What if I want to change?' he asked.

She shook her head. 'I can't ask you to do that.'

'You're not asking me. I'm offering.'

'No. Don't make any sacrifices, because you'll regret it later. Anything you decide has to be because you really, really want it. You can't live your life to please other people.'

'I don't want you to leave,' he said. 'Stay.'

'If I go home to Scotland, at least I'll have my family round me to help with the baby. If I stay here, I'll be struggling on my own,' she pointed out. 'It makes sense to leave.'

'So you want to keep the baby?'

She dragged in a breath. 'You can actually ask me that after what happened at work today, when that poor woman lost a baby she clearly wanted very much?'

He winced. 'Sorry, that came out wrong. I don't mean that at all. Just—we didn't plan this, did we? Either of us. We haven't talked properly about what we want out of life. We've been taking this thing between us one step at a time.' He dragged a hand through his hair. 'I'm making a mess of this, but we need to talk about it, and I can't let you just walk away from me—and the street really isn't the right place to discuss this. Your place or mine?'

'I guess yours is nearer,' she said.

'Mine it is, then—and there's no pressure. We'll just talk things through, and then, if you want me to drive you back to yours afterwards, I will.' He blew out a breath. 'Just talk to me, Isla. You once said to me that you weren't a mind-reader. Neither am I. And I really need to know what's going on in your head.'

She looked at him, and for a nasty moment he thought she was going to refuse; but then she nodded.

They walked back to his place in uneasy silence. He tried letting his hand accidentally brush against hers, but she didn't let her fingers curl round his, so he gave up. Maybe she was right. Maybe they needed to do this with a clear head, not let the attraction between them get in the way and muddle things up.

'Can I get you a drink?' he asked once they were in his living room.

'No, thanks.'

Were they really reduced to cool politeness? But then he found himself lapsing into it, too. 'Please, have a seat.'

He noticed that she picked one of the chairs rather than the sofa, making it clear that she didn't want him right next to her. He pushed the hurt aside. OK. He could deal with this. He needed to give her a little bit of space. Clearly she was upset and worried, and all the hormonal changes of pregnancy weren't helping the situation one little bit.

Hoping that she wouldn't misinterpret where he sat, he chose a seat on the sofa opposite her. All he wanted to do was to hold her and tell her that everything was going to be all right. But how could he promise her that, when he didn't know that it would be anywhere near all right?

What a mess.

He didn't even know where to start. Emotionally, this was a total minefield and it was way outside his experience. So he fell back on the thing he knew he was good at. Being a doctor. Maybe that would be the best place to start. 'Are you all right?' he asked. 'I mean, are you having morning sickness or headaches?'

'It's not been brilliant,' she admitted.

'How long have you known?'

She took a deep breath. 'I did the test nearly a week ago.'

So she'd had a week to get used to the idea and work out how she felt about it, whereas he'd only had a few scant minutes—and it wasn't anywhere near enough. 'When you thought you had the bug that was going round?' he asked.

'Except it wasn't that.'

Now he was beginning to understand why she'd backed off from him—because she'd discovered she was pregnant and she'd been scared of his reaction. Because he'd told her often enough that he didn't want kids. He just hadn't told her why. And maybe it was time he explained. 'I'm sorry,' he said. 'You should've been able to tell me. And I feel bad that I'm not approachable enough for you to have said anything before.'

'We didn't exactly plan this, did we?' She bit her lip. 'And we were careful.'

Not careful enough. The only guaranteed form of

conception was abstinence. 'Do you know how pregnant you are?'

'The test said more than three weeks. My last period was very light, but I thought…' She shrugged. 'Well, obviously I was wrong.'

'Isla, I don't know what to say,' he admitted. 'I really wasn't expecting this.' He raked a hand through his hair. 'And, after a day like today…'

'I couldn't keep it to myself any longer,' she said. 'Not after today. Because what happened to that poor woman made me think, what if it had been me? I hadn't really let myself think too much about the baby and what options I had. But after sitting there, holding her hand while you told her the bad news, it became really clear to me what I wanted.'

To keep the baby. She'd already told him that. But what else? Did she want to bring up the baby on her own, or with him?

And what did he want?

He'd had no time to think about it, to weigh up the options. He'd always been so sure that he didn't want children. So very sure. But now he was going to be a dad, and he didn't have a clue what to say.

'I've been trying to work out for the last week how to tell you. I knew it was your worst nightmare,' she said, almost as if she could read his mind. But then she frowned. 'But what I really don't understand, Harry, is why you're so sure you don't want kids. You're so good with them at work—and at the wedding, you were great with little Evan. And when we went away, you were lovely with that little girl on the beach who stood on the weever fish—you told her a story to keep her mind off how much her foot hurt. You'd make such a great father. I don't understand why you'd cut yourself off from all that potential love. Is it because you have so many brothers and sisters, but you didn't grow up with most of them?'

'No.' He blew out a breath. Maybe if he told her the misery that had haunted him for years, she'd get it. 'Do you remember the little boy who'd eaten his grandfather's iron tablets?'

'Yes.' She looked puzzled. 'Why?'

'And you remember I told his grandmother that toddlers were unpredictable?'

'Yes.'

'And I know that's true, because I've walked in her shoes,' he said softly.

She stared at him. 'What, you had a toddler who accidentally ate iron tablets—one who died?'

'Not my toddler and not iron tablets and no death, but something bad happened, something that's haunted me ever since,' he said. 'I was eleven. Mum had just popped out to the shops and she asked me to keep an eye on my sisters. Maisie was five, Tasha was two, and Bibi was a baby. I thought it'd be all right. I put Maisie and Tasha in front of the telly—there was some cartoon on they both liked—and I was doing my homework at the dining room table. French, I remember. Then Bibi started crying. Maisie came and told me the baby was all stinky, so I knew I had to change her nappy— I couldn't just leave her crying until Mum got home. I thought the others would be fine in front of the telly while I took the baby upstairs and changed her.'

'What happened?' she asked softly.

'I forgot to close the stair gate,' he said. 'Tasha got bored with the telly and decided to come and find me. I had the baby in my arms, and I saw Tasha get to the top of the stairs. She was smiling and so pleased with herself. Then she wobbled and fell backwards. Right down the whole flight of stairs. Before I could get to her. Everything happened in slow motion—I could see it happening, but I couldn't do a thing about it. And then she was just lying there at the bottom of the stairs and she wasn't making a sound. I thought she was dead and it was all my fault.'

'This is your middle sister, yes? And she wasn't...?'

He shook his head. 'She survived.' Though she hadn't made a complete recovery.

'Harry, just about anyone would struggle to look after three children under five, and you were only eleven years old at the time,' Isla pointed out. 'You were doing your best. You were busy changing the baby. You weren't to know that your two-year-old sister would fall down the stairs.'

'I know—but if I'd closed the stair gate it wouldn't have happened.'

'Or she might have gone into the kitchen or the garden and hurt herself there instead,' Isla said. 'You're right about toddlers being unpredictable, and you can't blame yourself—plus it's so easy to see things differently with hindsight. It's not fair to blame yourself. What did your mum say?'

'She came home to find an ambulance outside our house with a flashing blue light,' Harry said, 'so she was pretty shocked—and her first words to me were that she'd trusted me to look after the girls while she went to get some bread and some milk, and why hadn't I kept a proper eye on them?'

Isla winced. 'That to me sounds like a panicky mum who isn't thinking straight.'

'She apologised later,' Harry said. 'She told me that it wasn't my fault.' He paused. 'But we both knew it was, and she never asked me to look after the girls again on my own after that.'

'I bet she was feeling just as guilty—she was the adult, and she'd left you in charge of three young children, when you were still only a child yourself,' Isla pointed out. 'And how far away were the shops?'

'A fifteen-minute walk,' Harry said. 'Not far—but it was long enough for me to nearly kill Tasha. I had bad dreams for months about it. I saw my little sister lying at the bottom of the stairs, her face white, and I couldn't see her breathing. I never wanted to go through fear like that again, and that was when I vowed that I'd never have kids of my own. I didn't want that responsibility—or to let another child down.'

Isla left her seat, came over to him and hugged him fiercely. 'You were a child yourself, Harry, and having that kind of a responsibility as a child is completely different from having it as an adult. And she was fine, wasn't she?'

That was the big question. 'The hospital said it was concussion and a broken arm.' He bit his lip. 'We thought she'd recovered just fine over the next few weeks. But over the months, Mum noticed that Tasha was always off in a dream world. When she got a bit older, if she was reading, you had to take the book out of her hands to get her to realise you'd been calling her.'

'Because she lost herself in the book?'

He shook his head. 'Mum talked to the health visitor about it. They thought she might have glue ear. But when the audiology department at the hospital tested her, they found out that actually, her hearing was damaged permanently.' This was the crunch bit. 'According to the audiogram, what was wrong was impact damage—so it had been caused by the fall. Because I didn't look after her properly, Tasha's on the border of being severely deaf, and for certain pitches she's profoundly deaf—she can't hear really deep voices.'

'Plenty of people cope with deafness,' Isla pointed out gently, 'and I get the impression from what you've told me about your sisters that they're all very independent.'

'They are,' he admitted. 'But don't you see? Her deafness was caused by the fall. It shouldn't have happened. And I feel bad that she's always had to struggle and work harder than everyone else. She was bright enough to pick things up from books, but half the time she couldn't actually hear what the teachers were saying. Even with hearing aids, it's difficult—when she's in noisy surroundings, it's hard to pick up what people are saying, especially if they have quiet voices or they're in her difficult range and she can't see their faces to lipread. She has to concentrate so much harder to pick up all the social stuff as well as cope with work.'

'Is that how she sees it?' Isla asked.

'Well—no. We fight about it,' Harry admitted. 'She refuses to be defined by her hearing. She says I'm over-protective and it drives her crazy.'

'Have you tried putting yourself in her shoes?' Isla asked softly.

'Yes. And I still blame myself. And I'll always remember how I felt, seeing her lying there on the floor, not moving. That choking feeling of panic.' He dragged in a breath. 'I see parents most weeks who are panicking as much as I did back then. Parents who are worried sick about a baby or a toddler with a virus or a severe allergic reaction. I think the fear's the same, however old or however experienced you are.' He paused. 'And I guess that's part of why I didn't want to get involved with anyone. I didn't want to risk things going wrong. I told myself that getting involved with someone, getting married and having kids…that wasn't for me.'

Isla swallowed hard. 'And then I came along.'

'And you changed everything,' he said. 'You made me see that things might be different to what I always thought they were. That, just because my parents had made mistakes, it didn't mean that I was necessarily going to repeat them.' He took a deep breath. 'So if I was wrong about that, maybe I'm wrong about other things, too. Like not wanting children.'

'So what are you saying?'

'I'm saying,' he said, 'that I need a little time to let it sink in and to come to terms with it. Right now, I'm still shocked and I feel as if someone's smacked me over the head with a frying pan. But give me a little time to think about it and get used to the idea. You've had a week, and I've only had a few minutes. I can't adjust that fast, Isla, no matter how much I want to. I'm only human.'

'I'm sorry. I'm being selfish.' Her eyes misted with tears.

She looked as if she was going to pull away from him, but he wrapped his arms round her and hauled her onto his lap. 'Isla. These last couple of weeks, I've been doing a lot of thinking myself. And this week I thought that you were avoiding me because you were working out how to dump me—'

'Dump you?' she interrupted.

'Dump me,' he repeated. 'I'd been thinking about us. About how I like being with you. About how my world's a better place when I wake up in your arms in the morning. About how you make me want to be brave and take the risk of a real grown-up relationship.' He paused. 'I had been thinking about asking you to move in with me.' He paused again. 'This is probably too little, too late. But I'm going to tell you anyway, because you can't read what I'm thinking. I was going to ask you to get engaged.' He swallowed hard. 'To take the really big risk and get married.'

'What? *You* want to get married?' She looked at him in utter shock.

'Yes.' He gave her a wry smile. 'I didn't believe it either, at first. But the thing is, I met someone. Someone I really like. Someone I really believe in and who seems to believe in me, too. Someone who told me that I was capable of really loving someone. She made me think about it properly for the first time ever.' He paused. 'And you were right. I am capable of loving someone. I love you, Isla McKenna. And, if you'll have me, I'd very much like to marry you.'

'Uh...' She stared at him. 'I think it's my turn to have the frying pan moment. Did you just ask me to marry you?'

'I did.'

'Me *and* our baby?' she checked.

'I believe you come as a package,' he said dryly.

'But—you—me—how?' she asked plaintively.

He stroked her face. 'Now I definitely know you're pregnant. The hormones have put a gag on all that strident Scottish common sense.'

'Have they, hell. Harry, you're allergic to marriage.'

'There's no immunoglobulin reaction, as far as I can tell,' he said, starting to relax and enjoy himself.

'You said you didn't want to settle down. Ever.'

'Tsk—are you so old-fashioned that you think it's only a woman's prerogative to change her mind?'

'Harry Gardiner, you're the most impossible—'

He judged that he'd teased her enough. So he stopped

her words by the simple act of kissing her. 'I love you, Isla,' he said when he broke the kiss. 'I might even have loved you from the first day I met you. But every day I've worked with you, or dated you, or woken with you in my arms, I've got to know you a little more and I've grown to love you a little more. And although I admit I'm absolutely terrified at the idea of being a dad—and I'm even more terrified by the idea that I might let our child down, the way I let my sister down—I know I'm going to make it work because you'll be at my side. And, with you by my side, I know I can do absolutely anything. Because I can talk to you, and you can make me see sense. And you can talk to me, knowing I'll always back you and take your part. We're a team, Isla. Not just at work.'

A tear spilled over and trickled down her cheek, and he kissed it away.

'Hormones,' she said.

He coughed. 'Wrong word. The one you're looking for has one syllable, three letters, and starts with the twenty-fifth letter of the alphabet. The middle letter's a vowel. And the last letter's often used as a plural. Got it?'

'You didn't actually ask me,' she pointed out. 'You said, if I'll have you, you'd like to marry me. Which isn't the same as asking me.'

'Yes, it is.'

She just looked at him.

He sighed, shifted her off his lap, and got down on one knee before her. 'If you're being picky about it, I also don't have a ring—and am I not supposed to present you with a ring if I do it the traditional way?'

'You said you'll back me. That's enough.' She flapped a dismissive hand. 'We don't need flashy gemstones.'

He laughed. 'Ah, the Scottish tartness is reasserting

itself. Good. Isla McKenna, I love you. And I'm still terrified out of my wits about being a dad, but I know I'll love our baby just as much as I love you. Will you marry me?'

She smiled. 'Yes.'

He coughed.

'What?' she asked.

'You haven't said it,' he reminded her. 'Three little words. And I've spent the last week in a bad place, thinking that you were going to walk out on me. I need a little TLC.'

'Ah, the three little words. Tender, loving care.'

'Three *smaller* words,' he said, giving her a pained look. 'Come on. I said it first.'

'I know. And I'm glad.' She smiled. 'I love you, too, Harry Gardiner. I think I did from the second you kissed me in the moonlight in Cornwall. And I admit that I, too, am just a little bit panicky about whether I'm going to be a good enough mum. But with you by my side, I think the answer's going to be yes. It's like you said. We're a team. Things might not always go smoothly, but we'll always have each other's back.'

'You'd better believe it,' he said softly.

EPILOGUE

Three months later

'WE SHOULD'VE ELOPED,' Harry said. 'How about I go and borrow a horse and a tricorn hat, kidnap you and carry you off to my lair?'

Isla laughed. 'Are the boys giving you a hard time?'

'Not just the boys. Five best men. *Five*. It's excessive. And then the girls accused me of sexism and demanded to know why they couldn't be best women. All of them.' He groaned. 'I can't possibly have eight best men and women on my wedding day!'

'As you're only going to get married once, none of them wants to miss out, so I don't think you have much choice,' Isla said. 'And I'm surprised your father hasn't tried to make it nine.'

'He did. He said I'd been his best man so I ought to let him be one of mine. I reminded him that he's already got a role as the father of the groom,' Harry said. 'But the others... They're supposed to let the oldest sibling boss them around, not the other way round. They're impossible!'

Isla laughed again, knowing that his grumbling was more for show than anything else. Since Harry had opened his heart to her, he'd also opened his heart to his brothers and sisters—and as a result he'd become much, much closer to his whole family. 'I love your brothers and sisters. They're so like you. Totally irrepressible.'

He groaned. 'So much for a quiet wedding. We really should've disappeared to Gretna Green.'

'Scotland? Hmm. I don't think that would've been quiet, either. And you do know my family's planning on teaching yours to party the Scots way tonight, don't you?'

'We definitely need to run away,' Harry said.

'I think it's a little too late for that. We're supposed to be in church in two hours. And you're not supposed to be here, much less talking to me through a closed door.'

'You're the one who insisted that it was bad luck to see me on our wedding day before you got to the church,' he reminded her. 'That's why I'm talking to you through a closed door. Are you quite sure we can't elope?'

'Harry, stop panicking,' she said. 'Go with the flow and let your siblings enjoy your wedding. Because you're only getting married once.'

He sighed. 'Our poor baby doesn't know what he or she has in store.'

'Oh, I think he or she does,' Isla corrected, 'and I think this is going to be the most loved baby in history.'

'And definitely by his—or her—dad.' Harry had been in tears at the scan, and had been a besotted father-to-be ever since.

'See you at church,' she said softly. 'And thank you for the beautiful necklace. It goes perfectly with my dress.'

'Well, you needed a "something new" to wear. It's traditional.' He coughed. 'It's also traditional to give your husband a kiss for a gift.'

'I will. At the altar,' she promised. 'I love you, Harry. And today's going to be fun. Really.'

And it was. Right from the moment Isla walked up the aisle on her father's arm, seeing the small church absolutely bursting at the seams with all their family and their friends from work, through to seeing the love in Harry's eyes as he turned to face her at the altar, through to everyone throwing dried rose petals over them both as they walked out of the church as man and wife.

The reception was even better. And Isla really enjoyed the best-men-and-women's speeches. Harry's brothers and sisters had clearly got together before the wedding and practised, because they all lined up on the stage behind the top table.

'The best man's speech is supposed to be short,' Evan said, starting them off, 'but we all wanted to be the best man and made Harry let us all do it, and we all want to say something so the speech won't be very short. It's funny, though. And I'm going to tell you a joke. What did the banana say to the monkey?'

The others all chorused, 'Nothing, bananas can't talk!' and did a little tap-dance with jazz hands, making everyone at the reception laugh.

Harry's siblings went in age order after that, with each of them telling a Harry story that made everyone laugh, though Isla noticed that Harry's middle sister seemed to have missed her slot.

But then, when Jack had finished speaking, Tasha took the microphone. 'My Harry story isn't a funny one. But it's about the bravest, best man I know. When I was two, I fell all the way down the stairs and I broke my arm. A few months later, we worked out that the fall had made me deaf in one ear, too. Harry's always blamed himself for what happened, but there's no way he could've rescued me when he was right in the middle of changing Bibi's nappy. We all think he's a superhero, but even he can't be in two places at once.'

Isla slipped her hand into Harry's, and squeezed his fingers.

'Without him, I wouldn't be a trainee audiologist, and I wouldn't be able to understand my patients as well as I do,' Tasha continued. 'And actually, I'm kind of glad it happened, because I know it was one of the reasons why he became a doctor—and the emergency department of the London Victoria wouldn't be the same without him.'

There were loud cheers of agreement from Harry and Isla's colleagues.

'And because he's an emergency doctor, that meant that he met Isla at work. We're all so glad he did, because she's the best thing to happen to him, and it's lovely to see my big brother get the happiness he never thought he deserved—but he really *does* deserve it.' She lifted her glass. 'So the best men and women all want you to raise your glasses now for a toast—to Harry and Isla, and may their life together be full of happiness.'

Harry stole a kiss from Isla as everyone chorused the toast. 'Yes. It's never going to be quiet, but it's going to be full of happiness,' he said with a smile. 'I love you. And our baby. And our chaotic, wonderful extended family.'

'Me, too.' Isla smiled back. 'I'm with you all the way. Always.'

* * * * *

COMING SOON!

We really hope you enjoyed reading this book.
If you're looking for more romance
be sure to head to the shops when
new books are available on

Thursday 24th October

MILLS & BOON

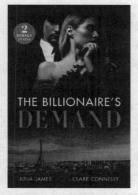

LET'S TALK
Romance

For exclusive extracts, competitions
and special offers, find us online:

f MillsandBoon

X @MillsandBoon

⊙ @MillsandBoonUK

♪ @MillsandBoonUK

Get in touch on 01413 063 232

afterglow BOOKS

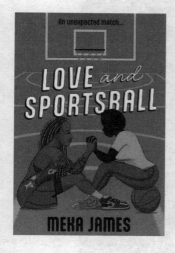

 Sports romance

 Sports romance

 Workplace romance

 Workplace romance

 One night

 Spicy

OUT NOW

Two stories published every month. Discover more at:
Afterglowbooks.co.uk